AT LOGGERHEADS

A Novel

KRISTEN NESS

EVENING POST
BOOKS

Published by

Evening Post Books
Charleston, South Carolina

First edition

Author: Kristen Ness
Editor: Elizabeth Hollerith
Designer: Gill Guerry
Cover Design: ebooklaunch.com

First printing 2023
Printed in the United States of America

A CIP catalog record for this book has been applied for from the Library of Congress.

ISBN: 978-1-929647-87-3

For

Mom and Dad

Sarah and Dale

Pete, Taylor, and Dylan

You are my home from beginning to end.

In my beginning is my end.

Home is where one starts from.

In my end is my beginning.

—**T. S. Eliot**

For most of the wild things on earth,

the future must depend on the

conscience of mankind.

— **Dr. Archie Carr**

Nature never did betray the heart that loved her.

—**William Wordsworth**

The idiom ***at loggerheads***, which usually functions as a predicate adjective, means *in a dispute.* Its origins are mysterious. Loggerhead originally referred to a stupid person, and in the seventeenth century, it took a new definition—*thick-headed iron tool*. When *at loggerheads* came about soon thereafter, it may have referred to the use of loggerheads as weapons. In any case, *at loggerheads* (*loggerheads* is always plural in the idiom) now implies harsh disagreement but not necessarily violence.

The singular *loggerhead* is mostly archaic. It now appears only in reference to the loggerhead turtle, a species of large sea turtle with a reddish-brown shell.

Grammarist.com

PROLOGUE

By the eggshell light of early morning in the last hot gasp of May, a teenage boy steered a johnboat along the curves and bends of a tidal creek. His younger sister perched on the bow with her face to the sky, curls lifted by a warm headwind. She looked out across miles of salt marsh coated with tall, golden-green cordgrass between Anders Isle and the South Carolina mainland. The licorice odor of pluff mud welled up, pungent and ripe, from the slick brown bank where a snowy egret tiptoed on stilt legs, stalking fish. The girl spotted buoys floating in the distance on flood tide-swollen water, marking their family's crab pots around jagged oyster reefs.

"There's one!" She pointed to the closest buoy.

The boy turned the boat in the direction of her outstretched, branch-thin arm.

He cut the engine as they approached the buoy and let the boat drift closer. Moving to the boat's center, legs planted wide for balance, he reached out to lift the crab trap while his sister peered over the boat's edge, waiting to see a cage full of large, claw-wielding blue crabs.

"Get the bucket ready." He grabbed the buoy with both hands.

Dropping the buoy into the boat, he pulled the rope taut with his right hand and gripped lower on the rope with his left. Bracing his feet against the ribs of the boat, he leaned back to haul the trap to the surface. But when his muscles strained for the first deep pull, the trap wouldn't budge. The boat pitched. He fell backward into its bottom and made it rock.

"Whoa!" The girl clung to the bow to steady herself. "What happened?"

"I don't know," he said. "The trap's so heavy. I can't pull it up."

"Maybe it's caught on something."

"Could be jammed against an oyster bed."

"So, try again." She brushed a strand of hair away from her mouth.

"Okay, hold on." He wrapped the rope around his hand for traction. "Ready? One...two...three..."

Yanking the rope with all his strength, he clenched his teeth as the trap's weight made his arms shake. Inch by inch, hand over hand, he raised the trap, as heavy as a laundry bag full of bricks.

It wasn't until he heard his sister scream that he looked down at the water to see what he'd pulled up.

CHAPTER

1

Brooke Edens didn't know how to find home again, until she did.

Home means different things to different people. Some people take home for granted, some run from it, and still others spend their lives in search of it. For many, home is an address, the four-walled structure of a house, the people who inhabit it, and the rooms carved out inside. For others, it's a feeling evoked by a group of people or a cherished activity. And for some, like Brooke, home is a deep connection to a place, a sacred spot on the map that conjures up a sense of belonging the way the moon pulls the tides.

Maybe it was the taste of her salt-kissed skin at the end of each day, or the sound of rhythmic ocean waves beating in her childhood dreams. Maybe it was the animal smell of marsh mud, or the sight of a dolphin's dorsal fin slicing through morning low tide. Whatever it was, it had long ago taken root in Brooke's deepest tissues and coalesced with her blood, so wherever she went, Anders Isle called her home.

A comma-shaped barrier island framing six miles of the slanted South Carolina coast, Anders Isle stretched from south to north, shielding plains of salt marsh and the lip of mainland from the push and pull of the steel blue Atlantic. Wide sandy beaches rimmed the island's ocean-facing side, and a swath of maritime forest on its north end was so thick with shadows it was perfect for hiding. Stories swirled about the history of its past inhabitants: furtive Native Americans, fugitive pirates, and colonial soldiers. Brooke grew up on Anders Isle with wind-sculpted trees, sea turtles, and with Drew Young, her constant—often more-than—friend. She knew the island's beauty in her bones.

Wild tangles of maritime forest sheltered the remote North End Beach—a fragile sea turtle nesting habitat—from encroaching light and noise of residents, vacationers, and development. As kids, Brooke and Drew often dared to ride bikes into the forest to climb through tunnels of crooked limbs and dig for sharks' teeth and fossilized shells in the gritty time-scarred dunes. Generations of people and wildlife thrived on and returned to the island. From sunrise to moonrise, Anders Isle protected, adapted, and moved imperceptibly between ocean and sky, as a barrier island was meant to do, all at once a sentinel to stand guard amid the changing of tides and a place to call home.

Brooke stepped onto the beach for her Saturday morning run. She tightened her ponytail, raised her arms above her head, and took a deep breath. Lungs full of tangy humid air, she exhaled into the heat of late May, watching a gull tilt on the wind. Her familiar island welcomed her with statuesque great blue herons and a wink of its salt marsh creek.

But something was amiss. Brooke didn't like the unexpected.

She started running toward the island's north end while the day brightened over the ocean to her right. Salty air cleared her head, crystallized her thoughts. Here she was again, on the same beach where she spent countless hours with Drew and sought comfort in nature as a child, playing outside until dark.

Brooke's earliest memories were of her island's beach, taking long walks and turning shells between her small fingers to study creatures inside them. By the age of ten, she could identify each marine creature and its common name: the brittle starfish tucked inside a velvety plush orange sponge, the domed armor of the horseshoe crab with its spider-like legs and stiff pointed tail, the sacs of whelk eggs strung together like quarter-size jewels on a spiraling necklace. She tried to decipher secret messages scribbled in sepia lines on lettered olive shells. The knobbed whelk slurped and spluttered water from its pudgy snail body whenever Brooke pulled it out of wet sand, retreating into its shell and closing its scab of operculum to keep out probing fingers.

Spiky sea urchins, robotic hermit crabs, the round bristly sand dollar—Brooke knew them all by name.

Before taking a single biology class in school, Brooke made her own mobile lab out of a red Radio Flyer wagon filled with buckets of collected specimens. Pulling the wagon from tidepool to tidepool, she stopped to show off the local marine life to fascinated tourists. The cannonball jellyfish, looking like a rubber bowling ball in a speckled purple-pink skirt, attracted the most attention. She laughed when she saw people poke at it with a stick in fear of being stung. Picking up the jellyfish with bare hands, she'd say, "See, you can touch it without feeling a sting. Its nematocyst stinging cells aren't strong enough to hurt humans." The cannonball jelly's scientific name—*Stomolophus meleagris*—was the first one she memorized from the many marine biology textbooks she checked out of the library.

Brooke's greatest sea treasure was the barb of a southern stingray, now displayed in one of the jars of shells in her apartment. She was thirteen when she pushed her way under the elbows of a small crowd on the beach to find herself almost eye to eye with a stingray spread flat on its back on the sand. It must've been as wide as her legs were long with a white belly glistening like wet tile. A barb jutted off its tail like a giant thorn. "Stay back," the fisherman warned, but when he looked away, Brooke reached out and ran her hand along the ray's winged side, feeling its sandpaper skin against hers. The fisherman twisted his hook out of the ray's down-turned mouth, making the ray flop around and whip its tail. The circle of staring people gasped. All eyes were on the menacing barb. But Brooke wasn't afraid. She wanted to come to its rescue, to carry it back to the safety of the ocean. Then the fisherman pinned its tail to the sand, cut off the barb, and tossed the ray into the ocean. "Show's over, folks," he said, smiling through sundried lips and too tan skin. When Brooke turned to leave, she saw the stingray's barb—as out of place as a thumb—discarded in a waste bucket. She plucked it out and slipped it carefully into her pocket. Walking away quickly, she explored the barb with tentative fingers, filled with a mixed sense of confidence and self-consciousness known only to those who carry a concealed weapon.

With a childhood full of courting sea creatures and yearning to protect them, Brooke glimpsed her calling at an early age. More than anything, she wanted to see a nesting loggerhead. In high school, she snuck out to the beach on summer nights to search for sea turtles, dragging Drew along with her. Their close friendship, easy and innocent most of the time, always seemed to be on the verge of something more. One June midnight near the north end, Drew reached for her hand as she told him stories about silly hermit crabs in her bedroom aquarium. Pulling her toward him until they stood silently face to face, he kissed her, leaving a question in the space between them. Just then, movement to Brooke's right caught her eye. A dark, boulder-size shadow lurched on the sand. There, a few feet away, a huge loggerhead heaved herself across the beach to nest. It was love at first sight. When she looked at Drew with wide open awe and delight, he asked, "Are you going to leave me for turtles?" She shrugged and slowly smiled, losing a little bit of him—of what might have been young love—that night, but finding a big part of herself. From then on, Brooke read everything she could find about sea turtles and tirelessly volunteered for a fledgling nest protection project until she left her island, and Drew, for college.

While Brooke's experiences in college, graduate school, and field research in far flung locations broadened her mind about sea turtles and people, science and relationships, they also focused her heart on her barrier island home, where loggerheads still nested, and where Drew still lived. After ten years away from the island where she was born, she returned to it—much like the loggerhead sea turtles she studied.

Loggerhead hatchlings imprint on their home—their natal beach—when they break free of their leathery eggs and scramble from their sandy nest pit to find the ocean, where they wander as nomads at the mercy of predators and other hazards. Only one in a thousand survives to maturity. After decades of life and hundreds of miles traveled at sea, an adult female loggerhead returns to lay her clutches of eggs near the same beach where she was born. Somehow—beyond all scientific odds and explanations—she finds her way home to begin the cycle anew.

Brooke returned to Anders Isle to find home again. Two years had passed since then—two summer turtle seasons, two lukewarm autumns, two snaps of winter, and two slow-blooming springs. Now, at age thirty-three, she ran along her island's beach, fighting a nagging dissatisfaction with her somewhat lonely, always-ordered life. Why was she such a plan-maker, a rule-follower? She wore her independence like a badge of honor, which tended to push people—men—away, at least those who didn't know her well. And then there was Drew. He knew her well, didn't he? There'd been a few hot moments between them in the past, moments Brooke remembered with nostalgia more than regret. But Drew always had other women—many other women. Recently, Brooke wondered how she compared to those other women and that thought came with a surprising bite of jealousy. She didn't know how to figure Drew out—or her feelings for him. Science trained her to observe, hypothesize, experiment, and draw conclusions. But matters of the heart couldn't be solved by scientific method.

Shell fragments crunched and popped in the sand beneath Brooke's shoes with each running step she took. She ran toward the island's secluded north end, where bottlenose dolphin pods fed in calm waves, where wide sea turtle tracks crisscrossed the beach, where turning tides washed away self-criticism. Her island seemed undisturbed by the passing of time.

But time would always be the true test of home, of love, of self.

What would endure?

Ahead, the strip of exposed shore—windswept and tide-washed—curved left at North End Beach, then followed the length of the surging inlet between Anders Isle and Taylor Island. Sunrise bled orange at the horizon. A pelican bobbed on the incoming tide. A lone bonnethead shark trolled the shallows. Brooke could close her eyes and run the beach to its end at the marsh creek. She knew it all so well—by memory, by heart.

Then she saw something in the distance, a shape that didn't belong.

Her scientist mind raced ahead of her long legs, analyzed the size and location of what she saw lying on the sand: big enough to be a body, and washed up above the high-tide line.

A searing dread burned in her throat as she moved closer, then stood still over a discovery she knew would change everything she loved about home.

CHAPTER

2

Brooke pounded on Drew's front door. Sand stuck to sweat on her lean legs and bloodstained forearm. Struggling to catch her breath after sprinting from the beach, she fixed her dark brown hair into a fresh ponytail. Drew opened the door, squinted against a slice of morning light. At six foot two, he was only a few inches taller than Brooke.

"Hey there," he said through a yawn, then grinned at her, half asleep and smelling like bed. "What're you doing here? It's so early."

"I tried to call," she said, winded, hands on her hips.

"Aw, I didn't hear my phone." Reaching out to give her a bear hug, he noticed her arm. "Is that blood?" He clasped her wrist for a closer look, eyes more alert now. "Are you okay?"

"I just tripped. You know me." She bent her elbow to see the bright-red scrape.

"Come in. I'll get you a Band-Aid."

"No, we need to go. I found something awful on North End Beach."

"At this hour, it better be a dead body," Drew teased.

Brooke pressed her lips together. She was *not* going to cry. "Someone cut out her spine as a souvenir and left her to die." She paused. "I need your help."

Drew felt her plea stab him in the gut. "What do you mean?" His eyes softened when he realized her hands were shaking. He couldn't stand to see her upset.

"Just come on." She wiped her bloody arm on her shirt. "We have to hurry."

Leaving the door open, Drew dashed to his bedroom. His quickening heartbeat pulsed in his ears. A dresser drawer ground on its runner; a clip clicked into place. Tucking his phone and badge in his pocket, Drew met Brooke on the porch. As Detective Sergeant of Investigations, he wasn't required to wear full uniform, but he still carried his pistol and other gear secured to his police duty belt. He hooked his hat onto his head, pulling it by the bill over his shaggy waves of blond hair.

"Let's go," he said, following her down the steps to his driveway.

Drew's white pickup sped a half mile to the mouth of a dirt road that wound through the sixteen-hundred-acre maritime forest. He glanced at Brooke, who seemed lost in thought with her face turned to the side window while the truck bumped along the road with a veil of dust in its wake. Where branches parted to show the island's northernmost point, Drew parked in a clearing cocooned by trunks and shadows of bordering trees.

Brooke led him along a beach access path between crests of head-high dunes, scanning the wide expanse of North End Beach. The tide was halfway in.

"There!" She pointed to a hulking, sand-encrusted mound the size of a coffee table.

Drew rushed over to find a female loggerhead sea turtle that probably weighed at least two hundred pounds. Her reddish-brown head and beaked jaws were lodged in the sand, disfigured by a gash that nearly split her head in half. Her top shell, normally fused with her spine, had been hacked from her back, exposing raw tissue to salt air. A white crust trailed down from one eye.

Drew crouched near the resting head. Not exactly a homicide. But seeing this mutilated turtle would be disturbing for anyone. For Brooke, though, he knew it was like finding a murdered pet.

He looked up at Brooke. "What happened?"

"I don't know." A tear slid onto her cheek. She swiped it away.

"I'm so sorry." Drew stood next to her, surprised to see her tearing up since she rarely cried in front of him. "Come here." Wrapping his strong arms around her, he held her close, felt her smooth hair against his jaw.

"I think it's Miss Biggy," Brooke mumbled into Drew's shoulder.

Trying not to laugh, he whispered, "Miss Biggy?"

When she gave him a look, he chuckled a little. His kind blue eyes shone like pieces of sea glass caught by sunlight.

"Stop it," she said, but finally let her tears flow, sad-laughing at the same time. "It's a cute name for our largest turtle mama."

Drew loved to tease her. He licked a tear off her cheek, which made her laugh harder. He laughed too, squeezing her in closer when she tried to wiggle away, until she did.

She sighed. "It isn't funny." She dabbed her face with her shirt. "None of this is funny."

"There's one funny thing," said Drew. "I thought you found a dead person out here. That's what I was worried about. So, the joke's on me."

Brooke smirked. "You never would've come if I told you it was a turtle."

"You're damn right about that." He smiled at her.

They both knew he was lying.

Drew attended events with Brooke in support of sea turtles—mostly to spend time with her—and learned to care about turtles because they meant so much to her. He would have come, even for a turtle. He would have come for her.

Brooke borrowed a pair of latex gloves from Drew's duty belt and bent down for a closer look at the turtle. Measuring and examining carefully, she dictated notes and took pictures with her phone from various angles.

"Was it a shark attack?" Drew watched her work.

"No, this isn't natural. See here, where her carapace, her top shell, is cut off? And this deep wound in her head? Someone killed her, which is an actual crime since loggerheads are a threatened species protected by state *and* federal law. Good thing I have a cop with me. Want to call it in?"

"Ha! You know I admire your work, Dr. Edens, but I'll be the talk of the station for years if I call in a dead sea turtle."

"Worth a try." Brooke winked at him. "But seriously, I need your help getting her to the aquarium for a necropsy. I already reported this to the South Carolina Department of Natural Resources and got the green light to move her since I'm certified to handle sea turtles and permitted to transport them."

"What are those white marks?" Drew pointed to a crusty streak on the side of the turtle's head.

"Her tears."

Drew frowned. "I have a blanket in my truck. We can use it to carry her."

Brooke noticed that Drew called the sea turtle "her" instead of "it." He removed his hat while he walked toward his truck and raked his fingers through his hair. Brooke smiled slightly at the familiar contrast of confidence and insecurity in his gait, allowing her hesitant eyes to linger on the form of his shirt against the toned shape of his shoulders and back.

Drew Young was borne of the sea. Brooke imagined he sprang from whitecaps as an infant and rode barrels in to meet his parents on the sand. The sea was his first love and would always be. Brooke knew she couldn't compete with the constant beauty of the Atlantic's rolling crests, the thrilling drum of her breaking waves. Drew's maiden sea called to him, calmed him, tamed his daredevil soul. He could never leave the ocean's side. He would be all wrong in a city.

Brooke adored Drew for that, for being who he was, for still living on the island where they grew up together. Each day when his work was done, he hustled to the ocean to surf or kiteboard. She watched him riding breakers in the late afternoon, wind wild in his hair. She found it hard to look away. His was a free, uncompromising spirit.

Drew and Brooke met in kindergarten, seated side by side in chairs attached to desks. During recess, when kids played cops and robbers, Drew always chose Brooke as the girl he was meant to protect; he whispered to her to stay hidden and promised to come back for her when it was safe.

They held hands in the lunch line.

When they were both six years old, Brooke marched into the kitchen and announced to her mom, "I'm marrying Drew and moving in with his family." Although their engagement faded without fuss, their allegiance to each other endured as a lifelong friendship complicated by attraction.

Growing up on the island, they lived a few blocks apart in wooden houses with saggy porches and peeling paint. As teenagers, they spent thick summer days languishing in the salt-worn boardwalk town, sipping milkshakes at the slanted shack that was Fat Andy's Fish Fry. When blinking fireflies ushered in night, they danced with friends on Front Beach Pier, or snuck into condominium swimming pools to take a dip in their underwear. On the beach, Drew taught Brooke how to read the wind and currents. She taught him how to read the sand. Behind the cereal aisle at the Sand Dollar Grocery and Sundries, they shared their first kiss—a cold grape-popsicle kiss—that lasted a few delicious seconds.

Something real connected them. A bond beyond friendship. A shy, fledgling love. Their lives unfolded and enfolded together, as predictable and inevitable as sets of waves rolling into shore, until Brooke earned a full scholarship to college in another state.

Leaving Drew for college was harder than leaving her parents. He didn't ask her to stay. He wouldn't. Her dreams were too big for their small town, too big for their maybe-love. But sometimes she wondered what she truly left behind all those years ago.

"This should work." Drew's voice snapped Brooke back to the task at hand. He carried a blanket thrown over his shoulder.

She took one end of the blanket to spread it out. "Thanks for your help."

"Anytime." He tugged her ponytail trying to cheer her up and stretched his fingers into a pair of latex gloves.

She smiled at him, glad for the easy intimacy still between them.

They struggled to lift the turtle carcass onto the blanket, then wrapped it and dragged it to the truck. After hoisting it onto the flatbed and tossing their used gloves into an old cooler, they drove to where the road emerged from the forest, straight and paved.

CHAPTER

3

"Hey, what's going on with Claire?" Brooke propped her feet on the dashboard. "I ran into her the other day at the farmer's market, but she clammed up when I asked about you. She couldn't get out of there fast enough."

Brooke was used to awkward conversations and false friendships with women Drew dated. Although she enjoyed being the only constant woman in Drew's life, his confidante and closest female friend, she accepted the distrust of his current girlfriends and the ire of those he left heartbroken. Two of his flings from last year, teacher Mimi Charles and nurse Tara Shultz, had been roommates until Drew came between them. Neither of them tried to get to know Brooke and both avoided her after things ended with Drew. The most recent, Claire Banks, a bartender from Atlanta, was just another one of the many.

Teachers, bartenders, nurses—they came and went, practically with the tides.

Drew smirked. "Oh, that ended weeks ago."

"So, what did you do this time?" Brooke folded her arms.

"It wasn't me." Drew gave her a side glance and smiled wide.

Brooke sighed. "Sure it wasn't." She rolled her eyes, pretending to be annoyed.

Drew just kept smiling.

Brooke nudged him playfully on the shoulder. "What am I going to do with you?"

He eased back into the driver's seat, one hand on the wheel. Brooke noticed his hand, just tan enough to hint at his life spent mostly outdoors, strength etched in veins and knuckles tightly defined, quick to fist. She always noticed his hands, especially when she watched him shape surfboards in his garage. His hands could catch wind in the curve of a kite, in the side of a sail. His hands knew how to build things, how to maneuver and press, how to sculpt and hold. His hands knew their way around a woman's body.

Drew's phone rang. He answered and listened while Brooke studied him. Faint lines deepened around his eyes.

"What is it?" Brooke asked.

Holding up a finger, he sucked in his cheeks, then said, "Yeah, I see."

She saw his obviously troubled face. But there was something else. Excitement? Anxiety? She couldn't quite tell. She stared at asphalt rolling swiftly under-tire. They were close to the connector bridge from the island to the mainland, but still a few miles from Anders Aquarium. She hoped Drew wouldn't leave her on the roadside with a decomposing turtle and speed off to a crime scene.

He hung up. She looked over at him.

"You aren't going to believe this," he said.

"What?"

He didn't answer, just gawked at the road, tightening his fingers around the steering wheel like he wanted to rein the truck in and keep it under control. Slowing to a stop, he started a U-turn.

"Where are we going?" asked Brooke.

"Anders Isle Marina."

"Why? What's going on?"

"That was Paul. Island Fire and Rescue got a call about two kids in the salt marsh," Drew said.

"Are they okay? What happened?"

"The kids are fine; it isn't them," he said. "They were crabbing, pulling up pots." He swallowed. "They pulled a dead body out of a tidal creek."

Brooke was sure she hadn't heard him correctly. "A dead body? A *human* body?"

Drew shot her a look. "Yes. Human."

"Oh my God," Brooke said.

"The older kid is just a teenager; he's the one who pulled it up. Paul said he panicked. His little sister went into shock. The Coast Guard and paramedics are on the scene right now."

"Those poor kids," said Brooke. "I can't imagine. Have you ever seen a dead body—I mean, like that?" Brooke corrected herself, but it was too late. She knew Drew was only thirteen when he saw his own dad's dead body in the open casket. At the funeral, Drew hugged Brooke for a long time. She remembered how she felt him exhale, felt his shoulders relax. But he didn't cry about his dad, not that day or any day. She cried about it because she cherished her own gentle dad and didn't like to be reminded of his mortality, but Drew's dad had been a mean drunk.

Focusing on the road, Drew nodded. "I've seen enough."

Brooke dropped her feet off the dashboard, sat up straighter. "Do they know who it is?"

"Not yet. There wasn't an ID."

"Was it murder?"

"Too soon to know," said Drew.

"I can't believe it. I mean, even in all my years as a field scientist in some wild and remote locations, I never came across a dead body. Has anything like this ever happened *here* before?"

"Definitely not on Anders as far as I know, but, about five years ago, a body washed up on the sandbar near Taylor Island."

"Oh yeah," said Brooke. "I remember seeing something in the news."

"It was a guy who jumped off the connector bridge. Could be something like that."

"Maybe," said Brooke, but she knew as well as Drew that if someone jumped from a bridge or fell off a boat, it would be reported. If someone was missing or lost at sea, there surely would be a plea for help, a mayday call, or at least a blip on the evening news. People kept track of each other.

Perhaps adrenaline from the morning discovery of the dead loggerhead clouded Brooke's judgment, but her first instinct was usually correct. Intuition needled through her like lemon juice in her veins.

This wasn't an accident.

Brooke and Drew didn't say much as they drove the short distance to the marina. Leaning back, Brooke looked through the side window at the miles of salt marsh. How did a dead body end up there? She and Drew played in those creeks as teenagers, lording over colonies of oysters and wading like birds, floating on inner tubes in swift waterways while salt dried on their skin. Now, death tainted the serene water. The thought made her shiver.

Drew swung his pickup into the marina's parking lot. Emergency vehicles and police cruisers blocked any view of boats or docks. Red ambulance lights still swirled in frantic recognition that something was terribly wrong. Drew wedged into a space beside an empty boat trailer. Brooke could practically see both excitement and worry coursing through him.

"All right," he said, starting out of his door. "I'll be back after—"

"Oh, I'm coming with you." Brooke pushed open her door.

"Well." He surveyed the area, then looked back at Brooke, but she had already climbed out and shut the door. Shaking his head, he met her at the tailgate. "This is one of those times when I need to get there before you do."

"I know," she said, matching his pace across the lot.

"Just don't touch anything. Can you handle it?"

While Brooke appreciated his protectiveness, she despised the question. "I was the only one on my research team in Hawaii who didn't throw up trying to find a tag on a decomposing sea turtle partially eaten by a tiger shark. And I've touched all kinds of *fresh* animal poop. So, yes, I think I can handle it."

"This is different. You really might feel sick."

"I won't."

"Don't try to be tough. Find a trash can."

"Sounds like fun," Brooke said, her curiosity piqued.

They wove between a fire truck and an ambulance to a wooden walkway above the docks where a small crowd gathered at the ramp entrance. People craned their necks to catch a glimpse of what was happening. Whispered conversations filled the air.

Drew flashed his badge to navigate through the crowd. "Anders PD," he said in his most official voice. Brooke remembered him playing cop in their elementary school games and stifled a chuckle.

Officer Walt Pickering stood guard at the yellow crime-scene tape across the ramp entrance. The newest rookie in the Anders Isle Police Department, Walt found pleasure in tasks that required brute force. His build was deceiving—a tall, thin frame made of nothing but solid muscle. Walt could split a board with his fist, but you wouldn't know that from looking at him. He broke his stoic pose to welcome Drew.

"Well, if it isn't the department's golden boy," Walt said, chewing gum.

"Careful, Rookie, you sound a little green." Drew gave Walt a knowing smile and shook his hand with a quick, all-business pump. "Where's the scene?"

"Dock eleven, behind the Johnsons' yacht." Walt watched Brooke following close behind Drew. "Who's this fine lady you've brought along on the job? You know you shouldn't mix business with pleasure." He winked at Brooke. Then his eyes drifted slowly down to Brooke's chest and farther down to the curve where her thigh disappeared under the hem of her shorts. She thought he might lick his lips.

Drew said, "This is Dr. Brooke Edens. She's a friend," Drew warned, "so keep your eyes on mine, Rookie."

"Nice to meet you," Brooke said.

"Pleasure's *all* mine." Walt grinned, letting his fingers graze the handcuffs on his belt while he continued to undress Brooke with his eyes. "Can I call you Brooke?"

"No." Brooke cringed. "Please call me Dr. Edens."

Undeterred by her tone, Walt went on, "What brings you here, Dr. Edens?"

"None of your business," Drew interrupted, recognizing Brooke's defensive posture. "Listen, Paul's expecting me. Do you mind?" Drew pointed to the yellow tape.

Gnawing his chewing gum, Walt reluctantly removed the tape, then stepped aside to let them pass. He gave a mock salute to Brooke and resealed the tape behind them.

Paul Asher walked along the dock toward Drew and Brooke, furrowing his brow beneath a shock of thick, black hair. His broad shoulders, military-straight posture, and flexed biceps stretched his shirt to the limit, making his defined pec muscles evident from a hundred feet away. Brooke would be intimidated by Paul's looks if his coffee-brown eyes didn't warm his other features and bring out a charm in him that always appealed to her.

Paul was a couple years older, but he and Drew became close in high school, relying on each other like brothers since neither of them had a father at home. Brooke only knew Paul through Drew, though she often wished to know him better. Engaging and gregarious, he had a sharp wit to offset the everyday stress of his work.

As he approached now, though, his demeanor was far from playful. Nodding a quick hello to Brooke, he clenched his jaw. When he spoke, it was with a measured, professional tone.

"Young," he said to Drew, and shook his hand, "you need to prepare yourself for this one."

"It's that bad?"

"It's bad. The body's been in the water and"—he glanced at Brooke—"we suspect this wasn't an accident."

Paul hesitated long enough for Drew to make eye contact with him. His look said that Brooke shouldn't hear the rest of their conversation.

"Brooke, I think you need to head back up to the parking lot," said Drew.

"Definitely," Paul agreed.

"No way," Brooke said, hands on her hips. "You aren't getting rid of me that easily."

"This is a criminal investigation now," Drew said. "I could get in a lot of trouble if I bring you over there."

"You didn't have a problem with it a minute ago," Brooke said.

"I did, but I just didn't stop you," Drew said. "From the sound of it, this could be a homicide."

"It's not something you want to see," added Paul.

Brooke crossed her arms.

"I have to go," Drew said, "but you can wait here. If you're allowed any closer, then I'll come back to get you."

"Fine," Brooke said. "I'll wait, for now."

Paul motioned for Drew to follow him. They walked the length of the first dock, heads bowed in conversation, then turned right at the Johnsons' yacht onto a narrower dock jutting out between boat slips.

Brooke cupped her hands around her mouth and yelled. "Don't forget about me!"

A few more steps, and they were out of her sight.

CHAPTER

4

Brooke waited on the dock. Above the tangle of treetops, the sun struggled to shine through a milky haze of sky, muted as the globe of a flashlight under a blanket. From her vantage point on a flimsy wooden bench nailed to the dock, Brooke watched two birds in an airborne dance, freefalling then inverted, dipping right then left to catch wind, their moves synchronized with perfection. Yachts and motorboats bobbed in their slips, resting until pleasure cruisers would take them out in the afternoon. Unlike the commotion surrounding dock eleven, the docking area where Brooke sat was quiet. Most fishermen were at sea this time of morning, departing before sunrise for the trek to the Gulf Stream. Brooke found herself peacefully alone, hidden from view of the crowded parking lot by the hull of a large boat.

She called Diane's phone, but it went to voice mail. "Hey, Diane. You won't believe what I found this morning at North End. I think it might have something to do with the missing turtles. Call me back. I'm at the marina. Long story. I'm sure you'll see it on the news. Talk to you soon."

Despite the grim details, the dead female loggerhead would surely provide clues as to the possible fate of the twelve others that disappeared from North End Beach in the past three years. Nothing about the missing loggerheads followed the nature of their nesting habits. Brooke and Diane anticipated more questions than answers from this summer nesting season. Brooke's scientist mind thrilled at the challenge of solving the riddle of the missing turtles, offsetting Diane's growing frustration with the whole situation.

This wasn't the first time Brooke called Diane with possible theories and news related to the turtle disappearances. But unlike her weekly cerebral updates and brainstorming calls, this time Brooke had an actual dead loggerhead to examine.

Brooke tried Diane's office number at the LPL, the Loggerhead Protection League. At barely eight o'clock, the office wouldn't be open yet, but Diane might be there anyway, especially if she'd been out that morning to look for tracks.

No answer.

Brooke hung up. She toyed with her phone, checking battery life and volume to be sure she wouldn't miss Diane's return call.

After a few minutes, she tried Diane's office number again.

Still no answer.

Setting her phone down, Brooke watched the same dancing birds tumble through the air, remembering the first time she met Diane.

Two years ago, Brooke moved back to the coast and into the position of Lead Sea Turtle Biologist for Anders Aquarium, where she directed the rescue and rehabilitation of injured sea turtles found anywhere from Virginia to Florida. In her doctoral and postdoctoral programs, she traveled to faraway places like Hawaii, Brazil, and Costa Rica to conduct field research with sea turtles. So, she was pleasantly surprised to find the Loggerhead Protection League right there on Anders Isle and immediately volunteered to be involved with local nesting sites and turtle conservation at the grassroots level.

When the nesting season started that May, Brooke set out just before sunrise for her first day as a volunteer, driving to the meeting point at the Sand Dollar Grocery and Sundries. She parked in the empty lot at 5:30 a.m. and waited in her car for the other volunteer to arrive.

The Sundries, as the locals called it, was an icon of Anders Isle. Opened during her grandparents' time, it stood proud, clapboards and all, through hurricanes and salt-heavy summer heat. Sanford "Sanny" Otis and his wife Marla inherited the shop from his father in 1975. Even with the hundreds of people who came through the Sundries in the decades since Sanny took over, he never forgot a name.

A limited selection of groceries filled displays on the store's right side, but fishing tackle and bait were the big-ticket items. The store's left side showcased the latest rods and reels, hooks, lines, buckets, and myriad other accessories. In the back shop, from separate coolers, Sanny sold bait to catch everything from blue crabs to bluefin tuna. It was well known among locals that there was no better bait in town.

When Brooke was growing up, the Sundries sported a soda shop behind the store with blue umbrellas, patio picnic tables, and a sweeping view of bowing sea oats and dunes sloping to the beachscape beyond. Marla Otis, in her pink polyester uniform dress, looking more like a candy striper than a waitress, served milkshakes, popsicles, soft drinks, and her signature item, the Sundries Root Beer Float. She often sat down with the teenagers to hear the latest gossip or wore roller skates to, as she put it, "add a little flair." The soda shop had been a favorite hang-out spot for island kids, a magnet and a safe harbor, where everyone felt welcome. Brooke heard that Marla gave up her famous soda shop role after being diagnosed with breast cancer in the late 1990s. The soda shop closed soon after that, and a shiny new Starbucks moved into the building next door. Marla beat her cancer, but, at almost sixty-five, she didn't have the energy to reopen the soda shop. Many things had changed on the island since Brooke's childhood, but the Sundries, even in its more limited form, still provided some comfort in its familiar façade.

Brooke flinched at a knock on her car window. She looked out at a T-shirt emblazoned with a giant sea turtle and a woman's thoughtful face just visible in the pre-dawn light. Pushing the door open, Brooke gave a sheepish wave.

"I'm sorry," the woman said. "I didn't mean to startle you."

"That's okay," Brooke said as she got out. "I wasn't paying attention. I haven't had caffeine yet since nothing's open this early." Brooke gestured to the dark storefronts.

"Tell me about it. I keep asking the Starbucks people to open half an hour earlier, or to just leave a cup of coffee on the sidewalk for me. I'll take it."

Brooke nodded and smiled. "I try to make my coffee at home, but it never tastes as good. I'm hopeless in the kitchen."

They both laughed the way people laugh in the company of strangers, to ease tension more than to acknowledge something funny.

"So, you must be Amy." Brooke held out her hand.

"Actually, no," the woman said, shaking Brooke's hand anyway. "I'm Diane Raydeen. Amy called around one o'clock this morning with a stomach bug and asked me to fill in."

"Well, nice to meet you, Diane. You really do need coffee if you were up at one and then again to come out here."

"I'm used to it. I get calls at all hours this time of year. I'm the LPL director, but most people call me the Turtle Lady. Nesting season just started, but it's already busy 'round the clock."

"I knew your name sounded familiar. I'm lead biologist for the aquarium's sea turtle hospital. I put together a list of people I need to reach out to and you're at the top."

"Small world," Diane said. She glanced at the Sundries storefront, "or more like a small town. You were bound to run into me sooner or later. So, welcome to Anders."

"Thanks, but actually, I grew up here."

"Oh, welcome back then. I've only been here for a few years, but I love the place. I can see why it would be hard to stay away."

"I've missed it, especially the beach," said Brooke.

"Speaking of, let's get out there and look for some tracks." Diane took out her notebook, pencil poised over a blank page. "Now, tell me your name."

"Brooke Edens."

A flicker of change crossed Diane's face. Her full lips twitched. Eyes narrowed. She paused for a second, pencil held still, before she wrote Brooke's name. "I've heard a lot about you." Diane continued to draw a chart on the page with precise, sharp motions.

"You have?" Brooke only returned to Anders last month and hardly had a reputation—of any kind—that would precede her.

"I've heard you mostly referred to as *Dr.* Brooke Edens." Diane kept her eyes on her notebook, squeezing her pencil hard enough to snap it in half.

Brooke chuckled, relieved. "Oh, so you've met Drew. Why doesn't that surprise me? He seems to meet every woman who sets foot on the island."

They both laughed, but this time Diane's laugh was tighter, a closed-mouth, high-pitched, distrustful laugh. She avoided eye contact with Brooke. Her hair was a mass of soft, black curls twisted onto the back of her head and held fast with a hair tie. Even though she was petite, about five two, curves in all the right places more than made up for her lack of height.

Diane slid her notebook into her backpack and retrieved a flashlight. Starting toward the beach access path, she motioned for Brooke to follow her. They walked behind the circle of flashlight as it skipped and shimmied over sand and palm fronds. A skittish ghost crab zipped into its hole.

"By the way, Drew had only the best things to say about you," Diane said, walking slightly ahead of Brooke and talking back over her shoulder.

"What a charmer."

"Yeah, well, it worked on me . . . for a few months, anyway."

"Really? You and Drew?" Brooke guessed that Diane was in her late thirties, at least a good five years older than Drew, but age wasn't an issue for Drew when it came to women.

Diane nodded. "It was pretty short-lived, but fun."

Brooke suppressed an uncomfortable pang of jealousy followed by a surge of her competitive streak, sizing up Diane to measure what Drew had seen in her. "Why short-lived?" she asked, but quickly felt she said too much. "I'm sorry. You don't have to answer that. I mean, we just met."

Diane laughed again. The tight, closed-mouth laugh. She walked beside Brooke where the path widened. "I don't mind. Haven't thought about it in a while. Turned out we didn't have much in common." While she spoke about Drew, she blinked her wide-set eyes in rapid succession like the wings of a frantic moth. "It was mostly physical, but I wanted something deeper. I guess I was too available."

"Ah, the kiss of death. The end of the chase." Brooke noticed her own relief to hear that Drew lost interest—his usual dating pattern.

"Exactly." Diane's eyelids fluttered. "And that was that. We decided we wanted to see other people. The romance screeched to a halt, but we man-

aged to stay friendly."

"Drew's great at being friends," Brooke said, "not so good at relationships."

"Yeah." Diane looked down. "It sure would've helped to have met you a year ago!"

"I wouldn't have been much help, really. I could tell you stories, but they'd only endear him to you. Drew just loves women." Brooke smiled at thoughts of Drew. "He's also the smartest guy I know, reads even more than I do, and that's saying a lot because the library is basically my mothership. Oh, it really used to bug me every time he aced a test in high school when I knew he barely studied, but things just come naturally to him. He's always been there for me. He's probably my best friend."

Diane let out a short huff. "That's funny because he said almost the exact same thing about you." She kept her eyes on the flashlight beam. "Do you know he keeps a picture of you in his bedside table drawer with an article from the local paper about your research?"

"No." Brooke's voice came out small and confused, but joy fireworked through her with each revelation. These were intimate details about how Drew saw her, things he wouldn't tell her and probably didn't want her to know. Maybe he thought about her as often as she thought about him. She wasn't going to ask why Diane had gone through Drew's beside drawer, but she was glad to know she was in it.

An awkward few seconds of silence passed between them while they walked. Brooke noticed a chill in Diane's mood, a guardedness that hadn't been there before.

The pattern had become such a foregone conclusion. Brooke expected that any woman who dated Drew wouldn't want to be her friend as long as she remained friends with him. As eager as she was to make friends, having been an only child, she was overly sensitive and wary about new female friendships based on a connection with Drew. But her introduction to Diane was pleasantly different: Drew wasn't the reason for it. He was already in Diane's past. Brooke and Diane shared a passion for protecting sea turtles; she hoped that would be enough to excuse her friendship with Drew.

The beach access path wound between dunes and spilled onto Front Beach.

Sand stretched forty yards to low tide and as far to the right and left as the eye could see. Twilight painted the ocean silver-blue, burning deep orange on the horizon, and fading up into straw yellow against the retreating evening sky. Two shrimp trawlers, dark specks in the distance, wore lights as bright as stars against the fiery backdrop of morning.

"Wow!" Brooke gasped, grateful to change the subject. "I forgot the spectacular sunrise on this island."

"My office." Diane swept her arm across the beach. "Of course, I have a regular office, too, but it doesn't *glow* quite like this one."

They walked left along the high-tide line toward North End Beach, watching the sand for field signs of a nesting sea turtle.

Brooke paused to snap a picture of the sunrise. "I remember getting up before dawn for swim practice most school days. Swimming was my thing. Well, swimming and sea creatures. Although sea creatures are more like my obsession." Brooke glanced at Diane and saw her nod while she listened. "Those mornings, I thought I was the first one in the world to see the light of a new day, watching the sun rise over the island. Like the sun broke open here, clean as an egg cracked on the edge of the sea, then spread out to cover houses and trees and the rest of the world."

Diane smiled. "A childhood full of nature's simple beauty."

"Exactly. As my dad would say: so much beauty my eyes are full. I didn't realize how unusual, how magical, it was here until I left for college. Up to that point, everyone I knew lived here. I'm sure we all took it for granted."

"You were lucky."

"And not too well off, which might've—ironically—been part of the luck, although my parents didn't see it that way," Brooke said. "My mom dreamed of bigger cities, full of universities and museums, where she could go to graduate school. She always wanted to be a college professor. But I came along, unplanned, and dad couldn't afford to leave his engineering job. I think mom never really forgave me for being born. Like it was somehow my fault." Brooke scoffed and shook her head. "But my dad's always been my champion. I guess my parents folded their dreams in dirty diapers and threw the whole mess out."

Brooke was sure she was talking too much, oversharing as usual.

Diane let out a short laugh with a look of both empathy and surprise. She warmed to Brooke. "Well, my parents did the opposite. They saved and planned to move to a small beach town. Out of the dustbowl of middle America to the freshness of the coast. All I heard about growing up was how lovely it would be to live at the beach. How everything would be so easy once we lived at the beach. My mother told me stories about creatures she saw when she vacationed at the shore as a little girl: hairy-bottomed sand dollars and conch shells with giant tongues, stick-legged birds playing touch tag with the waves. Because of her stories, I fell in love with nature. Even though I didn't see the real ocean for the first time until I was fifteen, I saw it all along in my mind."

"Did your family finally move to the beach?"

"No," Diane said with a flutter of blinks. "My father got sick when I was in high school, was in and out of the hospital for treatments. Pancreatic cancer. He died during my senior year. His treatments wiped out most of my parents' savings, but even if my mother had the money, she wouldn't want to live at the beach without him."

"I'm so sorry." Brooke deflated, choosing her words carefully. She couldn't imagine life without her dad, whose warmth and easygoing guidance countered her mom's cold push for perfection. Maybe the common ground between Drew and Diane was a shared understanding of such a loss. "That must've been hard."

"There really isn't any way to explain the feeling. And it all happened so fast. Within six months of his diagnosis, he exhausted treatment and a home nurse was assigned to, as they put it—*make him as comfortable as possible*—during the final weeks. The painkillers made him hallucinate. I know this sounds strange, but some of the best memories I have of those last weeks with him are the days when we sat in his room together and he told me about the cat he saw in the window. I played along because it made him happy, and sometimes I even pretended to see the imaginary cat before he did, just for laughs. And we did a lot of laughing. That's what I choose to remember most."

"I'm sure he'd be proud to see you now, living at the beach and protecting loggerheads," Brooke said.

"I wish he could visit me here. He would revel in the seclusion—and birdwatching. I think a lot of my decisions about what to do with my life were guided by his death, like I picked up where he left off."

"What about your mom?"

"Oh, she loves to visit, gets here for most holidays. She remarried five years ago and still lives in my hometown in Ohio around the corner from my younger brother, his wife, and their two boys. What about your parents? Do they still live here?"

"No. They moved away when I went to college. Not far, just to Charleston, about an hour from here. Mom grew up there and wanted to be closer to her mother and sister. My dad's parents had passed away by then, and he was ready to move to a bigger city."

"So, they found a piece of their dream after all," said Diane.

"I think they did. At least, mom seems happier. She takes courses at College of Charleston and might go for her master's. Dad's happy if she's happy. Maybe that's the best we can hope for—to live a big dream on a smaller scale." But even as she said it, Brooke knew she'd have a hard time doing it. She was groomed from a young age to never let anything—or anyone—hold her back. She heard her mom's voice in her head, almost as a warning, and always full of regret from unexpected life experience: "Being a woman might be a glass ceiling in the world of work and one you can certainly break through, Brooke, but being a woman isn't as limiting as being a mom. Be sure to find your purpose and achieve your dreams *before* you have children. While womanhood is just a ceiling, motherhood is a box." And Brooke listened. She grew up determined to prove her worth. *Motherhood is a box.* Brooke understood. She put her mom in a box. And she still felt guilty.

It took about forty-five minutes for Brooke and Diane to walk their designated section of beach while looking for a mama loggerhead's telltale track. When a female loggerhead comes ashore to nest, she moves slowly, alternating her curved flippers to pull her heavy body across the sand. She might pause, lift her head, and listen, making sure it's safe to keep going. In her wake she leaves a crawlway of two parallel churned paths resembling tire tracks of a bulldozer separated by the flat drag mark of her belly. Each crawlway, like footprints, provides field signs of her movements on the beach. Sometimes her crawlway snakes and loops across the beach while she looks for a perfect nesting spot. Claws on her front flippers scratch deep V-shaped grooves in the sand with the V opening in the direction of her crawl to identify the track as an entrance or exit crawlway. An entrance crawlway shows her progress from the ocean toward the dunes and often leads to a shallow body pit where she turns and shovels sand with her hind flippers, digging and sculpting a deep lightbulb-shaped egg chamber. Facing away from the ocean, she settles into a trance while laying her clutch of about one hundred soft-shelled eggs as round as ping pong balls, then buries them all with more scooped and tossed sand. An exit crawlway shows her journey back toward the ocean to be lifted by folding waves and swallowed into the tide, leaving her offspring to hatch and survive on their own.

There wasn't any sign of a crawlway that morning. As Brooke and Diane reached North End Beach, sunlight crept over the horizon like liquid gold spilled onto the canvas of sea. Two birds darted into view. Their boomerang-shaped wings and tapered bodies torpedoed in an airborne tango.

Diane pointed to the birds. "Look at those!" She watched them fly, her eyes wide and focused. "They're magnificent!"

The birds cut left and right, slicing through sky, at first in unison and then splitting into acrobatic tumbles through the air.

"What are they?" Brooke asked.

"Swallow-tailed kites. They're the most adept fliers of all raptor species, often described as the coolest bird on the planet. I'm such a bird nerd." She smiled. "They're common in South Carolina, but I haven't seen them *here* before."

"Why do you think they're here now?"

Pursing her lips, Diane shook her head. "I really don't know," she said, hands on her hips and still looking up.

Brooke didn't know it yet, but during their friendship she would come to learn that it was rare for Diane to admit to not knowing something.

Although they didn't find turtle tracks that day, Brooke found it easy to open up to Diane. She found in Diane not only a longed-for female friend but also the older sister she never had.

After that day, dancing birds always made her think of Diane.

CHAPTER

5

"Let's go, boys! Move your asses! I'm not getting scooped on this one."

Walt Pickering watched as Bella Michaels, lead reporter for Local News 2, scurried across the parking lot from a van crowned with a giant satellite dish, cameraman and light tech close on her high heels. With a svelte figure and perfectly symmetrical, almond-shaped eyes, her name was well-deserved. She smoothed the lap wrinkle in her skirt and adjusted her form-fitting blouse while trying to keep her balance on sand and gravel, then pushed her way into the crowd gathered near the entrance to the docks.

"Excuse me." She side-stepped through a small gap in the last row of onlookers. "Excuse me. Local News 2 coming through. Please make some room."

"Whoa! Hold it right there, little lady." Walt held up his hand and puffed out his rookie chest. "This is as far as you'll be going."

He stood between Bella and the yellow crime-scene tape.

"Don't you know who I am?" Bella touched her collarbone.

"I don't care who you are." Walt felt the full weight of his power settle in his shoulders. "This area is off limits. No media allowed past this point."

"I'm sorry." Bella softened. "Let me start over. I'm Bella. And you are?" She extended her hand.

"Officer Pickering." Walt gave a perfunctory shake.

"Well, Officer Pickering," Bella said, her voice breathy, "it's very important to me to get this story. As you can see, we're the first news crew here. It only seems fair to let us have a closer look."

Walt found it difficult to remain professional in Bella's presence. She leaned toward him while she spoke, watched him with hypnotic eyes, and finished her request with a slight pout. Intoxicating perfume emanated from her clothes and hair.

"Rules are rules," he said. "I didn't make them, but that's the way it is."

"Haven't you ever broken a rule? Or bent one just a little?" Bella teased.

The news crew set their equipment down behind her, already tired of the banter.

Not sure how to respond, Walt cleared his throat, aware Bella was flirting. "Yes, I mean, I bent a rule here and there, before I became a cop."

"Then you understand." She pounced. "Sometimes it's the right thing to do. And if the rule isn't broken, only bent a little, then you're still doing your job and allowing me to do mine. What do you say? Can you help me get a closer look?"

She fixed her eyes on his, waiting. Her eyes weren't the only ones on him. The onlookers, unable to see dock eleven, turned their attention to Walt and Bella. Walt felt their judging stares, the importance of remaining in control.

"I'm afraid I can't do that." He stiffened. "You and your crew will have to wait here with everyone else."

Bella leaned closer. "Is there *anything* I can do to change your mind?" Her voice purred with seduction. She brushed her fingers along her neck and through silky strands of blond hair curled at her shoulder.

Walt couldn't believe his luck and, at the same time, his unfortunate position. This woman would stop at nothing to get her way, and he was supposed to stop her. Before he could tell her the list of erotic favors he had in mind, they were interrupted by the clatter of two more news crews crossing the parking lot.

"Looks like you'll have to change my mind next time." Walt pointed to the approaching reporters.

"That's a shame," Bella said with a hint of a smile. "For you, Officer Pickering, there won't be a next time."

As quickly as she warmed up to Walt, Bella composed herself to leave. She pushed her way through the crowd without looking back. Her camera crew picked up their gear and followed her.

Deflated by Bella's rejection, Walt crossed his arms and spit his gum over the railing into the water. From now on, there would be no further discussion; his command would be final. Fool him once, maybe, but not twice.

Bella set up for her report in the parking lot, close enough that Walt could hear every word. When the camera light snapped on, she spoke intently into the large microphone, punctuating each sentence with an expression of rehearsed concern. Her live report was instantly beamed to televisions across the region.

This is News Flash Live on Local News 2. I'm Bella Michaels. We're at Anders Isle Marina, where investigators are on the scene of a potential homicide discovered early this morning. Usually a quiet island, even with the seasonal flow of tourists, Anders Isle seems an unlikely place for murder. In fact, this is the first on record in decades. As you can see behind me, paramedics and policemen are here at the marina, along with the Coast Guard and Island Fire and Rescue. We don't know the number of victims or any potential suspects at this time, but we're waiting for details from the authorities. Local News 2 is continuing to follow this breaking story and will bring you the latest as we get it. I'm Bella Michaels reporting live from Anders Isle Marina. Stay tuned to Local News 2 for the best in local news.

CHAPTER

6

Above dock eleven, the thud of a circling news helicopter provided a constant pulsating soundtrack pierced by occasional gull cries. A 42-foot near shore lifeboat rubbed against its fenders where it was tied off to dock cleats with coarse lines. On board the boat, several Island Fire and Rescue crew members stood near a blue tarp draped over an object as bulky as a washing machine.

Two children huddled in blankets on a bench while paramedics swarmed around them with blood pressure cuffs and thermometers. Drew looked at the teenage boy, trying to remember where he'd seen him before. As a small island cop, Drew often came across gangs of young teenagers out too late at night and up to no good. Usually, he sent them home with warnings about trespassing and noise ordinances, knowing how it felt to be a teen stuck on a quiet island. There were only a few occasions when he'd taken further action for underage drinking or stolen property.

"Are those the kids who found the body?" Drew asked.

"Yup," Paul said. "The Willis kids, Mac and Cecilia. She's still in shock."

"How old is she?"

"Ten, I think."

"Damn." Drew frowned.

"Hey, I saw your mom the other day walking a big dog," said Paul. "Is she in town?"

"She was here for a few days. Brought her latest soon-to-be-husband number four, I think. I lost count. Her other two dogs just ran around yipping. Cute little ankle biters." Drew shook his head. "I like the dogs much more than the boyfriends."

"Detective!" A voice called from behind them. They turned to see a short, square-built man waving his whole arm at Drew while shuffling in their direction.

"Oh great, Sampson's on this one?" Drew complained to Paul. "You should've warned me. He must be about to piss his pants with excitement."

"At least he's thorough," Paul said.

"Yeah. A thorough pain in the ass."

Patrol Officer Mark Sampson hustled toward them, clasping a notebook to his chest. He flashed a jolly smile at Drew while his eyes—magnified by the thick lenses of his glasses—registered pure glee. A halo of buzz-cut blond hair encircled the balding spot on the crown of his head. "Good to see you, Detective, very good," he said through puffs of breath, his face and underarms visibly sweating even at that early morning hour. "The chief assigned me to assist you on this investigation. I'm at your service." He shook their hands with his perspiring palm.

"So it seems." Drew surreptitiously wiped his hand on his pants. "Well, the coroner is on the way, and we were just about to take a look at the body." Drew gestured to the boat.

"Man or woman?" Sampson fidgeted with his notebook.

"A female victim," said Paul. "I was one of the first responders."

"A rare case for our little island, isn't it?" Sampson asked. "The first homicide on record, I think."

"It is," Drew agreed. "So, let's get started. Sampson, you wait here to show the coroner where to go. After that, talk to the kids who found the body." Drew pointed to the Willis kids. "Find out what happened this morning."

"Of course." Sampson's face, already red from the heat generated by his own nervous energy, blushed an even deeper shade that spread from his neck to the top of his balding head. "Thank you, Detective."

"No need to thank me. It's part of your job now," Drew said.

Sampson nodded dutifully and scribbled something in his notebook, taking post to watch for the coroner.

When Drew reached the boat ladder, Paul pulled him back before he even put his foot on the rung. "Drew, wait, before you see her body." Paul squared his shoulders to Drew.

"Come on, Asher, you never call me by my first name," Drew said, a half-grin on his lips. "I know it'll be bad. Maybe some crabs found her before the kids did. I might not be an expert yet, but this ain't my first rodeo. I'm ready. If you can handle it, believe me, I can."

"It isn't the state of her body." Paul put his hand on his friend's shoulder and looked him straight in the eyes. "Drew, you know her."

CHAPTER

7

Brooke continued to wait on a slim dock extending into the marina like the tine of a giant fork. She scrolled through email on her phone, bounced her leg, and checked the time while she waited for Drew, or Paul, or a call from Diane . . . so long that the bench where she sat made wood swirl imprints on the backs of her thighs. Wisps of hair stuck to the nape of her neck, pasted there by the humidity of the overcast day. The boat behind her groaned in its slip as a few lazy swells rolled under its hull.

Then, from behind her, she heard a voice that made her breath catch. Caldwell. Her heart began to race. How long had it been? Almost two years?

The last time Brooke crossed paths with Caldwell was a few months after she called off their engagement. That day, she drove four hours inland to Charlotte, North Carolina, and didn't realize her meeting was in the same building as his office. Their encounter in the lobby was brief, awkward. He made an excuse to leave—head bowed, and hands shoved in his pockets—with a demeanor far from the arrogant law student, the bold Caldwell Castor Madden, Jr., she remembered from all the years they dated. He seemed nervous, but maybe she read too much into it. She, on the other hand, was surprised to see him, but not uncomfortable. Everything's easier for the person who chose to leave. She'd been so sure of her decision, yet she left the building flustered, haunted.

Now, she heard Caldwell's drawl from across the docks, and each word was once again imbued with his good old confidence. She shuddered when she saw him trotting in her direction along the length of a wooden railing that bordered the marina yard and overlooked a boat ramp. Noticing the pale skin tone of his arms and legs against a pink polo shirt tucked into khaki shorts, Brooke guessed he spent most of his time in the office, which didn't surprise her. His brown hair, cropped around his ears and clean-shaven above his collar, barely stuck out from under his hat. Caldwell yelled to the driver of an SUV, who shifted into reverse and maneuvered a sport fishing boat on its trailer toward the water. Two men stood in casual business clothes at the top of the boat ramp, each with arms crossed, dark sunglasses, and loafers planted shoulder width apart. They nodded and made conversation with a third man dressed in a coat and tie.

Caldwell didn't see Brooke. She couldn't decide if she wanted him to. It would be easy enough to duck behind a boat, hide from view, but that seemed silly after all that had happened between them. He must be over her by now. Knowing Caldwell, she was sure he didn't waste much time moving on. Still, she hesitated to find out.

"Lookin' good," Caldwell told the SUV driver, popping a thumbs-up. "Let's get her in the water."

He reached the corner of the overlook railing, leaned out, and motioned for the driver to steer the boat to the far dock in front of a neighboring restaurant. The ramp to Brooke's docking area was still cordoned off because of the investigation and eager media. At the railing corner, with his back to her, Caldwell was so close to where Brooke sat that she could read *The Heritage* printed above the adjustable back strap on his hat.

She held her breath.

Please don't turn around, she thought.

Please don't turn around.

That instant, in Brooke's hand, an upbeat ringtone blared from her phone. She dropped it and watched in horror as it tumbled across the dock toward the water.

"Shit!" She lunged to catch it, landing with a *thud* in a full body sprawl on the hard dock, her phone pinned under her right hand. The shrill ringtone, on high volume, repeated itself. Brooke closed her eyes. Silencing her phone, she lowered her forehead to rest on the warm wood of the dock, did not move. It was probably Diane calling back at the *worst* possible time.

"Hey! Are you okay?" Caldwell's syrupy voice sounded much closer, worried.

"I'm fine." Brooke kept her head down while half waving in the direction of his voice.

"Brooke?" Caldwell asked, syrup gone from his voice. "Is that you?"

She winced. "Yes, it's me." Opening her eyes, she lifted her head, looking up to where Caldwell—clean-cut, square-jawed, soft hands—stood against the overlook railing fifteen feet above the dock where Brooke lay. "Hi," she said with feigned surprise.

"Well, hey there." Resting his forearms on the railing, hands clasped together, he leaned forward, smiling. His sunglasses hung loose around his neck. Brooke felt his slate blue eyes focused on her. "What're you doing?"

"I fell."

"I can see that." He chuckled, cheekbones and dimples popping. He found her clumsiness adorable.

Sighing, she pushed up from the dock to sit cross-legged and brushed her free hand on her shorts while clenching the phone in her other hand. "I mean, my phone fell. I dropped it, and I was trying to catch it before it went in the water."

"Okay."

After a few seconds of awkward silence, Brooke got to her feet.

"But what're you doing *here*?" he finally asked.

"Oh, I'm waiting for . . . a friend." She purposely omitted Drew's name. Why did she do that? She didn't have to worry about Caldwell's suspicions anymore. Besides, he'd been the one more likely to stray in their relationship. Let him be jealous.

"The foot ramp is blocked, you know. Something big going on over on those docks." He pointed in the direction Drew and Paul had gone. "You should see the hoopla in the parking lot. We could barely get to the ramp. I doubt your friend will be able to get down there to meet you."

"He's already down here," she said, and left it at that.

Caldwell's eyebrows knitted together under the bill of his hat. He looked around for her friend. "Okay, then. Never mind."

"Will you be in town for long?"

"Nope. Got here last night for dinner and going back to Charlotte tonight. Business stuff." He jerked his head toward his boating companions. "I'm showing those knuckleheads some island real estate and good fishing. Can't wait to get out there and wet a line."

"Sounds promising." Brooke rubbed her elbow. "So, I take it business is good?"

"Definitely. Real good. I brought in one of the firm's biggest clients— pretty unusual for an associate."

"That's great." Brooke knew he wouldn't bother to ask about *her* work, *her* life. His self-centeredness remained the same.

"Mr. Madden, we're ready to go!" The driver hollered to Caldwell from the sport fisher, now docked and loaded with coolers and fishing gear.

"On my way!" Caldwell waved to the driver, then turned back to Brooke. "I hate it when he calls me Mr. Madden. I look around for my dad. But that would be Senator Madden, wouldn't it? Not such a bad title." He grinned.

"Not bad at all." Brooke smiled.

"Well, I guess I better get going. Don't want to keep the big fish waiting." He paused, softened. "Good to see you, Brooke."

"You, too. I'm glad things are going so well for you."

Caldwell kept grinning, all dimples and cheekbones, and tipped the bill of his hat to her.

Brooke watched him disappear behind a building and reappear at the opposite docking area. He waited for the three men to step onto the sport fisher before unleashing it from the dock and climbing aboard. From her dock, Brooke heard the engine guzzle and spin while Caldwell backed the boat into the waterway. As they pulled away, she saw that one of the casually dressed men was Linwood Kingston, a prominent local real estate developer referred to in certain circles as "Mr. Kingpin."

CHAPTER

8

On the deck of the Island Fire and Rescue boat, Drew and Paul stared down at the blue tarp in front of them. Paul nodded to his crew members, who unhooked bungee cords and pulled the tarp aside to reveal a wire-framed crab trap rusted from overuse in saltwater. Tied to the top of the trap with crude knots was the body of an adult female, fully clothed, her shirt torn open at the neck. A thick rope, brown with age, wrapped across her right shoulder, torso, and pelvis; crossed under her through the trap; extended from her left shoulder to her crotch; and was secured with a double knot. Her sneakers, still on her feet, had double knots eerily similar to those that bound her to the trap. Her pruney skin, wet and wrinkled, looked in death much as it would have in life after several hours in a bath. Dark, slick hair framed her pallid face, making her features seem pasty and plain. Her hazel eyes—wide open and startled—bulged like those of a fish out of water; her taut expression pled for a gasp of air.

Drew recognized her immediately: Diane Raydeen.

He didn't know whether the sight of Diane's body itself or the fact that he knew her was to blame for his violent need to vomit. Drew thought about her family and friends. How would they handle this? How would he tell Brooke? An intense wave of disgust and confusion rose through his insides. No, he thought, it wasn't confusion. It was an emotion embedded in him from early childhood, its barb twisted too deep to remove. He recognized the itch of it, the pain and prickling as it grew stronger. Not confusion, but anger—red, searing anger born from the profound helplessness he felt as a boy each time his drunken dad abused his mom. Sometimes his dad spewed a tirade of ugly words, other times he spoke with his fists. Drew rubbed his left cheek where he took a hit for his mom at the age of ten. Three years later his dad lumbered out of the house after another beating and drove full highway speed into a tree. The official report said cause of death was blunt force head trauma. Most assumed he fell asleep at the wheel. But Drew hoped some dagger of remorse made his dad turn the tires off the road on purpose that night.

Drew's stomach wrenched and burned as though he'd swallowed fire, its flames licking his throat. A metallic taste—old pennies and brass—swelled in his mouth. Lips open, clutching his ribs, Drew shivered with a dry heave and spit. His eyes watered.

Paul stood in silence, didn't recoil. He'd seen dead bodies in far worse shape than this one. "You okay, buddy?" He patted Drew's back.

Drew sniffed and swallowed. "Yeah. I'll be all right." He shook his head, took a deep breath, and continued to stare down at her.

Lifeless. Gone.

Finally, moving closer, Drew slid his hands into latex gloves to learn what he could from her body and opened his phone to photograph and dictate his findings. His training took over. Years of practice for a moment like this. The signs of death—objective and impersonal—would be his guide: pallor mortis, algor mortis, rigor mortis, livor mortis. Paleness of death. Coolness of death. Stiffness of death. Bluish color of death.

With detective eyes and a keen memory for details, Drew touched her face and neck, speaking his preliminary observations into his phone. "Skin is pale, cool to the touch. Most notably, no rigor in jaw or neck, where it usually sets in first, which means death was recent." He took a photo, then crouched down to move the hem of her shorts away from her skin for a clear view of her upper thigh. "Bluish-purple livor mortis in the back thighs and lower buttocks consistent with body's current supine position, but not conclusive. Body still could have been moved after death since lividity can take at least thirty minutes to settle. When I pressed the bluish skin, color receded and then returned, which confirms recent death. I'm guessing we're between two- and six-hours post-mortem."

Drew stood and leaned over to look in her eyes, ignoring flashes of her gaze back at him from when life had been in those now-dead pupils. Lifting one eyelid, he saw tiny bursts of red on white where delicate blood vessels had ruptured. "Corneas are clear, more proof of recent death, but eyes show signs of asphyxia." Probing her scalp and working his way down, he paused at her throat. "No visible head injury, no blood on clothing, no lacerations or gunshot wounds. Possible early signs of bruising around neck, but too early to tell for sure. Nothing indicates an obvious struggle by victim to escape from the ropes. She was probably dead before she was tied up. Saltwater washed away or contaminated most external fluids, hairs, fibers, and fingerprints."

Stepping back from the body, Drew stripped off the gloves and stuffed them into his pocket, noticing Paul again as though snapping out of a trance.

"Impressive," Paul said, clapping his buddy on the shoulder. "But I'm sorry. What a damn shame. Who would do that to her?"

"I was going to ask you the same thing. Any ideas?"

"Not a single one." Paul motioned to his crew to replace the tarp over the body.

"She wasn't the kind of person who made enemies." Drew watched the body disappear under the tarp, conflicted by his need to remember every detail for the investigation and his urge to forget everything he just saw. "Tied up that way, it's pretty clear someone didn't want her to be found, but I'm almost certain she was either dead or unconscious when she went underwater."

"I hope so," Paul said. "That's the kind of thing nightmares are made of—drowning in such shallow water you could reach up and feel fresh air on your fingertips."

"Stop, Asher. Jesus." He looked at the tarp, unable to blink away the image of Diane's still body. "We'll know more once we have the cause of death and any forensic evidence."

"Speaking of, where's the coroner?" Paul asked.

"Right behind you," said a gruff voice, so close even Paul flinched.

Drew and Paul turned simultaneously to meet the coroner and found themselves face to face with a middle-aged woman, a clear mismatch for the gruff voice. She peered at them with dark brown eyes set close together in a dark brown face. Bunched spider-webs of wrinkles rimmed her eyes and made her face appear to be stuck in a permanent squint. A shoulder bag, large enough to hold a couple melons, hung almost to her knee, emphasizing her squat, round build. Rummaging through her bag, she pulled out two lint-edged business cards.

"Terry Caufman." She handed a card to each of them. "I'm guessing you're authorized to be here?"

Her voice, while abrupt and commanding, belonged more to a male smoker pushing fifty than to a woman of any age. Distracted by the underlying rake-on-concrete rasp in her voice, Drew found it difficult to concentrate on the meaning of what she said.

"Well?" she asked, growing impatient with their blank stares.

"Of course," Drew said, clearing his throat and glancing at her business card. "Yes, Terry, of course we're authorized to be here. I'm Detective Young, Anders Police." He offered his hand, which she shook, but she looked at it and then at him—unimpressed.

She turned to Paul. "And you are?"

"Paul Asher, ma'am. I'm with Island Fire and Rescue."

Paul didn't even offer his hand. Something about her sour attitude and disapproving voice made him as apprehensive as a good kid sitting in the principal's office.

The coroner nodded in response to their introductions. She shoved one hand deep into her oversize bag and yanked it open wider with her other hand, sifting through its contents. After a few seconds, she sighed and glared into the bag, stretching her arm to its deepest corner. Finally, she found a pack of cigarettes and released the bag from her grip.

Tucking a cigarette into her teeth, she held the pack out to Paul and Drew. "Shmoake?"

They both declined. She lit up and took a long drag, then turned her head to exhale into the passing breeze.

"So, let's see what we've got here." She reached for the tarp. "This is my favorite part of the job," she said around the cigarette in her teeth.

They couldn't tell if she was kidding.

"Hold it." Drew had planned to share his initial impressions with the coroner, but it seemed she might be offended. Better to wait and see if her conclusions were the same as his. Test her thoroughness. Sampson could take notes. "Let me get my assisting officer to observe."

"Well, now, get your act together already," the coroner said, glaring at him and sucking on her cigarette.

Drew hurried to the ladder and climbed down to the dock. He didn't want to see the body—*Diane's* body—again. Etched in folds of his memory were images of that same body, naked and warm and smooth, quivering under his hands; her back arched to invite his kisses from her neck to her stomach; her legs wrapped around his waist, feet locked against his back, holding him in.

He remembered her in snapshots.

Seductive.

Alive.

The livid skin, the crab trap, the pallor, the dead-fish stare—none of that belonged in his mental pictures of her. He shook his head, but he couldn't erase what he'd seen.

"Did you see her?" Sampson waddled toward Drew with such haste his pants legs made loud swishing sounds like clothes in a wash cycle.

"I did," Drew said, stone-faced. "How could I miss her?"

Sampson cocked his head. "That's an odd question, but I guess the coroner might be hard to miss, as blunt and"—he searched for the right word—"*stout* as she is. I'm surprised you'd come right out and say it."

It took Drew a second, but he didn't let on that he'd mistaken the subject of Sampson's question. Embarrassed by his preoccupation with images of Diane's body, he forced a smile.

"I didn't mean anything by it. The coroner seems very professional. Actually, I came down here to find *you*. I want you to be there while she makes her observations. I already saw all I need to see."

"I'm on my way, Detective. And I tried to get a statement from the boy, Mac, before he went to the hospital with his sister, but his mother showed up in a fit."

"Any luck?" Drew asked.

"No. Nothing new. I got as far as the part where he pulled the body up before he started shaking. His mother insisted he'd been through enough for now."

"I'll follow up with them later, but I doubt the kids are involved. Seems they were in the wrong place at the wrong time."

"Perhaps, although the boy said it's their crab trap."

"It is?" Drew sensed a lead.

"Yes, Detective. Yes, indeed. Apparently, it wasn't by chance they found the body."

"Well, that's a good start."

"Thank you." Sampson beamed and fingered the notebook tucked under his arm, then glanced up at the boat deck. "I better not keep the coroner waiting too long or she might smother me with her giant purse." Sampson chuckled at his own joke.

Drew humored him with a grunt of amusement but didn't smile. This investigation wasn't business as usual; it was personal. He wanted each detail handled with the utmost precision—by the book. He would find this killer, and when he did, he wanted everything in perfect order to make this case a slam dunk.

"You're right," Drew said. "I would hurry if I were you. Be sure to keep a chain of custody for any evidence she removes."

"Will do." Sampson mounted the boat ladder. Perched mid-climb, he looked over Drew's head to the turn in the dock. "Get ready, Detective. Here comes the boss." With that, Sampson scaled the last two rungs and hurtled out of sight.

Chief Abraham Mullinax strode along dock eleven with the air of a king approaching his throne. His serious *kneel before me* expression was known to intimidate even the most seasoned cops in the department. It was clear he believed he deserved every bit of it. Part Bible Belt Baptist and part mama's boy, Mullinax was born and raised in a backwater town surrounded by cypress swamps deep in the Lowcountry. He was long-boned with knobby joints, a puzzle of mismatched parts—big feet and hands, narrow shoulders, bowed legs, and a face as pocked and bulbous as a potato. But, despite his incongruous appearance, he commanded attention with his walk. It seemed he could cross a twenty-foot room in four steps. He exuded arrogance and wore his authority like a cape.

"Just the person I was looking for," Chief Mullinax said to Drew, more upbeat than usual, which made Drew nervous. He squeezed Drew's shoulder and patted him a few times on the back.

"Hi, Chief." Drew took a deep breath.

"Seems we have an all-time big investigation on our hands." The chief rocked back on his heels.

"We do."

"Are you on top of it?"

"I think so."

"Don't think, son, you've got to know."

"Yes. I'm on top of it. I viewed the body, made some observations, and met the coroner. Sampson's with her now."

"Excellent. I'm sure Sampson will help with whatever you need, but you're the lead detective for this investigation. The mayor and maybe even the governor's office will be bearin' down on us to find a suspect. I don't want to let them down. First murder there's been on our quiet little island since anyone can remember. I intend for us to solve it."

"I've got Sampson under control."

"Good. You know how he gets bogged down in details. We need to stick to the big picture. Is this your first homicide case?"

"First one I've been in charge of, but I've assisted on county homicides. I know the drill."

"Well, anything you need, you just ask. I want suspects. No mistakes. Don't fuck this up, Drew."

"I understand." Drew swallowed hard. He knew this was the chief's way of placing trust in him.

"And I don't want you or anyone else talking to the goddamn media. I'll handle all public statements."

"Hey, I'm camera shy anyway, Chief."

"With that pretty boy face?" Mullinax shook his head. "Not a chance."

Drew shrugged. He suspected Mullinax wanted to be the face of the investigation. His potato face would be on television screens across the region, possibly even across the country. In the public eye, the chief's devotion to the case was certain to bring him recognition beyond any of his boyhood dreams.

"I'm going up there to see this for myself." Mullinax scowled at the boat deck. "I want you on the scene until the body's transported out. Got it?"

"Got it, Chief." Drew watched Mullinax ascend the boat ladder and swoop over the side of the boat. Feeling sweat bead around his nose and eyebrows, Drew exhaled. This was more than he bargained for as a small island detective, but he wanted justice for Diane. He thought of his dad, his mom, and all those nights when he could only be a witness. Whether or not he was able to solve this crime, at least now he had the ability and the position to do something.

CHAPTER

9

At noon, Drew found Brooke pacing the length of the dock where she spent the morning waiting for him.

"Finally," she said. "I was about to swim home."

"Sorry that took so long."

"You were supposed to come back to get me."

"I couldn't get away. Strict orders from the chief," Drew said.

"You could've called." Brooke threw up her arms. "At least Paul remembered I was here. He said you'd be a while, but I didn't know he meant hours."

"I had to do my job," Drew said. "Besides, you really only stuck around to find out what was going on."

"That curiosity lasted for the first hour. Then I needed to do *my* job by getting the sea turtle to the aquarium for analysis. Remember?"

"Oh, shit. I completely forgot."

"That's what I thought."

"Listen, the turtle is the least of my problems right now. I'm dealing with an actual homicide, and the chief is on my back to find a suspect as soon as possible. On top of that, I have a neurotic patrol officer as an assistant and an agitated, chain-smoking coroner." Drew wiped his forehead.

"So, it's really a murder? Do they know who it is?"

"I can't talk about it right now." Drew looked down so quickly she might not have noticed if she didn't know him so well. He slumped his shoulders.

"Not here. I shouldn't have said anything."

"No. *I* shouldn't have said anything. You're doing me a favor with the turtle, so I'll stop giving you a hard time. Just do what you need to do."

"I need to wrap things up in the parking lot. Then we'll head to the aquarium."

"Lead the way."

In the parking lot, the press thickened around Drew and Brooke. Anxious reporters stuck microphones in their faces and spit questions at them. Drew waved them off and dragged Brooke by the arm behind him.

They approached a transport truck as Sampson shut the rear doors. He scribbled something in his notebook.

"Are we all set here, Sampson?" Drew asked.

Sampson adjusted his glasses. "Yes, Detective." He glanced for a second at Brooke. "Everything's in order. They're taking the body to the cooler until tomorrow."

"Tomorrow?"

"Yes, tomorrow." He glanced again at Brooke. She turned her back on their conversation and feigned interest in the stewing media. "The chief asked the coroner to move the autopsy up a day to Sunday. It took her a full three cigarettes to agree to it. That lady smokes more than she talks."

"No kidding," Drew said. "Okay, well, good work. I want you to be at the autopsy tomorrow. We need every detail."

"Of course, Detective. I'll be there."

"You can give me the highlights afterward. And take lots of notes."

"I always do." Sampson raised his notebook.

"This afternoon, I'm going to the hospital to try to get more information from the Willis kids," said Drew. "I'll be sure to tread lightly with their mom. You head to the station to man the tip line. I'll meet you there at five o'clock to discuss leads and evidence."

Sampson nodded. "See you later, Detective." He shuffled to his car.

The transport truck pulled out of the parking lot as the first rumble of thunder boomed from the darkening eastern sky. The wind picked up. Lines clanked against the masts of moored sailboats. An ominous storm front—a massive tidal wave cloud—inched toward the marina.

The sky thundered again. Brooke and Drew looked up as the oblong cloud cast its gray shadow on the day. She was sure he was thinking what she was thinking: there's a rotting turtle in his pickup truck. Brooke knew Drew didn't want to clean up a mess any more than she wanted rain to wash away possible evidence on the turtle.

"We have about five minutes before it starts to pour," Brooke said.

"Less than that." He pulled his keys out of his pocket.

"I don't think we'll beat the storm to the aquarium, but we better try."

A bolt of lightning flashed, followed by a thunder crack. Fat raindrops began to fall far apart. One landed on Brooke's arm.

"Run!" said Drew.

They sprinted across the lot to Drew's pickup, rain coming harder now. Brooke stopped at the tailgate.

"What're you doing?" Drew yelled from the driver's side door. "Hurry up and get in!"

She stared into the bed of the truck. Rain poured down, drenched her hair, streamed across her cheeks.

Drew ran to where she stood blinking rain from her eyes. Clothes soaked. Then he saw what she saw.

The back of the truck was empty.

The turtle was gone.

CHAPTER

10

"Y'all might've heard my dad's presidential campaign is targeting the South this month," Caldwell said to his guests while they bumped along in a four-seater golf cart on an unpaved road through Taylor Island.

"Yeah, love his slogan: *Get Mad!*" said Bud Gibson, a local real estate broker and one of Caldwell's college fraternity brothers. "How's that going?"

"Well, just the other day he was going door to door to meet people upstate when he came upon this one farmer who had his whole arm up a cow's ass. This fella was so eager to meet my dad, he actually pulled his arm out of the cow, gave it a few wipes on his overalls, and reached out to shake hands."

The other men in the golf cart howled.

"What'd your dad do?" Bud asked.

"Shook hands with the man, of course," Caldwell said.

"I'll be damned if that isn't gettin' down and dirty to meet folks," Bud said.

"Good ol' Senator Madden. Nobody's ever been more tailor-made for politics," Linwood Kingston said, adjusting his tight belt around his gut.

"He'd be a damn good salesman, too, if he ever gets out of politics," Bud added.

"Sales? Aw, hell, that's what politics is, my boy. They're all for sale." Linwood patted Bud on the shoulder.

The golf cart moved at a snail's pace compared to the smooth speed of the sport fishing boat from which the four men had come. A looming thunderstorm forced them ashore only a few hours into their fishing expedition. Storms on the coast usually blew through in a matter of hours, so Caldwell suggested they head to his family's beach house on Taylor Island instead of returning to the marina.

Taylor Island sat across the inlet from Anders Isle. Accessible only by boat, Taylor catered to an exclusive crowd of landowners, including Caldwell's family, whose vacation home had been one of the first built on the island a decade earlier. Caldwell and his guests waited out the storm at the Madden's beach house and now toured the island by golf cart to admire the private residences, most of which were the result of deals with Linwood Kingston's company. Linwood always enjoyed a chance to see his developments in person. His company, the largest of its kind in South Carolina, executed property deals with such streamlined precision and in such volume, he rarely had time to see all the development sites, construction, or even the finished products. Linwood hadn't been to Taylor Island in almost a year.

"Just up ahead is the homeowners' club—Taylor Island Golf Resort—better known around here as the Tiger Club." Caldwell pointed to the first rolling fairway just visible through clustered points of palmetto fronds and sawgrass. "The golf course is consistently ranked in the top twenty nation-wide. Fantastic views, and never crowded."

"You know, I was at the Muni the other day with a client when some kid ran out on the fairway and stole our golf balls," Bud said. "Goddamn kid just ran out of the bushes, grabbed the balls, and disappeared on his bike before we could even get one leg in our cart to chase him."

"What'd you do?" Linwood asked.

"What could we do? The kid was long gone by the time we made it through the front nine."

"More importantly, why are you taking clients to the Muni?" Caldwell asked with a sour expression. "Those craphole greens are like puttin' on dirt. You might as well play a round at the local putt-putt."

"Excuse me, what's the Muni?" Ben Feldman, last of the foursome, was a painfully polite young gun sent down from Boston by Art Ogletree, a well-known and famously successful real estate tycoon.

"The Municipal Golf Course. It's open to the public," Caldwell explained.

"Oh, I see. Better to be at a private club then?" Ben asked.

"Always," Caldwell said.

"So, you guys do a lot of your business on the golf course, too?" Ben asked.

The other three men squinted at him as though he came from another planet.

"You're in the South now, my boy. Every business meeting is a prelude to a round of golf," Linwood said.

"Or a cover for one," added Caldwell.

The men laughed.

"That's the way our clients like it," said Bud.

"I'd be willing to bet more business is done on the golf courses around here than in all the conference rooms in the state," said Linwood.

"I can't tell you how many times I've called up clients for lunch and parlayed it into an afternoon on the course," said Bud. "Golf course deals are the reason business casual dress is the norm for our work week."

"I don't think I've worn a suit in months," boasted Caldwell.

"Yankee over here could learn a few things from us, starting with the meaning of business casual." Linwood gestured to Ben Feldman's suit. "That coat and tie is just plain overdressing for the occasion."

"Aren't you hot?" Bud asked Ben.

"Not really," said Ben, adjusting his tie, "just a little uncomfortable."

"Caldwell, you must have something back at the house this poor boy can wear so his clothes don't give him away as the Yankee he is." Linwood patted Ben's shoulder to smooth over the teasing.

"Didn't Art warn you about these knuckleheads?" Caldwell asked Ben.

Ben shrugged. "I thought he was kidding."

"Oh no, two things we never kid about in business—money and tactics," said Bud.

Caldwell snorted. "You're full of shit. *Tactics*? What would those be . . . our handicaps?"

Bud, Linwood, and Caldwell erupted in laughter. Ben smiled a thin, goofy smile, trying not to worry about being the butt of this gang's jokes.

CHAPTER

11

Brooke and Drew were quiet during the drive to Drew's house. With the truck's AC blowing full blast, Brooke shivered. Her wet clothes stuck to her skin. She remembered being soaking wet and riding in Drew's car in high school after a long day at the beach. The nose of his surfboard hung between them in the front seat. They talked and laughed around it, barely able to see each other. Then they just held hands below the board and didn't say a word, letting the warmth between their palms stoke their thoughts. She wondered how he'd react if she reached for his hand now. But she didn't.

From the side window, Brooke watched one beachfront mansion after another pass by along the main road, their multiple levels wrapped with porches. The new owners of her parents' old house on the island tore it down to build a modern three-story rental property, which seemed to be the trend. She marveled that many of the new giant houses were second homes for their owners, occupied during summer months but mostly vacant mid-fall to mid-spring.

The outside of Drew's house wasn't worth a second look. Made entirely of cinder blocks painted beige, with a flat roof and a mildew-stained awning over the front door, it probably hadn't been updated since it was first built some sixty years earlier. Fortunately, overgrown bushes hid most of it from view.

Inside, however, its charming rooms seemed without corners, as the walls met behind stacks of books arranged on furniture gathered as haphazardly as a crowd around a campfire. Each room opened with the surprise of a treasure chest, welcoming exploration. Layers of shells collected on tables. Library-size bookshelves shared the walls with framed photographs and maps. A surfboard leaned against an armoire.

Brooke stood near a coffee table topped with a pile of surfing magazines. She loved the cozy clutter of Drew's house, but she never knew where to begin to take it all in—whether to sit down or wade through. Looking around his house invoked in her the same hesitation and curiosity as reading a friend's diary without permission. His life spread around her in pieces. She'd been in his house countless times—he always invited her in—but she still felt like a trespasser.

Drew brought her a T-shirt. It smelled like sunscreen and soap. Like him. She went to the bathroom to change into it.

Even surrounded by his own things in his own house, Drew couldn't find a sense of calm. He wrung his hands and ruffled his hair, then pulled a curtain open. Gray daylight filled the room but didn't brighten it.

When Brooke came out of the bathroom, Drew faced her.

Taking a deep breath, he said, "It's Diane."

"Well, it's about time. Where's my phone?"

"No, hold on." Drew moved some clothes off the closest chair. "Maybe you should sit down."

"Why?" Brooke asked without sitting.

"Please." He put his hand on her shoulder.

"What's wrong?"

"Diane isn't on the phone. She's, well . . . it's Diane. The body they found this morning. It's Diane. She's dead."

"What?" Brooke let out a nervous chuckle.

"I'm so sorry. I didn't know how else to tell you. And I couldn't let you see her. Not like that."

"No, no, it can't be Diane." Brooke shook her head and closed her eyes for a few seconds. "I just saw her the other day. I called her this morning. She called me back while I was on the dock. Well, I thought it was her, but

I dropped the phone."

"Brooke." Drew rubbed her arm to comfort her. "Listen, Diane didn't call you. I saw her body. Somebody killed her."

Backing away from him, she settled like a falling leaf on the edge of an armchair, bracing herself with both hands. She stared at a stain on the carpet. Tears welled. Struggling to speak through quivering lips, she looked up at Drew. "You knew it was her all morning, and you didn't tell me? Paul must've known, too."

"How am I supposed to tell you one of your best friends is dead?" Pulling Brooke to her feet, Drew hugged her, rocking her gently. "I wanted to find the right time, the right place. I knew you'd be more upset than all the rest of us put together."

Brooke sobbed on his shoulder. He could feel her tears wet his neck.

Stroking the back of her head, he said, "We'll find out who did it."

But he knew murder cases had gone cold with far more evidence than this one, and he wondered whether they actually would.

After a good cry and a glass of water, Brooke stood at Drew's open front door, where just that morning she'd come to get his help. This day already felt like the longest day of her life.

"Are you sure you don't want a ride to your car?" Drew asked for the third time. "It's on my way to the station."

"No, thanks. I'll walk. I need some fresh air."

Drew looked reluctant to let her go. "I'll call you later."

"Okay." Brooke knew he might call, or he might forget to call, depending on what he was doing later.

Rainwater pooled on the sidewalk, dripped from stiff fronds of sabal palm trees, and hung as mist in the air. The day felt ten degrees cooler under the concrete, post-storm sky. Brooke walked a mile to where she parked her car that morning before her run, before her predictable Saturday routine became anything but. First the dead turtle, then its mysterious disappearance, and finally Diane—it was all too much. The disorientation left Brooke grasping for something familiar to hold on to, something to keep her from passing out or screaming with anger.

It was early afternoon. Normally, she finished her run first thing in the morning, returned to her apartment, showered, and ran errands. She usually grabbed lunch and took it to the beach, where she read a book or collected shells. In late afternoon, she visited the aquarium to check recovering turtles and follow up on research from the previous week.

Today, Brooke couldn't imagine relaxing on the beach. And she wasn't hungry. But the thought of spending time in the quiet, windowless belly of the aquarium appealed to her. Being in the company of sea turtles seemed an appropriate way to mourn Diane.

Driving along the main road in silence, she watched scenery pass by, trying to remember the last time she saw Diane alive. Was it two days ago? No, three. Three days ago, Diane met Brooke for their weekly Wednesday morning walk on Anders Isle to patrol for turtle nests. Their walk progressed as usual—stretches of conversation broken only to pause and study markings in the sand. They talked about their lives and work. Three days ago, Diane wore green cargo shorts and a pale blue patterned tunic. In the wind that day, her tunic fluttered around the shape of her body the way feathers shimmy on a tropical bird. Nothing about the day or about Diane warned of her coming fate. If anything, her more-chipper-than-usual mood screamed "new romance," but she denied any blossoming love interest, claiming the arrival of turtle season was reason enough for high spirits. Three days ago, radiant Diane searched for her beloved turtles—and now, she was gone.

On the connector bridge to the mainland, Brooke drove faster to avoid thinking about the spartina grass and marsh creeks all around her, interwoven to the horizon. *Diane died out there*, in one of those creeks against the slick, packed mud. Blinking away tears, Brooke gripped the wheel tighter.

The Anders Aquarium parking lot—too small for the growing popularity of the tourist attraction—overflowed with cars. A rainy Saturday on the coast meant a big visitor boom for the aquarium. Parking in an employee spot in the back lot, Brooke used her security code to enter through the basement door below throngs of tourists and out of sight of the staff. She stole away to the sea turtle hospital, where each hot-tub-size tank held an individual turtle.

The hospital program began five years before Brooke joined the aquarium staff. Its mission to rescue, rehabilitate, and release meant that most of the turtles in the hospital would eventually be sent home to the ocean upon full recovery and new rescues would rotate into their places. The latest addition was Cedar, a green sea turtle named for the creek where he was found. A boat strike on top of his shell, directly over his spine, had almost been a deadly injury and required CT and MRI scans at a local veterinary clinic partnered with the aquarium. Cedar rested in his tank while Brooke cleaned his wound and stroked his barnacle-covered shell.

After an hour of cathartic rounds to check turtle patients, Brooke received a hotline call from *Bonnie*, a shrimp trawler headed to port at Dylan Creek Marina in Anders City. Set up in partnership with the South Carolina Department of Natural Resources, the aquarium's hotline encouraged the public (especially fishing vessels) to report injured sea turtles directly to the hospital's staff, all of whom were certified by the SCDNR to handle sea turtles; it accounted for more than half of the turtles treated annually by the aquarium's hospital. People called the hotline about injured sea turtles as far south as Jacksonville, Florida, and as far north as Delaware Bay. Brooke was relieved this call would be a local rescue.

"*Bonnie*, what's the problem?" asked Brooke.

"I've got a turtle here, ma'am. It's in bad shape," said the shrimp fisherman through a crackling connection.

"Do you know what caused the injuries?" asked Brooke.

The shrimper didn't answer right away. After a few seconds of silence, Brooke asked, "*Bonnie*, are you still there? What are the injuries?"

"I'm still here, ma'am. There's a flipper that's got pretty cut up from what I can see."

"Where did you find the turtle?"

Again, silence. Brooke pressed for more information. "*Bonnie*? I'm only here to help the turtle, not to get you in any kind of trouble. Can you tell me more about it?"

The shrimper cleared his throat. "It was caught up in my gear, in the shrimpin' net."

"Do you have a TED?"

"No, ma'am. We're plannin' to put one in, but we don't have one yet."

That explained his hesitance. Without the Turtle Excluder Device, required by federal law, he was shrimping with an illegal net.

He continued, "We been out here shrimpin' all mornin' with no problem, then we got this turtle in the last net of the day. I just couldn't put the turtle out to die when it's my fault it's gotten hurt."

"I'm glad you called," said Brooke. "We can help."

"Are you gonna report me? 'Cause I can't afford no fines. What if this here turtle dies?"

"No, *Bonnie*, please listen: all I want is to save that turtle. If you bring the turtle to me, I'm not going to report you. I promise. Just get the turtle to me and go get a TED. Will you do that for me?"

The connection hissed with a few seconds of silence while Brooke closed her eyes and bit her lip.

"All right, ma'am," the shrimper agreed.

Opening her eyes, Brooke smiled. "Thank you, *Bonnie*. You're doing the right thing."

Before they disconnected, Brooke jotted down details of the scheduled three p.m. pick-up at Dylan Creek Marina and gave the shrimper instructions for basic turtle care while enroute.

Bonnie arrived in port twenty minutes past the scheduled pickup time. The shrimper relinquished the badly wounded turtle, an adult female loggerhead. Her torn front flipper evidenced her struggle to break free from the net, which left her lethargic and weak. The shrimper, his neck sunburned dark red, thanked Brooke for her help. She noticed his eyebrows, unruly and muppet-thick, and a deep dimple in the center of his chin. He shook her hand, his calloused palms hard and sharp against her softer skin.

Brooke transported the turtle—who she named Bonnie—to the aquarium, where she measured, weighed, photographed, and examined the injured loggerhead. Bonnie received fluids, antibiotics, and pain medication while resting on a "waterbed" of foam in a tank with a clear side window. Brooke cleaned Bonnie's flipper laceration with a special vacuum closure instrument to lightly suction out any infectious material. On any other Saturday, Brooke would assign a staff member to watch over a newly rescued turtle, but today she wanted to care for this turtle herself. Maybe if she could save Bonnie, she could begin to make peace with the fact that nobody had been there to save Diane.

CHAPTER

12

Through the open door to Cecilia's hospital room, Mac Willis saw Drew before he had a chance to knock. Mac stiffened. His mother rose from her seat beside the bed, rubbing a knot in her lower back. She stepped between Mac and Cecilia, who stopped watching television and craned her neck to see what was going on.

"Mrs. Willis?" Drew approached her with a gentle walk. "I'm Detective Sergeant Young with Anders Isle PD."

"You can call me Nadine," she said sheepishly. "I know you have questions, Detective, but I didn't expect you here so soon." Nadine turned to give her children a reassuring smile.

"I'm sorry to disturb you, but I need to interview your children while the details of this morning are still fresh in their minds. Is Cecilia feeling better?"

Frowning at Drew, Nadine reached over to pat Cecilia's hand. "A little bit better, thank you, but I just don't know that CeeCee is feeling better enough to talk about what she saw."

"I could start with your son. He could tell me what happened. Then I'd only need to speak to Cecilia if I'm still missing information. Is that okay with you?"

Mac pretended not to hear the detective's suggestion, concentrating instead on the blaring television commercials while slumping in his seat to appear more relaxed. He wished he could jump into the television the way that guy in Mary Poppins jumped into sidewalk chalk drawings. CeeCee made him watch that movie at least three times. It was a girly movie, but that chalk drawing guy sure knew how to escape.

Wary of Drew yet unsure whether she was allowed to say no to him, Nadine took a deep breath and glanced at the wall clock. Almost four p.m. Why wasn't her husband back from the cafeteria yet? She didn't want to be the one to make this decision. "Before you talk to Mac, do I need to get a lawyer or something? I'm not sure about how all this stuff works."

"You're welcome to get a lawyer any time you want to, but your children aren't suspects, and they aren't under arrest. I'm only here to ask them about what they found, the plain facts. That's all. This is strictly part of our routine investigation—gathering facts. And, of course, because they're minors you can be with them the entire time."

Nadine sighed. "I guess that'll be fine. Can we at least stay in this room? I'm not leaving CeeCee alone."

"Yes, of course."

"All right then. Let's get it over with. Mac, sit up straight. The detective wants to ask you some questions."

Grabbing the remote control from the side table, Nadine muted the television. Drew side-stepped around the bed and settled in a chair stuck in the corner without much leg room. He sat at an awkward angle to Mac but did his best to appear comfortable and in control. Mac sat on his hands and bit his lower lip.

"Let's see," said Drew. "Officer Sampson, who spoke to you this morning, told me you left off at the part where you pulled the crab trap to the surface."

Cecilia sucked in a quick breath and clenched her mother's hand. Nadine glared at Drew and turned the television volume back up to distract Cecilia.

Drew, seeing Cecilia focused on the screen, lowered his voice. "Can you tell me what happened next, Mac?"

Mac hunched his shoulders and looked down at the floor while he answered. "We saw the body, me and CeeCee, but CeeCee saw it first. She was already screamin' and cryin' before I had a chance to let it go and let it sink back down underwater. I didn't know what to do. CeeCee just kept screamin'. Then she started to shake like she was cold. A boat came out of nowhere 'cause they heard the screams, and one of the guys on the boat had a phone, so he called 911 when I told him what we found."

"Did you lift the trap up again after that?"

"No, sir! I sat with CeeCee and tried to calm her down while we waited for help. The rescue people got there fast and pulled up the trap, and I couldn't even look at it. I never seen anything like that dead body except in movies."

"And I hope you never have to see anything like that again," said Drew. "Now, just clear up a few things for me if you don't mind. How often do you check the traps?"

"'Bout every other day, but most of the time Dad comes, too. He's a shrimp boat captain. He's been teachin' me how to pull traps so I can help when he's out shrimpin'. I've only done it about five times by myself."

Nadine added, "He wasn't supposed to be out there this morning without his daddy's permission." She eyed Mac and shook her head.

"I see," said Drew. "Well, Mac, why didn't you ask permission?"

"Dad was out on his boat for an overnight shrimpin' trip. I was gonna surprise him."

"Sounds like you had good intentions," said Drew.

Nadine pursed her lips.

Drew continued. "So, before this morning, the crab trap in question was last checked . . . Thursday?"

"Yeah," answered Mac.

Nadine cleared her throat, giving Mac a disapproving look.

"Yes, sir," Mac corrected himself.

"Was your dad with you when you checked the trap Thursday?"

"Yes, sir," said Mac.

"Was Cecilia with you Thursday?"

"No, sir."

"After you checked the trap Thursday, then what did you do with it?"

"Dad put fresh bait in it, and we lowered it back into the creek."

"And you didn't check that trap again until this morning, correct?"

Before Mac could answer, Joe Willis darkened the doorway. "What the hell's going on here?" He looked first at Drew, then at his wife.

Nadine bristled. Attempting to ease the tension in the room, she said, "Joe, this is Detective Young from the Anders Isle Police. He needed to talk to Mac and CeeCee."

Joe walked to the foot of Cecilia's bed, stopping beside his wife. The stink of shrimp followed him into the room. His ruggedly handsome face, rimmed with a beard shadow, resembled a weather-worn Ben Affleck.

Drew stood up. "Nice to meet you, Mr. Willis. I'm sorry to barge in on your family like this."

"The hell you are. Now you listen here, Detective, my son didn't do anything wrong, and he doesn't have to answer to you."

"I don't mean to upset you. I'm not accusing your son of anything," said Drew.

Nadine placed her hand on her husband's forearm. "Joe, he was just asking some standard questions."

Joe grunted. "Honey, please, I don't need to argue about this here." Pulling his arm away from his wife's grasp, he said to Drew, "Bottom line is you shouldn't be talking to my son without talking to me first."

"You're right," said Drew. "I would've talked to you first, but I didn't know you were here."

"Course I'm here. My daughter's in the hospital. Where else would I be?"

"I thought you were out on your boat today." Drew leveled his eyes on Joe. "Weren't you on an overnight shrimping trip?"

"Yeah, I was, but that was last night. We got back to the marina this morning. I came straight to the hospital as soon as I heard about all this mess."

"Well, that's my mistake then," said Drew.

"I reckon it is," said Joe.

"Anyway, I'll be going now. I have what I need," said Drew. "I appreciate your time and, again, I'm sorry for the intrusion." He started for the door. "Oh, one last thing, Mr. Willis." He turned back around. "What's the name of your boat?"

"*Bonnie*. Boat's named *Bonnie*."

CHAPTER

13

On his way to meet Sampson at the station, Drew stopped at the Sundries to grab a late lunch. Beside the front door, Oliver Tack sat on a shaded bench and ate a third of his sandwich in one bite, chewing slowly with his giant mouth and washing it down with a gulp of soda. Everything about Oliver was big—he towered above most men with broad, sloped shoulders, his hands were like baseball mitts, and his midsection bulged under his shirt like a tire. Even seated on the bench, his torso and long thighs showed his height. Oliver was a super-sized man.

Drew didn't know Oliver well; not many people did. Oliver kept to himself. Rumors swirled about Oliver and his odd behavior. He was seen walking alone at night on the connector bridge overdressed for exercise or mumbling to himself in the grocery store while making sudden manic dashes for canned beans and frozen dinners. He paced the sidewalks of the historic district, fiddling with a dial on his handheld radio. Some of the locals thought he escaped from a mental institution. Others claimed he was a war veteran suffering from bouts of PTSD. The kinder gossipers called sightings of Oliver the embellished imaginings of small-town folks with small-town minds, defending him as eccentric, not crazy. Regardless of what they thought of him, most people in and around Anders had heard of Oliver. Drew chalked all that up to the chitter-chatter of locals, wary of a harmless misfit. Oliver seemed shy and aloof, nothing more. But Drew had never been good at reading people.

Oliver grinned at Drew through his mouth full of food. "Late lunch for you, too?"

"Yeah," said Drew. "Did you leave anything in there for me?"

Oliver huffed and guzzled down the rest of his drink. "You're lucky I'm not that hungry today." He smacked his lips, then wiped his mouth with the back of his big hand. "Hauling cargo at the port kicked my ass. I need sleep."

"It's been a long day," said Drew.

"Damn right."

The front door jingled when Drew pulled it open. He nodded to Oliver. "Have a good one."

"You, too." Oliver took another giant bite of his sandwich.

Inside, the Sundries was quiet. An array of premade sandwiches and pasta salad filled a refrigerated display case beside the checkout counter. The Sundries always offered take-out deli food, but on Saturday Sanny and Marla Otis made twice as much for the influx of fishermen and tourists, so they usually had leftovers well past the normal lunch hour. Most Saturdays, Drew counted on the Sundries for at least one meal.

Sanny saw Drew eyeing the sandwiches. "Howdy, Drew. We've got the ham 'n' cran for you today. It's buried in there somewhere." He winked. He often hid Drew's favorite sandwich under a stack of pasta in the corner of the case—especially on Saturday—to be sure it survived the crowd. Sanny had been saving sandwiches for Drew since Drew was a teenager.

Drew found his ham and cranberry sandwich, putting it on a tray with a bag of chips and sweet iced tea. "Thanks, Mr. Otis. You know this is the best sandwich in the state."

"I can't take credit for it," he said with a humble shrug. "It's Marla's cranberry sauce. Tastes like Thanksgiving on a bun, doesn't it?"

"It sure does. How is Mrs. Otis?"

"Mighty nice of you to ask after her, Drew." Sanny beamed. "She's splendid, bright as a ray of sunshine. Just the other day she made a bouquet of fresh flowers cut right from her garden. Flowers seem to sprout from every inch of dirt she touches. The most beautiful purples and yellows you ever did see."

"That's nice. I'm glad to hear she's doing well."

"And what about you?" asked Sanny. "Some awful news I heard about Diane. It's a tragedy. You must have your hands full."

"Yes, I do. We do. It's a big case."

"I'll say, wasn't she a friend of the lovely Miss Brooke? I saw them in here a time or two."

"They were friends, very close friends."

"That's a shame. Please tell sweet Brooke we're thinking of her."

"I will."

"You know, I always thought you two youngsters would end up together, like two little love birds when you were teenagers."

Drew blushed. "More like I was a lovesick bird around her."

Sanny puckered his lips. "Nope. I don't think so."

"Well, maybe you saw something she didn't, Mr. Otis. Anyway, those days feel like a lifetime ago."

Sanny snorted. "Son, you don't know what a lifetime feels like." He pinned Drew with a forgiving, grandfatherly look that read *you are too young to be wise*. "Listen to me—I sure am showing my age, rambling on like an old man. You go sit down, Drew; enjoy that sandwich. And good luck with the investigation."

The door jingled. Sanny and Drew turned.

"Well, strike my britches if it isn't Mayor Patterson McPhee." Skipping around the counter, Sanny greeted the Anders Isle mayor with a warm hand-shake and a squeeze on the shoulder.

"Sanny, my friend," said Mayor McPhee. "Good to see you."

"You, too, Pat. You look well." Sanny motioned to Drew. "Pat, do you know Drew Young? He's Detective Sergeant for the island police."

"Yes. Good to see you, Detective Young." Mayor McPhee shook Drew's hand.

"You too, Mayor," said Drew. "All of us at the department appreciate your efforts to increase our funding."

"It's the least we can do to thank you for your important service. I always say, the island can never be too safe. Lord knows, we need the police now more than ever. This latest incident . . . well, my office received more calls today than the whole month combined, and May is one of our busiest."

"I'm sorry to hear that," said Drew.

"I just want to be able to tell people we've caught the killer," said Mayor McPhee. "Do you have someone in custody yet?"

"It's an ongoing investigation. I can't talk about it." Drew took a napkin from the dispenser.

Sanny piped in, "Now Pat, don't pressure this fine young man. The island's in good hands with Drew. I've known him all his life—but don't get me started. You know me: you ask me what time it is, and I'll tell you how to make a watch."

Smiling, Drew shook his head. He didn't disagree. Sanny made many watches for Drew in their encounters over the years. Excusing himself, Drew carried his tray to a round table near the window at the front of the store. He sat down to eat and noticed Oliver was gone from the bench outside. Although he wasn't trying to eavesdrop, Drew could still hear the conversation at the counter.

"So, what can I do for you, Pat?" Sanny asked the mayor.

"Wish I could say I'm here for a friendly weekend visit, but I came on business. I'm sure you're following the news about Senator Madden's presidential campaign."

"Of course, I am," said Sanny. "I like that he's pro-business, and Marla likes his pro-environment platform. Her nature-loving ways have rubbed off on me over the years. We try to do our part, but it sure would help to have a president who cares about both the economy *and* the earth."

"You're right, Sanny, and that's just it," said the mayor. "The senator's campaign manager called me an hour ago. When Senator Madden heard the news about the murder of one of our island's most environmentally aware citizens—a woman dedicated to protecting sea turtles—he felt compelled to show his support as we deal with our loss. He's planning a visit to the island this Friday that dovetails with his previously scheduled private event on Taylor Island."

"Well, fiddle-dee-dee! That's exciting news!" Sanny slapped his hand on the counter. "I hope he's planning a stop at the Sundries."

"Even better, I think," said the mayor. "He needs a meeting point, a rally location of sorts. I thought of your parking lot. It's one of the best-known spots on the island. What do you think? The rally will likely get national media coverage."

"Are you kiddin' me? I couldn't be happier to help out."

"Then consider it done. I'll let the senator's people know."

From where he sat beside the storefront window, Drew watched a mother and daughter flip-flopping along the sidewalk to the beach access path with bags full of towels and toys. Eating his sandwich, he wished he hadn't overheard the mayor's news about Senator Madden.

He knew the Madden family all too well from the years Brooke dated Caldwell, Senator Madden's only son. According to Brooke, Senator Madden and his wife were the quintessential political duo—charitable, accomplished, ambitious. Caldwell was desperate to follow his father into politics, but he lacked eloquence and struggled with feelings of inadequacy in striving to please his parents. Brooke said Caldwell's refusal to make his relationship with her a priority over his family's high expectations had been a big part of why she broke up with him.

Although Brooke—who always made determined lists and took methodical steps to achieve her lofty goals—shocked everyone when she threw out her plans for marriage, Drew was proud of her for putting her own happiness first. He met Caldwell a few times, cornered him in a bar once for flirting with another woman in front of Brooke, and told him he wasn't good enough for her. She acted strange around Caldwell, not like herself. Then she left him and came home, and Drew's life seemed to brighten with her return.

Mayor McPhee paused at Drew's table on his way out of the Sundries. "You're one of the good guys, aren't you, Detective Young?"

"I like to think I am," said Drew, puzzled by the question.

"That's what I thought." The mayor pushed the front door and held it open for a second. Wagging his finger at Drew, he proclaimed with a confident grin, "The good guys always win."

CHAPTER

14

"Hello, Detective." Officer Sampson sat upright at his desk, clutching his open notebook with both hands as Drew walked into the police station.

"Hey." Drew tossed his keys and wallet onto his own large desk in the corner and half sat on its edge, facing Sampson. He crossed his arms. "So, let's recap what we have so far. You start."

"Okay." Sampson placed his notebook flat on his desk. "Apparent homicide, pending details of an autopsy to be performed Sunday morning. Victim is Diane Raydeen, thirty-eight-year-old white female. Exact cause of death is still unknown, pending autopsy and—"

"Please," Drew interrupted. "Tell me something I don't already know. And just talk to me. You don't need to read your notes word for word. Let's start with evidence."

Sampson looked at Drew with a blank expression, then down at his notebook, where he didn't find anything more to say.

Sensing Sampson's discomfort, Drew filled the silence by sharing his part. "I coordinated with our crime lab techs to analyze the crab trap and ropes as well as the victim's clothes and any trace evidence found by the coroner. Since the body was found in the water, we don't really have a crime scene, but I got a search warrant for the victim's apartment anyway and sent Forensic Services to gather any evidence that might lead us to a person of interest. They'll report to us when they're finished."

Sampson nodded, taking hurried notes while Drew spoke.

"Any leads from the tip line?" Drew asked.

Flipping to an earlier page of notes, Sampson referred to it with his finger. "Yes, actually, one promising call. A bartender at School, that new restaurant in Anders City, said he saw a woman who he thinks was the victim at the bar last night. A man sent her a drink, which she refused, then the man sat next to her to strike up a conversation, which seemed to end abruptly. The woman paid her tab and left without finishing her drink."

"That's something." Drew let the call buoy up his hope for a new lead.

"What about the kids who found the body?" Sampson asked, eyes eager behind his glasses. "Did you talk to them?"

"I spoke with the Willis boy, Mac, at the hospital. He seemed nervous, but truthful. The trap belongs to his family and hadn't been checked for a couple days. His father, Joe Willis, is a commercial shrimp fisherman and captain of a trawler named *Bonnie*. He was out on an overnight shrimping trip until this morning. He got back to the hospital room at the end of my interview with Mac and was *not* happy to see me there."

"What do you mean, Detective? Was he acting like he had something to hide?"

"Not exactly. He seemed to be protecting his children from questions that might upset them."

"And that's all it was?"

"I think so." The chief's voice rang in Drew's head: *Don't think, son, you've got to know.* A flutter of panic filled his chest. For the first time, Drew feared he might fail at his job. Before this, he glided through most typical cases—theft, vandalism, misdemeanors—with a bare minimum of effort. This time the case—his case—was homicide, too important and too personal. He needed a suspect. The chief would expect nothing less, but all Drew had so far were vague recollections of a local bartender and the gruff first impression of a protective father.

Drew rose from his casual seat on his desktop and began to pace. Sampson turned to a clean page in his notebook, watching Drew and awaiting further instruction.

"We need a plan." Pivoting at one end of the room, Drew pointed at Sampson. "I want you to follow up on the Joe Willis lead. Check out his alibi."

"Where does he dock his boat?"

"Dylan Creek Marina." Drew paced back to Sampson's desk, continuing to dictate. "Head over there and find out when he left port yesterday and when he came back today. Let's see if Captain Willis really was on an overnight boat trip. I'm going to School to have a chat with the bartender."

"All right, I have my orders."

"And you're going to observe the autopsy tomorrow morning at ten a.m.," Drew added.

"I'll be there, Detective."

"Let's hope we get a clear cause of death. Call me with details as soon as you can. I'm meeting with the chief at three o'clock tomorrow afternoon to brief him on the investigation."

"The chief? Working on a Sunday?"

"Yeah, I know, kind of like God himself deciding to forego Sunday rest. It's crucial we have our act together by then. I don't want to let him down."

"Nobody does."

CHAPTER

15

School Bar and Grill occupied a corner building in the ten-block enclave of restaurants and shops known as the Anders City Historic District. Praised by food critics for its unique fusion of southern cuisine and sushi-style presentation, School brought a hip urban-chic ambiance to the otherwise traditional charm of Main Street. The place had been a hit from the day it opened. Unlike any other restaurant in town, School's kitchen closed at midnight and its bar kept drinks flowing until the last patron stumbled out—even on Sunday. Visitors flocked to the upscale nature of School's food and service as compared to the usual screened porch, paper-plate fish fare. Everyone from the oldest barber in town to the newest state legislator could be seen at School. It was *the* place to see and be seen.

Drew, however, didn't care much for School. He tried his best to avoid any trendy establishment with an enforced dress code that excluded jeans and flip-flops. He opened the heavy oak door to a Saturday-night crowd packed into the entryway and bar. Dressed in plain clothes—dark gray slacks and a crisp blue collared shirt—Drew blended well with the crowd. He stepped between couples and around clusters of people standing at high tables. Two frenzied bartenders shook drinks and filled glasses for the throng of people trimming the thirty-foot bar. The thought crossed Drew's mind that this might not be the best time to speak with the bartender, but he needed information. Police business certainly trumped the next drink order.

The caller was named Jack. Drew flashed his badge to catch the closest bartender's attention.

"Is there someplace we can talk in private?" Drew shouted as he approached, but his words were lost in the din of music and chatter. The bartender pointed to a door behind Drew marked *Employees Only* and ushered Drew into a windowless office and storage room.

Inside, the bar noise subsided to a low background drone. Drew introduced himself, then asked, "Are you the one who called the tip line?"

"Yes. I'm Jack."

When they shook hands, Drew noticed Jack's sleeve of tattoos and judged from his boyish face and lanky build that he couldn't be much older than twenty-five. "Thanks for contacting us. I'd like to ask you a few questions if you don't mind."

"Go for it," said Jack.

"First, what makes you think the woman you saw is the victim?"

"Her picture was on the news this afternoon. She looked just like the woman I served last night. The news said her name is Diane, and the woman at the bar was Diane."

"How do you know?"

"I carded her." He wouldn't look Drew in the eyes while he said this.

"Really? She was thirty-eight." Drew gave Jack a skeptical look. "What aren't you telling me?"

Jack shuffled his feet, hesitating. "Well, man . . . it's sort of embarrassing."

"What is?"

Looking down, Jack hooked his thumbs in the back pockets of his black skinny jeans. "I thought she was hot," Jack admitted. "That's why I remember her and the guy who ended up hitting on her."

Drew chuckled. "I see. Nothing to be embarrassed about. We've all been there."

"I guess so." Jack shook his head. "I just got worried when I saw her picture on the news. Maybe if I'd talked to her, she'd still be alive."

"You're doing the best thing you can to help at this point."

"Yeah, that's true."

"Tell me more about the guy who approached her at the bar."

"He was pretty far gone, you know, real drunk."

Drew nodded and listened.

"He sent her a drink, but she didn't want it. When he saw her turn it down, he moved to the seat beside hers and slurred a few sentences at her. I couldn't hear what he said."

"What did he look like?"

"Tall, fit. In his mid-twenties."

"You said he'd been drinking and ordered a drink for her. How did he pay for his drinks?"

"Um"—Jack thought for a second—"Probably credit card."

Bingo, thought Drew.

"Do you have a copy of his receipt?" asked Drew.

Jack's eyes lit up. "It's in the safe. You're the *man*! Why didn't I think of that?"

"Hey, that's my job." Drew smiled at his good luck.

"I'll go get it."

A wave of noise tumbled into the small room when Jack opened the door to leave. Drew's phone rang.

"Talk to me, Sampson. What did you find out?"

"Well, when I first got to Dylan Creek Marina, a dock hand recalled that *Bonnie* was out overnight, but couldn't remember specific times. He sent me to the marina house to review the manual log, which is this ratty three-ring binder full of barely legible handwritten notes about the comings and goings of boats docked at the marina. The last two log entries for *Bonnie* indicated they left the marina at 5:00 a.m. yesterday, Friday, and returned at 10:15 a.m. today."

Drew sighed. "All right then, it seems Captain Willis was out shrimping like he says."

"His alibi checks out."

"It looks that way. Even so, make copies of the log entry pages. I want to show the chief."

"I have copies in hand right now. I'm heading back to the office."

"Good work, Sampson. Keep it up. Leave the copies on my desk. I'll review them tomorrow."

Drew slid his phone into his pocket and gripped his forehead, rubbing his temples with his thumb and middle finger. One lead, gone. He crossed his arms, leaning back against a supply shelf to wait for Jack to reappear with the magic receipt, the winning lottery ticket in a search where the odds of finding a suspect stacked against him with each passing minute.

The door opened with a whoosh of music and cool air from the bar. "Here it is, man. My manager found it at the top of last night's stack." Jack handed the receipt to Drew. "I probably wasn't supposed to look, but the name's on there."

Drew unfolded the receipt and scanned it. He looked up fast at Jack. "Are you *sure* this is the right guy?"

"Positive. His tab was the last one I closed before I clocked out around midnight. Why? Is something wrong?"

"No. Nothing's wrong. Just keep this between us for now, okay?"

"You got it, man. No problem."

"Can I keep this receipt?" asked Drew.

"Sure. I already asked my manager, plus, we keep an electronic copy."

"Thanks, Jack." Drew shook Jack's hand.

"Glad I could help." Jack opened the door to leave.

Following Jack into the bar's bustle and hum, Drew looked again at the name on the receipt, the name of the biggest jackass rookie cop in the department: *Walt Pickering.*

Drew waded across the crowd to make a swift exit from School, suppressing the rage that welled up as he imagined scenarios of what happened between Walt and Diane. Bursting through the heavy front door, he almost toppled an older couple on their way in. He apologized and crossed the street to his truck, calling Brooke as he climbed into the driver's seat. It was time for him to ask her some tough questions about Diane's personal life—who she dated, who she blew off, and who might've wanted her dead. If anyone knew, it was Brooke.

But Brooke didn't answer. When his second call also went to voice mail, he couldn't help but drive in the direction of her apartment on Anders Isle.

CHAPTER

16

Brooke sat in a folding chair beside the recovery tank where Bonnie, with her bandaged flipper, rested in shallow water. As each hour passed, Brooke intended to go home, but she stayed another hour and another. Midnight had come and gone. She couldn't sleep. Her carefully planned schedule for the day—and for her life—no longer seemed to matter. For the first time, Brooke didn't know what to do next. Diane's death sapped the importance out of routine tasks that usually gave Brooke a compass, control. More than anything, Brooke felt numb. Her emotions seemed disconnected from her body. She watched Bonnie wave her healthy flipper in slow strokes—back and forth, back and forth—sending flat ripples across the tank.

Less than a year ago, in mid-September, Brooke and Diane sat on Front Beach beside a loggerhead turtle nest, waiting for hatchlings to emerge. They both wore Loggerhead Protection League T-shirts with cargo pants. Diane brought a large utility bucket and a backpack, a powerful flashlight with a removable red filter, latex gloves, and a listening device—the essential tools of any Turtle Lady.

Each nesting season lasted from May through August. During dawn patrol, turtle team volunteers located potential nests by searching for bulldozer-like crawlways in the sand where a mama sea turtle had dragged herself ashore overnight. Her buried clutch of golf-ball-size eggs wasn't visible from the surface. Volunteers notified Diane, who found the nest by following the crawlway to a body pit and pushing a T-shaped metal rod into the sand until she felt it give way into the hollow of the egg chamber. The nest was then numbered and dated on one of three stakes connected with orange tape to form a triangle around the nest's location.

Approximately sixty days later, the "nest-sitters" visited the site each night to check for a depression in the sand above the nest, a sign of turtle hatchlings digging around in the egg chamber below and causing loose sand to fall down inside the chamber. With the listening device, they amplified underground sounds to hear the scratch of baby turtles on the move and to better predict when they would come out. Sometimes a hatchling scout popped its thimble head out of the sand to check for favorable conditions. Eventually, the nest "boiled" with sand-caked palm-size turtles scrambling over each other, spilling onto the beach, and shuffling fast toward their first taste of ocean. Diane and Brooke, with gloved hands, gently brushed off any stuck hatchlings and lifted them free. Within a few days of a boil, each nest was inventoried to count eggshells, determine survival rate, and release any stragglers.

Baby turtles used moonlight's reflection on the ocean to navigate their way to the waves, but on cloudy or new moon nights, a strong flashlight served as a false moon for guiding them. Brooke had been "the moon" before, knee-deep in midnight waves, holding a bright flashlight beam high above her head to lure hatchlings toward her and out to sea. She remembered the tickle and peck of their small bodies bumping into her ankles while they swam past her into darkness.

The nest they sat beside last September had been found by a volunteer in late July. The nesting season last summer yielded only four viable nests on Anders Isle, none of which were found at North End Beach. Three years earlier, the nest count was almost forty, with more than half found at North End. In only three years, the number of nests on the island plummeted to single digits.

That September night Diane said, "What worries me is that the nests we're lacking aren't showing up on other islands nearby." She sighed into the wind; her profile silhouetted against moonlit breaking waves.

"I know," Brooke said. "It would make more sense for our turtles to nest in the *region* of their natal beach if not on the *exact* beach where they were born." She scanned the nest with the red beam of her flashlight, saw only still sand.

"And," continued Diane, "what about the dead-end crawlways—no nest, no stranded turtle, and no exit crawlway back to the ocean? I don't get it. I recorded those as false crawls, but they don't follow the usual pattern. I guess the exit tracks might be washed away by high tide—or remember the *flying turtle*, where the wind blew drier sand over the tracks, so it looked like the turtle flew away?"

Brooke laughed and nodded, then became thoughtful again. "How many dead-ends has it been now?"

"Twelve in three summers." Diane shook her head in disbelief.

"That's inexplicable," said Brooke. "You know, most quirks of nature exist by design. A squirrel can't find about seventy-five percent of the acorns it buries, but that's because the squirrels are planting new oak trees."

"Ha!" said Diane.

"And what about the world's tallest man who saved the life of a dolphin because his arm was the only one long enough to reach into the dolphin's stomach to remove a plastic obstruction. Amazing!" Brooke said. "But twelve missing sea turtles can't be nature's doing. There isn't a reason for it. Mother Nature, unlike human nature, doesn't make mistakes. Most perceived mistakes in nature almost always serve a purpose."

They both paused to think. Then Diane said what they'd been too afraid to say before now. "I think someone's taking the turtles."

Diane told the wind, the moon, the ocean, and the night sky: *I think someone's taking the turtles*. She didn't expect to know who, not right away, but she and Brooke knew it was the truth.

And now, Diane's voice echoed through Brooke's memory . . . *I think someone's taking the turtles*.

Sure, the thought had crossed Brooke's mind that humans were to blame—poachers, pranksters, teenagers—but how would they do it, and why? Loggerhead sea turtles wouldn't sell for much, especially if they were dead. Their eggs were far more valuable, but none of the nests had been disturbed. Was the dead turtle she found this morning related to the other turtle disappearances? And who took that dead turtle out of Drew's truck?

While she puzzled over the missing loggerheads, Brooke watched Bonnie open her eyes and move her good flipper in slow strokes. Van Morrison's "Into the Mystic" played on the radio. It was Brooke's favorite song because it had been her dad's favorite song. It filled her with longing for ghostly fog horns she heard as a child in the middle of the night, for lasting romantic love, and for coming home. Humming the chorus, Brooke stood up to get a better look at Bonnie, but Bonnie stopped moving as soon as she saw Brooke and eventually closed her eyes again. Brooke sat back in her chair, felt the lack of sleep seep into her head. Her eyelids grew heavy. When her favorite song ended, she turned off the radio and turned on the small television in the corner to try to stay awake.

Even well past midnight, Diane's murder still led the local breaking news. No doubt this was one of the biggest stories in the history of the island. The reporter stood in front of Anders Isle Marina, which was lit only by spotlights from various news crews still on the scene. Brooke noticed the live ongoing coverage was interspersed with helicopter footage from Saturday morning that panned across the docks and parking lot, showing the Island Fire and Rescue boat, uniformed officials in action, and people bunched here and there. Although the reporter must have been digging for information all day, she looked fresh and determined during her special report. Her feline eyes and soothing voice made even the worst news more bearable.

> *This is News Flash Live on Local News 2. I'm Bella Michaels. Behind me is Anders Isle Marina, where officials spent the morning investigating the death of a woman whose body was recovered from the marsh by Island Fire and Rescue. The woman has been identified as Diane Raydeen, a thirty-eight-year-old resident of Anders Isle. Nicknamed "the Turtle Lady," Ms. Raydeen was Director of the Loggerhead Protection League, a nonprofit dedicated to preserving the island's loggerhead sea turtle population. Ms. Raydeen's death is considered a homicide at this time.*
>
> *In the most recent breaking news, our sources confirmed tonight*

that presidential candidate U.S. Senator Caldwell Castor Madden Sr. from North Carolina plans to visit Anders Isle this Friday before a previously scheduled private event on Taylor Island. A spokesperson for Senator Madden's campaign told us the senator was saddened by the news of such a terrible loss for a close-knit community of advocates for sea turtles and the environment. To show his support, Senator Madden plans to hold a "Get Mad" rally this Friday at noon at the Sand Dollar Grocery and Sundries on Anders Isle. I'm Bella Michaels, reporting live from Anders Isle Marina. Stay tuned to Local News 2 for the best in local news.

Brooke groaned, wishing she hadn't heard the news. Politicians would use any excuse to hold a rally in lockstep with their own platform, and Senator Madden was no exception. His "Get Mad" campaign slogan wasn't a bad play on his name, but it felt gimmicky. Perhaps the senator truly believed his own talking points that development shouldn't be at loggerheads with the environment, that healthy economies are necessary for healthy ecosystems, and vice versa, but it remained to be seen what he would actually do about it.

To be sure, Diane's death lent an emotional element to the issues, one the senator needed and would certainly exploit to his full political advantage. Brooke could see him at the podium, raising a fist while he urged people to *Get Mad* about sea turtle habitat destruction or to *Get Mad* about violence against women. She saw right through it all, saw politics for what it was—a circus in which each candidate vied for attention; performed as ringleader, acrobat, clown; did whatever they could do to win the admiration of the audience and, ultimately, their votes.

Pushing away thoughts of Caldwell and his family, Brooke switched to a late-night show but spent more time thinking about Diane than following the program. She closed her eyes and drifted to sleep.

When she woke to a splash on her foot, she didn't know how much time had passed. The recovery tank water sloshed against the side, rolled over the edge, and hit the ground, spraying her ankle again. Bonnie swam along the top of the water, lifting her head and stroking with ease. Brooke let out a sigh of relief at the sight of the strong-swimming, beautiful marine reptile.

Drew often joked about Brooke being like a sea turtle, especially when she moved from land to water at a swim meet. Once she almost fell off the starting block at the 200-yard individual medley heat before setting a state record for the fastest time. Water was her element. She learned to swim by jumping off a dock to her dad. She could free dive to almost forty feet. She even lost her virginity in a swimming pool.

Bonnie and Brooke watched each other for what seemed to be a full ten minutes before Brooke grabbed instruments to check the turtle's vitals. Bonnie, surprisingly, didn't shy away this time. She waited patiently in the water while Brooke prodded at her and treated her wounded flipper. Brooke had earned Bonnie's trust along with a timely reminder of her purpose: to save and protect sea turtles.

When Brooke finally looked at the clock, it was 2:33 in the morning. She pulled a cot out of the supply closet and found a blanket stuffed on a shelf. The television droned in the corner. When she closed her eyes to sleep, Diane's voice met her in the darkness.

I think someone's taking the turtles.

CHAPTER

17

The whistles of morning birds and a whitewash of dawn woke Drew from his cramped sleep in the reclined driver's seat of his pickup. For a few seconds, he didn't remember where he was. Then the events of the previous day rushed at him like head-high breaking waves—Diane's dead body, Brooke's distraught expression, the chief's expectations. His head pounded. His mouth felt full of chalk. He swallowed and yawned, wiping the corners of his lips with his thumb and index finger. The edge of his kneecap ached where it had been pressed against the door handle all night.

Through the windshield, he saw Brooke's apartment door. Her front light wasn't on; her car wasn't in the parking lot. He called her phone again, still no answer. It wasn't like Brooke to be out all night. He should've insisted yesterday that she stay with him, as upset as she was about Diane, and he would've slept on the couch.

Where could she be at six a.m.?

Under normal circumstances, his first guess would be Diane's apartment. Only two other places came to mind: the beach and the aquarium. Brooke had a bad habit of going out to the beach alone at all hours of the night to watch for turtles. He had warned her many times that she shouldn't have a false sense of security on the beach. Being naïve could get her into trouble. She was too quick to see the good in people, even crazy people, and nothing was more dangerous than a crazy person. He couldn't imagine she'd risk her own safety with Diane's killer still on the loose.

That left the aquarium.

Shoving the key into the ignition, Drew drove from Brooke's apartment on the island to the aquarium on the mainland in Anders City. When he turned into the back lot, he was relieved to see Brooke's car covered in a film of dew. He parked, stepped out of his truck, and felt every ache and tight muscle. It was obvious from the wrinkles across his pants and collared shirt that he'd slept in his clothes. He wanted a breath-mint and a drink of water.

Walking through still morning air, Drew remembered the last time he went to the aquarium with Brooke about three months ago. She showed him one of the turtle hospital's loggerhead patients named Molly. They entered the aquarium that day through the exterior basement door, which at the time was barely locked by a loose doorknob. Drew urged Brooke to install better security measures, especially because she was there—often alone—at all hours of the day and night.

When he reached the door this time, he was satisfied to find the loose doorknob had been replaced with a new handle and a keypad lock. An intercom system on the wall beside the door gave instructions for visitors. In addition, a security camera trained on the doorway provided a clear view of anyone at or near the basement door.

Drew grinned. No wonder Brooke spent the night here. This place was safer than most people's houses. A bubble of pride lifted his battered spirits. In a job that could be thankless and unforgiving, he accomplished one small but important thing: he protected Brooke. He was a cop, after all.

Drew pressed the intercom button, tucked in his shirt, and licked his lips. After ten seconds without an answer, he pressed the button again. The intercom crackled and hissed.

"Hello? Is someone there?" asked Brooke, voice raspy from sleep.

"Brooke, it's me," Drew said. "Sounds like you slept as well as I did last night."

"Yeah, it was a long night. What're you doing here?"

"Let me in and I'll tell you all about it."

"Okay. Wait for me by the door. I'll be just a few minutes." The door buzzed and unlocked. Drew entered the dim underbelly of the Anders Aquarium. Pumps hummed. Warm air hung thick and humid like earth's salty exhale.

Shaking off the last remnants of sleep, Brooke stretched her arms high over her head. She took a deep breath. Bonnie appeared to be making a swift recovery. Brooke bent over the utility sink to wash her hands, then filled them with water to splash her face and rinse her mouth. She patted her skin dry with a paper towel. In the mirror over the sink, she smoothed her hair down and pulled it back into a ponytail. Her eyes looked puffy, but morning looks didn't matter to Drew. As teenagers, he saw her in the morning every time they met up on the beach for Drew's early surf sessions and Brooke's study of island fauna. Of course, she looked much younger in the morning back then.

Brooke found Drew waiting by the basement door. He greeted her with a big hug, holding her longer than usual. "I was so worried about you," he said. "I called your phone a bunch of times. Were you screening my calls?"

"No. Don't be silly. My phone barely gets a signal down here." Brooke led Drew along the hallway to the turtle hospital.

He tugged playfully on her ponytail. "You don't look like you spent the night in the aquarium."

"Thanks." She smiled. "I didn't plan to stay overnight."

"You mean you did something you didn't *plan* to do?" he teased.

Brooke looked over her shoulder at Drew, amused and a little hurt. She wanted to be more spontaneous around Drew. "You know it's too early to start picking on me." Pulling open the door to the hospital, she let Drew hold it for her. "Besides, am I really that controlled by my plans?"

That was a loaded question, and Drew knew enough not to answer.

They entered a room full of tanks and sea turtles.

Brooke rolled her eyes. "Well then, speaking of plans, what kept you from getting a good night's sleep? Big plans with the latest Mrs. Right Now?"

"Um . . . no, but I guess I deserve that." Drew shook his head and grinned. "You're going to feel really bad when I tell you I slept in my pickup in front of your apartment last night."

Brooke gasped. "You did *not*!"

He looked her straight in the eyes, nodding slowly.

Gripping her forehead with one hand, she squeezed her eyes shut. "I'm such a jerk. Forget I said anything. I can't believe you did that. Why?"

"I was worried when you didn't answer your phone. I needed to talk to you. Then when you weren't home, I got really worried, so I thought I'd just wait for you. Turns out that took all night."

"I'm so sorry. I didn't mean to worry you. I only came to the aquarium to escape for a little while, but a hotline call came in about Bonnie." She gestured to the sea turtle in the nearest recovery tank. "I ended up at Dylan Creek for a rescue pickup, then stayed on overnight watch. I guess I didn't want to be alone."

"Did you say *Bonnie*?" Drew glanced at the sea turtle gliding along the top of the water.

"Yes. This is Bonnie." Brooke moved next to Bonnie's tank.

"Where'd she get that name?"

"I named her after the shrimp trawler that brought her in."

"Yesterday?"

"Yes."

"Do you remember what time?"

"Around three-thirty. Why?"

"Trust me. Are you sure about the time?"

"Almost positive, but I wrote it down." Brooke walked to the desk. Rifling through some papers, she found the note about *Bonnie*. "Here." She handed the note to Drew and pointed out the times. "The call came in at 2:16 p.m. Saturday, and we scheduled a pickup for three o'clock, but the boat was twenty minutes late."

The *Bonnie* note felt thin and fragile in Drew's hand. It was a key piece of evidence against the one person—Captain Joe Willis—who had just become a potential suspect in the biggest case of Drew's career. He clasped the paper between his fingers like a glass egg. "I'll need to take this with me," he managed to say after a few beats of silence.

"You can have it." Brooke noticed his pleased expression. "Does this have something to do with Diane?"

"You didn't hear it from me." Drew folded the paper, careful not to crease the handwriting.

"So, you have a suspect?"

"Not exactly, but we're closer now."

"And that's what you wanted to talk to me about—a boat?"

"No. Not at all," said Drew. "This," he held up the folded paper, "is what we call a break." Looking at Bonnie swimming in her tank, he shook his head in wonder.

"Well then, what burning questions made you camp out at my apartment and track me down this morning?"

Drew slid the paper into his back pocket and took a deep breath. "What do you know about Diane's personal life?"

Brooke squinted, pursing her lips. Curious, she asked, "Why? Was she in some kind of trouble?"

"Not that I'm aware of. I need to know who she was dating or who she recently broke up with. That sort of thing."

"Oh. Um . . . she wasn't dating any one person really. She told me about a few flop dates from a couple months ago, but that's all."

"Do you know why she went to School Bar and Grill Friday night?"

"I have no idea," Brooke answered. "The last time I saw her was Wednesday morning. I guess I spoke to her once on the phone after that, maybe Thursday afternoon—I'm not sure—but she didn't mention any plans for the weekend." Brooke's cheeks flushed. Her throat tightened. The realization of Diane's death anchored deeper in the pit of Brooke's stomach. She'd never again talk to Diane, never again walk on the beach with her in search of turtle tracks. Tears welled and threatened to fall.

Drew put his arm around her shoulders and pulled her in. "Thank you, Brooke. I know this is hard."

"I still can't believe she's gone." Brooke wiped the tears away, fighting a quiver in her voice. "And I can't believe I've become such a cry-baby."

Drew laughed a little, giving her a reassuring squeeze. "Aw, you're a cry-baby, but it's okay. So much is happening. I'd be surprised if you weren't crying all the time."

She smiled. "Last night, I thought a lot about Diane. What if I can't protect the turtles as well as she did?"

"Are you kidding me? That's just nonsense. Not only do you have a PhD but also you love sea turtles more than anyone I've ever met. Look at the lengths you go to for them. The turtles around here are the luckiest on the planet. Hell, you even got me up early yesterday for the sake of one, and that one was already dead."

"Yeah, well, apparently someone else wanted that dead loggerhead more than I did," Brooke said. Diane's voice again: *I think someone's taking the turtles.* In an instant, two thoughts snapped together. Brooke straightened up and dried her eyes. "Diane and I thought maybe someone's taking loggerheads from the island. In the past few years, we've seen a dozen tracks that led to nothing. The turtles simply vanished from their paths on the beach. And then yesterday the dead one disappeared from your truck. What if we're right?"

"What if you are? See what I mean? The turtles are in such good hands with you."

"Drew, you know taking loggerheads is a crime, especially if they're being killed."

"One crime at a time. I have my hands full with this murder investigation, but I promise I'll look into the turtle problem after this. Plus, a dead one is hardly proof of a crime."

"Come on," said Brooke. "Her shell was clean cut from her back. Her head was bashed in. That was done on purpose. Someone killed her. Someone's probably killing all of them." Brooke looked at him, wide-eyed, thinking out loud. "And for what? Loggerheads aren't the usual target species, they aren't as marketable as other sea turtles like hawksbills. And, besides that, sea turtle eggs are even more in demand. Why kill the adult before she lays her eggs?"

"Whoa, okay, hold on." Drew patted Brooke's back. He could almost see her thoughts churning. "I know it looks bad and you're eager for answers. I know how impatient you get when you have a scientific puzzle to solve. But, even if you're right, we don't have the dead turtle, so we don't have evidence of a crime."

CHAPTER

18

Sunday morning in Charlotte, North Carolina, meant churches packed with people from all walks of life. Some came to worship, others to socialize. The Madden family did both at St. Peter's Episcopal, where they'd been attending services, baptisms, confirmations, graduations, weddings, and funerals since the time their family burst onto the political scene three generations earlier. They even had their very own pew in the second row. After church each Sunday, the Madden family, all five of them—Senator Madden, his wife Lydia, son Caldwell, and teenaged twin daughters—enjoyed brunch at Charlotte Country Club, then Lydia took the girls shopping while father and son played golf or tennis.

Even though it was one of the hottest days of the year so far, Caldwell and his dad chose to play tennis rather than ride from hole to hole in the comfortable shade of a golf cart. Senator Madden's ego smarted from his losing tennis record against his son. He wanted an opportunity to earn a W.

Spry and fit at age fifty-eight, Senator Madden's black hair was only peppered with gray, but any indication of a health problem could prove catastrophic to his presidential campaign—best not to risk a heat stroke or heart attack. So, they agreed to play one set instead of multiple, which meant a shorter duration of play with the winner being the first to win six games by a margin of two.

Serving at thirty all and leading five games to four, Caldwell tossed the ball high and whipped his serve down the center line for an ace. Senator Madden shook his head.

"Match point, Dad." Caldwell smirked while he steadied himself to serve. "Get in ready-to-lose position."

"Careful, Junior." Senator Madden bent forward on the baseline. "Pride comes before a fall."

Caldwell ripped his serve to the far corner of the service box, but his dad managed to return it. Meeting the ball at the net, Caldwell volleyed it back at such a sharp angle his dad couldn't run it down before the second bounce.

Game, set, match. Another win for Caldwell.

Raising his arms in the air, racket held high, Caldwell ran a lap around his side of the clay court. Senator Madden waited patiently at the net, arms folded across his racket head, watching with amusement as his son showed off. Caldwell finally jogged over and shook his dad's hand. They both caught their breath and filled paper cone cups with ice-cold water from the cooler beside their court. They drank the first cupful, refilled, and sat on a bench between the courts in the shade of an umbrella.

"I believe you missed a call or two there, Junior." Senator Madden raised his eyebrows in mock accusation.

"I'll have you know, I have twenty-twenty vision," Caldwell boasted. He swallowed his cup of water in one gulp.

"Well, in that case, you cheated," Senator Madden teased.

They'd been reciting the same lines for a couple decades, an old joke from Caldwell's junior tennis days.

Caldwell crushed his paper cup in his fist. All jokes aside, he wished his dad would give him a simple *good match* or *congratulations* after a win. Their usual banter diluted his victory.

Senator Madden toweled sweat from his face and neck. "Linwood called me last night to rave about the fishing trip and the tour. You must've shown him a good time yesterday."

"The fishing didn't amount to much, but I thought he'd like to see the island real estate," said Caldwell, grateful to Linwood for the call. "He said he hadn't been over to Taylor Island in almost a year."

"Well, he always tells me the best investments are the ones you can stand on. You impressed him, and believe me, I've known Linwood for a long time—that's hard to do. You should keep in touch with him, Junior. I happen to know he's in the market for a new firm to handle his land deals. You could double the business for your firm's South Carolina real estate group." Senator Madden winked at his son.

Caldwell smiled. "Thanks for the tip, and for making all the fishing trip arrangements. Bud almost kissed me when I asked him to come along. He told me he's been trying to get a meeting with Linwood for months. Even Art Ogletree's guy, Ben, loosened up and was having a good time by the end of the day."

"I can't say I'm surprised that Art sent one of his minions in his place. I just hope you're keeping Art happy. He could have his pick of firms, and he doesn't seem too big on second chances."

"Don't worry, Dad. Art's files are my top priority. He's probably one of the biggest clients my firm has ever had. We'll keep courting him and his companies like they're our only clients. I certainly have the partners' attention."

"You know what they say: it's not *what* you know that matters, it's *who* you know."

Caldwell cringed hearing one of Brooke's most hated sayings. He blurted, "Guess who I ran into at the marina yesterday?"

"Who?"

"Brooke."

"Ah, the one that got away." The words hit Caldwell like a punch to the gut. He wished he hadn't said anything; his dad wouldn't dream of letting this drop. "I always liked that girl. Strong-willed, smart—although she wasn't so smart when she broke up with you." The senator smiled and gave his son a firm pat on the knee. Caldwell grimaced. "What's Brooke up to these days?"

Caldwell hadn't the slightest idea. He didn't ask her. "I don't know. I only saw her for a few minutes." He rubbed out a ball mark on the clay with the sole of his shoe. "We were late getting on the water because the parking lot was jam-packed. I found out later a woman was supposedly murdered."

"I heard about that—such a shame. I'm going to Anders Isle this Friday for a Get Mad rally in her honor."

"You are?"

"It was a last-minute schedule change, but it's the least I can do. She was a big proponent of the environment, tracked sea turtle nests, and even had a small local following. You know they called her the Turtle Lady. Catchy name. I think the people who liked her will like my environmental platform."

Caldwell didn't respond. On the one hand, he admired his dad's political optimism, his ability to find the political silver lining in any given situation. On the other hand, he felt uneasy about the idea of using this woman's death as an opportunity to excite the environmental base.

His dad continued with enthusiasm, "After the rally, we're attending a fundraising dinner and roast at seven o'clock at the Tiger Club, hosted by a select crowd of my campaign supporters. And by 'we' I mean your mother, me, and *you*." He nudged Caldwell.

"I don't know, Dad. It'll take me almost four hours to get to Anders from Charlotte. Then I'll still have to catch the ferry over to Taylor. I can't leave work early Friday for a dinner party."

"Sure, you can, Junior. And I'm expecting you to be at the rally, too. Just take the day off. Tell those partners the place will be chock-full of wealthy potential clients. You can bill the time as business development. Isn't that how you big-firm lawyers do it?"

"Not exactly. Plus, I'm still an associate. I don't get to decide when to take a day off for business development."

"You already bring in more business than some of the partners, right?"

"Well, yes, but the bulk of that work is for Art."

"So, they know you're making *lots* of money for the firm, and that's all they really care about. And if it isn't enough for them that you're wooing new clients, you tell them Senator Madden requested his son's presence to help with his presidential campaign. That should shut 'em up."

Caldwell sighed. "We'll see." He hated relying on his dad's name for his own success. At times he worried that all his accomplishments, all he had, including his sense of self, had been inherited. From his prestigious law firm job to his access to the social elite, from the beach house to his own politics and religion, he was the next generation of Madden family men, an extension of established beliefs and a pawn to carry on the reputation of his family name. Nothing about Caldwell was self-made. He didn't have an individual identity. He, alone, would never be good enough.

CHAPTER

19

Drew left the aquarium early Sunday morning, drove home, took off his shoes, and fell into bed still wearing his rumpled clothes. It wasn't even eight o'clock when his head hit the pillow. He needed some good rest before going to the office to prepare for his meeting with the chief.

Four hours later, Drew's phone rang and woke him from the depths of dreamless sleep. He fumbled for it on the bedside table and managed to answer on the third ring.

"She's preggers!" announced a loud, gravelly voice, familiar and androgynous, laced with a hint of sarcastic enthusiasm.

A bolt of fear shuddered through Drew. This was the call most single men dreaded—the call to commitment—the call to inform the lucky stud that he knocked up one of his latest flings. Wide awake now, Drew sat on the edge of his bed, blinking his eyes to adjust to the light. His heartbeat pounded in his ears. "Who is this?" he finally asked.

"Terry," said the voice.

Terry? Drew thought back to his recent dates. *Terry . . . Terry . . .* Nobody came to mind. He started to sweat. There was an obvious pause in the conversation.

"Terry *Caufman*," added the voice, "Coroner?"

Drew exhaled hard. "Yes! Of course! Okay."

"Boy, you scare easy, Detective."

"You keep sneaking up on me."

"Aw, I'm sorry." Terry cackled. Drew could tell she was smoking. She sucked in and blew out. "So, your dead girl here—Diane—was pregnant."

Drew took a sharp breath punctuated with a pang of guilt. He still wasn't in the clear. "How pregnant?"

"About thirteen weeks."

He made a quick mental calculation. It had been at least six months since he last slept with Diane. He shut his eyes with a sigh of relief.

"What do you think about that?" Terry asked, then sucked on her cigarette.

"It's motive," said Drew.

"Tell me about it. I have four kids—all boys," she said while holding in her smoke. She exhaled and cackled again.

Drew didn't find any of this to be funny, least of all the fact that Diane had been pregnant when she was killed. Just another complication to add to an already difficult case. "Did you determine cause of death?" he asked.

She sucked in, then blew out for what seemed to be a full five seconds before answering, "Homicide by strangulation."

"How sure are you?"

"Positive." She sucked in, blew out. "She's got a fractured hyoid bone— that's the U-shaped bone in the neck—clear evidence she was strangled to death. I also found bruises around her neck, deep purple lividity, burst blood vessels in her eyes—all proof of asphyxia. There's no indication of any other trauma to the body. No evidence of rape. Other than the pregnancy, nothing unusual turned up in my examination of tissues, fluids, bones, stomach, bladder, intestines, and internal organs. I clipped her fingernails and supplied right- and left-hand samples to the crime lab to be analyzed for foreign DNA under the nails. The toxicology report came back negative for drugs and poison with only a trace of alcohol in her blood. From what I can tell, time of death was around 5:00 a.m. Saturday morning. She was dead before she went in the water. No water in her lungs. So, she didn't drown."

"Strangulation is an intimate form of murder. Maybe the murderer knew her? The father of her child?"

"Yeah, maybe. But it's also a convenient way to kill someone—quick and easy. No need for a weapon, no premeditation. So, the murder might've been in haste, unplanned."

"Good point. Crime of opportunity." Drew chided himself for sounding like the novice homicide detective he was. He worried his book smarts and limited hands-on experience weren't enough to prepare him for leading this investigation. The vice of potential failure gripped his head again, but he refused to let it show.

Terry said, "Unfortunately, I've seen more than my share of murder cases."

"I guess you have." Drew glanced at the clock—ten past noon. Needing to hurry to get to the office before the chief arrived, he stood, feeling for the receipt and note in his pocket, reassured to find them still there. "Thanks for the highlights, Terry, but you really didn't need to call. Sampson's going to tell me all this in his briefing."

"What can I say? I love the chance to call and chat. It gets sort of lonely in my line of work. Lots of people around, but none of them can carry on a conversation, if you know what I mean. At least they don't care if I smoke."

Drew laughed a little, despite his lingering exhaustion and mounting dread. "Even so, Terry, you should do something about that smoking habit. It'll kill you."

"I appreciate your concern, Detective, but I've seen far *better* things that'll kill me." She sucked in, blew out, and hung up.

CHAPTER

20

By Sunday afternoon, Brooke was exhausted. Her usual boundless energy and worker bee discipline, deeply ingrained in her by a childhood spent in competitive swimming, had been worn thin. Before a swim meet, she ate Fun Dip or dry Jell-O mix for a quick jolt of pure flavored sugar fuel. Now, she only wanted a nap. Although she managed to piece together a few hours of restless sleep overnight on the cot, the aquarium basement had been cold, and the blanket wasn't long enough to cover both her shoulders and her feet at the same time. One end or the other slipped off to give her a chill, waking her through the night. She was completely emotionally drained from the past thirty hours—it was all just too much.

She drove to her apartment and trudged toward her door through sun-dappled trees and the distant laughter of children that did nothing to lighten her mood. Going inside, she waded into the stink of spoiled bananas and mildew. Yesterday, she threw away the brownest bananas, leaving a good one on the counter for after her Saturday-morning run. On top of the dryer, a wet red towel had been mildewing for three days. She stood in the foyer and stared at it. *Just another thing to do*, she thought, grateful she didn't have a pet.

Drew had been right when he talked her out of adopting that blue-eyed rescue kitten at the Humane Society's booth last year. She wanted a furry companion, especially a lonely rescue kitten unwanted by its mom. "Let the kitty go," Drew said. "You can't even keep a cactus alive, Brown Thumb."

Brooke pouted and placed the kitten back in the pen, walking away fast to escape its plaintive meows. Drew apologized later, sensing her hurt feelings. But he'd been right. She had a brown thumb. Her lack of a maternal instinct was either nature or nurture, but given her mom's attitude about motherhood, Brooke was pretty sure it was the latter. That cat would probably be dead by now.

Just like the sea turtle.

Just like Diane.

Brooke dropped her keys and phone on the kitchen counter. She slid out of her running shoes and slowly pulled off her socks, stuffing one in each shoe. As she opened the refrigerator for a snack, her eyes settled on a picture stuck to the freezer door: Brooke with her arm slung over Diane's shoulder while Diane waved at the camera. The picture was taken last summer after the first turtle nest of the season had boiled. They sat by that nest for five nights in a row before the hatchlings finally decided to make a frenzied run for the ocean. In the picture, they both smiled wide from the rush of doing their part to protect more than a hundred loggerhead offspring.

Brooke let the refrigerator door drift shut. She lost her appetite. Tears came fast and hot, filled her eyes, and blurred her vision. She walked to her bedroom and buried her head in a pillow. There, in the yellow glow of curtain-filtered daylight, in the loneliness of her own bed, Brooke cried. She hadn't cried so hard since the day she realized she was going to leave Caldwell.

Love was a lot like death, unpredictable and illogical. Neither could be controlled or fully understood. And Brooke now knew both could inflict the same kind of pain borne from an acute sense of loss. She lost Diane to death; she lost Caldwell in spite of love. It had hurt just as much to fall out of love with Caldwell as it did to fall out of life with Diane.

Were these tears from the wound un-scabbed by seeing Caldwell or from the fresh wound made by Diane's death? Although her own change of heart precipitated her loss of Caldwell, the change was nearly as sudden.

More than two years had passed since then, but she still clearly remembered the day she knew it was over.

On a warm, stagnant Friday afternoon in March, Brooke waited at Charlotte Country Club for Caldwell to finish a round of golf with his dad. She and Caldwell were in Charlotte for the weekend, looking for a place to live. It was a half-hearted search on Brooke's part since she knew she couldn't do her work in Charlotte, an inland city near the center of the state line between North Carolina and South Carolina and at least a three-hour drive to the nearest beach. The night before, they had another argument about Caldwell's decision to apply to take the bar exam for North Carolina instead of South Carolina, one he made the previous fall when he secured a job in the Charlotte office of one of the biggest firms in the country. He was proud of earning an offer from such a prestigious firm based on his own resume, which landed—with a little help from his dad—in the hands of the managing partner. Of course, Brooke knew the real reason Caldwell's parents wanted him close to home was to keep him readily available to help with his dad's upcoming presidential campaign.

Until the job offer, Caldwell planned to practice law in South Carolina and to move with Brooke back to the coast where she could do her work. Then he promised Brooke the move to Charlotte would be temporary—a springboard to a job in South Carolina—a few years at most, but she still wasn't happy about it. What was a marine biologist supposed to do three hours from the nearest coast? Plus, Caldwell's parents often manipulated him. She feared that once he settled in, they'd make it impossible for him to leave. And then what? A mortgage? Kids? Each next step would take her farther in the wrong direction, keep her in the wrong place.

Sitting under a gazebo at the country club pool, she was reading *National Geographic* when she saw a monarch butterfly caught in the rafters. The gazebo, open on all sides for panoramic views, was topped with a large pyramid-shaped roof. The butterfly flew up and hit the ceiling head-on with a loud *tap!* Then it fluttered sideways and bumped into a column separating the spaces of open air. *Tap!* Frantically beating its orange and black wings with dizzying, arrhythmic patterns, the butterfly dove right, left, up, down, but it couldn't escape the covered structure. Over and over, it careened into the rafters, the columns, and even the floor. *Tap! Tap! Tap!* Brooke held her breath, hoping with each swoop the butterfly would escape. At last, with a deep dive and a bat of its wings, the butterfly soared between two columns into fresh air, alighting on a bush in the distance. Brooke exhaled.

That's when she noticed her own heart beating faster. Absurd as it seemed, at that moment in her life, Brooke knew she *was* the trapped butterfly. The enclosure that kept her in was the life Caldwell had built over and around her, on all sides, and she just wanted to find the open spaces of air, to get back home to where she belonged, by the ocean, on her beloved island. She looked at the magazine in her hands. Her mother's voice pounded in her head against the beating of her own heart: *Be sure to find your purpose and achieve your dreams. Motherhood is a box.*

The next day, she broke off her engagement.

And in the wake of her decision, she felt the same surge of sorrow and disappointment and loss she now felt about Diane's death.

Love and death defied illusions of control. Diane knew that. She lost her dad at a young age and struggled to find lasting love. She warned Brooke that things don't always go according to plan. Brooke should've listened.

After a good cry, Brooke rolled onto her side and curled up. She sniffled. Sleep eluded her. She couldn't stop thinking about Diane and Caldwell, death and love and turtles and Drew. For so long she'd been thinking of Drew, especially since she moved back to the island and found out he kept a picture of her in his drawer. He knew her the way she was as a girl and as a young woman, the way she always wanted to be—optimistic and driven, bold and accomplished, unaware of disappointments ahead and unchanged by them. When she was with him, she became—in his eyes—more herself. His presence was her time machine to the past they shared and to all that might have been.

Timing was the enemy of romantic love between them. They wrestled with attraction, mostly in high school, and since then only on a few occasions. Brooke wondered if Drew still thought of her that way, if he ever wanted her the way she often wanted him. She'd been the one who hesitated to get involved with him when he'd tried so hard in the past, the one to leave him behind for college, the one to date and almost marry someone else. She convinced herself he didn't have feelings for her since he was interested in a new woman every week. What made her any different from the next one?

But Drew had always meant more to Brooke than all the rest of the men she knew. Even while she dated Caldwell, she often thought of Drew, especially during rough patches in her relationship. On windy days, she imagined Drew kitesurfing, wind caught in the curve of his kite while it dipped and rose and pulled him across foaming waves. He was a large part of what made the island feel like her home. Could there be more to her feelings? What if she returned to the island not only to be near the beach and turtles and place she loved but also to be near Drew?

As quickly as those thoughts of Drew flashed in her mind, she dismissed them as ridiculous. Maybe it was a defense mechanism to push him away, or maybe her inner cupid missed her heart by a sliver of arrow. She did love Drew. They'd known each other almost their entire lives. But was she *in love* with him? She didn't know.

She suspected Diane had been in love with Drew. Something about the way Diane's expression brightened when she talked about him and the way her eyes lingered on him a few seconds too long betrayed her emotions. Brooke knew they dated briefly a few years back. Diane's love for him appeared to have been the toughest love of all—unrequited—and as time passed, Diane's feelings seemed to wear away until she didn't say much at all about Drew and didn't look at him the same way. He might've broken her heart like he had so many others.

But what did it matter? All of Diane's love and heartbreak died with her.

So why couldn't Brooke, for once, just take a risk and follow her longing heart instead of her overanalyzing head? Wouldn't it be better to end up heartbroken than alone?

With those questions swimming in her mind, Brooke finally drifted to sleep.

112

CHAPTER

21

Drew parked in front of Anders Isle Police Station between two cars: one belonging to Chief Mullinax and the other to Officer Sampson. The chief was an hour early for their three o'clock meeting. Why was Sampson here? Drew didn't invite him. Maybe the chief did? Everyone knew Sampson would take any opportunity to impress Mullinax. He thrived on the approval of others, especially his superiors. Despite his social awkwardness and general aim to please, Sampson was well aware of his value to the department. He would be as swift as the next guy to self-promote, even to the detriment of a colleague.

Stepping out of his pickup, Drew felt warm rushing wind on his face. Steady wind at twenty knots under a pale blue, cloudless sky made for perfect kitesurfing conditions. He wished he could spend his Sunday afternoon on the ocean instead of in a meeting with the chief. Mullinax would surely find something Drew missed. Drew's chest tightened; a pang of regret stung his side. He couldn't believe Diane was pregnant. Sampson must've found out about the pregnancy that morning. Why didn't he call with an update after the autopsy? It wasn't like Sampson to forget.

Drew swore under his breath. Late even though he was early. Walking into the station, he rehearsed the facts of the case in his mind. A manila folder tucked under his arm held his paperwork, the School receipt, and Brooke's note about *Bonnie*'s arrival time. At least he had some evidence of potential suspects.

Chief Mullinax paced in his glass-walled office with the door closed, shouting into the phone. Sampson, shuffling papers at his desk, glanced up at Drew to nod hello but otherwise avoided eye contact. Drew found that to be odd behavior for the usually eager Sampson.

"What's going on?" Drew stopped beside Sampson's desk. "Why didn't you call me about the autopsy?"

Sampson looked past Drew to see Mullinax still on the phone, then shifted his eyes down to his papers. Clasping his hands in his lap, he bounced his leg under his desk. "Well, Detective, um . . . the chief said he wanted to know first."

"Know what first?" Drew clenched his teeth and kept his eyes focused on the bald crown of Sampson's head.

Stalling, Sampson looked at Mullinax's office again, but wouldn't look at Drew. "The autopsy results."

"Why?" Drew waited.

Sampson sat stiff-lipped and started to sweat.

Pressing his index finger hard onto the desktop, Drew said, "Let's get something straight. You report to me on this case no matter what. I'm to know everything you know. Okay?"

Sampson nodded.

"Besides, you can spare me all this drama." Drew walked toward his desk in the corner. "I already know she was pregnant."

That got Sampson's attention. He looked up, bug-eyed, his mouth half open as though he meant to speak but the words dissolved on his tongue.

The chief's office door flew open. "Well, well, well. Here he is at last." Mullinax's stern potato-face aimed at Drew, gaunt with disapproval. "I just spent the past twenty minutes on the phone trying to cover your ass, son."

Drew swallowed hard, remained standing beside his desk chair. Did he cross a line in an interview with a witness? Did someone complain? He couldn't imagine what he'd done to require the chief's cover.

"I want to know one thing." Mullinax fumed, his feet planted firmly in his office doorway and long arms crossed over his chest. "Why the hell didn't you think it was important to tell me you were fucking the victim?"

The chief's question shot across the room at Drew like a flame-tipped arrow and struck him square on the forehead. Drew flinched, then froze. Stunned. He looked at Sampson, who sat as still as a wax figure, staring at his computer screen. Drew took a deep breath. He hesitated to answer Mullinax. Any answer would be the wrong one. He'd been ambushed. How did they know? Drew's silence only angered the chief.

"Don't stand there like an idiot," Mullinax said. "Start talking."

"It's over," Drew managed to say.

"Well, no shit, son. She's dead." Mullinax laughed, a few sharp snorts, the kind of laugh made for distraction just before throwing a swift sucker punch.

Drew swallowed. "I mean, it's been over for a while. We dated a few years ago, broke up, then slept together a few times after that, but that ended, too."

"Who ended it?"

"Well, she did, technically, the last time, but I was going to if she didn't."

"When was the last time?"

"About six months ago. In November."

"And where were you Friday night?"

"At a friend's house for dinner, then home after that. Please, Chief, you can't think I had something to do with—"

"Save it, son. I'm about one millimeter from tossing your ass off this case and suspending you for good measure. Did you know she was pregnant?"

"Not until the coroner called me this morning." Drew glared at Sampson, who clearly fed Mullinax some dirty details and assumptions behind Drew's back.

"Good. Did you kill her?"

"No! Of course not!"

Mullinax squinted at Drew, his dark eyes stuck deep in his potato face.

"I'm sorry, Chief." Drew looked down. "I should've told you all this before."

"You're damn right you should've. Your omission made a mockery of my department and of this case. Forensic Services called to inform me they found clear evidence of your presence in the victim's apartment. They lifted fingerprints, sent them through the database, and found that some belonged to you. I had to convince them they were wrong to suspect you, but I'll tell you what: I wasn't so sure myself. I'd have a helluva time believing your story if it didn't match up so closely to hers."

"Hers?" Drew looked up at Mullinax, perplexed. "What do you mean?"

"Mark?" Mullinax fixed his dark eyes on Sampson, who didn't respond right away. "Sampson!" Mullinax yelled and clapped his hands to break Sampson's fear-induced trance.

Sampson startled in his chair, "Yes, Chief, sir?" He fumbled around in a stack of papers on his desk.

"Show Drew what we have."

Sampson reached into a file box, pulled out a red hardback book, and handed it to Drew.

"Behold, the victim's journal," said Mullinax. "It's all there, son. The details of your on-again/off-again whatever-you-wanna-call-it. Lucky for you, she didn't embellish too much, and her timeline matches what you just told me."

Drew flipped through golden-edged page after page of Diane's handwritten innermost thoughts. The sporadic entries skipped weeks at a time, but each was long and personal. "This is—well—an unexpected relief."

"Right," said Mullinax. "It's a relief only because it helps you this time. Son, listen to me, as a general rule, never date a woman who keeps a journal. She's an observer. She'll write down all your dumbass mistakes and make them permanent. It'll get you every time."

"Yes, sir." Drew wasn't going to argue the fact that he didn't know she kept a journal. He paused on the last entry—dated Friday, the day before her body was found. "Did you read all these entries, Chief?"

Mullinax scoffed. "Do I look like I have time to sit around reading warm fuzzy journal entries? Mark flagged the pages I needed to see."

Drew asked Sampson, "Was there any mention of Walt Pickering?"

"No," said Sampson. "I don't recall . . ."

"Walt?" interjected Mullinax. "Why?"

"Pickering was the last person seen with the victim at School on Friday night."

That did it.

Mullinax raised his fists in the air, howling a guttural, furious "NOOO!"

to the ceiling and the heavens beyond. His neck veins bulged like hoses. Drew and Sampson braced for the tirade to come. Pointing an angry finger at Drew, Mullinax bellowed, "I don't care who you horny rascals screw on your own time, but you better damn well tell me about it when it involves the biggest case of my career! I'm running a police department, not a frat house!" Mullinax stomped into his office as he said, "Get Walt in here, NOW!" and slammed the door so hard it shook the office walls.

Drew sighed and looked down at his desktop, his throat dry and gritty. He respected the chief and hated to disappoint him.

Chief Mullinax had been with Anders Isle PD since Drew was a kid and had been the only one to recognize the abuse happening in Drew's family. Mullinax often made excuses to stop by the Young household for an unannounced visit. On several occasions, he even arrested Drew's dad to create a record of abuse when the normal protocol would've been to force Drew's mom to seek a restraining order. Mullinax knew from his own childhood experience that a mother leaving an abusive father was unlikely and would actually put her in greater danger of being killed.

As a child, Drew knew he could call the chief whenever things got bad at home. Based on a call from Drew, Mullinax was the one in pursuit of Drew's dad the night he drove off the road to his death. Drew wondered if Mullinax blamed himself for the accident—or the suicide—whichever it had really been. Drew didn't regret making the call that night, and he would be forever grateful to Mullinax for answering—that night and every night.

Over the years, Mullinax became Drew's only real father figure, and the primary reason Drew chose to go into law enforcement. Now, Drew wanted nothing more than to impress the chief by solving this case.

Drew sat in his chair, picked up the desk phone, and called Walt.

On the second ring, Walt answered. "Yo! This is Walt."

"It's Drew. I'm at the station with the chief. He wants you to come in." Through the phone, Drew heard music pumping and metal clinking in the background.

"When?" asked Walt, distracted.

"Right now."

"What for? Listen, I'm at the gym about to lift and, get this, these two fine ladies doing yoga moves on the floor keep looking over here with some serious sex-me-up eyes between their dog bends or whatever. I might get more than just a workout today; you know what I mean?" Walt snickered. "Can I be there in an hour?"

"No." Pressing his lips together, Drew inhaled slowly through his nose to stave off frustration. "I don't care if you're in the middle of a pajama party with Playboy bunnies. You'd better walk into this office in the next ten minutes. Chief's orders." Drew hung up before Walt could protest.

"Detective," Sampson said sheepishly. "I'm sorry about . . ."

"Stop." Drew held up his hand to deflect Sampson's words. "I'm in no mood to talk."

"I know. I just want to tell you I put the copies of *Bonnie*'s log entries on your desk."

"Fine." Drew found the copies. From his manila folder, he removed Brooke's note about *Bonnie* and set it next to the log entries.

Spread before him in paper evidence was a timeline that didn't match up. According to the marina log entry, *Bonnie* returned to Dylan Creek Marina at 10:15 a.m. Saturday. Brooke's note, however, put the boat coming into port at 3:00 p.m. Saturday. Brooke further explained to Drew that *Bonnie* was twenty minutes late. Therefore, the crew actually arrived at Dylan Creek Marina at 3:20 p.m. Saturday. Brooke was there to watch the boat come in. At the same time *Bonnie* arrived in port Saturday afternoon, Drew was meeting with the Willis family—including shrimper Joe Willis—at the hospital, where Joe stated that he returned from his trip Saturday *morning*.

Drew leaned back in his office chair. Joe Willis appeared to be caught in two lies. First, his boat came into port on Saturday afternoon, *not* Saturday morning. Second, and most importantly, he wasn't on board.

CHAPTER

22

Mullinax hunched over an open folder at his desk, deep in concentration. Reading through reams of notes, he touched his index finger to his tongue before turning each page.

Drew wondered if their meeting to discuss the investigation would still happen as planned. There was more to the evidence than what Diane's journal said about Drew's sex life. Joe Willis was clearly a person of interest. Drew hoped the details about *Bonnie* would defuse tension between him and the chief. And what part did Walt play? Had he been seeing Diane? The man who got her pregnant would certainly be a potential suspect.

Diane's red hardback journal lay in the middle of Drew's desk. He picked it up but hesitated to open it. She'd been a private person. Discreet. A keeper of secrets. To read her naked thoughts on paper felt like a violation of her privacy, even in death. But her words might provide answers about her killer. Plus, Sampson already combed through it, so why shouldn't he? Drew knew her far better than anyone else in the department. Well, except maybe Walt. Perhaps Drew would see something nobody else could. Opening her journal, he fanned through the pages, stopping on the last entry.

Friday, May 26th
Long day! A volunteer called around sunrise about a crawlway
on North End, but I couldn't find a nest. A false crawl. Mama

crawled about halfway to the dunes before she turned back to the ocean. Something bothered her? Bad timing? We were so sure we'd find a nest this week. Office pool on which night it will be is up to $65. Looks like this mama's planning to nest over the weekend. My money's on tonight and I'm almost never wrong.

Spent the rest of the day at the office—paperwork and too many phone calls. Some days it feels like the phone is glued to my ear! The best call of the day came just before lunch: we got the federal grant! The Loggerhead Protection League is the official recipient of the coveted Endangered Species Research Grant! $100,000—I can't believe it! Can't wait to tell Brooke. Also, taking Cindy to dinner tonight since she did the bulk of the grant writing. We scored a last-minute reservation at School! I'm really in the mood to relax and enjoy a good meal.

Diane's lilting voice emanated from her writing as though she was reading the words to him. Drew wondered if, while she wrote, she ever considered who might later read her entries.

Diane's last entry didn't raise any suspicions to help the investigation, but at least now he knew why she went to School the night before her death. The rest of it was just turtle talk.

Brooke would enjoy reading Diane's journal, but Drew didn't want her to see it. Brooke didn't know about his ongoing *thing* with Diane—and Drew didn't want her to know. She'd think too much of it. He saw Diane as just a friend for fun and casual sex—nothing more. Brooke didn't see sex that way. For her, sex was about being *in love*, making love, and all the emotional connection with it, which was why, even though Drew and Brooke flirted with each other, even when they hung out on the beach at night or at dawn in high school, even the few times they kissed and made out in the past, they never had sex.

Drew flipped to a flagged page, tempted to read Diane's musings about their trysts. He only made it through one sentence before Walt walked into the office, wearing sweatpants and a faded basketball jersey. Placing the journal on his desk, Drew leaned back in his chair and bit the insides of his cheeks to contain an onslaught of angry questions. He glowered at arrogant Walt.

Walt gnawed on a piece of chewing gum and blabbed into his phone, oblivious to Drew's stare and the relative silence in the office. Sauntering to his desk, he chewed and gabbed about girls at the gym while he shoved his free hand down the back of his sweatpants to scratch his butt.

Just then, the chief swooped out of his office and pointed at Walt. "You! Hang up!"

Walt almost choked on his gum in his haste to end the call.

Mullinax asked Walt, "What's this I hear about you being the last one seen with our murder victim?"

Walt balked, wide-eyed. "I didn't know that lady." His eyes darted from Mullinax to Sampson to Drew.

"Drew thinks you did," said Mullinax.

Walt's mouth fell open. Red blotches sprouted across his face and neck. He clenched his hands into fists, nostrils flared, spitting words at Drew, "Are you trying to pin this on me? I'll knock your golden-boy head off!" Walt strained to hold back the words he really wanted to say, biting his tongue in front of the chief.

Drew stood up and waved the School receipt at Walt. "I just report it like I see it. According to the School bartender, you bought Diane a drink the night before she was found dead. I have the receipt right here with your name on it."

"That's such bullshit!" Walt protested, but with less conviction. Backing off, he crossed his arms and shook his head, looking down at the floor. He hated being provoked but hated his own foolish temper even more.

Mullinax stepped between them. "Let me see that." Plucking the small receipt from Drew's fingers, he studied the black-and-white print of Walt's name. "Well, Walt, it does appear you have some explaining to do." He peered at Walt, prepared to hear the worst.

Agitated, Walt scratched his bicep then rubbed the nape of his neck. He scoured his few lucid memories from Friday night. "I had a lot to drink, Chief," Walt confessed. "I might've bought that lady a drink, but I bought drinks for lots of ladies that night. I don't remember any of their names. And, if it matters, I totally struck out and went home alone."

"You're telling me it's just a coincidence?" asked Mullinax.

"I'd call it really, really bad luck," said Walt.

"Wait a minute," Drew interjected. "If you were so drunk, how can you be sure you're innocent? What if you did something, but you can't remember? Maybe you blacked out."

"Gimme a fuckin' break. I may be a lady killer, but I'm not an *actual* lady killer. Obviously, nothing happened *in* the bar, and I think I'd remember if I murdered some lady during the two-block walk from School to my apartment. Oh yeah, and then somehow got her body from downtown to a creek in the marsh without any witnesses and without a boat." Raising his arms in surrender, he announced to the room, "I was drunk, not homicidal."

Mullinax was convinced, and relieved. He already knew from the crime lab that none of the other fingerprints in the victim's apartment were a match to any other officer in his department, but, after being surprised by the news about Drew, he wanted to be damn sure. "All right, that's the end of it." He tossed the receipt back at Drew. "I don't want any more finger-pointing. Stop wasting my time." He turned to Sampson. "Wait in my office, Mark. We'll be there in a minute."

Sampson clutched his notebook and adjusted his glasses before shuffling into the chief's office.

Mullinax continued, "Walt, you'll give a buccal sample as disqualifying evidence. We'll get some DNA kits tomorrow."

"But, Chief," whined Walt.

"No excuses," said Mullinax.

"Whatever." Resigned to the fact that a rookie must do as he's told, Walt cut his eyes at Drew and stalked back to his desk, stung by a stray bullet in the crossfire of office politics. He knew Drew was the chief's favorite. Walt slouched into his desk chair and sat brooding, tired of defending himself.

"Walt," said Mullinax, shooing, "go home."

That was one command Walt was happy to hear. "Yes, sir." He popped back up to his feet, hurried to the door, and gave a mock salute to Drew. "Later!"

Almost as quickly as he arrived, Walt was gone, along with the lead that seemed so promising to Drew less than twenty-four hours earlier.

Mullinax pinned Drew with a squinty-eyed stare. "You're on thin ice, son. First you don't say anything about being involved with the victim, and next you attempt to drag Walt into it based on some weak evidence."

"It was a legitimate lead, Chief." Drew raked his fingers through his hair. "I'd suspect the last person seen with a victim no matter who it was, but I just happen to know Pickering and his *way* with women."

"You jumped to conclusions. I know Walt gets on your nerves; he's brazen and obnoxious, but don't let him get the best of you. I need you to stay focused. You can do this. Got it?"

Drew nodded, bolstered by the chief's confidence in him.

"And you'll give me a disqualifying DNA sample tomorrow, too," said Mullinax, hands on his hips. "Grab your notes and get in my office for a briefing. I hope you have something more to show me."

Drew lifted the manila folder from his desk—thankful it wasn't empty—and walked into the chief's office, settling into a chair next to nervous Sampson.

Mullinax sat behind his wide desk, cracked his knuckles, and cleared his throat. "So, here we are." With his knobby elbows propped on the desk, he clasped his long-fingered hands under his chin. "Mark, you're up first. You reviewed the report from Forensic Services. Tell us what else they found in the victim's apartment."

"Oh, Okay," Sampson stammered while he looked at a printout of the report beside a page of his scribbled notes. "When the search unit arrived at the apartment, there was no sign of forced entry, but inside it was clear someone had been looking for something—open drawers and cabinets, overturned furniture, scattered clothes and papers. The victim might've been home at the time, but any visible signs of a struggle were lost in the mess. After processing the scene, the forensic evidence is inconclusive as to whether the victim was killed in her apartment."

"Here's the thing," Drew interrupted. "She kept a key hidden under a flowerpot by the front door, so the perpetrator didn't need to break in. The key was in an obvious place. Easy to find, easy to use, which makes it impossible to know if she let someone in."

"The report mentions that key." Sampson added. "They also found her driver's license, credit cards, and car keys in a small purse on the kitchen counter."

Drew said, "So someone was looking for something, but we don't know what, or if it was found. I'm even more concerned about Diane's phone."

"Why?" asked Mullinax.

"Nobody can seem to find it," said Drew.

Mullinax raised his eyebrows. "Interesting. You have my attention."

Drew asked Sampson, "Forensic Services didn't find it at her apartment, right?"

"That's right, Detective. Not in her apartment. Not in her car."

Drew continued, "I sent a search team to scour the area of the tidal creek where her body was found, to look for any evidence, but they found nothing. Her phone is still missing. Of course, it's possible her killer took it before stashing her body."

"Do you think that's what someone was looking for in her apartment?" asked Sampson.

Drew leaned forward. "Well, the way her apartment was turned inside-out, it's unlikely since a phone is usually left in plain sight on a table or at most inside a drawer."

"What about her office?" asked Sampson.

"I thought of that, but she was at School that Friday night after work. There's no way she'd go out without her phone, so I doubt she left it at her office, but I'll double-check. Plus, her car and her bike were both at her apartment, along with, as you said, her purse with her driver's license inside. The bartender at School told me he carded her, which means she had her license, so she at least made it home after dinner. But she might've brought someone home with her, perhaps the father of her child, or she might've gone back out again." Drew reasoned. "Another big problem is that we just don't know exactly where she was killed. There isn't a specific crime scene to process."

"Damn." Mullinax scowled. "We don't have much to go on so far." Straightening in his deep chair, he drummed his fingers on the desk. "Well, it is what it is for now. Let's keep pressing on." He steepled his fingers and looked at Drew, two deep lines creased his forehead between his eyebrows like an upended equal sign. A frown tugged at the corners of his mouth. "I'm almost afraid to ask, son. Do you have any other leads besides Walt?"

The flimsy manila folder felt too light in Drew's hands as he opened it to reveal the last shred of hope for the case—and likely for his career. If this lead fell through, he'd fail at his job, and fail the chief. He wanted so badly to prove himself with this case and to find justice for Diane. The chief probably gave Drew this case as a test, an opportunity for trial by fire, maybe even to groom him to take over one day. Drew did everything he could think of, but he wasn't a seasoned detective. He didn't even know what he didn't know. Self-doubt cast its heavy shadow. The evidence against shrimper Willis was hardly direct; it was circumstantial at best. And, to top it all off, Drew stumbled upon the discrepancy in the *Bonnie* timeline by sheer luck. He hoped lady luck would be loyal.

Taking a deep breath, Drew mustered up his most confident voice. "Yes, I have another lead, a much better lead."

"Well, let's have it," said Mullinax.

Drew slid the marina log entries and the *Bonnie* note across the spotless desktop until they were within the chief's reach. Sampson squirmed in his seat. Mullinax took the papers as Drew said, "Sampson helped with this lead."

Sampson adjusted his glasses and sat back in his chair, watching Drew with newfound appreciation.

Drew stood up and began his brief, "Joe Willis, a commercial shrimp boat captain, owns the crab trap where Diane's body was found. Yesterday, Joe told me he was on a Friday overnight shrimping trip on his boat, *Bonnie*, and got back to the marina mid-morning Saturday. Those two papers in your hands are copies of the Dylan Creek Marina log entries for *Bonnie*, showing the boat left port Friday morning and returned Saturday morning around ten o'clock. So far, so good for shrimper Joe, right?"

Mullinax nodded, spreading the log entries side by side on his desk.

"That's what we thought, too." Drew gestured to include Sampson. "But this morning I uncovered evidence that leads me to believe Joe lied about his alibi. You'll see a note there from a witness who received a call from *Bonnie* to meet the boat at Dylan Creek Marina. She watched *Bonnie* arrive in port at 3:20 p.m. Saturday. I can confirm Joe was at the hospital Saturday afternoon, claiming he'd been there since morning, which means he couldn't have been on board the boat. He wasn't on an overnight shrimping trip Friday night. And that makes Joe Willis a potential suspect in this case. I want to know where he was and why he lied about it."

Placing one hand flat on the papers, Mullinax pressed the fingers of his other hand onto the creases between his eyebrows. "Drew," he began, then folded his arms on the desk and leaned forward. Drew held his breath, poker-faced, the empty manila folder trembling slightly in his hands. "I'm impressed. Good work, son! And you, too, Mark." Mullinax leaned back in his chair. Lacing his long fingers behind his head, he smiled, showing a band of gums above his big-toothed grin.

Mullinax rarely smiled in the office. Drew figured he'd just seen too much in his decades of work to find anything to smile about.

"Thanks, Chief." Drew exhaled. "We need to ask Joe some questions as soon as we can, but I want him to agree to come in voluntarily, get him talking to see if his alibi holds up. Do you want to see the interview?"

"Absolutely," said Mullinax. "Call me when you have him."

Perched on the edge of his seat, Sampson beamed up at Drew with the hope-filled expression of a dog sitting for a treat—alert, committed, thankful. "What about me, Detective?" Sampson hugged his notebook, pleading eyes magnified by his glasses.

"You're coming with me to get our man." Drew gave Sampson a reassuring pat on the back, taking full command of the department's most important investigation.

CHAPTER

23

Late Sunday afternoon, Brooke woke from her nap to waning sunlight cast in orange blocks across her bedroom wall. For a few seconds, she didn't know the time, the day, or why she was in bed in her running clothes. She rarely slept in the middle of the day.

Brooke's mobile phone rang where she left it in the kitchen, restoring her to the present moment. Reality was a dead loggerhead found and lost, Diane gone forever, injured Bonnie, and work to be done. On the next ring, she sat up too fast. Dizziness dimmed her vision. She blinked at grains of darkness filling her eyesight and threw off the covers, answering her phone just before the call went to voice mail.

She was surprised to hear Paul Asher's voice. He worked a second job as a security guard for the Port of Anders City between his shifts for Island Fire and Rescue. His call to the turtle hospital hotline had been forwarded to Brooke's phone. He told her he saw a sea turtle floating near the loading docks at the port and couldn't tell if the turtle was alive or dead. Before Brooke could fully wake up and come to her senses, she agreed to meet him at the port's south entrance gate.

No need to shower—turtle rescues could be messy, especially one near a shipping area. She'd most likely end up in the water or at least covered in turtle muck. But since Paul would be there, she made a hurried effort to brush her teeth, braid her hair, and change clothes, then left her apartment without even turning on a light.

Brooke parked her car at the aquarium, loaded the aquarium's pickup truck with turtle transport equipment, and drove it toward the Port of Anders City. Sunlight flooded through the windshield and filled the air with a golden haze in the final bright hour before sunset. At the port's south entrance gate, Paul waved an arm from the window of his jeep and motioned for her to follow him, leaving another guard on duty.

The Port of Anders City was ten times larger than Brooke imagined. Although she had lived in the area most of her life, she could only see the port from a distance. There was no way to tell how big it was from the outside. Paul drove through a maze of train-car-size containers, each painted a solid color, stacked five-high and two-deep without any discernible pattern to their placement. If she lost sight of Paul's jeep, she would surely be lost for days in the endless acres of storage. She sped up to stay closer. They took a right turn off the main road then a left onto a narrow side road sandwiched between two towers of containers that rose to the sky like multicolored buildings. The side road ended at a wide thoroughfare edging the river, where several container ships were docked. Blue container cranes stood tall along the river like a row of giant steel giraffes. Turning right onto the thoroughfare, they passed several warehouses before parking near the last berth adjacent to a T-head pier.

Paul stepped out of his jeep. His easy smile—showing ruler-straight teeth above a wedge of tongue—looked like the start of a laugh. Sunglasses complimented the square shape of his face.

"Twice in one weekend," Paul said, smiling while he talked. "We really need to stop meeting like this."

Halfway between their vehicles, Brooke gave him a light hug. "Don't take this the wrong way, but I wish I hadn't seen you at all, especially yesterday." Her smile faded.

"I know. I'm so sorry about Diane."

"Thank you," said Brooke.

"I wanted to tell you, but Drew insisted he had to be the one."

"Drew," she said, shaking her head. "He was right to wait. I would've tried to see her if I found out while I was on the docks. Now, I appreciate those few extra hours of not knowing." Brooke slid a strand of hair behind her ear.

Their thoughts filled a beat of silence.

"Oh, let me show you the turtle." Paul walked toward the edge of the thoroughfare, where a vertical concrete wall dropped into sloshing water.

They leaned over the wall's lip to look down about ten feet into a saltwater berth. Small waves lapped against the wall.

Paul said, "I saw it right in here."

"When was that?" asked Brooke.

"About half an hour ago, but another guard said it's been coming up in the same place all afternoon. That's why I thought something might be wrong with it."

"Good call. Sea turtles don't usually float around in one spot, especially a busy terminal like this." Brooke noticed the sun sinking closer to the horizon. "Would you grab the flashlight out of my glove compartment? I'll keep an eye on the water."

"Sure." Paul walked over to her truck.

Brooke watched for any sign of the turtle. A water rescue required patience. While a sea turtle on land could be slow and quite easy to catch, a sea turtle in the water swam with the stealth and agility of a seal. Often a distressed turtle could elude rescuers for hours, making the task of saving the turtle more of a delicate waiting game than a hasty rush to action.

The berth's deep, dark water was fit for the giant hull of a container ship. A turtle caught in these busy waters could have any number of injuries, from bacterial infections to motorboat-blade lacerations, from debilitated turtle syndrome to entanglement in fishing gear. Brooke wasn't sure what to expect. She needed to see the turtle to determine the best method for capture.

Paul returned with the flashlight and followed Brooke's stare into the choppy water. A steady breeze whisked away the day's heat and humidity.

"There it is." Paul pointed.

Brooke spotted the faint oval shape of a shell rising from seaweed-green depths just before a scaled head surfaced. She recognized it immediately as a loggerhead by its bulbous head and beaked mouth. With labored breath, it hovered and floated more than it swam.

Leaning over the wall for a better look, Brooke concluded the turtle wasn't caught on anything underwater. "It appears to be a juvenile weighing about fifty pounds," she said, "a pocket logger."

"A what?" Paul chuckled.

"That's our nickname for the small ones." She smiled at the turtle with sympathetic eyes. "Adult loggerheads can weigh five times as much. But even though this one will be lighter to lift, I need to figure out how to maneuver it up from the berth. My dip net isn't long enough."

Brooke had an idea. While Paul kept an eye on the turtle, she went to the truck and tied long ropes to the corners of a tarp. She explained her rescue plan to Paul and with shared concentration they moved in step with each other like a waltz.

As the turtle paddled in weak strokes on the surface, Brooke and Paul held ropes on opposing ends of the tarp and lowered it down the wall, letting water weight it down until they managed to slip it under the turtle. Walking along the wall, they carefully skimmed the water until the turtle was caught in the tarp-sling. Brooke braced herself on the wall to pull up her end at the same time as Paul pulled up his until they safely scooped the turtle onto dry land.

The turtle wasn't well, as a healthy turtle probably wouldn't cooperate with such a tenuous capture. Since the turtle was a juvenile, its gender couldn't be determined by external characteristics. Brooke crouched to examine more closely. "It's covered in typical freeloaders—marine leeches, leech eggs, barnacles." She showed Paul. "But here in its mouth, see that J hook? This is what we call a hook-and-line injury. Someone reeled in this turtle and cut the line. No wonder this pocket logger is so lethargic. Its digestive system shuts down after an injury in the wild, so it hasn't been foraging as usual. Gas builds up in its intestinal tract and makes it float. Poor thing."

"Will it be okay?" asked Paul.

"Oh, I think so. We'll do an x-ray and exam at the aquarium for a clear view of the hook and any underlying conditions, but we should be able to remove the hook with light sedation. No surgery." Brooke smiled at Paul.

"Thanks to you, we found this little one in time."

"Well, that's great. Glad to help." He removed his sunglasses when the sun set, and now Brooke saw his warm brown eyes shift from the turtle to her face. "What do we do now?"

"I have a transport tub in the truck bed. Do you mind carrying the turtle to my truck?"

"No problem."

Paul lifted the turtle. Its fifty pounds barely flexed his arm muscles. Brooke secured the tub and turtle in the truck bed and closed the tailgate.

"Thanks again. I'll need to follow you back—" Brooke was interrupted by a loud clatter coming from a warehouse on the other side of the thoroughfare.

In the dusk, someone moved between the two closest warehouses. Paul grabbed the flashlight and cast its beam into the alley. They saw the backside of a large pair of pants as the man wearing them bent over.

"Who's there?" Paul yelled across the thoroughfare at the pants.

The man stood up—a shirt and head materializing above the pants— almost as tall as the warehouse doorway beside him, and nearly as wide. He turned around, raising his thick arm to shield his eyes from the light. A wooden crate lay askew in the alley behind him, where it apparently slipped off its ride on a rolling platform dolly.

"Oliver?" asked Paul. "Is that you?"

"Yeah," said Oliver, swiping at the light beam. "You tryin' to blind me? Get that light outta my face."

"Sorry." Paul turned off the flashlight. "We heard some noise."

"This damn crate came loose."

"Need some help?" asked Paul.

"Nah, I've got it." Oliver bent over, lifted the crate with ease, and slid it back onto the dolly. Waving his giant hand at them, he rolled the dolly into the warehouse.

Paul clicked off the flashlight and handed it to Brooke. "That's just one of our cargo inventory specialists. He's out here all the time."

Brooke nodded. She recognized Oliver and his oafish mannerisms. From time to time, she saw him walking on the connector bridge. Even on the hottest summer mornings, he was bundled up in several layers of clothing, taking labored steps as though trudging through knee-deep snow during a blizzard. She often felt sorry for him.

"I'll show you the way out," said Paul. "Good to see you again. Let's hope the next time is for something fun." He smiled again, his on-the-verge-of-laughing smile.

"Yes, please." Brooke smiled back at him as she climbed into the aquarium truck.

Tossing the flashlight onto the passenger seat, she followed Paul's jeep in a U-turn to change direction on the thoroughfare. When her headlights panned across the warehouse into which Oliver went, she saw a large number eight painted on the exterior wall. She decided Eight was as good a name as any for the newly rescued pocket logger.

CHAPTER
24

Brooke left Eight in the care of staff members at the aquarium and went home to her dark apartment. A soft night breeze carried summer sounds of frog songs and bird calls through palmetto trees and across the lawn, stirring nostalgia and loneliness from the depths of her heart to the forefront of her mind. As soon as she walked into her apartment, Brooke turned on all the lights—porch light, kitchen track lights, and five lamps in her bedroom and den. With her world illuminated, her sadness slunk back into shadows, at least for the moment.

When she picked up her phone to call Drew and tell him about the turtle and Paul, she noticed a missed voice message from earlier. The number, vaguely familiar, had a 919 area code for central North Carolina. Her first thought was NC State University. The aquarium sent severely injured sea turtles to vets at NC State in Raleigh for surgical procedures or intensive care hospitalization. They sent two last week, both with near-fatal lacerations from motorboat blades. Brooke expected a call with an update on those turtles, but not on Sunday. A Sunday call could mean bad news.

Checking the voice message, she heard Caldwell's smooth southern accent. Of course—he had that 919 number since law school at UNC Chapel Hill. She deleted him from her contact list just so she wouldn't have to see his name whenever she scrolled through. "Hey, Brooke. Good to see you yesterday. We need to stop running into each other in public places with no time to talk and too much to say. So . . . um . . . I was thinking maybe we should meet on purpose this Friday. I'll be down at Anders Isle for my dad's rally at noon. Will you meet me afterward? We could . . . um . . . get coffee or something and catch up? So . . . just let me know if that works for you. Talk to you later, I mean, when you call back, or on Friday. Okay. Bye."

Sitting on the couch, she replayed Caldwell's message. Three times. It infuriated her that he didn't bother to leave his name. He assumed she'd recognize his voice and the context. His call, while a nice gesture, was also an intrusion. Did she say or do something at the marina to make him think they need to talk? He sounded nervous the first time she heard the message, but by the third time she couldn't be sure whether he was nervous or just distracted. Either way, he held on to his charm. She scolded the small part of herself that was now looking forward to Friday. How many times had she forced down bubbles of doubt since the day she decided to leave him? Everything between them was well in the past, and she wanted to keep it that way. Now, suddenly, he was present again, encapsulated in her phone. She deleted his message. She wasn't going to return his call.

But it was too late. His voice brought back memories of their happiest times together—long walks and picnics on campus; slow dancing in his cramped kitchen until pasta boiled; standing mid-sidewalk kissing in a sudden summer downpour; and spooning each night, his arms wrapped tightly around her while they slept. Of course, Brooke idealized the good times. Happy memories of Caldwell were so much easier to recall than their many fights and disappointments, his out-of-whack priorities, the nights he forgot to call and came home hours later than promised. For such a long time she clung to happy memories to justify staying with him, until one day she just let go. Escaped. Her abrupt end to their engagement left a lot unsaid between them. What good would it do to rehash it all now? Did he want to be friends? Did he need closure? Brooke's sadness crept out of the shadows when she realized she wanted now more than ever to be able to call Diane.

The only time Brooke cried in front of Diane was a couple of months after they met, during a conversation about Caldwell. Another brilliant sunrise ushered in a Wednesday morning on the island while they searched for log-gerhead tracks. Wednesday morning walks became their ritual. Each week, they started out together at dawn with nothing but sand beneath their feet, bags in hand to pick up trash, and time to talk. An hour passed in a flash while they shared stories about childhood, parents, dating, favorite books, ambitions, and funny happenings—whatever came to mind. They debated current events and explored religion and history. In a short time, Brooke felt closer to Diane than to any other female friend. Even so, they consciously skirted two topics—Diane didn't say much about Drew, and Brooke didn't say much about Caldwell.

But that particular Wednesday, Diane noticed Brooke's solemn demeanor as they walked across cool sand.

"Are you okay?" asked Diane.

"Yeah," Brooke said quietly, looking straight ahead. "I'm fine."

They walked a few more steps in silence. Diane eyed Brooke. "Hold on." She stopped Brooke with a gentle hand on her shoulder. "You're not fine. What's wrong?" Searching Brooke's face, Diane tried to make eye contact, but Brooke turned to watch the little waves. Tears blurred Brooke's vision, then rolled wind-blown across her cheeks. Brooke sniffled. Diane rubbed her back and asked again, "What is it?"

"It's Caldwell." Brooke wiped away a spill of tears. "This Saturday would've been our wedding day."

"Oh, Brooke, I'm so sorry."

All Brooke had said about Caldwell was that they were engaged until she called it off.

"Sometimes I think I made a mistake," Brooke admitted, tears free-falling while she took a deep breath. "Breaking an engagement is one of those things I can't ever undo or redo. My choice set a whole series of events in motion that landed me here and Caldwell there. All the plans I made fell through."

"Plans tend to do that," said Diane. "What happened?"

Tucking some loose hair behind her ear, Brooke watched the water. She folded her arms. Nobody asked her what happened, well, nobody who didn't already know too much to be unbiased. She wasn't sure how to sum it up without breaking down. Brooke hesitated to answer Diane but desperately wanted to confide in her. Wouldn't Diane expect to hear something bad had happened to justify such a drastic change of heart? For too long, Brooke had been rolling her decision over and over in her mind like a snowball that grew larger with each doubt-packed revolution until its size forced out thoughts of anything else. Maybe Diane could offer perspective, empathy, or at least a shoulder to cry on. Maybe some relief from the pressure of snowballing doubts.

Brooke spoke to Diane but kept her face to the ocean as though giving a monologue, one she never rehearsed. "It wasn't one specific thing, but a hundred small things that wore on me. Finally, I realized I was living Caldwell's life and not my own. I knew it wouldn't change, not after marriage. In fact, marrying him probably would've been the end of me. He wanted a wife, kids, and the whole white-picket-fence-suburban-life. I just felt rushed. I remember when I used to watch my mom wash dishes. She smelled like freshly cut celery. Standing in front of the kitchen sink, her apron tied loose across her lower back, yellow rubber gloves up to her elbows, she would stare out the window, day after day. I wondered what dreams she dreamt while her hands rubbed a dish towel on a china plate. What other unlived life did she see through that window in the afternoon? And at night, when the light in the kitchen sent her own reflection back to her and she studied her face, was she happy with what she saw? She probably wished to be someplace else, doing something else. I didn't want to end up washing dishes at a kitchen sink in a house with an unwanted child, haunted by my lost dreams. And then there was the day I saw the trapped butterfly and decided to break our engagement." That was the first time Brooke had told anyone about her mom's regrets and the fateful butterfly. She was ashamed to confess she based a life-altering decision on what might've been a silly analogy to an insect's fluttering confusion.

But Diane just linked her arm with Brooke's and stood beside her. They gazed out over the calm morning sea. "Well, my mother used to say there's a difference between living and *living*," said Diane. "I didn't truly understand what she meant by that until my dad got sick. Even though you can breathe in and out, or do the daily chores, you might not feel *alive*. It sounds like you understand that difference now, too."

Brooke nodded. Diane opened her arms and hugged Brooke. In the instant of Diane's embrace, Brooke felt her snowball of doubt begin to melt, leaking from her eyes as grateful tears until she saw once more that she'd been right all along. Her eyes dried. Her mind cleared. And in the midst of the wide beach on the island she adored, with the music of purring waves and chanting gulls playing on salted wind, Brooke felt alive.

Although she couldn't call Diane, Brooke could call on memories of her. Remembering Diane shored up the breach in Brooke's dam of emotions. That same mix of comfort, connection, and reassurance swept through her now, as it had two summers ago when she wept in Diane's arms.

She stopped ruminating on the couch and drifted into her bedroom, to the dresser. She kept her few pieces of nice jewelry tucked in the back corner of a drawer behind a stack of pantyhose her mom bought for her that she would never wear, all of them still in their unopened packages.

Reaching into the back of the drawer, her fingers brushed over two small velvet boxes: the blue topaz necklace her dad gave her for high school graduation and a pair of real pearl earrings from her mom for her twenty-first birthday. She touched the top of a thin rectangular box that held an elegant diamond tennis bracelet, a long-ago Valentine's Day gift from Caldwell. She wore the bracelet only once, to a dinner party with Caldwell's parents, and spent the whole evening conscious of its cold rub against her skin like a handcuff. Brooke bit her lower lip as her fingers wrapped around the smooth edges of the last box, a square mahogany jewelry box with a delicate clasp, fit into the back corner of her drawer. She worked it around the other boxes and out from under the pantyhose.

Inside the mahogany jewelry box, pinned to a plump satin pillow, was the butterfly brooch.

Diane lent the brooch to Brooke five months ago for a black-tie New Year's Eve party at the aquarium. Brooke went to the party with an architect she was seeing at the time. It was their third date and her most formal event since the many fancy parties she attended with Caldwell. Brooke talked to Diane enough about the architect to give away her interest in him and her desperate need for hair and makeup.

The day of the party, Diane came over with makeup bags full of hair gadgets and products. Brooke only used mascara and lipstick for her usual dress-up routine. She didn't even own a hair dryer. Diane, on the other hand, practiced in the art of the makeover, had been making herself up from bed-head to beauty each morning since she was a teenager and seemed to have more styling stuff than the local drugstore.

Between sips of wine, Diane curled Brooke's hair, swooping part of it up into a silver barrette. Like a pro, she dabbed makeup here and there, brushed on blush and eye shadow, rolled mascara into Brooke's long lashes, and applied eyeliner, lip liner, and two blended shades of lipstick. Admiring Brooke's transformation, Diane hurried her into dress and heels and guided her to the full-length mirror tacked to the bedroom door. It took Brooke a few seconds to recognize herself in the striking woman reflected in the mirror.

Setting her wineglass on the dresser, Brooke pulled her shoulders back, rubbed her lips together, and smiled. "Wow, Diane, you have talent. Where've you been my whole life? I could've used your help."

"Nonsense," said Diane. "You make it easy for me because you're naturally beautiful."

Brooke rolled her eyes. "Natural, yes, but hardly beautiful."

"Oh, who're you kidding?" Diane stood next to Brooke to point out her finest features. "Look at your big brown eyes rimmed with just the slightest hint of jade green. Your cheekbones are to die for. And what certain architect wouldn't want to kiss those full, pouty lips?" Diane raised her eyebrows.

They laughed.

"Well, thank you!" Brooke beamed. "Could you record all that flattery so I can replay it when I need it later?"

"Listen, you look so gorgeous Mr. Architect isn't going to know what to do," said Diane while she bent over to retrieve something from her makeup bag. "But I do have just one more finishing touch."

She handed a mahogany jewelry box to Brooke.

"What's this?" asked Brooke.

"Open it," urged Diane.

Brooke gently unlatched the clasp and lifted the top on its hinges. Inside was a brooch the size and shape of a small butterfly, its cushion-cut blue sapphire body centered between gem-encrusted lace wings. The platinum arched plaque, set throughout with small rose-cut diamonds and sapphires, caught light and showered sparkles across the wall and ceiling.

Brooke looked at Diane, lips parted in awe. "Is this . . . real?" She gulped.

Diane chuckled. "Yes, it is, all of it—diamonds, sapphires, platinum."

"It must cost a fortune! Where did it come from?" asked Brooke.

"It's a family heirloom," answered Diane with a flutter of blinks. "I'm lending it to you."

"I don't understand." Holding the box with both hands, Brooke looked down at the blue butterfly.

"I remember the story you told me about Caldwell and the butterfly. I know you sometimes struggle to make peace with your decision. I want you to have this brooch for a while as a symbol of how brave you are, especially as you get back into dating, which can be hard on anyone's self-esteem. Wear it tonight and keep it for as long as you need a reminder of the butterfly that set you free."

"Oh, Diane, that's so thoughtful. Thank you, really, but I'm too nervous to wear something this expensive. What if it falls off or breaks? What if I lose it?"

"Don't be silly. You're the most responsible person I know."

"But not the most graceful," warned Brooke.

Diane laughed. "Well, you know you're a lot like a sea turtle that way, clumsy on land, agile in water. But we all have our faults." She slid the butterfly brooch from its box and pinned it to Brooke's dress. "There, now you're ready."

"Thank you, Diane," Brooke said again. "It's perfect."

"You're welcome."

Brooke touched the wings of the butterfly brooch. "I have a feeling this will be a great new year."

Diane handed Brooke her glass of wine while raising her own glass to toast, "To a fresh new start."

"To new turtle hatchlings," said Brooke.

"And new romance." Diane winked.

"Cheers!" They chimed glasses, and each drank a dose of hope with their swallow of wine.

Now, Brooke stood in her bedroom in the same spot beside the dresser where, five months earlier, she and Diane made their toasts for the New Year. The butterfly brooch sparkled on its perch in the mahogany jewelry box in Brooke's hands.

She'd been wrong. This wasn't a great year. In fact, it was a terrible year—and not even half over. For every toast they made that New Year's Eve, the opposite happened. Brooke didn't make any fresh new starts but kept on with her same daily routines, same comfortable habits. It remained to be seen if any new turtle hatchlings would be born, but there wasn't yet a single loggerhead nest on Anders Isle. As for new romance, things with the architect fizzled out before February and dates since then were few and far between. Even the hope and friendship of five short months ago was gone.

They didn't toast to life, but now Diane was dead.

And, to top it all off, Caldwell was back.

So, Brooke did what she always did with Diane's butterfly brooch. She stroked its sculpted ridges, its diamond-and-sapphire wings, then gently unpinned it from its cushion. With the cold, faceted gems pressed flat against her palm, Brooke squeezed the brooch in her fisted hand, closed her eyes, and whispered, *"Brave."*

CHAPTER

25

Caldwell didn't buy his own coffee on Monday mornings. Instead, he played office politics. He could medal in the sport.

Every Monday morning, Percival Jones, the partner in charge of the real estate practice group, walked the hall and stuck his head into select office doorways to invite associates to join him for a trip to Starbucks. The coffee call came sometime between eight and eight-thirty as a means of rounding up those associates who were—in Percival's opinion—committed to the law firm, purposely excluding the slackers who arrived at work at nine or didn't bill enough. Caldwell made a point of being seated at his desk by seven-thirty sharp each Monday morning and wouldn't leave his desk until he stood to follow Percival for coffee.

Recently, Caldwell had been the first associate Percival would invite. Percival even allowed Caldwell to recommend fellow associates, an honor that lifted Caldwell a notch in the pecking order. Percival picked favorites, and Caldwell was his new favorite. The coffee group strode past the open office doors of the unchosen without a sideways glance. Off they trotted, Percival surrounded by a gaggle of admiring associates vying to take the lead in witty conversation. Percival always bought the Monday-morning coffee, but the associates knew that he expected one—if not all—of them to at least offer to pay. And they all offered, reaching for wallets and loose bills until he waved them off. It was a well-rehearsed rite of passage, and the associates indulged the partner no matter how ridiculous it seemed.

The Monday morning after Caldwell's business fishing trip to Anders Isle, the coffee group included Percival, Caldwell, and three other associates. Their conversation on the way to Starbucks jumped from sports to politics to the latest stock market fluctuations. But on the way back, the talk was all business.

Percival and Caldwell took the lead while the others lagged, gabbing about their workloads.

"How did things go with Kingston this weekend?" Percival asked Caldwell.

"Fishing was rained out, but I think I have him on the hook."

"Reel him in." Percival pantomimed a reel with his coffee cup.

Caldwell nodded and smiled. "I will." He looked down at his feet, which suddenly felt much heavier. They walked a few steps in silence, Caldwell eager to think of something to say to keep Percival's attention. "I have a conference call this morning with Art Ogletree."

That worked.

Percival arched his brow, taking a sip of coffee. "About what?"

"His projects. He wants an update."

"Well, whatever he wants, by all means, you do it," said Percival, a demanding bite in his voice. "Did I know about this call?"

"I sent an email to you about it and put it on your calendar." Caldwell knew that wasn't enough.

"I didn't see it. Next time tell me in person. Do I need to be on the call?"

"No," said Caldwell with little conviction. "I'm just giving him a quick status report for each deal."

"That's right. Keep it brief," said Percival. "You have to be the duck."

Caldwell hesitated, wracking his brain to remember something about a duck, then gave up. "What do you mean?"

Percival wet his lips with a sip of coffee. "When a duck glides across a pond, it moves with ease, smooth, barely a ripple in its wake. Do you ever notice its webbed feet paddling furiously underwater?"

"Um . . . no?" answered Caldwell, but questioned his own answer, still puzzled by Percival's point.

"Exactly." Percival pushed the elevator button. "All you see is the duck—its color, its size, maybe its speed on the water. As a lawyer, you should aspire to be like the duck with your case work. The client should never notice the furious behind-the-scenes leg work you do for each case. It should appear to the client that the case moves forward effortlessly and without issues, like the duck gliding on water. We don't need to overwhelm clients with legalese and mundane details of every minute we spend on a case. They pay us to take care of all that stuff, so they don't have to think about it."

Caldwell humored him. "Good one. I'll remember that." The duck isn't the animal he'd choose to be—or most clients would want him to be—as a lawyer. The lion, the shark—any predator—made more sense. But Caldwell wanted to be a partner, and if he had to be a duck to do it, then a duck he would be.

Percival walked onto the elevator, associates crowding in around him. They watched each floor number blink on a digital screen while they rode to the top. Swallowing a hot gulp of coffee, Caldwell considered asking Percival to join the call after all.

By the time the coffee group splintered into their various offices along the hall, Caldwell had ten minutes until his nine o'clock conference call with Art Ogletree. Percival paused in Caldwell's doorway, pointed at him, and said, "Be the duck."

"Be the duck," repeated Caldwell, forcing a smile.

He hoped he could be.

The phone rang at five minutes to nine, but Caldwell didn't recognize the number. Clearing his throat, he arranged his notes for the Ogletree investments and picked up the receiver. "Caldwell Madden."

"Junior, I have good news," said Senator Madden. He barked an order to someone in the background, "Call him back. Tell him *again* that we're *not* doing it."

"Dad?" Caldwell tried to refocus his father's attention.

"I'm here, just in the middle of a hectic Monday morning. So, listen to this," he began.

"Dad, I can't talk now. I have a really important call any minute."

"Who could be more important than your dad?" Senator Madden teased.

"Art Ogletree," said Caldwell, even though he knew he didn't need to answer.

"Ah, yes, my favorite Bostonian. Tell him hello for me. I'll see you at noon today—rally on The Green. Don't forget." He hung up before Caldwell had a chance to respond.

As stupid as it seemed to Caldwell, *be the duck* worked as a calming mantra while he waited for Art's call. He repeated it in his head—*be the duck*—*be the duck*—and soon regained confidence.

The phone rang again at exactly nine o'clock. This time, Art's number, which Caldwell had memorized. He took a deep breath and answered, "Hi, Mr. Ogletree. I was expecting your call."

"Oh, please call me Art." He was casual about putting them both on a first name basis even though Caldwell hadn't been on a call with Art alone before.

Art had a reputation for being kind, even generous, to new friends and business associates—until one made a mistake or dared to cross him. Talk of his explosive temper almost invariably followed mention of his internationally recognized name. Unfortunate souls who'd been on the receiving end of his wrath in the past were quick to warn newcomers of Art's extreme mood swings, his tendency to cut someone out of his big business deals—and his life—as quickly as he let them in. It was all or nothing with Art. But most people—drawn to his easygoing, gregarious first impression and his staggering wealth—took their chances with his fiery nature.

"Well, Art, I enjoyed meeting Ben this weekend." Caldwell's voice felt tight as he measured each word. "We didn't have much luck with fishing, but I hope he enjoyed the trip."

"He told me it was fantastic. I think he was most impressed by the real estate tour. I get the feeling he isn't much of a fisherman." Art chuckled. "Thank you for your Southern hospitality."

"My pleasure."

"I'm sorry I couldn't make it. Something came up."

"Your assistant left a message. You just let me know when you want to cash that rain check. I'm happy to show you around anytime."

"Very good," said Art. "I look forward to it. And tell your father I plan to play a round of golf with him when I come down to Taylor Island this weekend for the campaign dinner."

"I'm sure he'll be happy to arrange it. He said to tell you hello."

"Same to him."

"So, shall we get down to business?" Caldwell reminded himself to be the duck.

"I'm all ears," said Art, which was funny because he was. His ears stuck out and stretched like shoehorns from his temples to his jawbones. Jokes swirled about Art's ears being the secret of his enormous success because he could hear the whisper of a deal from across the country. Those in his inner circle snickered when he boasted about being a good listener. Nobody dared to comment about his ears to his face. Even if he was aware of their unusual size, Art wasn't self-deprecating and fancied himself handsome.

Caldwell was too nervous to laugh. Thank goodness. He began his status report with Project Flood, a townhouse complex in an upscale suburb of Raleigh. Like many law firms, Caldwell's firm used arbitrary project names to maintain confidentiality in all communications about a project. The real name of a development wouldn't be released to the public until units were ready to be sold.

Art liked to name his projects in the Carolinas after catastrophic natural disasters.

In two short minutes, Caldwell summarized the other three Ogletree developments: Project Tornado and Project Thunderstorm, both high-rise luxury condo buildings in uptown Charlotte, and Project Earthquake, a hotel resort development just off I-77 near Rock Hill, South Carolina.

Art sounded pleased. "Good work, Caldwell, everything appears to be in order down there in the Carolinas. Let me know when we wrap up Project Flood. I want to start selling those units as soon as possible."

"I'll call you when the signed originals get here Wednesday."

"Super. Talk to you then." He hung up.

Leaning back in his chair, Caldwell blew out a sigh of relief. The call lasted a total of seven minutes. Brief. Caldwell kept the review cordial, uncomplicated, and succinct. Just the way Percival liked it.

Caldwell was the duck.

CHAPTER
26

At half past nine, Brooke inched her car over the connector bridge from Anders City to Anders Isle, stuck behind a line of drivers with out-of-state license plates and boats in tow. The locals called them "summer slippers" because they only rented boat slips from May to August. Brooke thought of them as a burden for both traffic and turtles, but she welcomed the forced slow approach to the island. She agreed to help the Loggerhead Protection League manage turtle team volunteers until the appointment of Diane's replacement, but she was in no hurry to visit Diane's office.

The connector bridge stretched its flat, straight concrete spine across the salt marsh, then arched over the Intracoastal Waterway. From Brooke's point of view, the rise in the bridge led up into clouds and sky like a runway. Brooke imagined speeding off its end, flying magically through the air over the island. Maybe Diane was up there somewhere, soaring with her father like the birds they adored.

The Loggerhead Protection League, known for short as LPL, began a decade earlier as a grassroots project comprised of concerned island residents. For the first few years, LPL members simply met at each other's houses to document loggerhead nesting patterns and discuss related issues. But as interest grew and a trained volunteer base developed, they needed more space, finding a central location for operations in a four-room wood house a block from the beach.

Parking in the sand and gravel side lot, Brooke looked at the LPL's screened porch. She had visited Diane at the office many times in the past two years of their friendship. They would sit in rocking chairs on the porch and talk about turtles—and life—while the sun sank into the arms of grand oak trees.

Brooke pushed open the front door of the office. A wind chime tinkled a cheerful, high-pitched flurry of notes.

Cindy looked up from her seat behind the reception desk. "Hi, Brooke. Nice to see you."

"You, too."

"Thanks again for helping out today." Cindy stood up, rounded the desk.

"You're welcome." Brooke accepted Cindy's quick hug, then glanced around the office at myriad loggerhead posters, books, and trinkets lining the walls.

Everything reminded her of Diane.

Cindy noticed Brooke surveying the place. "It's all loggerheads all the time in this tiny house."

"Home sweet home," said Brooke.

"That's what Diane called it."

"I know. I heard her say it so many times I can almost hear her saying it now."

Cindy's eyes watered. "I'm sorry." She placed her hand on her chest. "I'm so upset about Diane. I went to dinner with her the night she was . . . well . . . I should've waited at the restaurant with her. I shouldn't have left her there alone." Reaching for a tissue on her desk, she wiped her runny nose and blotted her tears.

"It's not your fault." Brooke touched Cindy's arm.

"Thank you for saying that." Cindy blew her nose and dropped the tissue in the trash can before composing herself. "Anyway, I know you two were really close."

"We were." Brooke thought she would be the one teary-eyed about Diane's death but found herself surprisingly composed. Numb. "It hasn't really sunk in yet."

"I know what you mean. It doesn't seem real. I keep expecting to see her hurrying in and out on turtle missions. When I heard the door, I swear I thought it was her."

"We all miss her." Brooke wanted to change the subject, trying to keep her sadness at bay. "So, how can I help?"

"Well, what we need most is a contact person for the volunteers."

"I can be that person."

"Thank you. That would be so great. I guess you know how it works?" asked Cindy.

"Only from a volunteer perspective. Why don't you give me the rundown?"

"Sure. So, volunteers patrol the beach in pairs, and each pair takes one of five sections of beach on the island. That means ten volunteers go out each morning to look for tracks and seventy total volunteers are involved over the course of a week. They keep regular schedules—walking on the same day and in the same section week to week—so you won't need to do much scheduling, but they'll contact you to find substitutes, or to let you know when tracks are found."

"I can do all of that."

Cindy narrowed her eyes. "Are you sure it isn't too much with all that's going on?"

"I'm sure."

"Well, thanks again. You're a lifesaver," said Cindy, but as the words came out, she realized too late she shouldn't have put it that way. "I'm sorry, I mean, we really need your help."

Brooke nodded. "I understand."

Cindy grabbed a stack of papers from her desk. "Here's the volunteer list and schedule." Handing the papers to Brooke, she hesitated. Brooke flipped through the pages, then looked at Cindy for the rest of the instructions. Cindy swallowed and asked, "What should we do about Wednesday?" She pointed a timid finger at the schedule in Brooke's hands.

"Wednesday?" Brooke's eyes followed Cindy's finger on the weekly nest patrol schedule. In the slot for Wednesday morning, Diane's name was listed just above Brooke's name for the North End Beach section. "Oh," Brooke deflated. "Right. I guess I thought . . . I don't know what I thought. I just hadn't thought that far ahead yet."

"You know what?" Cindy added quickly, offering a sympathetic smile. "We'll figure something out."

"Okay." Brooke looked down at the page, stung by the prospect of walking alone on Wednesday—and every other day.

"That's really all there is to it for now." Cindy sat at her desk. "I'll send out an email to let the volunteers know you're filling in."

"Great. Thanks." Gazing across the room at Diane's closed office door, Brooke took a deep breath. "Do you mind if I spend a little time in there?"

Caught by surprise, Cindy bobbed her head. "Sure . . . I mean, sure you can go in."

Brooke took a few slow steps toward Diane's office. On the door, a name plate bore Diane's name and title etched in professional type. Brooke's heart sank. Would it always hurt whenever she saw or heard the name Diane? As much as Brooke wanted to run out of the house and away from the onslaught of all things Diane, a deeper mission urged her into the office. She must continue to search for answers about the dead-end loggerhead tracks. If there was one thing Diane would want Brooke to do, it would be to find out what happened to the twelve loggerheads that crawled ashore on Anders Isle and vanished.

The door swung inward, revealing an organized office dedicated to the adoration of sea turtles. Inspirational loggerhead posters wallpapered the room. A bookshelf sagged beneath the weight of textbooks stacked like bricks, interspersed with a dozen turtle statues made of everything from crystal to bronze to tin cans. The corkboard on the wall beside Diane's desk held pictures of individual turtle hatchlings making their way into the ocean, pictures of nest sitters from previous summers, and the same picture of Brooke and Diane that hung on Brooke's freezer, the two of them beaming from the thrill of watching hatchlings scamper to sea by the light of the moon. She swallowed hard, beat down her sorrow.

Sitting carefully at Diane's desk, she turned her back to the pictures on the wall. Over the past three years, Diane documented the loggerhead disappearances. Brooke just needed to find Diane's files. Pulling open desk drawers, she found only office supplies. There wasn't a free-standing file cabinet or any other piece of furniture to hold files or notebooks. Maybe the files were in another part of the house?

Brooke swiveled in the chair, looking through the window at Front Beach in the distance. So many houses and buildings crammed the beachfront, she couldn't see the dunes. She remembered a time growing up when it had been just the opposite—miles of rolling dunes broken only by a house or two. A lot had changed on the island since then.

Her phone rang. Pulling it out of her pocket, she saw Drew's name on the screen.

"Hey," she said, "tell me some good news . . . *please*."

"Thank you," said Drew.

"What?"

"Your information about *Bonnie* is the biggest break in Diane's case so far."

"Really? There's a break in the case? But I shouldn't get credit for that, you should."

"*We* should. Your work is as much a part of it as mine."

"Well, you're welcome, and thanks. That *is* good news."

"Also, I need your help again," said Drew.

"What can I do?"

"We're on our way to pick someone up for questioning. Can you come to the station to identify the fisherman who was on *Bonnie* when you got the turtle?"

"Sure."

"I'll let you know when we're headed back so you have time to get over to the island."

"I'm already here . . . in Diane's office."

"Why?" asked Drew. "I thought you were at the aquarium."

"I'm filling in until they find a replacement."

"Really? Are you okay with that?"

"Yes. It was my idea. It isn't easy, but I know Diane would want the LPL to keep up with the turtles no matter what."

"Are you sure that isn't too much too soon?" asked Drew.

"I think it'll be therapeutic."

"All right, just . . . don't push it."

His concern was touching. "I'll be okay."

"Okay," Drew conceded. "Actually, one question since you're there: do you see Diane's phone anywhere?"

Brooke searched the desk, opened drawers, scanned the bookshelf and floor. "Hold on. I'm looking."

"Oh, and if you find it, don't touch it. Use some of those gloves you wear for the hatchlings and drop it into a bag for me."

"Sure." Standing up, she bent over to look on the floor immediately in front of the desk, the part she couldn't see from behind the desk, but didn't see a phone anywhere. Instead, wedged under the front of the desk was a cardboard file box labelled in black marker as: TURTLE FILES.

"Did you find it?" asked Drew.

"Nope. No phone in sight." Brooke walked around the desk to reach the file box.

"Oh well, worth a try," said Drew. "So, I'll text when we're at the station and you can come on over. Will that work?"

"Yes. See you then."

"Okay, later."

Pocketing her phone, Brooke opened the file box. Inside, she found notebooks labeled for each turtle nesting season—May through August—for the past three summers when female loggerheads were disappearing, twelve in all by the end of last season.

Brooke wasn't living in Anders when the strange dead-end turtle tracks began to appear three summers ago, but she'd been there for the bulk of the disappearances since then. Each new season was worse than the last. Three loggerheads vanished in the first season, another four in the summer after that, and five more last summer.

Female loggerheads usually nest for one season out of every three years and lay an average of five nests per season. If those twelve missing loggerheads were killed, then the current population nesting on Anders Isle would have been nearly wiped out in three short years.

The dead loggerhead Brooke found Saturday would be unlucky thirteen.

Diane and the LPL kept quiet about the disappearances, afraid of public backlash and the embarrassment that would befall them if they admitted to failing at their one and only mission. A faction of LPL members speculated that the suspicious crawlways causing all the fuss weren't made by loggerheads, but by a rogue group of local teenagers playing pranks.

One night, a week before the discovery of the first dead-end crawlway, Diane came across a group of four teenage boys partying on North End Beach. She crashed their party while searching for a loggerhead she expected to see nesting near the dunes. The boys were drunk and rude. She asked them to move the party inland, explaining how their noise and laughter and phone lights could scare off turtles coming ashore to nest. They jeered at her, sloppy and cussing, feeding off each other like a pack of wild animals, telling her they couldn't care less about some stupid turtles. What they didn't know was that Diane happened to be dating a cop at the time—Drew. That night, the whole gang of teens was arrested for underage drinking. Plus, it turned out they stole the golf cart they rode in on.

The bust made headline news on the island and gave each boy motivation to learn enough about loggerhead turtles to cause problems for Diane. All it took was a Google search to yield volumes of details about loggerhead nesting habits, including pictures of crawlway tracks.

Diane told the LPL members about her run-in with the boys. Some of them agreed with her decision to alert the police, but others thought she went too far. A week later, the first mysterious entrance crawlway appeared on North End Beach. Those who disagreed with Diane questioned the authenticity of the crawlway, claiming the boys faked it to get revenge. Battling their doubts, Diane pointed out grooves and drag marks that could only be made by a large sea turtle and certainly couldn't be imitated with such precision by a group of teens. Some said the boys must have caught the turtle and carried it farther down the beach to release it. Diane argued that the boys had no way to predict where to find a turtle mid-crawl on the beach. But her analysis of the situation fell on deaf ears. She didn't have a better explanation. The crawlway itself was the only evidence that a turtle might've come ashore and disappeared. Even after the second and third mysterious crawlways were found that season, the LPL continued to be plagued by infighting . . . until the following summer, when four more crawlways led to nothing.

By the end of the second season, most LPL members united behind Diane, convinced loggerheads were, in fact, disappearing. But it was too late. They lost two nesting seasons of precious time and evidence and had to wait until the next summer to begin an investigation. By then, many disgruntled members cycled through to other assignments or organizations. None of them felt as compelled as Diane to find a cause for the supposed disappearances. Nobody, including Diane, wanted to inform the public. It remained a mystery known only to the LPL and its inner circle of turtle friends.

Brooke opened the notebook from last summer, when the island had a record low number of loggerhead nests and a total of five dead-end crawlways. Diane described each discovered crawlway on a table, including the date, time, beach zone, crawlway width, and GPS coordinates for a nest location, or, in the case of the mysterious crawlways, the end point of the turtle tracks. She added notes underneath each table with details about the weather, other environmental factors impacting nesting habits, and whether the nest had been relocated.

According to Diane's notebook, the first dead-end crawlway last season appeared in mid-May, ironically, on the morning of Mother's Day. The crawlway, found on North End Beach, measured thirty-eight inches across and stretched almost to the base of the dunes. The notes below the table read: "*M/L-1*: Missing Loggerhead, first of the season" with a description of the crawlway as normal, and a large question mark at the bottom of the page.

The four others were spread through the months of May and June, all located on North End Beach. Diane's notes were the same for each: a table with measurements, shorthand labels *M/L-2* through *M/L-5*, brief descriptions, and a big question mark. If Diane had any theories about what was happening to the loggerheads, she didn't include them in her notes.

But Brooke heard Diane's theories firsthand.

Only two theories seemed plausible to Diane. As much as she hated to admit it, the crawlways could have been the work of vengeful teenage boys. Although it seemed to be an extreme effort, especially for a bunch of kids with short attention spans, that theory would be the best scenario for the turtles. The other theory, the more likely and more upsetting of the two, was that someone was taking the turtles. If that was the case, the twelve missing loggerheads were probably dead, a thought that caused Brooke to choke up almost every time they talked about it.

"Brooke?" Cindy gently knocked on the door, then cracked it open.

"I was just finishing up in here." Brooke stacked the notebooks in the file box and closed the lid.

"I'm going to get some coffee. Do you want anything?"

"No, thanks," said Brooke. "I'm on my way out, too."

"Oh, okay."

"I found this box of files I'd like to review. Mind if I take it with me?"

"Fine with me," said Cindy.

Carrying the box, Brooke followed Cindy out of the LPL house into bright Monday morning sunlight.

CHAPTER

27

Sampson rode in the passenger seat of the unmarked police car. "So, Detective, what's your theory about Joe Willis?"

"Classic jealous ex-lover." Drew parked at Dylan Creek Marina.

"Really? You think Joe had an affair with the victim?"

"Maybe, or just a one-night stand. He was obsessed. She rejected him. He became enraged and—*whamo!*—he snapped and killed her. If he couldn't have her, nobody could. He seemed like the type to have a temper."

"You think the baby was his?"

Drew shrugged. "Could be, or she told him there was someone else and used the pregnancy as an excuse to end things. Either way, I think it's an affair gone bad."

"I don't know, Detective. I don't know." Sampson unbuckled his seat belt. They got out of the car.

"What don't you know?" asked Drew.

"It's just, well, the victim . . . why Joe Willis? I don't see it."

"Who knows? No explaining physical attraction. He could pass as the ruggedly handsome type. A real sea-cowboy."

"I guess some women are into that." Sampson took hurried steps to keep up.

Drew shook his head. "And it always seems to be the women you least expect."

Dylan Creek Marina spread along the wide mouth of the creek where it spilled into the harbor. Sampson and Drew climbed a set of stairs to a covered plank porch flanking the sturdy shingled marina house. Commercial fishermen registered their boat information with the marina and entered daily departure and arrival times in a manual log anchored to a wooden podium on the porch. A few pencils dangled from strings tied to the binder, their tips dull from overuse.

Last night, when Drew showed up at the Willis residence, Nadine Willis told him Joe was out on an overnight shrimping trip and would return by ten o'clock in the morning.

Sampson opened the binder to the first page of entries. "I don't see *Bonnie* listed today. Must not be back yet."

"When did they leave Sunday?" asked Drew.

Sampson turned to the next page, but it was blank. He flipped through a few more pages—all blank. "Today's the only day in here."

"Why's that?"

"I don't know, but we can find out." Sampson pointed to the marina house.

In the air-conditioned office, a fresh-out-of-college intern eagerly offered them the log pages from the previous week. He pointed out entries for *Bonnie*'s departure at 5:00 a.m. Friday and her arrival at 10:15 a.m. Saturday. In the last column, the initials *JW* were penciled in for both entries. Drew already had copies of these entry pages, but the originals would be better evidence.

Sunday's log was the top page in the binder. Sampson and Drew found the entry for *Bonnie*'s departure at 2:00 p.m. Sunday, *JW* in the last column.

"Looks like he's out on the boat," said Drew, tapping his finger on Joe's initials. "Let's go to the docks."

At Drew's request, the intern printed the registration details for *Bonnie*, which listed Joe Willis and Mr. Riley Broom as the boat's owners and co-captains. Then the intern directed them to dock fifty, one of the commercial docks mooring shrimp boats.

The air stank like the breath of a thousand oysters. A cluster of shrimp boats were tied off alongside the dock, the first of which was *Bonnie*. On the aft working deck, two men yanked ropes and nets, moved equipment, and sorted their catch. Drew and Sampson approached the boat unnoticed.

A flapping group of hungry gulls squawked above the stern, waiting to dine on discarded scraps. Pelicans perched on nearby pilings to gulp down leftovers. Two masts rose like giant antennae from the center of the 55-foot outrigger trawler, and two booms jutted out diagonally over the stern with lines and trawls strung between them, the great green nets hauled in and hanging down loose and empty.

One man on the boat yelled to the other, "Hey, Joe, grab that cooler in the wheelhouse."

"Got it," Joe yelled back from somewhere on the far side of the boat.

"Excuse me," Drew called out, catching the attention of the man on the bow. "Are you Riley Broom?"

The man squinted at Drew and rubbed his bulbous nose. "I'm Riley." Moving to the boat's edge, he cupped his hand above his woolly brows to shade his eyes. "Do I know you?"

"No, Mr. Broom," said Drew. "I'm Detective Young, this is Officer Sampson, Anders Isle PD. Is that Joe Willis on the boat with you?"

"Yeah, Joe's my co-cap'n." Riley wiped sweat from his sunburned neck and coughed. "We just got back. Did we do somethin' wrong?"

"We're trying to figure that out, Mr. Broom. We'd like to speak to both of you."

"Joe!" Riley yelled over his shoulder. "Police are here!" Leaning over the rail of the boat with a worried frown, he lowered his voice. "Is this 'bout the turtle nets?" His beady eyes shifted to Sampson, back to Drew.

"The what?" asked Drew. He looked at Sampson, who shrugged.

Before Riley could explain, Joe ducked around the rigging in the back of the boat. He casually worked his way along the rail to stand beside Riley on the bow across a slit of saltwater from where Drew and Sampson stood on the dock.

Joe looked at Drew. "Well, I guess I'm not all that surprised to see you again, Detective. What's this about?"

"Will you and Mr. Broom come with us to the station to answer a few questions?"

"Is this about my son? Because I can tell you he's sure as hell scared straight."

Joe balled a dirty towel in his hands and tossed it at a bucket on the deck.

"I'm sure he is. We need to clear up some things for our investigation. It would be best if you both come with us voluntarily."

"What does Riley have to do with this?"

"We'll give you more information at the station, where we'll have some privacy." Drew cocked his head at the other commercial shrimp boats moored close by.

Joe crossed his arms. "And what if we don't?"

"Well, if you refuse to talk to us, that sure will make me suspicious. I don't want to have to detain you just to ask some questions."

"Joe, please," said Riley, begging with his eyes. "Let's go. Let's cooperate. I don't need no arrest on my record."

"They're not gonna arrest you, Riley. This has nothing to do with you."

"I think it might, Joe. I think I mighta said something could get us into trouble."

Joe cut his eyes at Riley in disbelief. "What're you talkin' about?"

Riley didn't say another word. He just looked down at the rail and picked at a splinter.

"So, will you come with us?" Drew asked.

Riley nodded fast, not looking up. Joe glared at Drew and Sampson, measuring their expressions, but they waited stone-faced for his answer. "Okay," said Joe. "We'll go with you."

"Thank you," said Drew, relieved. "Smart decision."

Joe pulled on the line tied to the piling to draw the side of the trawler against the dock. Drew noticed the bright white sheen of rope against Joe's tan, calloused hands. While the fishermen climbed from the boat to the dock, Drew stepped out of the way and saw that all the other lines tied off at dock fifty were stained a dark brownish yellow from regular use.

"Is that a new rope?" Drew pointed to the clean white line strung between *Bonnie* and the dock.

"Yup," said Joe. "Have to replace 'em from time to time."

"It looks *brand*-new," commented Drew. "When did you get it?"

Joe studied Drew's eyes. "Yesterday—Sunday—before we went shrimping."

"Where did you buy it?"

"I got it over on Anders Isle at the Sundries." Joe held Drew's even stare. Shrugging off the answer, Drew nodded casually. "Okay."

The fishermen followed Drew and Sampson, first to the marina house, where Joe made a log entry for *Bonnie*'s return time, then to the parking lot, where they ducked into the back of the unmarked car.

CHAPTER

28

At the station, Joe Willis and Riley Broom sat in separate interview rooms in metal chairs facing bare tables. A ceiling-corner-mounted video camera recorded every move and sound. The doors remained open between the main office and the interview rooms, signaling to the men that, not being in custody or under arrest, they were free to leave at any time.

Drew and Chief Mullinax agreed it would be best to convince Joe to come to the station willingly, without arresting him. The evidence against him—a potential false alibi and the body found tied to *his* crab trap—was damning in the eyes of those looking for someone to accuse, but the same evidence could be explained as coincidence or blamed on another person, especially by a bulldog defense attorney, if it got that far.

Bottom line, there was room for reasonable doubt, and they couldn't risk arresting the wrong man. Island residents, the media, potential tourists, and politicians at all levels of the government food chain waited for answers, for resolution, for the capture of a suspected murderer. Mounting pressure showed on the chief's face in the observation room while he looked through the one-way glass at Joe and Riley.

In one room, Joe lounged back in his chair, his hands stuffed in his pockets and legs spread wide. He sat still, looking first at the wall, then up at the ceiling. Disinterest soured his face. In the other room, Riley couldn't have been more opposite of Joe in both position and demeanor. With his chair pulled up so close to the table's edge that his chest pressed against it, Riley sat at attention, hands clasped in front of him, and watched the doorway. One leg bounced under the table. Sweat speckled his temples and neck.

Drew assigned Sampson to question Riley, wanting to observe Riley's responses in prep for interviewing Joe. Having a disarming humility, Sampson had the best chance of putting Riley at ease.

Sampson entered Riley's interview room and closed the door. "Mr. Broom, I'm closing the door to keep our interview private, but I want to remind you that you're not under arrest. You're free to leave at any time."

Riley nodded, flattening his hands on the table.

Sampson began with a statement of the date and their names. Leaning casually against the wall, he spoke in a conversational tone. "Okay, Mr. Broom, this will be a simple question-and-answer session. Tell me everything you know. Anything relevant. Be sure to speak each answer clearly for the recording. Do you understand?"

Riley nodded furiously and clasped his hands together again.

"Please speak your answers, Mr. Broom."

Widening his bloodshot eyes, Riley swallowed. "Okay. Yes, yes, I understand," he said, flustered by making a mistake on the very first question. He took a deep breath and looked up at Sampson.

"Is it true that you and Joe Willis are the co-owners and co-captains of the shrimp trawler named *Bonnie*?"

"Yes."

"How long have you and Mr. Willis owned the boat?"

"'Bout five years now."

"And during those years, have you and Mr. Willis gotten along?"

"Sure, we get along."

"Would you say the two of you are friends?"

Riley hesitated. "Um, yeah, we're friends." He scratched at the skin behind his ear.

"Well, as co-owners and co-captains who get along—as friends—do you and Mr. Willis always go out on the boat together?"

"Not always, but mostly."

"Give me an example of a time when *you* decided not to go out on the boat. What was your reason?"

"Uh, lemme see." Riley rubbed at a mark on the table, looked up at the ceiling. "One time I pulled my back out building a wall around my yard. I was laid up in bed for a couple days. Joe went without me. We have a crew that helps out, a rig man, headers, so he wasn't alone. But the thing is, see, shrimpin' is my life. I'm a shrimper. That's what I do. So, I wanna be out there, at sea, haulin' in the catch. I don't like to miss work."

"What about Mr. Willis? Would you say he feels the same way?"

"Aw, Joe, hell—I don't know—I mean, he's got a family, kids, and all that. I reckon his work is important to him, but maybe not as important as other things."

"Does he miss trips on the boat?"

"Sure, of course. Usually for family reasons. But when it happens a lot in one week, he always offers me days off to make up for it. I just don't have any use for days off."

"How often does it happen a lot in one week?"

"Not very often except in summer—May, June, July. That's when his kids are out of school. It's usually a last-minute thing—family stuff comes up."

"When was the last time Mr. Willis missed a trip?"

Riley thought about the question for a few seconds, then smiled. "Friday." He nodded.

Behind the one-way glass, Drew and Mullinax exchanged looks. Drew pinched his chin between his thumb and index finger, rocking slightly from heels to toes, eager to burst into Joe's interview room and force some answers. Mullinax's paw-hand rested heavily on Drew's shoulder, holding him in place.

"So, Mr. Willis wasn't on the boat with you this past Friday?"

"That's right." Riley continued to smile.

"Why does that make you smile?"

Riley's grin turned into a snort-laugh. He cleared his throat and tried to keep a serious face. "The reason's kinda funny. See, Joe's son was goin' on his first real date Friday night. Joe wanted to be there, see him off, make sure he kept his curfew and all that. He said he needed to give his son some advice, you know, give him *the talk* 'bout the birds 'n' bees." Riley chuckled again. "I told him his son surely knew all that stuff by now. I mean, the kid's sixteen. He probably already rounded a few bases! But that didn't matter to Joe 'cause he wanted to be a good dad and be there for his kid. He's always talkin' 'bout how much he wants to give his wife and kids a good life. Anyway, Friday was an overnight trip, we had a full crew, so I told him I could handle it without him."

"When did you return from the overnight trip?"

"Not 'til Saturday afternoon, 'round three o'clock, I think. I don't know the exact time."

Sampson cleared his throat and glanced at the one-way glass. "So how did things go on Friday for Mr. Willis's son?"

Riley paused, his face a mask of surprise. "You know, I forgot to ask him. He didn't bring it up. I guess that means it went fine."

"Well, Mr. Broom, thank you for your candid answers. Let's take a break." Sampson walked briskly to the door. "Do you mind waiting here while we speak to Mr. Willis?"

"No," Riley answered, and Drew watched Riley's whole body appear to relax.

Sampson joined Drew and Mullinax in the observation room. "He has no idea what he just told us."

"Good work, Mark," said Mullinax.

An impish grin spread across Sampson's face. "Thank you, Chief. Thank you." He stood with his hands on his hips, swelling with pride, and nearly patted himself on the back.

"You're up, Drew," said Mullinax like a coach sending in his star player.

Drew watched Joe through the glass, gauging his attitude from his body language. In general, he looked pissed off.

Joe's lanky body overwhelmed the small stiff chair. Each time he tried to adjust to fit one part of his body, another part hung off at an awkward angle. He didn't look around the room, but kept his eyes fixed on the doorway. Although he'd been sitting there for less than ten minutes, he scowled with the impatience of someone waiting five times longer.

Closing his eyes for a second, Drew took a deep breath, preparing himself for the challenge of interviewing a potential murder suspect the same way he prepared for the danger of a kitesurfing session in gusty, shifting winds. A rush of fear and excitement fed his confidence. Thrill beat hard and fast in his chest.

Drew walked into the interview room, closed the door, and informed Joe that he wasn't in custody and was free to leave.

Joe stiffened and sneered. "But if I leave, then you'll arrest me, right?" He picked at a dried shrimp flake on his pants.

Bristling at the comment, Drew replied coolly, "You're not under arrest. I think we'd both like to keep it that way."

Joe rolled his eyes.

"Are you ready?" asked Drew.

"Sure."

Drew made the usual introductory remarks before he began. "Mr. Willis, your children made a terrible discovery Saturday morning. How're they doing?" Drew sat on the metal chair across the table from Joe.

Joe's eyes, full of contempt and distrust, searched Drew's face for some sign of insincerity, but didn't find any. He softened a bit to discuss his children. "My son's doing better. He was scared shitless by the whole mess and won't be pulling up crab traps any time soon, but he's doing okay." Pausing, he shook his head. "Cecilia's having nightmares." He frowned.

"I'm sorry to hear that. I hope things get better for her."

"Yeah, thanks."

"Mr. Willis, do you know why we asked you here for questioning today?"

"Nope. I thought my family already told you everything they know."

"You're right. We did get the information we need from your family, but we need more information from you."

"Like what?"

"Well, to begin with, it'd be helpful if you can confirm our timeline, since your family's crab trap is part of the crime scene." Drew didn't add that the crab trap wasn't technically a crime scene. Best to reveal just enough to get Joe to talk.

"I'll try." Joe straightened himself in the rigid chair and leaned in with his arms folded on the table.

"Good enough." Drew sifted through his notes, reading one of the papers. "At the hospital, your son told me the last time you baited the crab trap was Thursday. Is that correct?"

"That's right. I took Mac out Thursday to check the trap and put in fresh bait."

"Was Thursday the last time you saw that trap?"

Cocking his head to one side, Joe squinted like he was trying to lure memories out of the depths of his brain. "Yup, Thursday." He nodded, then covered his mouth with one rough palm and rested his chin in his cupped hand.

"And you were on an overnight shrimping trip from Friday to Saturday. Is that correct?"

Joe tightened his lips and rubbed his nose. "Yes."

"What time on Friday did you leave for the overnight trip?"

"Around five o'clock in the morning."

"And what time did you return Saturday?"

"Ten fifteen. There's a log at the marina."

Drew expected to hear about the log from Joe. It would be the best evidence to support his alibi. He feigned surprise. "That's right. I almost forgot. I have those log entries in my file." Drew thumbed through his folder. "Here they are." Scanning the pages, he read, "*Bonnie* is logged out at 5:00 a.m. Friday and logged back in at 10:15 a.m. Saturday." Drew slid the pages across the table to Joe and pointed to the *JW* at the end of each entry. "Are those your initials?"

Joe looked at the log pages. "That's me—JW—Joe Willis."

Nodding, Drew picked up the pages. "That's what I thought. So, you were out on your trawler, *Bonnie*, when someone killed the victim and tied her to your family's crab trap, and your children pulled her up."

"Unfortunately, yes."

"Well, Mr. Willis, I'd say that was actually *fortunate*, not unfortunate. If you hadn't been out shrimping then you'd probably be our prime suspect, considering a dead woman was found tied to your crab trap."

"I meant *unfortunate* because of my kids, because I wasn't there to help them." Joe became flustered. "I should've found that body instead of them."

"True. That was unfortunate . . . for them." Drew paused to make his point. "So, who would do something like that? Why use a crab trap? And why use *your* crab trap?"

"How should I know? Isn't that your job?" Joe's nostrils flared.

Drew raised his hand in surrender. "I'm sorry. You're right. Forgive my confusion, but I still can't seem to make sense of all the facts." Opening his folder again, he referred to the note from Brooke. "For example, you said you returned from your trip at 10:15 Saturday *morning*, but I have a statement here from a witness who watched your trawler come into the marina at 3:20 Saturday *afternoon*, about the same time you and your family were meeting with me at the hospital. How do you explain that?"

"I don't know what you want me to say. I got word my kids were in trouble Saturday morning. I went to the hospital straight from the marina. Maybe Riley took *Bonnie* back out that afternoon. He'd stay at sea for good if he had his way. We had some of the best shrimp runs to start the season last week. Riley couldn't get enough."

"I guess that's one explanation. I just wonder if it's the truth." Drew pulled his shoulders back and ruffled his hair with a sigh.

Joe glared at him.

Drew continued, "So, we talked about the timeline for Saturday and the log entries, but there's just one more thing that bothers me, one small problem with your story." Drew stared at Joe to deliver the question he thought was sure to provoke a telling reaction. "If you were out catching shrimp Friday night, then what happened with your son's first date?"

Joe's forehead tightened up between his eyebrows. He held Drew's stare. "What're you talking about?"

"Your son's first date—this past Friday night—Mr. Broom told us all about how you wanted to be there for your son, to give him the big talk, right?" Drew chuckled a little. "Mr. Broom said that's why you couldn't go shrimping Friday night."

Shaking his head, Joe looked down at the table and muttered a few expletives under his breath. He smirked and leveled his eyes on Drew again. "Riley Broom is a damn fool and a drunk. He doesn't know what day it is half the time, especially after a good swim in the bottle and a few nights at sea."

"Wait a minute. You expect me to believe you were actually on the boat Friday night, but Mr. Broom just doesn't remember because he was too drunk and disoriented?"

"No. I expect you to believe I was on the boat because I'm telling you that's where I was, because the log entries tell you that's where I was, and because my son didn't have his first date last Friday night, he had his first date the Friday *before* last, and Riley can't keep it straight. Riley told you the wrong Friday. Just show him the log entries." Joe pressed his lips together—smug and defensive—and sat back so hard in the small metal chair that the force of his body moved the chair a few inches, making its legs screech against the tile floor.

Drew deflated.

The door opened. Sampson stepped in with one hand still on the knob. "Sorry to interrupt, Detective. Someone's here to see you."

Relief welled up in Drew's chest. "Excuse me, Mr. Willis. I'll be back in a few minutes."

"Whatever." Joe raised his arms.

Drew followed Sampson out of the room.

As they rounded the corner, Drew saw Brooke standing in the main office. He felt light-headed, then lead-footed. Anger paralyzed him. If Brooke wasn't there, he'd probably topple the nearest desk. But she was there, smiling at him and giving him that look she always gave him, all big-eyed admiration and trust.

Drew and Brooke usually hugged with ease, but the surroundings kept them both reserved. Brooke waited for Drew to lead her through the process of being a witness.

Touching Brooke's shoulder, Drew introduced her "Officer Mark Sampson, this is Dr. Brooke Edens."

"We met," said Sampson. "She told me she came at your request, Detective."

Drew nodded and looked at Brooke. "She's the one who saw *Bonnie* dock at the marina Saturday afternoon. I want her to point out which fisherman was on board." He turned to Sampson. "Here, take these log entries. After Brooke makes her ID, go in and ask Mr. Broom about these. We need to figure out which one of them is lying."

"Got it." Sampson darted to his nearby desk.

Drew dreaded going back into the observation room to face the chief. *You can't think, son, you've got to know.* All Drew knew was that he lost control of the interview with Joe. He lost control because he *thought* he had the true facts, but he didn't *know*. It was a classic mistake; one the chief warned him about time and again.

Drew exhaled, leading Brooke to the observation room door.

"Are you okay?" she asked in a whisper.

"Fine," said Drew, his sallow expression telling Brooke the exact opposite. "Just bear with me."

Opening the door for Brooke, Drew followed her into the dim, cramped observation room. He introduced Brooke before Mullinax could scold him. Her presence dampened Mullinax's fuming frustration. Looming in the corner of the observation room like a thick tree trunk, Mullinax pursed his lips to hold back a mouthful of orders, keeping his eyes on the one-way glass.

Drew gave Brooke a quick orientation. "The two men you see in those rooms are here for questioning. They can't see you or hear you. Do you recognize either of them as the shrimper who gave the turtle to you Saturday afternoon?"

One man wore the vexed expression of someone being repeatedly poked. The other, who would be cowboy-handsome after a clean shave and scrub, looked bored.

Brooke pointed to the first man, Riley Broom. "That's him."

"Are you sure?" asked Drew.

"Positive."

As if on cue, Sampson walked into Riley's interview room to begin the second round of questions.

"Should I go?" Brooke whispered to Drew.

"Wait at my desk, please, if you have time. I want to get your statement in writing. This shouldn't take much longer."

"No problem." Brooke quietly slipped out of the room.

Sampson reached over Riley's shoulder and spread the log entries on the table in front of him. "Do you recognize these papers, Mr. Broom?"

Riley leaned over the rows and columns of sloppy penciled entries. "They look like pages from the marina log."

"Exactly," said Sampson. "Earlier, you mentioned Mr. Willis wasn't on your overnight shrimping trip this past Friday because his son had a big first date. Is that right?"

"That's right." Riley seemed perplexed.

"These papers are log entries for this past Friday and Saturday. Do you see the entries for *Bonnie*?"

Riley lifted one page with his shaking hand, then flattened the paper on the table and scanned each row with one trembling finger, stopping on the first entry for *Bonnie*, Friday morning at 5:00 a.m. "Here's one."

"Can you read the initials of the person who made that entry?"

Riley slid his finger across the entry row until he found the initials *JW* penciled in the final column. He looked up suddenly at Sampson, then down again at the initials. "Those are Joe's initials?" said Riley, more as a question than an answer.

"And what about this entry?" Sampson pointed at the page for Saturday and tapped his finger on the *Bonnie* entry at 10:15 a.m. "Who made this one?"

Riley stared again at Joe's initials in disbelief. His answer bubbled out like a croak. "Joe."

Sampson sat down in the chair across from Riley, removed his glasses, and swiftly rubbed the lenses clean. "I'm confused, Mr. Broom. You said Mr. Willis wasn't on the Friday-night trip, but these entries indicate he was. So, tell me, what should I believe?"

Riley hunched over the table. "Um, I don't know." He wrung his hands in his lap; his shoulders shook. He squirmed like a fish on the hook. But after a few seconds, Riley's face brightened. He straightened in his chair. "Believe whatever Joe told you."

Exasperated, Sampson threw up his hands, red blotches spreading across his cheeks. "I'm trying to figure out if I can do that. That's the point. That's why I need to know what you're telling me. Think for yourself, Mr. Broom."

"I don't know what I'm telling you. Joe and me, we always go by the log entries. That's Joe's rule. I must be wrong 'bout Friday. It must've been a different Friday. I told you. I'm a shrimper and that's my life. I'm on the boat so much it's easy to mix up days and weeks. That's all I can say."

"You said you returned to the marina Saturday afternoon from your shrimping trip. Why isn't there a log entry for *Bonnie* on Saturday afternoon? Why does *Bonnie's* Saturday entry have a morning arrival time when several other boat entries listed ahead of it have afternoon times? The arrival times are out of order for that day."

Riley hung his head. "I don't know."

"Do you have a drinking problem, Mr. Broom?" Sampson pushed for a decent response. "Is that why you can't remember simple facts from only a few days ago, can't keep your days straight? Are you a drunk?"

Shaking his head, Riley kept looking down at the tabletop.

"Please speak your answer, Mr. Broom."

"I don't know." He continued to shake his head and look down, his body collapsing in total defeat, like he would curl into a ball if his stocky torso would physically allow it.

"We're finished here, Mr. Broom." Sampson jabbed the table with one stiff finger. Drew marveled at Sampson's control; even his anger was repressed, confined to a single finger. He stood mechanically, collected the log entries, and left Riley alone in the interview room.

Drew, on the other hand, could use some self-control when it came to certain things. He seethed in the observation room, ready to burst through the glass and strangle Joe and Riley until they choked up the truth. But he was kept in check by the chief's watchful eyes, until Sampson came in.

"Can you believe these two?" blurted Drew. "We can't get a straight answer out of either one of them!"

Sampson shook his head and removed his glasses to wipe sweat from his forehead. "Sorry I had to cut it off like that, but I think I got all I could."

Mullinax remained a silent, foreboding shadow in the corner.

"Damn it!" Drew paced. "All I need to know is whether Joe was on that boat, and I still don't *really* know. They're hiding something, and that was our chance to figure it out." Groaning, Drew shoved both hands into his wavy hair.

Mullinax spoke up. "That's enough. You better pay attention because your fisherman's about to leave." He pointed to the interview room, where Joe was on his feet, heading for the open door.

Drew spun on his heel. "I'm arresting him." He pushed past Mullinax and Sampson.

"You'll do no such thing," ordered Mullinax.

"He's lying to us!" Drew hesitated at the door. "He wasn't on that boat."

"You can't prove it, and until you can, I won't let you arrest him and make a circus of this case, son."

Drew sucked in his breath.

"Now," said Mullinax, "Get out there and arrange for transportation to take Mr. Willis and Mr. Broom back to the marina. Mark, tell Mr. Broom he's free to leave." He turned to Drew, pinned him with serious eyes. "Find me some better evidence and pray the media doesn't catch onto this."

With Mullinax's words hanging in the air, they spilled out of the observation room into the main office, where Walt Pickering and a couple other uniformed officers were coming in from their morning patrol. Mullinax trudged into his office and slammed the door.

Walt raised his eyebrows at Drew. "Uh-oh, golden boy, did you make the chiefy mad?"

Ignoring Walt's comment, Drew held three fingers up in Brooke's direction, trying to let her know he would only be busy for a few more minutes. Walt's eyes followed the gesture and landed on Brooke.

"Well, well, well," Walt teased Drew, loud enough for the other officers to hear him. "I see you brought your girlfriend to work again today. Or is she here to see me? My, she is one *fine*-looking lady!"

"Shut up, rookie. Stop making an ass of yourself." Drew said with a smirk while he hurried out to the parking lot.

He caught up with Joe just as Sampson escorted Riley out of the building and waited while Sampson rounded up a couple officers to drive the fishermen back to the marina.

Drew and Sampson stood alone in front of the station. Drew's tense expression made it obvious he was replaying the interviews in his mind, figuring out how to catch Joe in a lie.

"So, what's next?" asked Sampson.

"Let's follow up on Joe's version of things," Drew instructed. "You go back to Dylan Creek Marina in an unmarked car. Don't let Joe or Riley see you. Get log entries for the Friday before last, the night Joe claims he missed a shrimping trip for his son's date, then hang around to see what our shrimpers do. Call immediately if you see anything suspicious."

"I'm on it."

"Great. I'm going to the Sundries. Mr. Otis never forgets a face. If Joe was in there buying a new dock rope on Sunday like he said he was, Mr. Otis will remember. And if it was another day, like, say, Friday night or early Saturday morning, Mr. Otis will remember that, too."

"It's a shame Mr. Broom doesn't have Mr. Otis's memory."

"Nah." Drew stuffed his hands in his pockets. "That would be too easy."

CHAPTER

29

Senator Madden stepped to the podium to address the rowdy crowd packed onto the lawn of The Green in uptown Charlotte, North Carolina. A roar erupted and rolled like thunder across the park. Supporters raised signs: "Get Mad about climate change!" "Get Mad for President!" "We're all Mad! Get Mad!" "Get Mad about the economy!" "Get Mad for change!" "Get Mad!"

Caldwell stood with his mom and sisters, who fanned themselves with paper flyers in the heat of high noon. He watched his dad beam and wave and bask like a sunbather in the attention of the moment. This was how Caldwell imagined the presidential campaign trail. He knew his dad had dreamed of being part of it for decades. It seemed the many years of determination and maneuvering were finally paying off. But one thing Caldwell didn't tell anyone was that his dad's drinking was getting heavy—and secretive—again. Caldwell recognized the signs: a bourbon bottle tucked in his dad's tennis racket bag, his dad's swollen words during late night phone calls, a highball glass hidden in a desk drawer. He even smelled alcohol on his dad's breath before the rally.

Ever since Senator Madden announced his run for president in March, he'd been swept into a whirlwind of campaign fundraising, speeches, rallies, media appearances, and platform debates. The road to the White House, intense and public, required stamina and an ego of steel. His "Get Mad" slogan became a motto for many Americans. It was memorable, spread easily, and served as a catalyst for his instant popularity. People were frustrated with the constant gridlock in Washington. They wanted action. They were mad for somebody to take charge. The wordplay on his name expressed a mood that separated him from the eleven other candidates in his party vying for nomination at the national convention the following summer.

The crucial southern states held primaries early in the election year, which meant Senator Madden needed to be known throughout the South in time to be leading the polls. Already the media labeled him a moderate Republican—a Rockefeller Republican—who spoke like he was from America and not from Washington. He started way back as a Southern Democrat before he switched his allegiance to oppose union infiltration and big government. Fiscally conservative and socially liberal, he appealed to the massive middle base of voters, independents, and even some liberal Democrats. By avoiding extremes that crippled candidates of both parties in the past, he planned to become a hybrid by standing for what he saw as the best aspects of each side and bridging gaps to placate Americans looking to vote for an individual rather than a party.

As the early frontrunner, Senator Madden had to work twice as hard to maintain momentum and keep his message fresh. The huge turnout at his rallies after only a few months of campaigning signaled a groundswell in the making. The more he rallied and spoke his mind, the more money flowed into his campaign fund. People were—above all—willing to pay to assuage their anger and to back a leader who would follow through on campaign promises.

At least, that was Senator Madden's explanation for his rise to the top, even though Caldwell knew his dad—like most politicians—believed campaign platforms were actually suggestions, not binding promises. Most Americans voted based on what was said but seldom paid attention to what was done. Senator Madden knew exactly how to manipulate the process in his favor.

Caldwell often heard warnings from his dad about people's preconceived notions of a senator born and raised in the banking city of Charlotte: a capitalist, a one-percenter, a religious conservative. Those misguided voters were the ones Senator Madden needed to impress the most with his pro-environment platform, his promise to protect habitats of endangered and threatened species, and his insistence that corporate growth and sustainable development were not mutually exclusive but co-dependent.

Senator Madden was in his element, center stage, center of attention.

As his speech reached its conclusion, Senator Madden lifted his gaze upward and said, "A healthy economy supports a healthy environment, and vice versa. Look around at these buildings on this clear summer day, these monuments to the greatest economy, to our land of opportunity. At the same time, remember the creatures you see and hear when you're out in nature, hiking a trail, walking a beach, or simply sitting in a rocker on your back porch. We have all the wonders of this earth and this country to enjoy today, but will our children—our grandchildren—have them tomorrow? Preservation is done through sustainable development, which is good for nature, and good for business. Capitalism doesn't have to be at loggerheads with environmentalism. So, call me an eco-capitalist or a capital-environmentalist or whatever label you want to come up with for this interdependence. Maybe you're an eco-capitalist, too, and you don't even know it. Because isn't conserving the environment in everyone's economic interest? Doesn't it make sense?"

People nodded, clapped, and lifted their signs higher.

He continued, "Think about the legacy we want to leave. Don't we want to be the generation who did something to reverse what is already an enormous level of consumption and pollution? Aren't we *mad* there is so much talk about change, about fueling our economy, or protecting our natural resources and fragile species, with very little action? And what about inaction when it comes to the topics of gun laws, immigration, and homeland security? The firestorms of debate fizzle out when it comes time to craft a bill or to enforce the law. I'm mad. I'm sick of politics as usual. And I think that if you aren't mad, then you better get mad. I'm not just talking about these issues, I'm demanding action. As your president, I'll prove we can *do* better. Get Mad! Get Mad for a better America!"

When Senator Madden finished, his fist pumped the air with each word of the chant, "Get Mad!" The crowd echoed him, encouraged him with their rally cry. "Get Mad!"

CHAPTER

30

After Brooke signed her witness statement, Drew offered to buy her lunch at the Sundries, where he was going to investigate the timing of Joe Willis's rope purchase. Sanny heard the door jingle and lit up when he saw Drew holding the door open for Brooke. "Well, lookie here! It's Drew and his Miss Brooke." He clapped with delight. "It's been such a long time since I've seen you two together. Marla!" he called in the direction of the kitchen, "Marla, come out and see who's here!" He smiled at them, a broad, cheeky smile that spread enthusiasm like wildfire.

"It's so nice to see you, Mr. Otis," said Brooke, suppressing a pang of annoyance at being called Miss, which made her feel like a teenager.

"You, too, dear. Drew was in here just the other day and your name came up." He nodded at Drew, who reddened enough that Brooke noticed it. "I heard about what happened to your friend. How're you doing?" Reaching across the counter, Sanny covered Brooke's hand with his own, his eyes welling with sympathy.

Brooke glanced down. "I'm okay." An easy answer she hoped was enough.

To Brooke's relief, Marla's sweet voice wafted into the room with the flowery scent of her perfume. "Hello, hello!" she said in a cheerful singsong tone. "How lovely to see you both!" Scooting around the counter, she gave them each a quick squeeze. With her hand still on Drew's arm, she looked up at him. "Drew Young, you just get more handsome every time I see you."

She winked at Brooke.

"Thanks." Drew's polite smile hid his embarrassment.

"So, what brings you in today?" asked Marla.

"How 'bout some lunch?" added Sanny.

Marla and Sanny looked expectantly at Drew and Brooke, their eyes warm and glimmering. They doted like grandparents on the boy and girl they watched grow up from elementary school children to young adults.

"Yes, we'd love some lunch," said Drew.

"Wonderful," said Marla. "What can I get for you?" She went behind the counter, retrieved her notepad, and perched her glasses on her nose, ready to take their orders.

"The usual for me," said Drew.

"Ham 'n' cran," Sanny told Marla.

"I know, honey." She rolled her eyes. "I've made a thousand of those sandwiches for Drew." She playfully bumped her husband with her hip. "And what about you, Brooke?"

"The chicken salad sandwich and a sweet tea, please," said Brooke.

"Sweet tea for me, too," added Drew.

"No straws," they both said, almost at the same time.

Brooke smiled at Drew, then said to Marla in a loud whisper, "I trained him well."

Drew admitted, "It was that picture of the plastic straw stuck in the sea turtle's nose. Pretty gross, and hard to forget."

"Hey, whatever works," said Brooke with a shrug.

Marla chuckled. "Okay, you two. I'll have everything ready in a few minutes."

Drew stepped up to the cash register. "It's my treat," he said, prompting Marla and Sanny to exchange knowing glances. He almost explained but thought he might disappoint them if he told them he wasn't on a date with Brooke. Instead, he launched into business. "Mr. Otis, I have another reason for coming in today. I hope you might remember a recent purchase by one of your customers."

"I'm glad to help if I can," said Sanny.

"Do you know Joe Willis?"

"Sure do. He's in from time to time for bait and supplies."

"Was he here this past weekend to buy some rope?"

"He was."

"Do you remember which day that was and about what time?"

"Let me see." Sanny shifted his eyes to the ceiling. "It was yesterday, Sunday. He stopped in about lunchtime." Nodding to confirm his own story, he looked at Drew. "Yes, that's right. Got a couple premade sandwiches and some rope."

"Oh. Okay," said Drew, surprised Joe apparently told the truth—at least about the rope. "I appreciate your help."

"It seems like I didn't give you the right answer," said Sanny.

"Well, it isn't the answer I was expecting, but it's still what I need to know," said Drew as he paid for lunch. "Thank you."

"You're welcome, of course, and please let me know if there's anything else I can do."

"I will."

"Marla will have those sandwiches ready in no time." Sanny smiled at his wife.

"Almost done," chirped Marla.

Drew joined Brooke with their sweet teas at a table near the front window. A few minutes later, Marla appeared with two lunch plates, each holding a sandwich and a pile of chips, garnished with a single pickle spear.

"Thank you," said Drew and Brooke in unison.

"You're always welcome, darlings." Marla lingered for a moment as if thinking about what to say. Then she held up a finger and dashed off to the back office.

Drew and Brooke were chewing their first bites of food when Marla returned to their table. "Before I forget again," she said, "I meant to bring this to the police station for lost and found, but I'll just give it to you, Drew, if you don't mind."

Marla handed a phone to Drew.

"No problem," said Drew.

"Thank you, darling." She left their table.

Drew pressed and tapped the phone until it turned on, displaying a photo of a sea turtle.

"Look at this." He held it up for Brooke to see.

She immediately recognized the photo. Her mouth dropped open. "Are you thinking what I'm thinking?"

He nodded.

Pulling out her phone, Brooke called Diane's number. The mystery phone in Drew's hand began to ring.

When Brooke hung up and they were finally able to take their eyes off Diane's phone, Drew looked around for Marla while Brooke picked at her sandwich, having suddenly lost her appetite.

Marla was wiping a nearby table.

"Excuse me, Mrs. Otis," Drew said.

"Yes, darling." She arrived at their table with her garden of perfume.

"I was wondering—where did you find this phone?"

"On North End Beach."

Brooke looked up from her plate.

"When?" asked Drew.

"Oh, it was a couple days ago—Saturday—during my usual morning walk."

"Do you know about what time you found it?"

"Well . . . probably around nine o'clock. I start walking at eight, and it usually takes me about an hour to walk to the point from here."

"And where exactly was the phone on North End Beach?"

"Up near the dunes." She puckered her lips in search of a more precise description. "It was near that last foot path, the one that leads from the beach to the shoulder of the forest road."

"I know which path you mean." Drew glanced over at Brooke, who shook her head in disbelief. "Thank you for turning in this phone, and for the information."

"Well, I just hope I didn't cause any trouble by keeping it for too long."

"Please don't even worry about that," said Drew.

"How are those sandwiches?" she asked.

"Delicious," said Drew.

Brooke nodded in agreement.

"Wonderful," said Marla. "Can I get anything else for you two?"

"No, ma'am," said Drew. "I think we're fine for now, thanks."

"Okay, well, just holler for me if you need anything."

"We will," said Drew.

When they were alone again, Brooke reached for Diane's phone, but Drew warned her not to touch it. Without an evidence bag, he improvised by wrapping the phone in a latex glove from his duty belt.

Brooke said, "You know what this means, don't you?"

"Something happened to Diane on North End Beach? Maybe she was killed there?"

Staring at the phone, Brooke nodded. "And it wasn't a coincidence."

"What wasn't a coincidence?"

"That I found a dead loggerhead Saturday morning at almost the exact same spot where Mrs. Otis found this phone. The loggerhead must be related to Diane's death. It wasn't a coincidence."

"You're saying the same person who killed the sea turtle also killed Diane?"

"Maybe. Think about it. Diane was probably out on the beach before sunrise at about the same time as the turtle. What if she saw something she shouldn't have seen? Clearly, whoever killed the turtle didn't want anyone to know about it. That's why the turtle disappeared from your pickup."

"That's a big what if . . . but it makes sense." He leaned back in his chair and crossed his arms. "You're good at this. Ever thought about being a detective?"

"Thanks, but no thanks." Brooke laughed a little. "I prefer being a scientist. I investigate life, not death."

"Well, I like your theory. It definitely gives us a possible motive."

They finished lunch while Brooke watched beachgoers tow coolers and kids across the Sundries parking lot to the beach access path. She often forgot her usual Monday was a vacation day for tourists on the island. By the time Drew and Brooke rose from their table to leave, a lunch crowd line stretched from the counter to the front door.

Outside in the heat of the day, Brooke shielded her eyes to gaze up at a news helicopter buzzing overhead. She gripped Drew's arm. "The news helicopter."

"What about it?"

"The news helicopters were there—at the marina—Saturday morning. I remember seeing a report on TV that night. I think it was Local News 2. The helicopter footage showed the marina docks and the *parking lot*."

Drew squinted at her, looking perplexed.

Brooke sighed at him. "The footage showed the marina parking lot, where your pickup was parked when the dead loggerhead was taken."

Drew put his palm to his forehead. "Of course! Great idea." Pulling his shoulders back, he took a deep breath. First, the phone, and now a potential new lead. "I can't wait to see the look on chief's face if I get this right."

"Well, there's one thing you already got right."

"What's that?"

"I *am* good at this." She smiled and strutted across the street.

Drew laughed and followed her.

CHAPTER

31

In the lobby of Local News 2, Walt sat in a modern leather-and-chrome armchair, drumming his fingers on his knee and pretending to take interest in a bronze statue on a podium. He looked in the direction of high heels clicking on marble to see Bella round the corner in a pencil skirt tightly hugging the curves of her hips and butt. She was even more gorgeous than he remembered. Her blond hair bounced against her shoulders with each step, her full lips spreading into a brilliant white smile when she saw Walt stand up. Her blouse was unbuttoned just enough to show the lace edge of her camisole across the valley of her cleavage.

All he could think about was a Victoria's Secret ad.

"Officer Pickering." Gazing at him, Bella reached out to shake his hand. "What a pleasant surprise."

When Walt shook Bella's hand, he lost all conviction to be tough. His usual arrogant machismo and his ability to form coherent sentences melted in her presence. Bella's hand slipped into his with ease, warm and firm and smooth as satin. Eying him seductively, she squeezed his palm while they shook hands and then, just as suddenly, slipped her hand away again, leaving only the heat of her skin on his.

"Can we talk outside?" Bella motioned to the door.

Walt nodded and followed her out to the sidewalk before speaking a single word. She turned to face him, standing so close that if he wrapped his arms around her in a swift second and pressed his lips to hers, she wouldn't have time to take a breath. Mustering every ounce of self-control to keep his hands by his sides, he concentrated on words to articulate the reason for his visit.

Bella leaned closer as if to confide in him and said, "I didn't expect to hear from you again since you put on quite an act at the marina."

"What do you mean?" Walt furrowed his brow. His police work wasn't an act.

"Friday night." Bella hinted. "At School?"

Walt's flat eyes registered nothing in his cloudy memory from that night.

She continued, "We met, well, you hit on me. Got my number and flirted shamelessly with me all night, calling me your *little lady.*" Bella clasped her hands together. "I thought we really hit it off until I saw you cozied up to another woman at the bar. Then you left without even saying goodbye, and I thought . . ." She stopped when she searched Walt's face and realized he had no recollection of the evening.

"I'm sorry," he finally said. "I don't remember. I had a lot to drink. I'm an idiot."

"Oh." She took a step back from him, looking down, then away. "I'm so embarrassed. I assumed, well, never mind."

"I'm just here about some news footage," Walt said, shifting his weight.

Clearing her throat, Bella snapped into her professional mode. Her voice chilled. "What exactly do you need?"

"Well, your news helicopters were over Anders Isle Marina Saturday morning to cover the murder story, right?" Walt noticed her mood change but pushed through the awkwardness.

"Yes."

"I need all your helicopter footage of the marina from Saturday between seven and noon."

"Really? May I ask why?"

"Not yet," he said. "It's an ongoing investigation, but I'd really appreciate your help with this."

The news media—local and national, television and print—had been stonewalled by authorities. Very little information leaked about the "Turtle

Lady Murder." Every news outlet was eager for any detail to dissect and analyze.

"And if I do this favor for you, what's in it for me? An exclusive interview about the investigation?" Sensing an angle, she perked up, her feline eyes fixed on him.

Walt wished he could say yes. He wished he could say yes to anything and everything Bella asked of him. Whatever he could do to make up for his stupid drunken forgetfulness. "Possibly." He played along, poker-faced. "I don't get to make that decision, but I'll tell you what: if you cooperate and that footage shows us what we need to see, then I'll do my very best to get you on the record with our lead detective."

"And if I don't cooperate?" she teased, warming up to him again.

"I'll eventually get the footage anyway by warrant or subpoena, but you'll create a big headache for me. You don't want to do that to me, do you?"

Bella pouted and shook her head. "No, I don't." Hands on her hips, she smiled at him. "I'll play nice."

"I *will* find a way to thank you." He grinned, holding her stare for a few long seconds. "But I play naughty."

She raised her eyebrows at his innuendo. "Promise?" Her lips curled into a bemused smile.

"Promise . . . *little lady*," he said with a wink.

Keeping her eyes on his, she took a few steps backward. "I'll go get that footage."

When she turned to enter her office building, Walt's gaze lingered on the curves of her skirt, following them down to the perfect definition of her calf muscles.

She knew he was watching her.

Walt chuckled to himself, imagining the many ways he would repay Bella's favor.

CHAPTER

32

Chief Mullinax leaned back in his chair to ponder Drew's report about the victim's phone and possible link to a dead loggerhead.

Sitting across the desk from Mullinax, Drew wondered what was going through the chief's head. On the one hand, he must be glad to have another clue. On the other hand, the discovery of the phone on North End Beach meant the murder might've happened there, on a public Anders Isle beach, where the crime scene would already be corrupted by any number of beach-combers. If Drew were chief, he would hope to find evidence placing the murder at the victim's apartment, which had been secured and preserved since day one. Between the relentless media probing for answers and the desperate mayor's office pushing for an arrest, this high-profile murder case was high stakes and high pressure. Plus, for an island touted as an unofficial sea turtle sanctuary, negative publicity about a mutilated loggerhead on the beach could result in backlash from both tourists and turtle-loving locals. But, for Drew, the mounting pressure and personal nature of this case only fueled his determination to solve it.

Mullinax righted himself in his chair and focused on Drew. "So, you sent Walt for the helicopter footage, right?"

"Yes," said Drew. "I just spoke to him. He's on his way back with uncut Saturday morning footage from the marina."

"And the victim's phone is being analyzed?"

"We'll get everything the tech people can find."

"What about the place where the phone was found? Have you been out there to look around for more evidence?"

"Well, that's what I need to clarify," said Drew. "We can search North End Beach, the beach access path, and the easement road because that's public property, but forensic evidence found there, like footprints or tire tracks, will be practically useless because anyone could've been there for any reason before or since Saturday morning. The rest of the north end is all privately owned land covered with maritime forest. I was about to contact the owner for permission to search the property, but I thought I should run it by you first."

"Because Linwood Kingston owns it?"

"I think so."

"You *think*?" Mullinax groaned.

"Hold on." Drew raised his hand to placate Mullinax. "I know I shouldn't *think*, I should *know*, but I *do* know the Kingston Company has owned the property for as long as I can remember. I just need some official confirmation they still own it before I can say I *know*. So, we can either spend time on a title search, or I can call the Kingston Company."

"We don't have time to waste. Make the call. Get Kingston's permission to do the search. Don't discuss any details of the case."

"And if Kingston doesn't own it?"

"Ask him who does."

"Okay then." Drew nodded. "I'll let you know what I find out." He left Mullinax's office.

As soon as the door shut behind Drew, he looked across the room to where Brooke sat beside his desk.

"Well?" she asked. "How'd that go?"

"He's in." Drew smiled. "He wants to see the footage and wants a search of the property near the beach."

"So, he likes the theory about the loggerhead connection?"

"I wouldn't say he *likes* it, but he sees it."

"That's good enough." Brooke beamed up at Drew. He knew she hoped this new evidence would solve Diane's case. She needed some measure of closure.

He put his hand on her shoulder. "I shouldn't be telling you any of this."

"Who am I going to tell? I want to find Diane's killer as much as you do. I won't do anything to jeopardize your investigation. Besides, I've been involved from the start—not by choice, but simply by circumstances."

"True, but you still shouldn't be here." He squeezed her shoulder gently and continued past her to sit at his desk.

"Just let me stay to see the helicopter footage."

"I don't know," Drew hedged. "That's not entirely up to me."

"Then tell whoever wants to know that I'm here on behalf of the logger-head." Leaning forward, she placed one hand flat on his desk. "It's just as important to my work as it is to yours to find out who took that turtle out of your truck."

Drew thought about her argument for a few seconds, then agreed. "Okay, you can stick around, but I want you to be a wallflower. And you have to leave after we see the footage. If we identify someone, nobody outside this office can know what you know until an arrest is made. That's for your safety and for the sake of the investigation."

Brooke raised her right hand like she was taking an oath. "I'm a wallflower, and I don't know anything. How's that?"

"Well, those are two things I never thought I'd hear you say," Drew teased.

"Ha, ha." Brooke stood up. "I'm going to get the turtle files out of my car. They'll make me look more *official*. Be right back."

While Brooke was gone, Drew called the Kingston Company. The receptionist put him through to Linwood's office, where a woman with a strong Southern accent answered, "Linwood Kingston's office. Marion speaking."

"This is Detective Drew Young with Anders Isle Police. I need to speak with Mr. Kingston about a piece of property we believe he owns."

"I'm sorry, Detective. Mr. Kingston is in the Bahamas till Thursday. Can *I* help you?"

"Maybe." Drew considered the best way to approach the subject without causing alarm. "I'm trying to find out if Kingston owns the maritime forest property on the north end of Anders Isle."

"Okey-dokey," said Marion. Drew heard her chair squeak. "I can look that up if you hang on a minute."

"Thank you," said Drew, relieved.

"Hmm, that's strange," Marion wondered aloud. "I could've sworn we still had that one, but I don't see it listed on here."

"So that means Kingston doesn't own it?"

"Usually that's what it means. I try to keep the database current, but Mr. Kingston has a bad habit of moving properties around and forgetting to tell me about it. Drives me nuts." Marion sighed.

"By any chance, does your database show who the new owner is?"

"No, see, that's the strange thing: I can't find the property listed at all. Hold on, let me try one more thing."

Drew heard Marion typing furiously.

Brooke returned with some notebooks and sat across the desk from Drew, flipping through pages while he waited on the phone.

Marion's key-taps stopped for a few seconds before she sighed again. "All I can find is a note that one of our companies transferred the property in 2008 to another one of our companies that doesn't exist anymore. I wasn't working here then, so I don't know exactly where it went from there. I'll have to ask Mr. Kingston about it and get back to you."

"That's fine. Thanks for your trouble."

Drew gave Marion his number, then hung up and rubbed his chin. He swiveled slightly in his chair, restless and contemplating the time it would take for a title search versus the time it would take for Marion to call back. He needed access to that property as soon as possible.

Brooke glanced up from the notebook in her lap at Drew's pained expression. "Wait a minute," she gasped. "Are *you* stressed?"

"We're in quicksand here. There's nothing solid." Drew shook his head.

"Nothing solid?" Brooke balked. "You just found Diane's phone and a possible motive with the loggerhead."

"We need a suspect before we can use a motive."

As if on cue, Walt strode through the door and stopped a few steps in. He raised his arms and a DVD gripped in one hand in victory and announced to the mostly empty office, "Mission accomplished!" Puffed up and proud, he looked around and saw Drew and Brooke were his only audience. Dropping his arms and rolling his eyes, he trudged across the room to Drew's desk. "Hey, golden boy, I'll trade you—this little DVD for that little hot-tee-tee." Walt cocked his head at Brooke.

Brooke ignored him.

"What's *wrong* with you?" Drew squinted at Walt, then stood up and snatched the DVD out of Walt's hand.

Walt laughed.

"Go set up the DVD player over there in the corner," ordered Drew.

"Okay, okay." Walt walked away, holding up his hands in mock surrender.

Drew knocked on Mullinax's office door.

"What is it?" asked Mullinax in a gruff voice.

Poking his head in the office, Drew held up the DVD. "We have it."

"Good," he replied without looking up from his paperwork. "Scan through it and come get me if you find anything."

"Yes, sir."

Drew inserted the DVD and gave Walt the remote to fast-forward through footage. An aerial view of Anders Isle Marina filled the screen, focused on dock eleven, where people swarmed and scurried around the Island Fire and Rescue boat.

Brooke stayed at a distance, still seated at Drew's desk, but within earshot should Drew see something.

The first half hour of news footage zoomed in and out on the same general docking area, as though the helicopter was hovering. When the activity picked up, the helicopter's view expanded and panned out to cover the whole marina—docks, marina shop, and parking lot. From the footage, it appeared the helicopter moved to a different, higher location that provided a more panoramic view of the scene.

Just past the thirty-minute mark on the footage, Drew spotted his pickup. "Wait," he told Walt. "Let it play."

Brooke perked up and looked at the screen, but she couldn't see it very well from where she sat.

While the footage rolled, Drew saw his truck pull in at the top of the screen. He and Brooke climbed out and walked across the parking lot. The helicopter's view held steady with the parking lot still visible in the top of the picture. A minute later, a faded gray pickup stopped behind Drew's truck. Two men got out. They casually approached the back of Drew's pickup, opened his tailgate, lifted the blanket-covered loggerhead, and carried it to their truck, undeterred by the arm-straining weight of the turtle. It took them less than thirty seconds.

"There!" Drew pointed at the men. "Pause it right there." He stared at the two men frozen on screen. One of them, obscured by a hat, was only visible from the back. But nothing hid the identity of the other one. He didn't even attempt to cover his face from buzzing news helicopters. Even from an overhead distance, his massive build and distinct facial features were clear. Drew clenched his teeth. "I'm getting the chief. Rewind it back to when they pull up."

Drew almost couldn't believe his eyes, or his luck. Lady luck, loyal lady luck—he owed her one.

Brooke tried not to leap out of her chair and dash across the room. Instead, she contained herself and snuck closer for a better look at the television. She was so quiet she startled Drew when he turned to get Mullinax and found her right behind him. Mouthing the word *wallflower*, she made him crack a smile.

Drew knocked on Mullinax's door while opening it. "Excuse me, Chief, but you really want to see this."

"I'm coming." Mullinax finished making a note. He rose from his desk and followed Drew into the main office, where he immediately noticed Brooke. "Why is Dr. Edens still here?"

"She needs to know what happened to the loggerhead," Drew explained, trying to sound nonchalant. "She's lead biologist for the sea turtle hospital and has to file reports about missing and dead loggerheads."

"Uh-huh," said Mullinax, hardly convinced, but he didn't make Brooke leave. Instead, he pointed to the television. "Show me. This better be good." Leveling his pursed potato face at the screen, he crossed his arms while the footage rolled into action.

They watched the two men climb out of their truck and steal the turtle. It only took those thirty seconds to flip Mullinax's mood from grim to downright giddy. He actually let out a few chuckles.

"What is it, Chief?" Drew hoped the chuckles were a good sign.

Mullinax gestured to the paused picture of the two men about to make a getaway. "It's the smoking gun, son. I'd imagine that's the clip we'll see over and over on the news after we arrest Oliver Tack and get the name of his partner in crime. Now we know those two are at least responsible for the turtle and, since our murder victim's phone puts her on the same beach as the turtle around the same time, it's very likely they're connected to the murder." Clapping Drew on the shoulder, he flashed another rare and toothy smile. "Dare I say—hot damn! We got our men! Well done!" He popped a thumbs-up to Walt, then patted Drew's shoulder again. "Good work tracking this down."

"Thanks, Chief," said Drew, smiling at Brooke, who kept quiet. She was happy to let Drew take credit. They both knew whose idea it really was, and that was enough for her.

Even Walt accepted Mullinax's praise graciously and without the usual snide remark aimed at Drew.

"So, you've both redeemed yourselves since yesterday, but don't think I forgot about your DNA samples. I want to officially rule you two out," said Mullinax. "The kits came in this morning. Grab a couple and come to my office. I'll do the swabs before you go make this arrest. It only takes a few minutes."

"Hold on. Why is golden boy giving DNA?" asked Walt.

"Standard procedure, Walt," said Mullinax. "Let's go."

"But surely *he* isn't suspected, is he?" Walt gasped sarcastically and looked at Drew with a smug grin. "What did I miss?"

Brooke remained a wallflower, as instructed, but waited with nauseating anticipation to hear Drew's answer. She wondered if wallflowers were allowed to pass out. She couldn't imagine why Drew needed to give a DNA sample.

Drew didn't speak fast enough.

Mullinax rolled his eyes. "For Christ's sake, Walt, the victim was pregnant, and Drew was fucking—pardon me"—he glanced at Brooke and toned it down— "having sex with her. Can we just get on with it now, please?" He stalked back to his office, leaving the three of them—Drew, Walt, and Brooke—in a stunned triangle.

Looking at Brooke's horrified face, Walt smirked. "I guess I'm not the only one who missed that." He left the room to get the DNA kits.

Brooke rushed to Drew's desk to collect her things.

"Wait!" Drew went after her, desperate to explain himself. "Brooke, listen."

She wheeled around to face him with hurt-filled eyes and a sharp edge to her voice. "How could you keep that from me? How could Diane keep that from me? She was pregnant? And sleeping with you! Was it your baby, Drew?"

"No. Listen, she was only three months pregnant, and we had sex—yes—but not that often, only a few times since we broke up." Drew stammered and said too much. "It was a casual thing. She ended it for good last November. And I didn't know she was pregnant until yesterday."

"Why should I believe you?"

Drew scrambled for an answer that might salvage Brooke's trust in him. "Don't believe me." He went to his desk, unlocked the file drawer, and took out Diane's red journal. "Believe Diane."

He gave the journal to Brooke. Even though it was against protocol to lend her a piece of evidence, Drew cared more about Brooke than he did about breaking the chain of custody.

Sunlight from the nearby window glinted off the gold-edged pages of the journal. Brooke placed it on top of the notebooks and clutched the stack to her chest. Looking at Drew, she parted her lips to speak, but nothing came out. Drew held her stare for a few seconds—stung by her raw disbelief and pain—until she turned and walked out.

CHAPTER

33

The road bordering the salt marsh on the back side of Anders Isle came to a dead end at Oliver Tack's house. Patches of maritime forest filled spaces around and between the few neighboring houses set far apart along the stretch of faded asphalt. On Oliver's small slice of property, two massive oak trees shrouded his house behind a screen of leaves and Spanish moss, their thick lower branches so old and heavy they rested on the ground in some places. Loblolly pines shot up like tufted toothpicks between the wedge-shaped tangle of red cedar and wind-bent yaupon holly molded by salt spray. Although stilts lifted Oliver's wooden house a story above the ground, the house appeared to be propped up and almost swallowed by crowded, overgrown forest.

Drew and Walt approached with caution. Two uniformed officers backed them up. They couldn't see the front of Oliver's house from the driveway, which helped with the element of surprise, but a blind entry was also dangerous.

With one hand on the grip of his holstered pistol, Drew walked through the yard, crouching under and stepping over the lowest oak branches. When he didn't see a vehicle to indicate that Oliver was home, he motioned for one back up officer to stay on the driveway and the other to circle around to the back of the house. He sent Walt to check the carport.

Ten seconds later, Walt returned, shaking his head and mouthing the word *empty*.

They climbed a flight of stairs on the side of the house to reach the front door, Drew in the lead with Walt close behind. Drew knocked hard on the door.

No answer.

Drew knocked again, harder this time, and yelled, "Police! Open up!"

Not a sound of movement from inside.

They had a search warrant for Oliver's house, issued at the same time as Oliver's arrest warrant, which gave them freedom to confiscate any evidence found inside, but Drew wanted to make this arrest. He wanted Oliver in custody. Oliver was the wild card. Without immediate family or any known close friends to keep him nearby, Oliver could go wherever, whenever. He could vanish.

Drew had called his friend Paul at the port, who confirmed Oliver wasn't at work. If Oliver also wasn't at home, where was he? Drew had to find him before he found out he was a wanted man.

"We're going in," said Drew.

Walt radioed this news to the two officers who stood guard outside the house—one in the driveway and the other in the backyard.

Drew broke through the lock with one swift kick, slamming the door against the inside wall. He pointed his gun into the dim front room. Dusty curtains and old bed sheets covered the windows. A tattered couch and stain-splattered armchair faced a television on the hearth. Piles of newspapers, magazines, and trash littered every table surface. The smell of coffee grounds mixed unpleasantly with an even stronger animal odor, something akin to wet dog and farm mud. Drew couldn't quite place the smell. He grimaced and tried to breathe through his mouth.

With their guns ready, Drew and Walt split up and stepped through the main level of the house, rounding each corner, and aiming to shoot. In less than five minutes, they canvassed the whole space except for one last room in the back corner of the house. They met at the closed door to the final room, where the odor was strongest. Based on the area they already covered, Drew estimated the final room to be about twelve feet square, probably a second bedroom.

Drew turned the doorknob. When the door squeaked open, things moved. In the pitch-black room, things scurried and scraped, making sounds like toenails on tile, skin rubbing cardboard. Drew and Walt braced their guns in outstretched arms, pointing blindly into the darkness. Their heartbeats raced. Drew pawed the wall for the light switch and flipped it on.

"Holy shit." Drew felt cold chills trickle down his back.

Staring at them from across the room was the menacing head of an adult American alligator with its armored, black hide—easily eight feet long—outstretched on a wide counter. Its eyes were frozen open in death, and its broad, rounded snout seemed to leer at them.

They dropped their guns and moved in stunned silence, looking around at the disturbing contents of the room.

Ten-gallon aquariums lined the floor and shelves, filled with all kinds of turtles, snakes, and salamanders. Drew recognized coiled copperheads and rattlesnakes, but he wasn't sure of the exact species of the other reptiles and amphibians. One aquarium held several active baby American alligators with distinct yellow bands on their solid black hides. They crawled over each other, tiny claws tapping and scraping the glass aquarium sides.

"What the fuck *is* all this?" asked Walt.

"I'm guessing we just stumbled into the black market," said Drew. "I'll bet these animals are being held for trade."

"Come on," said Walt, holstering his gun. "Who would want a salamander when they could have an elephant tusk or something? Isn't the black market mostly out of Africa?"

"No, it's everywhere," said Drew. "All it takes is demand from people willing to pay big money and you bet the poachers and smugglers will find a way to supply."

"So, Oliver's a poacher?"

"He's probably a poacher *and* a smuggler. Poachers do illegal hunting and trapping. Smugglers do the transporting and trading. It looks like Oliver does both."

"And you're telling me these turtles and snakes and gators are worth a lot of money?"

"Oh yeah, especially if they're protected or endangered species, which I'm guessing these all are. The rarer the animal, the higher its black-market price. We're talking thousands of dollars per animal in some cases."

Walt surveyed the room and marveled at aquariums full of thousands of dollars.

Drew thought of Brooke. She was the one who told him all about poaching and the black market. Would she be able to forgive him for keeping secrets about Diane? He didn't mean to hurt her. If he could go and see her right now, he would. He wanted to, but he had to solve this case. He was an inch away from figuring it out.

Walt radioed the other two officers to let them know that nobody was in the house. "Just a bunch of freaky gators and snakes."

"We need to round all this up. I'll call the chief to find out how to handle living evidence, if you start taking pictures."

"You got it."

"And thanks," said Drew, grateful they were able to work together to make such a crucial discovery. "I know we've had our differences, but you really had my back out here."

"I was just doing my job." Walt shrugged off Drew's olive branch.

"Well, good job, then." Drew had to let Walt be Walt.

CHAPTER

34

Fat Andy's Fish Fry, a hopping diner at Front Beach on the main drag of Anders Isle, welcomed Drew and Paul with a haze of fryer smoke hanging like cloud cover under the dimly lit ceiling. Hardly more than a shack, the Fry's walls were covered with a layer of old license plates, framed newspaper articles, and random metal junk dredged up by fishermen and put on display as vintage decor. The Fry had been a fixture on Anders Isle for as long as Drew could remember, feeding teens by day and a friendly bar crowd at night. Locals adored it, ignoring the grumbles of newer, fancier residents who complained about it being an eyesore.

The cooks greeted Drew and Paul by name, laying breaded flounder fillets in cast iron skillets to make the Fry Fish Basket, a favorite of the regulars. Drew relaxed into their usual booth just as a plate of hush puppies appeared on the table with two cold beers.

"Damn, I love this place," said Paul, taking a long swig of his beer.

"You say that every week, Asher." Drew dipped a hush puppy in the Fry's special sauce and bit into the thick ball of deep-fried cornmeal batter with a soft crunch.

Paul reached for a hush puppy. "You look much better than the last time I saw you."

"No kidding." Drew drank his beer. "I wasn't expecting to feel sick. First time that's happened to me on the scene."

"Well, you're tough, but you're also human, and Diane wasn't just another dead body. I haven't rescued or identified someone I knew before. You handled it fine." Paul smiled while he talked and followed each bite of food with a chug of beer. "I mean, you didn't actually blow chunks, so that's something."

Drew laughed. "Yeah, there's the silver lining."

"You must have the autopsy results by now. What happened to her?"

"The details are still under wraps, of course, so you didn't hear this from me," Drew said, lowering his voice with a quick glance around. "Strangulation."

Paul widened his eyes mid-sip, then swallowed his mouthful of beer and replaced the bottle on the coaster. "That's . . . shit, that's awful, man. And Oliver might be involved?"

"Could be. We linked him to some other criminal activity, enough for an arrest, which is why I need you to keep an eye out for him when you're working security at the port. But I seriously doubt he'll show up for work, especially if news breaks that he's a wanted man."

"Oh, you can be sure I'll be watching." Paul wiped his mouth with a paper napkin. "I'm on day shift there tomorrow and Friday."

"Great, thanks. I need him in custody."

"No offense, but how the hell are you going to prove who did it when the body was submerged in water and there isn't a weapon or a bloody crime scene anywhere?"

Shaking his head, Drew finished his beer and said, "I have no idea, but I'm going to."

Even in the dark corner of the room, Paul could see the shine of determination in his friend's eyes. A minute of silence passed between them until their Fry Fish Baskets arrived with lemon wedges and generous heaps of coleslaw. They ordered another round of beer.

"I saw Brooke yesterday," Paul said while he forked a steaming piece of flaky golden-fried flounder. "She came out to the port to rescue a sea turtle."

"Really?" Drew thought this topic wasn't much better than the last one, since he caused Brooke to leave the station that afternoon on the verge of tears. "She loves her sea turtles." He managed to smile.

"And she really knows her stuff." Paul winked at his buddy, knowing Drew's soft spot for Brooke. "I bet she's wild in bed. Smart women are the best lovers."

"Stop, Asher." Drew tossed a piece of hush puppy at Paul's shirt. "You always go there. It's not like that with Brooke."

"Hey, gets a reaction from you every time, so I know you think about it." Shoveling a piece of fish between his teeth, Paul chomped on it and grinned at Drew. "She's hot."

Drew smiled and shook his head, accepting Paul's teasing, then took a long sip of beer to fill the emptiness he felt at the thought of Brooke. He screwed things up.

CHAPTER

35

Well past midnight, Drew pushed open the door to his dark house after a long day of searching for Oliver Tack, eating with Paul, and returning to the station to review every shred of evidence he had so far. He couldn't stop thinking about the hurt look on Brooke's face when she found out about him and Diane. He had called her three times already, but she didn't answer. And she didn't call back.

Drew's head throbbed. His feet ached. He wanted a hot shower and some sleep. With his mind preoccupied, he swung the door closed behind him. It shuddered to a sudden stop. Spinning around, he saw a man's outstretched arm propped against the door, holding it open.

"Who's there?" Drew shouted, aiming his gun at the doorway. Adrenaline coursed through him. "I'm pulling the trigger in two seconds!"

"Don't shoot! Please! Don't shoot!" The man waved his arms through the open doorway in surrender, then hesitantly stepped into view under the porch light with his arms raised above his head.

It was Joe Willis.

"What the hell are you doing here? Trying to get yourself killed?" Drew glared at Joe and lowered his gun but kept it ready.

"I'm trying *not* to get killed," said Joe with a hunted look in his eyes, arms still raised. He glanced nervously over his shoulder. "Can I come in?"

"Sure, yes, come in." Drew holstered his gun and stepped aside to let Joe pass. "And you can put your arms down now."

Joe lowered his arms while Drew switched the lights on and locked the door.

"I didn't know where else to go," Joe said. The confident swagger had been completely wrung out of him. He cowered in the shadow of some unseen threat, some lurking danger that clung to him like the stench of the shrimp he fished each day. "I've done things I'm ashamed of. I know things I shouldn't know. I'm worried they'll come after me and my family, so I'm turning myself in."

"Wait. Slow down," said Drew. "What're you talking about?"

"The Turtle Lady."

Drew froze mid-stride. His mind raced. "What about her?"

"I know who killed her. And who killed the turtles. I know everything."

It took a second for Drew to process what he heard. Here it was—the connection he and Brooke hoped to find between the dead turtle and Diane's murder. Joe claimed to know it all. As tired as Drew was from the day's events, he felt a surge of energy. Solving this murder case would be both a professional victory and a personal relief. But Joe wasn't a friend and might be saying things out of desperation. Drew had to be deliberate in his approach, pushing for information, asking probative questions, but ultimately letting Joe tell his story.

Drew blinked and wiped his sweaty palms on his pants, feeling skeptical.

"Sit down." Pointing Joe to an armchair beside the coffee table, Drew sat on the couch across the table from Joe, ready to test him. He leaned in and propped his elbows on his knees, leveling his eyes at Joe. "Let me get this straight. You show up here in the middle of the night to tell me you know what happened, but you wouldn't admit to anything when you were at the station. I don't get it. Why come clean now? Why didn't you tell us what you knew from the start?"

Joe looked down at his lap. "I should've told you, but I thought if I said anything, I'd put my family in danger. Then I saw the cops over at Oliver's house and knew I'd be next. As soon as you caught him, *he'd* tell you I was in on it."

"Hold on. How did you see us at Oliver's house? Where were you?"

"On my johnboat in the marsh." Joe looked up at Drew. "I was on my way over to tell Oliver I'd been questioned to figure out what to do. But when I saw the cops there, I knew I was in even bigger trouble."

"What do you mean?"

"Oliver warned me not to tell anybody what we were up to. He'll think I gave him up. He told me plenty about guys in his poaching rings and the money they make. They won't think twice about killing me or my family because of what I know."

Joe's hands trembled where he gripped the chair.

Drew sat back and crossed his arms. "I need to know what you know."

Joe snorted and shook his head. "I might be scared, Detective, but I'm not stupid."

"Okay, listen, Joe," said Drew, growing frustrated, "It's late, and I'm tired. I'm not going to argue with you. You came to me. So, what do you want?"

"I want protection for me and my family."

"All right."

"And I can't go to jail. My family needs me. I support them."

"Well, maybe you should've thought about that before you got involved with all this."

For a split second, Drew thought Joe might lunge at him, but Joe just looked down at his lap. "I know. I really fucked up."

After a few beats of silence, Drew said, "I'll call a couple officers to park at your house tonight and stay around the clock, but any charges against you will depend on what you did. I can't cut a deal; that's what the lawyers do. But I can tell you that your cooperation will help you. Right now, I just want to talk to you about what you know and get your statement as a witness. Okay?"

Joe nodded, looking up at Drew with his face sagging. "I'll tell you everything as soon as you get some cops over to my house," said Joe. He sniffed, pinching the bridge of his nose. Drew could see his resolve to make things right.

Drew made a few calls and waited for confirmation that officers were at the Willis residence.

Meanwhile, Joe called his wife to let her know that cops would be watching the house, but, despite her prodding questions, he didn't tell her why.

Within ten minutes, protection was in place for Joe's family.

Drew set his phone on the coffee table in voice-record mode. "Your statement will be recorded. Do you understand and agree?"

"Yes, that's fine."

"Please state your name."

"Joe Willis."

"Mr. Willis, you're here because you have information related to the homicide of Ms. Diane Raydeen. Is that correct?"

"Yes."

"In your own words, tell me what happened."

"Well, this past Friday night we went out to look for a loggerhead turtle on North End Beach."

"Who's 'we'?"

"Me and Oliver Tack. He told me a female loggerhead would probably be coming onto the beach to lay eggs overnight Friday, or sometime during the weekend, and we should get over there. He knows a lot about those turtles. He's been doing this kind of stuff for a long time."

"What kind of *stuff*?"

"Poaching. He bragged about all the different animals he caught or killed over the years—gators, turtles, snakes, birds. It never seemed to bother him. I guess it should've bothered me, but I got used to it. The money was *real* good. I kill shrimp and fish for a living. I didn't see the harm in killing some turtles to support my family."

Drew cringed, thinking of how Brooke would react to that justification.

"It was like hunting," Joe continued.

"But you knew it was against the law to poach loggerheads, right?"

"Yeah, I knew that, but it didn't seem like a big deal. Oliver said all that'd happen if we got caught is we'd get fined."

"Or go to jail. I guess he didn't tell you that part."

"No, he didn't," said Joe. "Besides, I just thought I'd do it a few times to pay bills and save a little money—you know, get us through the tough times—and then I'd stop."

"How long have you been poaching?"

"This is my fourth summer. And I only poach loggerheads. That's it. I'm not doing it the rest of the year and not any other kind of animals. Just so you know."

"Does loggerhead poaching really make enough money to outweigh the risks?"

"Hell, yeah." Joe leaned forward and lowered his voice. "Oliver paid me forty thousand bucks for each one. And we got about four a summer. That's one hundred sixty grand each summer for hardly any working time. I made almost half a million dollars in just three summers! Do you have any idea how long it'd take me to make that kind of money catching shrimp?"

"No, I don't."

"Well, a hell of a lot longer than three summers of part-time work. One turtle earns me about as much as a year of shrimping, so you do the math. With the money I made, I got out of debt and fed my family and got insurance and still have enough left over for savings."

It was a stunning amount of money. Forty thousand dollars per turtle—and that was just Joe's cut. Oliver must be paid even more. Drew didn't know how this amount compared to other poaching fees, but Oliver seemed to be plugged into a circle of extremely wealthy—and *powerful*—collectors to garner such huge profits. Brooke would tell Drew the going rate for loggerheads on the black market—assuming she ever spoke to him again.

Drew brought the subject back to Diane's death. "Getting back to the night in question, you and Oliver Tack went out to North End Beach to look for a loggerhead. Then what happened?"

Joe scratched the back of his neck and shifted his weight in the chair. With his head semi-bowed, he looked up at Drew, his forehead creased as he recalled the events of the past Friday night and the images that had rattled him awake through two sleepless nights since then. He harbored a nightmare from which he could never truly wake, so he told Drew what he saw. "We went to look for a loggerhead on North End after dark, just like we did every time. When we got to the beach, we split up to sit in our usual spots in the dunes about a hundred yards apart. We did a lot of sitting and waiting. Some nights we sat all night and never saw a turtle. That night, we sat there until around five in the morning—Saturday morning. We were about to call it quits when Oliver snuck over to where I was sitting and motioned for me to follow him. He said he saw a loggerhead coming out of the water and waited for it to get halfway up the beach to be sure it didn't have time to turn back and escape. That was our usual routine. I followed him to kill the turtle."

Joe swallowed hard, shame flickering across his face.

Drew used Joe's pause to ask a question about something that perplexed him. "How could you and Oliver see a loggerhead in the dark over such a large stretch of beach?"

"Night-vision goggles. I know, it sounds crazy, but Oliver had 'em, and he swore it was the only way."

"Okay," said Drew, grudgingly impressed. "Go on."

Joe fidgeted in his chair, then continued. "Oliver led me to where he saw the turtle, which had crawled almost to the dunes by then. It was a huge female. The biggest I'd seen. I wondered if the boat would be able to hold me and Oliver and that giant turtle. But I didn't have long to think about it because dawn was bearing down on us. We had about thirty minutes before the beach would be too light for us to kill the turtle, get it to the boat, and make a clean getaway. That's when Oliver raised the shovel high up and brought it down on top of the turtle's head with a crack. It only took one blow."

Joe hesitated and looked down at his lap.

This cold description left Drew wary of what would come next in the story. He wasn't sure he could handle hearing the details of Diane's death presented in the same emotionless tone Joe used to describe the bludgeoning of a helpless sea turtle. Drew took a deep breath, determined to stay calm and not react until Joe finished. He needed the whole story for this statement to mean anything to the investigation.

"Everything would've gone as planned, just like the other times—kill the turtle, carry it to the boat, and get the hell outta there." Joe didn't look up from his lap. He shook his head. "But we heard a scream like nothing I'd ever heard. We both jumped. I think the scream started at the same time Oliver brought down the shovel on the turtle, or maybe right after. I don't know. It all happened so damn fast even though I remember it in slow motion. That woman's scream—a long, drawn out 'Noooo'—like she was in agony, as loud as a siren, like demons of hell were swooping in on us. Her scream was so close, too close—forty, maybe fifty feet away—coming from down the beach behind Oliver. His back was to her, but I saw her standing there—a dark woman shape—screaming at us, screaming for that turtle. I couldn't move. I just watched. Oliver turned to look at her and dropped his shovel. That's when she stopped screaming and took off running toward the dunes. Oliver ran after her. I didn't know what he was doing, and it all seemed unreal. He went crazy. At first, I thought he was chasing her off, trying to scare her, but he must've caught her and knocked her down behind the dunes because all I could see was her legs kicking, then they twitched a few times and went limp. And that was it. He killed her. He fucking killed her right there, and I didn't do a damn thing to stop him."

Sweat shone on Joe's forehead. He wiped it away with his palm and exhaled hard, clasping his hands together to control his shaking. When he finally looked at Drew it was with a mixed expression of fear and relief—eyes both pain-stricken and unburdened.

It took long seconds for Drew to believe what he had just heard and to keep his anger at bay. He had a job to do.

This was it. This was an eyewitness account of murder—the most damning evidence Drew could hope to find. He had to muster up some seed of empathy for Joe to keep him talking. He'd have to find a way to keep Joe alive until a murder trial at some later date when Oliver would face the wrath of a jury box full of real people with real emotions who would hear Joe on the witness stand, telling them what he just told Drew.

But, right now, Drew needed more. "I know this must be hard." Drew attempted to coax Joe back to facts and away from guilt and shame. "You couldn't have known what Oliver would do. And maybe you didn't do anything to stop him then, but you *are* doing something now by talking to me."

Joe nodded. "Yeah. Putting a fucking bull's-eye on my back."

"I think you would be in more danger if you didn't come forward. It would be easy enough for Oliver or one of his gang to get to you without the protection we can offer you—protection for you *and* your family."

Joe nodded again.

"Okay," added Drew. "Tell me the rest."

Joe squeezed his eyes shut for a few seconds like he felt a muscle cramp. "I don't have a clue how a man's supposed to act after he kills someone, so I don't have a comparison for what I saw, but my guess would be Oliver didn't act like most people would. It crossed my mind he might've done that sort of thing before, because he didn't seem bothered by it or scared about the consequences. After he killed that woman, he walked over to where I was. It was light enough by then that I could see his eyes—this hollow, distant look—and his mouth was shut so tight I could hardly see his lips. When he said something to me, he seemed to talk through his teeth, and he just hissed an order at me. 'Cut its shell off,' and tossed his carving knife at the dead turtle next to me. There was no way in hell I was gonna ask why. I figured he had something in mind, some reason. Anyway, I wasn't thinking. I was just doing whatever I could to get out of there. I cut shells off lots of turtles we killed before, but we usually did it after we got the turtle off the beach and back to the dock. There wasn't much time to do anything with the sun coming up. I didn't want Oliver flipping out and killing anybody else. So, I did what he told me to do. While I cut the shell off, Oliver carried the dead woman to our boat. Then I saw him waving at me and motioning for me to come on. I only had a couple more cuts to make, but I just left the whole turtle there and ran to the boat. Boy, that pissed him off. He pointed down the beach where I saw—far in the distance but headed our way—a person walking a dog around the bend to the North End. He cussed me out and told me to get the shell and at least we'd get paid. He said if I didn't hurry up and get that shell, he'd leave me there on the beach. So, I rushed back to the turtle, finished cutting, and lugged the shell back to the boat. We had to leave the rest of the turtle behind. We just didn't have time. As soon as I stepped foot in the boat, Oliver sped into the marsh creek where we found some cover."

"Did you ever ask him why he told you to cut the turtle's shell off on the beach instead of helping you take the whole turtle to the boat?"

"I did ask him later, and he said he knew it was getting too light on the beach—well, first he said, 'fuck you,' and then he said it was too light, and he wasn't sure we could get the dead woman and the turtle into the boat at the same time. Since the turtle was too heavy for either of us to carry alone, he thought I could at least carry the shell by myself, and then we could both go back for the rest if we had time. But with someone walking our way on the beach, we didn't."

"So, you went to the marsh creek, and then what?"

"We had to put the body somewhere. We couldn't pull the boat up at the marina with a dead body in broad daylight. So, I suggested we stash the body in the marsh, tied up to one of my crab pots, which would hold it underwater out of sight in a place where we could find it again that night and deal with it then. We used the rope from the johnboat. It was all we had. When we docked the boat, we used a rope from the dock to tie off the boat, which is why I ended up getting a new rope."

"I see. Had you ever seen the victim before that morning" Drew fished for any hint his prior theory about an affair might be true. It seemed unlikely, given the turtle angle, but Diane had been pregnant and, so far, they didn't know who got her that way.

"Hell no, I never saw her before in my life."

"Do you think Oliver knew her?"

"I don't think so," Joe said. "The way it happened—she surprised us. It was the worst timing of her life."

"Yes, it was. I was just curious. It's a small island. You never know who knows who. Would you be willing to give a DNA sample we could compare to other evidence to confirm your story and rule out any possible personal contact between you and the victim before her murder?"

"I guess so."

Drew nodded. "Good. Tell me what happened next."

"Well, after we docked the boat, Oliver wrapped the turtle shell in a tarp and tossed it in the pickup bed. We drove to North End Beach, which took about a half hour, to get the rest of the turtle. We figured it was easier by land where anyone who saw us would probably think we were animal control if we acted like we were supposed to be there. But we were too late. When we drove past the beach access path, we saw a couple people carrying the turtle to their truck."

"I know that part." Drew smiled. "One of those people was me."

"You're shittin' me," said Joe, blanching. "That was you? Hell, I hadn't slept at all the night before, and didn't pay much attention to the faces. I just saw a man and a woman."

"Yup. That was me and a friend of mine who studies sea turtles. And I think I know the rest. You and Oliver followed us to the marina, where you took the turtle out of my truck."

"That's right."

"But you failed to notice the media helicopters buzzing around, recording your every move."

Joe sighed. "Yeah, we were wiped out." He shook his head. "So, that's how you got us?"

"Well, yes, eventually. There was a lot more to it, but that's how we got Oliver. We couldn't identify you from the news footage. But it wouldn't have taken us much longer to figure it out."

"Really? You think so? How were you going to explain my alibi? The marina log entries show I was out on my boat when all this happened. Your sidekick seemed convinced."

"I didn't believe your alibi. I could tell by your partner's face he expected to see something different when we showed him the log entries. That's when it hit me. The return times were out of order and the entries were all in pencil—easy to erase, easy to forge—and kept out in the open for a week, which you knew, and which gave you easy access for tampering. But I couldn't prove it. Riley made the entries on Friday and Saturday, but you went back and changed them to fit your story—adjusted the time and signed your initials. Then you attacked his credibility, so he'd go along with your changes."

"Not bad, Detective. Still, you have to admit, I just made your job a whole helluva lot easier by showing up here tonight."

"Yes, you did. Thanks for that." Drew stopped the voice recorder.

"I hope you'll remember this when it matters most."
"You did the right thing. That always matters most."

CHAPTER

36

Tuesday morning came too soon. Troubling thoughts of Drew and Diane woke Brooke throughout the night. She ignored Drew's phone calls yesterday and didn't call him back. He left voice messages with apology after apology, but each one only made her feel worse than the last. *Sorry* was just a word, after all; it didn't undo what was done.

Diane's journal lay on the dresser, unopened. Brooke glared at it from her bed. Her sadness about Diane was pierced by a deeper hurt, a bitter disdain for the secrets harbored by her supposed friend. The journal probably contained more information than she wanted to know about what went on between Drew and Diane, but she was curious. She wanted to confirm what Drew told her about the casual nature of the relationship, but at the same time she didn't want to be tortured by details.

Her phone rang on her bedside table: Drew. Rolling away from the phone with a frustrated sigh, she closed her eyes. "Leave me alone," she said out loud to the walls of her bedroom, trying to smother the little voice in her head that said he must really care about her to call so many times.

A chime from her phone indicated a new message. Brooke reluctantly opened her voice mail and listened to Drew's fourth message in less than twenty-four hours.

"I know you don't want to talk to me, Brooke. I'm sorry about all this. Really, I am. I should've told you about Diane, but I just didn't know how.

The last thing I ever wanted to do was to hurt you." Brooke imagined him fidgeting the way he did when he was uncomfortable or self-conscious. "Besides being sorry, I also need your help. It's for the investigation. This is such bad timing. I'm not trying to trick you into calling me back. I promise. I think I just found out why the loggerheads have been disappearing. Do you have the dates when those turtles went missing? If you do, please call me back. I won't ask you to forgive me again, not now, but I'd really appreciate your help. Okay. Thanks. Bye."

Brooke sat cross-legged on her bed by the end of the message. Tossing her phone onto the covers, she looked out the window. Sunlight seeped across grass, clung to bushes, coated the tapered trunks of palm trees, and slowly brightened dawn into full morning.

In three short days, Brooke's life shifted from dim dawn to full light. Not becoming brighter, necessarily, but certainly more enlightened, disillusioned. Diane's death propelled Brooke into discovering truths both upsetting and intriguing—about local loggerheads and murder and secret attractions. If Drew knew something about the missing loggerheads, did that mean he also knew more about Diane's murder? If he didn't get Diane pregnant, then who did? Surely, that person would be a suspect. Why did Diane keep it all a secret? As much as Brooke's heart ached, she wanted justice for Diane and for the turtles.

Brooke stepped out of bed and crossed the room to her dresser. If she was going to help Drew, she wanted to know more about what really went on between him and Diane. Could she trust him again? To figure that out, she needed to see the relationship from Diane's point of view.

Before she could talk herself out of it, she picked up Diane's journal. Riddled with flagged pages, it felt light in Brooke's hands. She opened it to the first entry.

August 9th
I celebrated my 38th birthday last night with friends at Anders
Crab House. Had a little too much to drink and felt tipsy walking
home, which would've been fine if I'd gone straight to bed. But I

got home feeling drunk and not at all tired, so I made the mistake (again) of calling Drew. All day I hoped to hear something from him—some sort of happy birthday or any acknowledgment he even knew it was my birthday, which I guess he didn't because I didn't hear from him. So, like a dummy, I called him at almost midnight after one too many glasses of wine. He didn't answer so I left a message—some overly happy drunken message about my birthday and being home alone—la-la-la. I don't even remember what I said. How embarrassing! All I know is I managed to get ready for bed and was about to drift off to sleep when I heard someone knock on my door. And there he was—Drew and his sexy grin—saying he was there to make my birthday wish come true, which must've been a reference to something I said in my message; something I couldn't remember. It was obvious he'd been drinking that night, too.

Anyway, we didn't waste much time talking.

My attraction to him is overwhelming. It's really crazy. I saw him in my doorway and my skin tingled. My heart sped up. I had butterflies in my stomach. I mean, really, I feel like a silly teenager with a crush. Before I could say three words, he grabbed me and kissed me, walking me backward and kicking the door closed behind him, all while kissing me. We couldn't keep our hands off each other—feeling and fumbling and kissing and undressing—just like every other time. He knows the way to my bedroom and led me straight to it. In under a minute, we were naked in bed—kissing and grinding and tangled in covers and clothes. We both came fast and loud. We really do have great sex. But the part I always struggle with is what happens afterward. I keep telling myself I don't have feelings for Drew anymore, but then we sleep together, and I want more. I want him to stay all night, talk about more than shallow events of the day or the latest news. I know he doesn't feel the same way. And I wish I didn't feel anything. The physical stuff is so delicious. Maybe it's just the woman in me, right? When will I learn? We've had these one-night episodes a couple times since we broke up and that's why it's so hard to get over him. I'm still in love with him.

And then there's Brooke. She's right in the middle of it and doesn't even know. So now, not only do I feel guilty for hurting myself with these quasi-one-night-stands but I also feel doubly guilty for keeping this from Brooke. I mean, I don't have to tell her, but we've become such close friends and she's always talking about Drew with a dreamy look in her eyes and it just seems like the right thing to do. Drew doesn't think so. When I mentioned telling Brooke, he made me promise not to. He said she wouldn't understand and would make much more of it than it is. He doesn't want her to know because he doesn't want to hurt her feelings or mess up their relationship. And that actually made me feel worse, because not only did he imply that what's happening between us really isn't much, but he clearly cares more about Brooke's feelings than mine.

What is it about men like Drew? I want to hate him, but he isn't doing anything that I'm not also doing. If he knew I was having these feelings, he'd probably just end things between us for good and that would be it—no more late night whatever—but I don't want to stop having sex with him. It makes me feel close to him. So, until I'm ready to stop, I'm just going to write everything down in here and not speak a word of it.

Note to self: burn this journal.

Brooke closed Diane's journal. She didn't want or need to read any more. In one entry, she learned enough about Diane's feelings for Drew, and Drew's lack of feelings for Diane. In fact, reading the journal made Brooke feel better than anything either of them could have said to her in person. Drew must've known that when he offered Diane's journal to explain. Parts of the journal entry—the details of the tryst and Diane's emotions about it—gutted Brooke with self-doubt and sour envy. She wished Drew desired *her* that way. But overall, the entry made it clear: Drew had only been in it for the sex.

Brooke felt a deep sense of relief that it wasn't a love affair.

Even so, the secrecy of it stung. She blamed them both for that but found her hurt turned to pity for Diane as the one being used in the situation.

As for Drew, well, she never knew what to do about Drew.

Although Brooke wanted Tuesday to be a normal Tuesday, nothing about any day had been normal since Diane's death. Attempting to find comfort in routine, Brooke dressed for work at the aquarium. On her way there, she took a call from an LPL volunteer who found turtle tracks and a possible nest on North End Beach. Brooke drove past the connector bridge and straight along the length of the island to the north end. If this turned out to be a new nest, it would be the first and only one on the island so far that season.

The prospect of a loggerhead nest both exhilarated and upset Brooke. While she was glad her beloved loggerheads persevered through their many losses over the years, she hadn't taken care of a nest on the island without Diane. It was another painful reminder of her absence—followed swiftly by the sharp betrayal now tainting Brooke's once-perfect perception of their friendship.

Rounding the last turn on the narrow road through the maritime forest, Brooke tried to quell her inner turmoil. She pushed aside thoughts of her last trip on the same stretch of road the morning she found the dead loggerhead, before she knew about Diane's death, when Drew was hers—always *her* confidant and *her* friend—and not Diane's dirty secret. But the burden of knowing transformed her attitude with such abrupt and sudden force, Brooke felt disoriented on an island she could once navigate in her sleep. Her own inadequacy weighed on her while she struggled to quiet her mom's critical voice in her head, her mom's disapproval when Brooke chose to pursue a career in science over swimming, when she decided not to marry the wrong person just for his family name and money.

Like so many times in her past solitary work, Brooke relied on nature to center her. The loggerheads pulled her attention away from draining intro-spection and back to the beach and the creatures she loved so much. Sugar-soft sand dunes fringed with sea oats rose beside the path to North End. Brooke left her shoes in the car and walked barefoot to the beach, where she saw distinct flipper-churned tracks in the shape of a giant V opening toward low tide waves and peaking at a body pit surrounded by thrown sand.

Brooke gently probed the concave pit with a metal T-shaped pole until it gave way into the hollow of a buried egg chamber. She found the nest! After marking the nest with a triangle of stakes and orange tape, she documented it in her notebook.

Lingering on the beach, she thought about Drew's message. He said he might know why the loggerheads were disappearing. Brooke couldn't wait to find out. After theories and speculation in hour upon hour of conversation with Diane, Brooke didn't want to waste any more time not knowing. If Drew had the answer, then Brooke would put aside her hurt feelings and talk to him.

Since she was only a couple of miles from his house, she drove there to see him face to face. The turtle file box from Diane's office bumped against the passenger seat. With each hour of distance from the revelation of Monday afternoon, Brooke realized her feelings of betrayal came less from the fact that Diane and Drew were sleeping together and more from the fact that neither of them told her about it. She convinced herself she would've understood. After all, who was she to judge? She wasn't dating Drew. They were free to do whatever they wanted to do. Why did they keep it a secret?

The more Brooke thought about their deception, the more her indignant pain got the best of her. By the time she reached Drew's house, she was mad. Jerking the car into park, she threw the top of the file box onto the floorboard. With three notebooks under her arm, Brooke slammed her car door shut and marched to Drew's front porch. Pausing, she took a deep breath, tried to calm down. The last time she was there, Saturday morning, her ordered life started to fall apart. Here she was again after three days that felt like months.

She knocked with normal force, despite a strong temptation to beat down the door in frustration. She was tired of being the *nice* girl, tired of being so damn self-reliant, and self-conscious. For far too long, she'd been playing the agreeable friend around Drew, trying to be good enough, keeping things light and easy even when she wanted and needed so much more from him. He was supposed to know her best, but she hadn't let him. She only showed him a version of herself. Being raised by a perfectionist taught her to hide her insecurities, her flaws. It was about time he knew what she really thought.

She knocked again, but nobody answered.

She rang the doorbell. Still—nothing.

Then she noticed the empty driveway. In her blind rush to the front door, Brooke didn't look for Drew's pickup.

She no longer felt emboldened, she felt silly, but also relieved she didn't say something she'd regret. The next time she saw Drew, she wanted to be composed and completely honest. Maybe even a little vulnerable. She clearly had some work to do between now and then.

Brooke left the notebooks on Drew's doorstep with a simple message:

These are the turtle files with tabs to mark disappearances. We need to talk.
—Brooke

CHAPTER

37

By Tuesday afternoon, word of a break in the Turtle Lady Murder rippled across Anders Isle to every media outlet in the Southeast and beyond. Speculation ran rampant about the anonymous witness who was the source of the lead. But nobody had as much detailed and exclusive inside information about the case as the lead reporter for Local News 2, Bella Michaels.

While other reporters and anchors slapped together commentary, repeated bits of fact, and clamored for more of the story, Bella Michaels and Walt Pickering repaid each other's favors in the fan-whipped privacy of Walt's studio apartment.

It was clear they were attracted to each other every time they met but being such similar creatures—deflecting emotion with charm and shifting seamlessly from flirtation to disdain—neither had been willing to make the first move. Desire was both their seat of power and their greatest weakness. Until they had a reason, an excuse, to give in to what they both wanted all along.

When the helicopter footage Bella gave Walt proved to be pivotal in the hunt for a suspect, Walt phoned Bella late Monday night to share inside information about the prime suspect and potential link to a major poaching ring. Although they were even—favor for favor—Bella asked Walt to meet her Tuesday for lunch, which they never ate, opting instead for a romp in Walt's apartment to satisfy their obvious and voracious appetites for each other.

They stripped and flung clothes in a tangled trail to Walt's bed—his pants, her skirt, his shirt, his boxers, her blouse, bra, thong—all while *Local News 2 at Noon* blared from the wall-mounted flat-screen television. The top story featured a replay of Bella's breaking news report, originally aired earlier that morning, in which she released the name of the suspect to the public and launched hundreds of frenzied spinoffs on stations across the country. Bella's serious-reporter voice cascaded from the television speakers and filled the room, in stark contrast to her loud moans and shrieks of delight—punctuated by Walt's dirty talk—from under the covers.

This is News Flash Live on Local News 2. I'm Bella Michaels. I'm standing on the street of a suspected killer. The house at the end of this Anders Isle back road belongs to Oliver Tack, who is now wanted in connection with the Turtle Lady Murder. This is the first substantial break in a homicide case that has captured the attention of both local residents and turtle lovers nationwide since the body of thirty-eight-year-old murder victim Diane Raydeen, known as the "Turtle Lady," was pulled out of a marsh creek this past Saturday morning. Ms. Raydeen was the Director of the Loggerhead Protection League, a nonprofit dedicated to preserving the Anders Isle loggerhead sea turtle population.

A warrant for Oliver Tack's arrest includes a charge for the murder of Ms. Raydeen as well as a series of charges for poaching and smuggling with intent to sell federally protected species. A search of Oliver Tack's house revealed a hotbed of animal laundering activity suspected to be linked to the international black market, including a room filled with live timber rattlesnakes, copperheads, eastern hognose snakes, snapping turtles, Blandings turtles, box turtles, North American wood turtles, and two yellow-spotted Amazon River turtles, which are federally protected as an endangered species. Also found was the head and hide of an adult American alligator and several live baby American alligators, another protected species.

A manhunt is currently underway for Oliver Tack. If you or someone you know has information about his whereabouts, please

*contact the Anders Isle Police Department. I'm Bella Michaels re-
porting from Anders Isle. Stay tuned to Local News 2 for the best in
local news.*

Bella gasped and giggled with pleasure, rolling onto her stomach, and stretching nude across Walt's bed, her hair a mess. She lay with one cheek on the
cool sheet and said playfully, "I think that makes it your turn."

Moving from the edge of the bed to lounge beside her, Walt pressed his
eager body against her from head to foot. "Damn, woman." He admired
her curves, running his hand from her shoulders along her velvet back to the
rise of her perfect ass. "I can't think. You officially fucked my brains out."

"Who needs brains when we can do what we just did?" She laughed.

Walt smiled. "Not me." And his hand groped between her thighs until she
caught her breath. "My turn." He pulled her onto her side with her back to
his stomach, sliding into her fast and hard while he kissed a path from her
neck to her parted, panting lips.   .

CHAPTER

38

"We still don't know who got her pregnant," Drew said while sifting through Diane's homicide file.

"Just be thankful the lab's rapid DNA machine already proved it wasn't you or Walt." Mullinax silenced the constant ringing of the phone on his desk.

"Oh, I *am* thankful. A machine that can interpret DNA samples in less than two hours is like magic." Closing the file in his lap, Drew looked at Mullinax and shrugged. "But I already knew it wasn't me."

"You seem to think that matters, son."

"I'm just saying, if we're basically declaring the case solved, the pregnancy is a big unknown to leave out there."

"According to the eyewitness account from Mr. Willis, who the victim was fucking has nothing to do with her murder. So, drop it."

Drew took a sharp breath. He couldn't argue with that, but he still wanted to know.

"Now," said Mullinax, "What about Oliver? I have a press conference in an hour."

"We're searching everywhere for him," said Drew. "We've circulated his name and photo to generate leads, but nothing substantial has come in."

"Nothing? Hell, everybody in a hundred-mile radius knows who he is by now."

Drew shook his head. "Not even a sighting."

"Stay on it. I want everyone on it. We need to catch him." Mullinax leafed through stacks of papers on his desk, agitated and tense. He pointed to the window, which looked out on a parking lot full of impatient media. "On top of those idiots, the poaching angle is blowing up on national news—turns out Oliver is one of the biggest middlemen in the international black market for reptiles." Mullinax snorted with satisfaction. "Our little operation here on Anders is being compared to New York's Operation Shellshock and the Operation Flying Turtle in LA. Did you know that?"

"I don't know what those are," Drew said.

"Well, I didn't either until I heard about it all over the news this morning. Apparently, they were huge black-market stings run by state and federal agencies. To think: our little department just pulled off what those agencies spent years setting up, and we did it by accident. Ha! That's what I call luck, son. Agents from the National Marine Fisheries Service already called to find out more about Oliver's connections. They want to set something up to take down the whole ring. And the mayor is breathing down my neck to get this guy off the streets. He says tourists are fickle." Mullinax repressed a smile.

Drew thought Mullinax might laugh out of pure glee to be in the eye of a national news storm. But with the thrill of victory came the crushing pressure to capture the elusive Oliver Tack.

Mullinax's expression changed. Stress and urgency etched darker shadows in the creases of his potato face. He looked at Drew, annoyed to see him just standing there. "Go!" He shooed Drew toward the door. "Find Oliver Tack!"

Slogging through a crush of cameras and microphones from the station door to his truck, Drew managed to escape the parking lot without a word. While he drove, he pondered where to look next. How could he find a man who was never part of the community, always outside of it? Nobody knew Oliver or his routines. Sure, stories and tall tales swirled, but most of the talk was exaggeration spurred on by curiosity and fear. Sometimes the oddball neighbor, the wild-eyed wanderer, turned out to be a quiet saint. Other times he turned out to be the monster everyone imagined him to be.

What Drew knew: Oliver wasn't at his house or his work—officers were stationed at both places. Oliver wouldn't dare try to hide in Anders City or Anders Isle, where he would be recognized easily by hundreds of watchful eyes.

In fact, he couldn't hide.

He had to keep moving.

And the best way to keep moving on the coast was by boat.

In South Carolina, all motorized boats and watercraft had to be registered or titled with the Department of Natural Resources; however, a search of Oliver's property and SCDNR records revealed nothing to prove Oliver owned a boat. The only vehicle registered to Oliver was a pickup—the one Oliver was driving at the marina when he and Joe took the dead turtle—abandoned at an Anders City shopping center soon after the hunt for Oliver began.

One person might know more about Oliver's access to a boat—Joe Willis. Joe said he and Oliver used a johnboat each time they poached loggerheads. And that johnboat was yet to be found.

Joe was in custody at Anders County Detention Facility about thirty miles west of Anders City. After his midnight confession to Drew, Joe went with Drew to the station for booking. Later, he was transported to county jail to await his arraignment in a day or two. As of that morning, Joe hadn't lawyered up. A court-appointed attorney would be assigned to him at the arraignment. Until then, Drew hoped Joe would keep talking. If he was telling the truth, then he'd benefit from Oliver being captured and brought to justice.

On his way to the county jail, Drew drove across the connector bridge from Anders Isle to Anders City. Looking out at the expanse of salt marsh in layered shades of green, slim cordgrass stems beaded with periwinkle snails stuck tight above a flood tide, he wondered how a place with so much beauty could also harbor a killer. The series of events from the past few days built up and broke over him like a rogue wave. He squeezed the steering wheel to corral his anger about Diane's senseless murder and the helplessness it dredged up from his troubled childhood, swallowing down the choke in his throat that made him want to yell every obscene word he could muster at a world where horrible things kept happening every day. And daggers of heartache came with any thought of Brooke because he wasn't man enough to confess his real feelings for her or to even be the friend she deserved. Speeding along the connector, he focused on his next steps, while all around him tidal creeks wove through a blanket of tall grass licked by sunlight to the horizon. Even with his pressing worries and anguish, Drew knew today's troubles would eventually pass and drift out to sea like dried marsh reeds on a king tide. He had to believe it would all work out. In the face of such awesome nature, the problems of one person, one place, seemed wholly insignificant.

By the time Drew parked in the county jail lot, the sun was halfway set. Inside, the institutional green room stank of antiseptic and nervous sweat.

Joe sat opposite Drew in a small cubicle, a thick pane of glass between them. A hunted expression lingered on Joe's face. Eyes darted. Lips twitched. His whole posture slumped under the invisible weight of what he'd done and seen. Picking up the phone receiver, he mumbled a defeated hello.

"How are you holding up?" asked Drew.

"I'm worried about my family," said Joe. "They're safe, right?"

"We have officers watching them 'round the clock."

"But you haven't found Oliver yet. Is that why you're here?"

Drew nodded. "I need to know more about the boat you and Oliver used. Whose is it? Where's it kept?"

Joe shook his head. A pained, sarcastic smile curled his lips. "Well, shit. Things just got a whole helluva lot worse for me. I didn't think that was possible. If he's out on that boat, I doubt you'll ever find him. And if you don't find him, I'm shit outta luck. I'm stuck with a jury looking at me as the only one around to convict."

"I'm trying to keep that from happening."

"Dumbest decision I ever made talking to you last night." Joe poked his finger into the glass at Drew. "Look where it's got me—locked in here while some maniac is out there plotting to kill my family." Joe's grip tightened on the phone.

"You did the right thing."

"Fuck the right thing!" Joe's words hit the glass divider like a wad of spit. "I got scared, that's all."

Drew stood up to leave. He wasn't there to put up with a tantrum, and he certainly didn't pity Joe's situation. Joe did this to himself. Drew just wanted to find Oliver, which would ultimately help Joe.

Before Drew took a step away, Joe knocked hard on the glass and gestured for him to come back to the phone. He mouthed the word "please" and pointed to the phone again.

Drew could almost smell Joe's desperation.

Reluctantly, he sat back down to listen to what Joe had to say. He picked up the phone. "What?"

"Dylan Creek Marina." Joe shifted his eyes from Drew to the corner of the cubicle and back again. "We docked the boat over at Dylan Creek. Oliver leased one of those summer slips. I don't know where he kept it the rest of the year. It's a standard johnboat, about twelve feet long. I guess it belongs to Oliver. That's all I know."

"Thanks," said Drew. "That should help us find him."

"Yeah," said Joe, unconvinced. "I sure hope so." He hung up and folded his hands on the table, looking down at them as though he couldn't believe those were the same hands that killed sea turtles.

Drew stepped into fresh outside air and a hug of summer warmth. Rolling down his windows, he let his pickup carry him—free and eager—back to the coast, back to the hunt for one small boat—and one very large culprit.

CHAPTER

39

Life in a high-powered law firm didn't change much with the seasons, except for summer. The month of May brought an influx of summer associates, usually eight to ten rising-third-year law students, all idealistic and gunning for work to show off their budding legal skills.

Caldwell loved the season of summer associates. He sloughed off nagging, low-billing cases on the pool of recruits. He took full advantage of the firm's inflated social calendar designed to portray an artificial work-life balance that didn't exist in big firm reality. Cocktail parties, long lunches, happy hours, and concerts became almost daily activities. As long as summer associates were kept busy and happy, firm associates were free—and expected—to participate in all the fun.

On the rooftop patio of Rí Rá, an Irish pub in downtown Charlotte, a summer-associate happy hour burst into full swing Tuesday evening. Caldwell stood in the middle of it and half listened to simultaneous conversations while a vertical strip of sunset faded between two skyscrapers. Looking up at towering glassy buildings painted silver-blue in the closing light of day, he followed their sleek stacks of windows to crowns of points and arches that rivaled even the beauty of the sky, feeling proud and satisfied to see his office window at the top of the tallest building. Like one of those windows, he was on top of the world, among the elite, and shining bright as the first visible star at dusk.

One of the so-called "summers" handed Caldwell another beer, and he brought his mind back down to the patio party. Caldwell couldn't keep the summers' names straight. Most of them had been in orientation since they arrived. Tonight was their first firm outing and first chance to socialize with attorneys outside the office.

In all, nine summers mingled with about twenty associates and a few of the more gregarious partners. Open bar, chips and dips, free-flowing drafts, and all-you-can-drink cocktails made for quite a party. Everyone was catching a buzz on the firm's dime.

Percival Jones cornered Caldwell. "These kids look like high schoolers. They're babies." Percival pointed to the nearest collection of chattering summers. They seemed to be playing dress-up in pressed suits and trendy ties, pencil skirts and high heels. Percival slurped a gin and tonic. He was already hammered, which brought out his grinning, mellow alter ego. "How'd we end up with such a young bunch? I'm not sure they can handle my files, if you follow me?"

"Aw, they're harmless," said Caldwell. "They'll do anything you want them to do, exactly how you want it done. Besides, we all started somewhere, right?"

Percival shook his head. "I won't admit I ever looked that green on the job. Now, you, I bet, about four years ago, you looked just like that guy over there." Percival pointed to a recruit with his coat off and collar unbuttoned, no tie, drinking a cold beer from the bottle and entertaining a ring of riveted female associates with some outlandish story that required exaggerated arm gestures.

"Me? No way. I wasn't that guy." Caldwell squinted again at the recruit. "I wasn't even a summer. Y'all recruited me during third year."

Percival smacked his lips. "Well, we couldn't turn down the senator's son and the promised business of Art Ogletree, the biggest real estate tycoon in the country, now, could we?" He pinched away beads of sweat on his upper lip and raised his glass for a toast. "To a good deal." His glacier blue eyes focused on Caldwell, a flat expression that could've been the stupor of an alcohol-soaked brain, indifference to the *deal* he just revealed, or pity for Caldwell, who didn't know about it.

Caldwell couldn't speak. He lifted his beer bottle enough to clink Percival's glass, going through motions, reeling from what he just heard. Percival's words clanged like cymbals in Caldwell's mind.

A good deal...Clang!

A good deal...Clang!

Percival tossed back the last sip of gin and tonic. "I need another drink." Pushing away from the table, he lumbered off on heavy drunken legs, patting shoulders and slurring greetings on his way to the bar.

Caldwell sat in slap-stunned silence, his perception of his ability and work life flipped on end. Sure, he worried his job offer had been partly based on his name, but he didn't expect a deal had been struck when a simple nudge would've been enough. His nagging suspicions were confirmed by Percival with such mean nonchalance it left him dazed. Everything he believed he earned on his own merit, the confidence he gained from what he thought was his own achievement, was all based on a lie, a farce. Caldwell was a pawn, accepted to the firm as a package deal to obtain Art Ogletree's business, now one of the firm's biggest clients. He felt exposed in a crowd, stripped of the little piece of identity he'd built for himself, and chained once more to the Madden family name.

One singular question bubbled up, boiled in his head: *Did my dad broker that good deal?*

But he didn't need to ask.

For his son's own good, to wrangle him ahead through the good-ol'-boy network, Senator Madden surely pulled strings and traded favors, held closed-door meetings, and delivered his friend Art Ogletree as a client to seal Caldwell's fate in a big firm. Senator Madden believed it was all about who you know. He based his career on knowing the right people and benefitted from those relationships whenever possible. Of course, he wouldn't think twice about doing the same for his son.

Suddenly, the surrounding towers didn't look like shining beacons of success. They were dark, ominous, and stone-cold, dividing the sky around Caldwell like giant steel prison bars.

CHAPTER

40

Tuesday night blew warm and blustery wind against Drew's pickup while he crested the connector bridge and descended to Anders Isle. Each gust pushed his truck off-center. Bracing the steering wheel, he held the tires straight, an unnatural sensation to him, fighting the wind instead of catching it. He longed to be kitesurfing, cutting across choppy waves, scooping wind in the curve of his kite, harnessing it, and riding fast and wild for miles and miles. After a day of dead ends and not a trace of Oliver Tack, Drew craved some wind-swept speed.

The moon winked between rushing clouds when Drew arrived at his front door to find Brooke's message clipped to a stack of notebooks. As soon as he got inside and flipped on a light, he dropped everything in the closest chair and called Brooke, relieved to know she wanted to talk. He couldn't wait to talk to her, but she didn't answer, so he left a brief message to thank her for the files and told her to call back anytime.

Starving, Drew peered into his virtually empty refrigerator: two eggs, half a bag of shredded cheese, ketchup, and a few bottles of beer. He whipped up a plate of cheese-covered scrambled eggs and popped open a beer, eating and drinking while standing at the kitchen counter. Taking a second beer to the couch, he drank a third of it in a couple quick gulps and grabbed the turtle notebooks.

The day had been a blur of searching for Oliver, following leads, and tying up loose ends. Based on Joe's witness statement, Drew sent the crime scene unit to canvass the area around the access path at North End Beach for any possible physical evidence, but they found nothing useful. The public space, covered with dry powder-soft sand, was too heavily disturbed by days of exposure to foot traffic, tides, and weather. He expected as much but knew better than to take a witness's account as absolute truth without some sort of corroborating evidence.

From the jail, Drew drove directly to Dylan Creek Marina in search of Oliver's johnboat, but the only record of the boat was a slip leased from May through August in Oliver's name with a general description of the boat—color, length, type—and nothing about the boat's use. Dylan Creek Marina didn't keep a log of the comings and goings of small watercraft like johnboats, especially not for seasonal boat slip renters, and nobody could recall when the boat was last seen in the slip. He put the marina attendant on alert to call him immediately if there was any sign of it.

Despite the lack of information about the boat, the trip to the marina wasn't a complete waste of time. Drew got copies of log entries for the past three summers to verify Joe's claim that he used overnight trips on *Bonnie* as a cover for nights he planned to poach loggerheads. If Joe was telling the truth, *Bonnie* would be logged out for an overnight trip every time a loggerhead was reported missing in the turtle notebooks.

Taking the log entries out of his case file, he began to compare dates with the tabbed notebook pages. Three summers ago, a total of three loggerheads vanished in June and July. The summer after that, four went missing, and last summer, five more. A total of twelve loggerheads disappeared in three years. All the dates of turtle disappearances matched up with overnight *Bonnie* trips. So far, the facts appeared to support Joe's story.

Across the island near its south end, Brooke sat in her apartment wondering about parts of the story that didn't make sense to her. All day, she heard news reports about Diane's murder, the poaching ring, and the involvement of Oliver Tack and Joe Willis. People were quick to accept poaching as a legitimate explanation without question, but Brooke knew better. She knew loggerheads weren't one of the highly coveted sea turtle species on the Endangered Species List. Why would anyone poach loggerheads? Why so many? The money alone couldn't be the primary motivation, not based on what she knew of the black market. The poachers weren't taking eggs, which were generally more valuable than female adults. If there were wealthy buyers involved, what was their attraction to loggerheads?

By far the most difficult part of the story for Brooke to understand was the senseless murder of Diane—her death a purported case of wrong place, wrong time—with reporters making snide remarks about her naïve sense of security to be on the remote North End Beach alone in the dim pre-dawn hours. Again, Brooke knew better. Diane was anything but naïve. She always took precautions when it came to personal safety and the sea turtle program. She wouldn't have been on the beach alone in the darkness of morning without a compelling reason. Although Diane took more risks in recent summers to prove her theories about the loggerhead disappearances—there were a few rare occasions when she couldn't find a walking partner and went out anyway at odd hours to search for turtle tracks—she at least made an effort to call someone (almost always Brooke) to walk with her in the dark or to let someone know where she'd be.

But she didn't call Brooke that day.

So why had Diane been there alone?

These were questions Brooke realized might never be answered, but she worried that they weren't even being asked. By all news accounts, the Turtle Lady Murder case was solved, with a manhunt underway for the prime suspect, Oliver Tack. Free-flowing praise for Anders Isle PD lauded Chief Mullinax and his team of officers as heroes for their swift results in the investigation and their bonus victory over a major poaching ring responsible for killing and trading innumerable endangered species in the eastern United States. In several reports, Drew was pictured, mentioned by name, and celebrated as the lead detective on the case.

Brooke supposed the outcome of the case was a success. Perhaps her lingering questions and doubts were simply her analytical mind in search of clean and tidy solutions. She wanted an answer for every question, expected her structured scientific method to apply to something beyond all rules of science: the heinous act of one human against another. What good would questions do at this point anyway? There wasn't any answer that could ever be good enough to explain Diane's murder in a way that made sense, in a way that made it easier to accept. Knowing why wouldn't make things better, wouldn't bring her back.

For grief, there is no remedy in science or law or justice.

There isn't even a remedy in time.

There is only grief.

Brooke put aside her questions and opened a paper grocery bag. Walking through her apartment, she filled the bag with things borrowed from Diane—three books, a lace scarf, and last but certainly not least, the beautiful butterfly brooch housed in its elegant mahogany box. She only wore it that one New Year's Eve.

The paper bag felt too light in Brooke's hand. There had been so much more shared during her friendship with Diane than could fit into a paper bag. These tangible items were only things, and things—even those as precious as the brooch—weren't a measure of the weight and value of a friendship. But they were all Brooke had left for now.

Tomorrow morning, she would give Diane's belongings back to her family.

Tomorrow morning, she would keep only memories of Diane.

Tomorrow morning, Brooke would attend Diane's funeral.

CHAPTER

41

Limbs of burly oak trees draped with manes of Spanish moss were bent around the small stone church on Anders Isle, where a standing-room-only crowd gathered to mourn Diane's death and celebrate her life. The preacher spoke of God and love and peace, but Brooke wished she could be walking instead on the beach with Diane, looking for turtle tracks, like they did every Wednesday morning. Whenever they found a crawlway and a nest, Diane humored Brooke's giddy enthusiasm. For Brooke, each nest was as exciting as the last, as exciting as the first, because it meant more turtle hatchlings and a healthy cycle of life for loggerheads. While Diane was the steady driving force behind the nest protection program on Anders Isle, Brooke's contagious passion for her work at the sea turtle hospital raised awareness of and attracted support for turtles at a faster pace and on a wider scale than ever before. Many volunteers and patrons over the years commented that Diane and Brooke were the ones who made them care about sea turtles. It was hard for Brooke to imagine saving turtles without Diane.

Brooke startled when someone tapped her shoulder. She didn't realize the service was over. She stood up, teary-eyed. As Cindy passed by, leaning into her husband, she grasped Brooke's arm.

People filed out of the church and into the courtyard, where Diane's family, all from Ohio, flanked the gate to receive hugs and hands and kind words. Brooke recognized Diane's mother from pictures but didn't know the other men and women huddled in the shadow of an oak. The family bowed their heads, blotted weeping eyes, and reached for people in passing. Brooke wondered if they found any comfort at all in the words and gestures of Diane's friends, most of whom were complete strangers to them.

Brooke struggled to keep from crying when it was her turn to clasp the warm hand of Diane's mother, knowing her own sadness from losing a friend paled in the presence of a mother burying her only daughter.

"Thank you for coming." Diane's mother looked at Brooke with a pleasant smile and reddened eyes, as though her tears were all spent, her phrase of gratitude an automatic response. She sandwiched Brooke's hand between her own hands.

"Mrs. Raydeen, I'm Brooke Edens. Diane was one of my best friends. I loved her very much. I'm so sorry for your loss."

The fog lifted in Mrs. Raydeen's eyes. Whimpering, she pulled Brooke against her soft chest in a full embrace. "My DeeDee talked about you all the time." She patted Brooke on the back, continuing to hug her. "It's so nice to meet you."

"You, too." Brooke's tears came fast. She didn't expect such warm recognition from Diane's mother.

When the hug ended, Brooke picked up the paper bag at her feet and gave it to Diane's mother. "These are a few of Diane's things I borrowed over the years. I wanted to be sure you got them."

"Thank you." Mrs. Raydeen nodded gratefully, opening the bag to look inside.

"There are some books and a scarf and your family's beautiful brooch. Diane lent it to me. I thought I should give it back to you in person."

"A brooch?" asked Mrs. Raydeen as though she had never heard the word before. Looking confused, she reached into the bag. "I don't remember DeeDee having something like that." She pulled out the mahogany box and gently lifted the clasp.

The butterfly brooch caught sunlight and scattered a flurry of sparkles inside the lid.

Mrs. Raydeen gasped. "Oh my, it's exquisite, but I'm afraid I've never seen it before."

This time Brooke was confused. "Are you sure?"

"I'm sure. I wouldn't forget this." Holding the brooch's box in both hands, she admired its shimmering flawless wings.

"I'm sorry for the mix-up. Diane told me it was a family heirloom."

Mrs. Raydeen carefully closed the box and handed it back to Brooke. "Then it must be another family's heirloom because it doesn't belong to us." She noticed the line of people forming behind Brooke, well-wishers waiting patiently to give their condolences. "I'm glad we met and wish we had longer to talk. You were such a good friend to my DeeDee. She admired you."

Brooke felt tears well up again. "I admired her, too. Your daughter was the big sister I never had. She'll be missed by everyone who knew her, especially me."

"Thank you, sweetheart." Mrs. Raydeen placed her hand on her chest as they parted ways.

CHAPTER

42

Drew eased his pickup along the curve of dirt road splattered with shadows from twisted limbs of ancient live oak trees so dense their canopies nearly blocked the sky. The maritime forest crowded the road, leaning and folding in on itself, salt-pruned and quiet. Shaded narrow paths meandered through thick undergrowth, stamped out by families of deer. Resurrection ferns coated the knotted arms of oaks like green fur.

Parking on the shoulder near the northernmost beach access path, Drew stepped out of his pickup to look around. The clearing opened on one side to a view of dunes and ocean framed by forest. Drew wanted to see the alleged murder location for himself, even though the crime scene techs didn't find any physical evidence during their search of the area. Since Joe said he and Oliver targeted North End Beach for poaching loggerheads, Drew hoped to find something, anything, to validate Joe's statement.

Ten paces took him from his pickup to the access path. Another ten paces between head-high dunes and he was on the beach, but still at least twenty yards above the most recent high tide line. Walking slowly, taking advantage of the bright mid-morning daylight, Drew paused to puzzle over marks and depressions in the sand. Each cluster of footprints was formless, innocent, untraceable. Everywhere he looked he saw only the usual stick-and-shell debris and aimless trails of people and animals enjoying the beach. Nothing looked suspicious. Nothing resembled evidence of a crime.

On his way back to his truck, he stood in the clearing with his back to the ocean, peering into the darkest recesses of the forest. The surrounding property was all private and Drew didn't pursue a search warrant after discovering the crime happened on the public beach, but he was here, so he might as well walk the property line and see what he could see. Based on the open field doctrine, he could use evidence found in a warrantless search of undeveloped property adjacent to a crime scene, especially where there wasn't a fence, a barrier, or even a housing structure.

He just wanted proof Oliver had been there.

Most of the tall weeds and grasses along the edge of the forest were impenetrable, clumped in bunches between saw palmettos, shrub thickets, and a variety of lichen-crusted trees. A screen of nature to keep people out. But something caught Drew's eye. About fifty feet into the forest, on the side nearest to the beach, he noticed a pink surveyor's flagging ribbon—usually marking a tree to be saved during construction—tied around the trunk of a live oak. Just beyond the flagged tree, a stack of dried palm fronds rested horizontally between the forks of two smaller oak trees, almost hidden completely by the camouflage of vegetation. The fronds were light brown, clearly dead, and wedged up in the trees about five feet off the ground to form the "roof" of what appeared to be a crude shelter.

Drew could barely make out a foot-wide path of bent and broken grass leading to the shelter. He followed it. Small twigs and sawgrass scratched against his pants. Under the palm frond roof, an oval space of forest floor was flattened to dirt and pine straw, large enough for a grown man to curl up on his side. The sight of it made Drew think of homelessness and desperation. A place where someone would go to sleep one off in the dark, or to hide out and stalk. The lean-to was man-made and felt dangerous, out of place in the wild.

Even more out of place were the crumpled beer cans falling out of a plastic bag under a bush and rusting into the ground among brittle leaves. Drew's skin prickled, his senses sharpened on alert, while he wondered if the person who built this might return or might be watching. He stood still to listen, but heard only the rustling wind, the shushing waves. Calls of birds and insects.

Satisfied with his finding, as random and unlikely as it was, Drew took a picture of the flagged tree and the shelter. Tugging the plastic bag open with one gloved hand, he collected all the scattered beer cans with the other, filling the bag and tying it up. He would take the cans to the crime lab for analysis in the off chance any prints were found to match Oliver's. And, if not, at least he cleaned up some litter in the process.

CHAPTER

43

Caldwell's eyes ached from staring at his computer screen. He sucked down his third double espresso. All morning and through lunch, he kept his office door closed and absent-mindedly thumbed through files on his desk. It would appear to passersby in the hallway that he was too busy at work to be disturbed, though he barely logged two hours of billable time. Whether it was the overload of caffeine or the constant replay of his revealing conversation with drunken Percival Jones from the night before, Caldwell couldn't concentrate. He usually excelled at office politics, but knowing the circumstances surrounding his hiring squashed his motivation and made any effort seem pointless. The firm would keep him because he came with Art Ogletree's business, a package deal. Caldwell could bill two thousand hours or only ten. It didn't matter.

To make things worse, the Project Flood documents arrived that morning. Caldwell owed Art a phone call about the project, but he kept putting it off. He glanced at the computer clock: 2:43. Each minute seemed to drag by more slowly than the last with the call looming as the largest obstacle to the end of his workday. If he could just muster up the professional attitude and necessary fear to call Art and get it over with, he could sneak out early and strategically leave his office door closed and his sport coat on his chair to create the illusion he was coming back.

Then Caldwell had an idea. Tapping computer keys, he opened the firm's file management database to access the scanned copies of the Project Flood documents. Instead of calling Art, he would email the signed documents to Art with a note about giving him a chance to review them and suggest a time for a phone call tomorrow. In five minutes, he could set himself free for the day.

The firm's file management database allowed quick and basic search requests by entering a specific project name or file number as well as more generalized or advanced searches by attorney name or client name. Caldwell entered *Project Flood* in the search field and a line item appeared with the project name and a list of documents attached to the file. After opening the documents to confirm they were in order, he was about to attach them to an email when one of the columns caught his attention. The column showed the client's name—*Art Ogletree*—as a hyperlink. Caldwell could open a list of every matter being handled by the firm that involved Art Ogletree. He hadn't thought about researching a client this way in the past, but he also didn't have a reason to care about any one client's business with the firm until now. Percival always gave Caldwell priority access to Art Ogletree's files, even allowing him to view billing details because Art was known for bringing up fees without warning. As needed, Caldwell could open a list of itemized billing for each of Art's matters using the database.

Curious about the value of the *good deal* that evidently formed the basis of his job, Caldwell clicked on the link to the Ogletree files to see how many matters Art had with the firm and what he was paying for them.

Exactly how much was Caldwell worth to the firm?

The cursor blinked and swirled while the database searched its files. Then a list of five open matters filled the screen. Accounts receivable for Ogletree matters came to a total of more than four hundred thousand dollars for just one month of billable fees. Over a single year, that would add up to millions. It seemed Caldwell was a *very* valuable good deal.

Caldwell scanned the list again. He reached for a folder on his desk, pulling out his summary of Art's real estate projects. There were only four on his list: Project Earthquake, Project Flood, Project Thunderstorm, and Project Tornado. The database showed a fifth project that wasn't on Caldwell's list:

Project Hurricane.

Since his first day at the firm, Caldwell was assigned to all of Art's real estate projects (now he understood why) under the guidance of Percival Jones. There wasn't another attorney at the firm aside from Percival who knew more about Art's business than Caldwell, but Caldwell had never heard of Project Hurricane. Usually, Caldwell and Percival were listed together in the database as managing attorneys for Art's matters—Percival as partner and Caldwell as associate; however, Project Hurricane listed only Percival and, most unusually, the file was password protected. Caldwell tried to open the Project Hurricane file using several different search terms, but each time he was prompted to enter a password to view details of the file.

Caldwell wouldn't dare to ask Art about the mysterious Project Hurricane for fear he'd appear either incompetent for not knowing as much as the client about a case or inappropriate for inquiring about an apparently confidential matter. Both scenarios would risk him being on the receiving end of Art's infamous wrath, a risk he wasn't willing to take. Instead, he printed the Project Flood documents for reference and called the general Ogletree Acquisitions office number.

When the receptionist answered, Caldwell asked, "May I please speak to Ben Feldman?"

He was put through to Ben, who answered with an expectedly timid, but professional, voice. "This is Ben Feldman."

"Ben, how's it going?" Caldwell asked in a casual tone usually reserved for close friends.

"I'm sorry. May I ask who's calling?"

"Caldwell Madden. We met this past weekend when I gave y'all a tour of Taylor Island."

"Oh, right, of course. I remember." Ben tried to sound relaxed, but only sounded more strained. "I enjoyed the tour." There was an uncomfortable pause. "Were you trying to reach Art?"

"No. Not yet. I want to talk to you first."

"Me? Oh, okay. What do you need?"

"Well, see, I'm the attorney down here for Art's projects in the Carolinas.

There's a project I need to talk to Art about, but I don't have the latest documents for it, and the partner on the case isn't available. I'm sure you know how Art will get if I'm not prepared and end up wasting his time. So, I'm hoping you can find the information I need."

"I'll do my best. What's it called?" asked Ben.

"Project Hurricane."

There was another uncomfortable silence. Caldwell couldn't tell if it was Ben's social awkwardness or something else until Ben finally said, with a tight, almost panicked voice, "I have to go."

And he hung up.

CHAPTER

44

Brooke spent Wednesday afternoon with the ocean. Walking barefoot on wet sand, she let saltwater run up around her ankles, calmed by the ocean's rhythmic heartbeat of breaking waves. Nothing soothed her more than being on the beach of Anders Isle.

In five short days, her routine-filled world had been flipped on its end and stopped making sense. It was all too much—Diane's murder and pregnancy, poached loggerheads, Drew's secret trysts with Diane, Caldwell's return, and now the mysterious butterfly brooch. Like her friendship with Diane that once seemed pure and untarnished, the brooch was now a mere trinket and no longer a source of strength. Its beauty seemed shallow and false. Something about it was an omission, a lie.

Alone and confused, Brooke didn't know who to trust. She looked out across the vast ocean, the same view she'd seen since her childhood. So many things changed on the island, but those were all at her back. When she faced the water's edge, there wasn't any indication of time or change. She could be four years old building a drip castle or fifteen being kissed. She could be a teenager collecting shells or her present self in need of an escape from the sudden upheaval of her quiet coastal life. The ocean remained the same. Brooke found comfort in its constancy.

She couldn't do anything about Diane's murder, or the loggerheads already lost. She couldn't change the things that happened between Drew and Diane or their secrecy that led her to question her friendships. She couldn't ask Diane about the brooch's true owner, and it didn't really matter anyway. All she could do was find a way back to her own life, purpose, and sense of home.

Down the beach, she saw a young boy poking a stick at a cannonball jellyfish washed up on shore. She smiled at the memory of collecting specimens in her Radio Flyer wagon. Reflexively, the cannonball jelly's scientific name escaped her lips: *Stomolophus meleagris*.

Brooke thought about the three voice messages she needed to return. The first from her mom, checking in again to make sure Brooke was taking care of herself and doing everything right. The second from Drew last night, his voice kind and consoling. He thanked her for the turtle notebooks and told her he'd be thinking of her during Diane's funeral. And the third from Caldwell, who sounded stressed and almost desperate. He decided to come to Anders a day earlier than planned and would arrive Thursday evening. He wanted to take her to dinner and asked her to call him back as soon as possible, which reminded her of being with him, when *everything* had to be done as soon as possible.

And still, somehow, through all her life changes and difficult decisions, these two men knew her best, held her closest, and cared most. Nobody was more surprised by that fact than Brooke.

Brooke's mom used to tell her not to count on anyone but herself. "We all end up alone," her mom would say, "And that's different from lonely." With a view of the ocean spread in front of her for as far as she could see, Brooke understood how to be alone. Being alone with the ocean felt natural to her. But loneliness had crept in more often since she left Caldwell, since her sudden loss of Diane. And Drew, her once-constant confidant, seemed apart from her now. She didn't want to be lonely. Actually, she didn't want to be alone either.

Her thoughts turned to turtles. She sighed. The LPL expected her help again today.

The sun sank lower into late afternoon while Brooke walked off the beach and back to the present day. Families trudged from the beach to the road, sweaty and sunburned, lugging strollers, buckets, umbrellas, and chairs. She wondered if they spent the day digging giant holes in the sand or building mounds of castles above the high tide line, unwittingly creating obstacles for a mama loggerhead on her trek to nest that night.

CHAPTER

45

Drew last saw Paul Monday night at the Fry. Since then, with the investigation in full swing, Drew had been too busy to eat much of anything that didn't come prewrapped in fast food packaging with a side of fries. So, when Paul invited him over Wednesday for an early dinner, Drew's stomach growled in anticipation of a home-grilled meal.

Drew knocked on Paul's front door. No answer. He rang the bell. "Asher? You in there?" Cupping his hands to his temples, he peered through the windowpane in the door.

"Back here!" Paul's voice came from the direction of the backyard.

Walking around the side of the house and through the gate, Drew saw Paul poking a spatula at burgers on the grill. Smoke streamed from the hunks of sizzling meat and dissipated through the air, intoxicating Drew's senses with a drippings-on-charcoal aroma and seared-beef flavor. He could almost taste the burgers with each breath.

"Hey, man," said Paul. "Beer is over there." He cocked his head at a blue Yeti cooler perspiring near the back door.

"Thanks," said Drew. "I'm starving. I didn't realize how hungry I was until I smelled those burgers."

"Good. There's plenty. Grab us a couple cold ones."

Drew pulled two cans from the cooler, wiping off flecks of ice. He popped them open and handed one to Paul.

Paul took a sip. "I'd say I haven't seen much of you, but it seems like you're on my TV every time I turn on the news."

"Ha! I tried my best to avoid that, but the chief likes the attention, so we all get dragged in with him. I'm just pissed we haven't found Oliver."

"Yeah, how's that going?"

"Nowhere." Drew chewed a chip around his words. "This is the biggest investigation of my life, but I'm chasing down evidence. I can't seem to get ahead of it. I'm doing everything I can think of to do."

"I'm sorry, man. That sounds frustrating. Lots of emergencies I deal with are pretty clear cut—a car accident or a shark bite—but it sounds like what you're looking for is more like the cause of a fire. It takes time to find a fire's source, you know—that bit of burnt cigarette or melted candle wax under a pile of ash and rubble. There must be a sign out there. You'll know it when you see it. Just takes time. That's probably not what you want to hear."

"It isn't. I wish I could be patient, but there's too much at stake with this murderer on the loose. Just today the chief lectured me about people fearing for their lives on the island and tourists canceling their plans to visit. All because Oliver is still out there and I haven't found him—at least, that's the chief's take on it."

"That's a load of crap."

"I know but try telling him that. Plus, he's done so much for me, I really want to do this for him." Drew shoved another salsa-laden chip into his mouth while Paul lifted burgers from the grill and slid them onto a plate.

"Well, forget about the chief for now and eat up." Smiling, Paul set the burger plate on the patio table next to heaps of lettuce leaves and tomato slices.

They each built a burger, sat down, and ate in silence for a minute before Drew asked Paul, "So what's new with you?"

"Not much. Same old shit. People are getting into all sorts of absurd trouble this week on land and sea. Earlier today we raced out on Jet Skis when a call came in about three people caught in a rip tide. But when we got out there, it was just a few dumbass teenagers trying to swim out to the breakers where they thought there was a sand bar to stand on. They were swimming back in with no problem when we rode up on them to help, had no idea they caused an emergency."

"Boneheads."

"Exactly." Paul laughed and took a bite of his burger. "My job pretty much exists because there are so many boneheads out there."

"I guess we were a couple of them, too, when we were kids."

"Oh, we definitely were. Especially that time we went surfing with the hurricane offshore. Today's call made me think of that. We talked Brooke into swimming out there with us. She got caught in that rip tide before we even realized what was happening. Remember that?"

"Oh yeah," said Drew. "I've had a hard time getting her into big waves ever since then." Drew had stuffed his face with burger, but still felt hollowed out at the thought of Brooke.

"Really? You can't get Brooke to do something your way? Doesn't she follow you around like your other girlfriends?" Paul joked, reaching for the chips. Drew didn't laugh. Paul looked over at him, noticed his drawn expression. "What is it, man? I was just kidding."

Drew cleared his throat. "Nothing, nothing." He half smiled.

"Right—okay—come on, tell me."

It was difficult not to trust Paul. Drew leaned back in his chair and took a long drink of his beer. "It's Brooke."

"Hasn't it always been Brooke?" Paul said wisely, without hesitation, without surprise, as though he already knew what was on Drew's mind.

Pressing his lips into a thin smile, Drew watched a drip of water roll down the side of his beer can. His memory flashed, a split-second image of the Brooke he knew so well—a ponytailed, big-smiling, doe-eyed girl—a smart, optimistic, sweet woman full of good. He cocked his head and said, as close to a confession of feelings as he could muster, "Yup."

"And when are you going to tell *her* that?"

"I don't know."

"Well, figure it out. We outgrew being boneheads, right? So, stop being one. You have to tell her what's up. If it's always been her, then let her know. See what happens. You only have her to lose."

"I might've already lost her. I always screw things up. She found out about me and Diane."

"I thought she knew you dated Diane."

"But she didn't know about the ongoing stuff . . . the random one-nighters here and there."

"So what? She's your friend, not your girlfriend. You can do whatever you want and not tell her about it. Your life, bro."

"You don't know Brooke the way I do. It's complicated. I deliberately kept my thing with Diane a secret from her and even told Diane not to talk about it. I think I wanted Brooke to see me as someone she'd want to be with. But maybe I'm not."

"Whatever. Cut through all that crap and tell her it's always been her. Believe me, you'll regret it your whole life if you don't. Remember Mandy?"

"Of course, how could I forget your many drunken nights of trying-to-erase-Mandy?"

"Exactly, and that didn't work. I still think about her, even after what? Five years? I was so stupid. I don't know what I was waiting for. I guess I thought we'd always have more time to figure it out. And then she left, and I didn't stop her. I let her slip away, and now she's married to some other guy. And I just have to live with that. And it sucks."

"That does suck," Drew said. Paul got it. He'd been through it. And he was also a big teddy-bear softy when it came to women. He was the marrying kind. "I wish I was as sure about Brooke as you were about Mandy. I mean, with Brooke it could be the real thing. I don't know if I'm ready for that kind of . . . *commitment*."

"Ugh, bro, that's such bullshit. You think long and hard about it. You almost lost her once. She was on her way down the aisle. And the look on your face when you told me she called it off . . . you were happier than I'd seen you in a *long* time. You don't even know how lucky you are to have another chance."

Drew had been elated when he found out Brooke was moving home. He even helped her move into her apartment. But after she was back in his life, he kept putting off any attempt to change their friendship into something more. He was afraid he'd lose her by wanting to have her.

He took another long drink of his beer and let himself imagine loving Brooke. Being with her always felt like home to him. Nothing felt better than that.

CHAPTER

46

Brooke's Wednesday nights used to be fun and full of potential.

There was a time—not too long ago—when she would be going out for the night at ten o'clock to see a band with friends at the Backstreet Pub in Beaufort, North Carolina. Every Wednesday, the same local bluegrass band played at the same gritty bar, and Brooke was there with most of the same people. But it never grew old. She lived the simple life of a grad student at the Duke Marine Lab, where Sly cooked up Southern food at its finest, intellectual curiosity fueled fiery romances, and night life was relished with delight by studious night owls. It was a carefree time when anything could happen.

As Brooke opened the front door of her bleak apartment at ten o'clock Wednesday night, it struck her that she couldn't remember the last time she'd gone out at ten. She missed those regular late nights with friends. For once, she didn't have anything pressing to do for work. Her Wednesday night was wide open but didn't feel free.

Brooke chose a movie and let familiar dialogue keep her company. She loved to watch her favorite movies on repeat, a habit of hers that annoyed Caldwell. With sounds from the television lightening her mood, Brooke approached her hall closet door. As organized as she was with her work and life plans, she was equally disorganized when it came to keeping house. Clutter collected in corners and on tables until she finally stuffed it all in the closet to keep it out of sight and mind. She still had several moving boxes she hadn't opened in two years. She hoped sorting through the closet might make her feel productive on this otherwise empty Wednesday night.

The closet door creaked open. Brooke was surprised that papers, boxes, books, and photo albums didn't tumble out on top of her. Stacked almost to the ceiling, clutter formed precarious towers, filling the small space from wall to wall. A shelf at the top of the closet was barely visible beneath even more boxes and papers.

Brooke felt overwhelmed. How would she begin to organize all this stuff? It was as though a door to her brain stood ajar to reveal memories packed like those papers in the closet. Each piece connected her back to somewhere or someone from her past. But she always felt better after the rare instances when she cleaned out and streamlined the dark, messy spaces in her home; the effect transferred to the dark, messy spaces in her mind. To that end, Brooke reached in and pulled out boxes, albums, and loose papers until it looked like her closet threw up all over her living room.

She fished out obvious keepers—photo albums and books—from the sea of could-be-trash items. After putting them in a nearby cabinet, she reached for one of the mystery boxes. The first box contained meticulously labeled and annotated hard-copy research about sea turtles from a paper she wrote in graduate school. It seemed wasteful to her now, all that paper covered with information she no longer needed. Maybe she kept it in the hope she'd need to refer to it again someday. This time she dumped it all into the recycling bin and opened another box.

Inside the second box were Brooke's good intentions: a list of people to whom she owed thank-you notes, the actual cards she bought to write them on, unsent tokens of gratitude, and photographs in an interlaced stack meant to be given to the smiling friends and family members in the pictures. This box oozed guilt. Brooke cringed as she read her overdue thank-you to-do list, embarrassed to see almost all the notes were related to events and gifts from more than a year ago, some even as old as three years. Her mom would be ashamed of her poor habits, but Brooke wasn't going to expect to change by hanging onto the list for another year or two. She had to accept that she just didn't write thank-you notes, which was much easier for her to do now that the week's events had propelled her into a more detached perspective. None of this would matter after she was gone. Who really cared now about any of Diane's unwritten thank-you notes?

But the pictures were more difficult to dismiss. She shuffled through snapshots of places, people, and events. Each photo made her smile, made her yearn—a dinner party with old neighbors, a sunset beach photo with Drew silhouetted against a blazing crimson sky, an assortment of candid moments in her life with Caldwell.

Resting on the bottom of the box was a Tiffany silver frame with an eight-by-ten photo of Caldwell, his parents, and his paternal grandmother, "Gam," his favorite grandparent. The photo was taken at Gam's eightieth birthday party. Gam taught Caldwell to play backgammon when he was six. He called the game Gam, thus the nickname. They played for hours whenever they were together. Gam could bake desserts that rivaled the finest bakeries in the country. Brooke loved her chocolate éclair cake most of all. And Gam loved Brooke most of all of Caldwell's girlfriends, as she told Brooke on several occasions, usually in front of Caldwell, to be sure he knew what he had.

In the photo, dimpled Caldwell stood between his dad and Gam, smiling at Brooke with his shaggy hair curled around his face. With gleeful expressions, his parents were looking to the right of the camera. Gam grinned without showing teeth. Her apple cheeks and shining eyes belied her age. She was looking up at Caldwell. Brooke framed the picture for Gam because she knew how much Gam adored Caldwell and would want a photo to remember that night, but Gam died suddenly only a few months after her birthday. Brooke didn't send the picture in time.

Brooke wanted to keep this picture, but she didn't need it on display. It was a harsh reminder not only of her lost relationship with Caldwell but also of her inability to express gratitude in a timely manner. These were people who almost became her family, but she didn't belong with them anymore. She took a long last look and, just as she was about to put the picture away, she noticed something attached to Gam's dress.

There is a split second between not knowing and knowing. Like the instant new parents find out their child is a boy or girl. The instant someone is diagnosed with cancer. The instant Drew told Brooke that Diane was dead. The instant Brooke heard that Diane was pregnant.

As short as it is and as long as it might feel, an instant can change everything.

In the photo she held dear, in a split second that sent waves of betrayal shuddering from her stomach to her heart, Brooke recognized what was pinned on Gam's dress. She saw it now as clearly as she'd seen it sparkling in its mahogany box. And the instant Brooke knew—she couldn't go back to not knowing.

It was the butterfly brooch.

It was Caldwell's family heirloom. Caldwell gave the brooch to Diane.

How did that happen? Were they seeing each other?

The picture frame smacked against the floor, making a single metallic bang like a gunshot. Brooke ran to the bathroom and fell to her knees. Gripping the toilet bowl, she dry-heaved. Bile stung her throat. Her eyes watered.

Caldwell was in Anders the weekend of Diane's murder. Brooke saw him at the marina that Saturday morning.

Was he the father of Diane's unborn child?

CHAPTER

47

After a belly full of dinner with Paul and a stop at the station, Drew sat in the quiet of his house. He checked his phone again for any message from Brooke, but she hadn't responded. Sinking into the couch cushions, he flipped through television channels until he stopped on an eleven o'clock news report.

The usual local crimes and tragedies led the news, including an update on the Turtle Lady Murder. A video clip showed Joe Willis emerging from the county courthouse, his arm shielding his face from the cameras. The anchor reported blandly that Mr. Willis made his first appearance in court with his attorney. Bail was set by the judge and posted by Mr. Willis late that afternoon. A grainy photo of Oliver Tack filled the screen, his name in bold below his grim expression, while the anchor relayed that he was a suspect still on the loose and urged viewers to call the number on the screen with any information about him.

Drew called Sampson to confirm security for Joe Willis. His primary witness needed protection until a future trial date.

"I'm on it, Detective," said Sampson amid sounds of rustling notebook pages and scribble. "We had one patrol car outside his house for his family, but I added a second one to guard him around the clock, at least until we find Oliver."

"Good," said Drew. "I told the chief about prints lifted from a bunch of beer cans I found near North End Beach. The crime lab matched most of them to Oliver through the FBI database. Turns out, Oliver's prints were on file from a criminal background check required for port employees who need a Transportation Worker ID Card. So, at least we have proof he was there. None of the prints matched Joe's. I assigned Walt to stake out North End overnight in case Oliver comes back. Other than that, I've got nothing else on him. You?"

"A few tip-line calls that turned out to be dead ends. I wasn't going to bother you about it unless we found something useful. Funny thing, though, evidently there's a guy named Lawrence Bell with a similar build to Oliver. Two callers mistook Lawrence for Oliver. We didn't find a connection between them other than their shared uncommon features, but I made a note of it anyway."

"Well, Oliver's face is being broadcast all over the place so somebody's bound to see something. He didn't just vanish."

"Let's hope so, Detective."

"Keep me posted," said Drew.

Dropping his head back onto the couch, he stared at the ceiling, took a deep breath. Any rest would be hard fought with the pressure of an open manhunt on his shoulders. And beneath that pressure, in the beating of his heart and at the forefront of his mind, a dull hunger-ache came with every thought of Brooke.

He couldn't find Oliver, but he could find Brooke. And he better find her fast, before he lost her again and for good this time. Paul was right. Drew felt lucky to have another chance. He had to stop wasting it.

A commercial blared from the television. Drew quickly turned it off and grabbed his phone, wallet, and keys. He nearly leaped out of the front door and down two steps at a time to his driveway before he looked up in haste to see Brooke standing by her car across the street.

His momentum rushed dizzily to his head when he froze to look at her: Brooke with a loose braid across her shoulder, casual jeans fitting her perfectly, and a wry smile that always made her seem amused by him.

But something was wrong. Her smile twisted into a pained expression.

"Where are you going?" she asked in a tight voice.

"To find you," he said.

"You are?" Shocked and relieved by his answer, she ran across the street and hugged him. Holding onto him, her arms wrapped around his chest, she squeezed him to her, engulfed by his familiar embrace. She sobbed.

"What's wrong?" He stroked her head and nuzzled his chin and lips against her soft hair, but she kept crying. "Shhh, it's okay." Rocking her slightly while hugging her close, he tried to calm her down.

It took a minute for Brooke to catch her breath and loosen her grip on Drew. She'd never cried that hard around him, or *on* him. Drying her eyes, she managed to say, "Diane was seeing Caldwell." Even as the words fell out of her mouth, they didn't make sense to her. Those two names didn't belong together that way.

"What?" Drew's astonished eyes searched hers.

"I went to her funeral this morning and—" Brooke's sentence broke into more distraught tears, but she wiped them off fast.

"Come inside." Drew took her hand and led her into his house. Grabbing two bottles of beer from the fridge, he handed one to Brooke and sat with her on the couch. "Now, back up, and tell me what the hell is going on."

Brooke spilled the whole story—from the day Diane lent her the brooch, to the funeral when Brooke discovered it wasn't Diane's family heirloom, to the framed photo—the missing link.

Showing the brooch and photo to Drew, then shoving them back into her bag, Brooke leaned against his shoulder. "Why would she do it? I'm so hurt and *angry,* I'm almost glad she's gone." She sniffled. "I know that's awful to say, but I don't care. All this time, I thought she was my friend. I thought I knew her. But she isn't who I thought she was at all. I wish I could just ask her why."

"Listen, Brooke." Drew paused for a second, unsure whether to continue. "There's something you should know about Diane."

Sitting up to face him, Brooke braced herself for what was sure to be more bad news. "Okay. What?"

He hesitated.

"Drew, what? Just tell me."

"Diane hated you before she ever met you." Drew shook his head; he didn't like to hear himself say it out loud.

Brooke drank the last of her beer and stared down into the top of the empty bottle in her lap. "Go on," she said without looking up.

"Before you moved here, when I was dating her, she was so jealous of you and suspicious of our friendship. It drove her crazy that I talked about you and that we called and texted each other. She wanted me to block your number on my phone, but I wouldn't do it. I told her I'd never abandon you like that because I've known you almost my entire life and I'd only known her for a few months. That really pissed her off. She flew into a rage and called you all kinds of names."

Tightening her grip on her beer bottle neck, Brooke thought about hurling it against the wall.

As though he could read her mind, Drew reached for the bottle, placed it on the table, and took Brooke's hand in his. "I didn't want you to know, but our biggest fights were about you. I defended you and our friendship. I refused to cut you out of my life, and she couldn't stand it. I mean, we had a lot of differences, but you're probably the main reason we broke up."

Brooke let go of his hand. "But then you kept seeing her off and on after that, right? Even after I moved here and thought she was my friend? Were you still defending me while you were sleeping with her?"

"No—well, yes and no." Drew stood up to get more beer from the fridge. "Yes, I slept with her a few times after that, but it was just a physical thing, and she completely changed her opinion of you. I thought you two were friends. She genuinely seemed to like you."

He handed Brooke another bottle. They sat apart on the couch and watched each other with eyes full of questions.

"So, she pretended to be my friend to keep you closer? When she couldn't have you, she moved on to Caldwell to get, what, some kind of revenge?"

"I don't think so. I have no idea what was going on with Caldwell, but with me, she wasn't plotting against you, she was just really . . . insecure. See, I called her Brooke by mistake. Not just once, but several times. And the last time, it was while we were having sex. That's when she finally ended our casual one-night thing and said she never wanted to see me again."

Brooke almost spit out her beer. "Well, no wonder." Taking a deep breath, she pondered the absurdity of it all. "How could you keep all that from me? How could she? I was right in the middle of your mess with her, and I didn't have a clue."

"She wanted to tell you about us, but I talked her out of it. I didn't want you to think I loved her."

"Why?"

"Because"—Drew shrugged— "I love *you*."

Brooke blinked, as though she mistrusted her own ears. "You do?"

"Always have, since the first day we met."

"But you never choose me."

"Huh?"

"All our lives, I watched you chase other women. I listened to you tell me how crazy you were about this or that girl, saw you when you claimed to love someone, the things you did and said and the way you acted. I think about how you are with me, and you don't act like that, like you've loved me all along." She shook her head. "Even those few times we made out in the past, when I thought you wanted me most, there always seemed to be another woman in the way. I wasn't enough. It just doesn't add up. You've treated me like a friend, so I accepted that's all I am."

"Have you been keeping track?"

"Well, sort of." Brooke took a drink.

"I'll save you the trouble. You can't study me to figure me out. I'm not predictable, and I'm definitely not perfect. Don't be so analytical about everything. Stop thinking so much and start feeling."

"I can't stop thinking. I'm a scientist. That's like asking me not to breathe."

"Listen to what I'm telling you, Brooke." Moving closer to her on the couch, he covered her hand with his. "It's finally you and me in the same place with everything ahead of us. Stop testing me, stop questioning me. You know me better than anyone else. And I know you." His fingers interlaced with hers while his eyes read the planes of her face. When their eyes met, he gazed at her. "You're pure beauty—inside and out—brilliant and kind. You don't see how you are, do you? But I do. I saw you worry over your choices even while you accomplished your dreams. I saw you leave and find your way home. Your friendship saved me over and over. You're my best friend. I don't just love you; I'm *in love* with you. I've been in love with you since we were kids. I've just been too scared or stupid to risk telling you. I only want *you*."

Squeezing his hand, feeling the warmth of their interlaced fingers, Brooke held his stare. "You sit there at the worst possible time and tell me what I've wanted to hear from you my whole life?"

"I know," said Drew. "My timing sucks, and I'm sorry, but right now I don't want to know what you think. I want to know what you *feel*."

Brooke sighed and dropped her eyes to her lap. "I guess, I'm overwhelmed." She turned her head to look at Drew. "There's so much—"

His lips were on hers before she could finish. He cupped her face in his hands, palms pressed lightly against her jawbone, and held her still. Kissed her softly. Their eyes closed.

"How did that feel?" he asked with their foreheads bowed together.

"So good," she said, eyes still closed.

"And this?" He lifted her chin and kissed her again and again. Only their lips moved. Sliding one hand up the nape of her neck, he spread his fingers into her hair and cradled her head like an apple, parting her lips with his tongue.

She opened her mouth to his, wrapping her arms around him. Their tongues tangled. Soft hums vibrated through their intense kisses.

When they paused—mouths open, breath heavy—Drew pulled her body against his and they held each other in a long hug, breathing together. His cheek brushed hers when he asked, with his lips to her ear, "How did *that* feel?"

"Like . . . love," she said, and he squeezed her tighter, so tightly she smiled from the pure joy of being hugged by him. She felt opened, set free. Planting a slow kiss on his cheek, she whispered in his ear, "I love you, Drew Young. You're the love of my life."

And his strong arms enveloped her, his mouth found hers while she grabbed him, kissed him, pulled him on top of her body. Desire bolted through them.

Rapt with heartfelt love, they gasped between fiery kisses.

At some point they let go enough for their eyes to meet, smiling the way new lovers do.

Revealed.

Drew rose from the couch and turned off the lights. Taking Brooke's hand, he led her to his bedroom. Moonlight through the window blinds cast their shadows across the floor. He undressed, reached for her. They kissed with passion and tenderness and need. He peeled off her clothes while trailing kisses along her bare skin and firm breasts, sliding his fingertips down her stomach, between her legs. Chills drifted across her body like sheets of wind. Exploring with hands and mouths, they followed each other's pleasure sounds and touches. She buried her fingers in his hair while he knelt to taste her.

Naked under the covers, his body over hers, eyes locked, then lips, he spread her legs, thrusting into her wetness. She wrapped her whole self around him, guiding him, wanting him, holding him deep inside. Connected skin to skin and soul to soul, the sensation was like swimming in the ocean at night. Waves rolled through them—waves they couldn't see in advance—lifted and dropped them. She clung to him. Their moans of ecstasy intensified their hungry kisses and quickened their aroused bodies until their unleashed desire erupted into pure explosive bliss.

Brooke kept her eyes shut and floated, swayed, tumbled in thrilling tingles that shuddered to her toes. And she couldn't recall the time or day or any of her worries because everything before *I love you* fell away from her memory to make room for every erotic second after.

CHAPTER

48

In the middle of the night, Brooke woke to the sound of a phone ringing from the other room. She'd fallen asleep on Drew, her head on his chest, her right leg draped over his. She could hear his heart beating. The sheets half covered them. Drew's arm across her back held her against him. She drifted back to sleep.

The phone rang again. It was Drew's. This time he rustled in the sheets and pulled Brooke closer in a full bear hug, waking her slightly, enough to make her laugh a little while she tried to maneuver to hug him back with his strong arms holding her down. They wrestled and tickled each other until they were kissing again in a sweet, friends-turned-lovers embrace. How well they knew each other already. Nothing was holding them back.

"Why did it take us so long to get here?" Brooke asked between kisses.

"Don't know, but we finally made it." Propping himself up on one elbow, Drew looked at her, smitten. "And can I just say—you're good in bed. I mean, *really* good."

Brooke gave him a playful smile. "Well, don't sound so surprised." She traced his jawline with her fingertips. "I love sex most with someone I love."

"Mm, lucky me." He kissed her again, kissed her lips and her cheeks and started down her neck. Excitement surged through her.

"Oh my . . . lucky me, too." She felt Drew smile against her skin while he kept kissing.

For the third time, Drew's phone rang. He stopped mid kissing-spree and groaned. "I better get that. Three times in a row is usually bad news."

"Don't go." Brooke tousled his hair and pouted while he unwound himself from her grasp.

He reluctantly left the bed, pulled on his pants, and reached his phone to see Sampson's name on the screen. "This is Drew."

"Detective, where are you? I've been calling for the past half hour!"

"At home." Drew could hear voices yelling in the background through the phone. "What's going on?"

"I'm so sorry, Detective. I don't know what happened." Sampson said over blaring sirens. "I'm at Dylan Creek Marina. You have to get over here. Joe Willis"—Sampson struggled to catch his panicked breath— "he's dead."

"Oh, shit." Drew deflated, then seethed. "Dammit!" He wanted to kick something. He clenched his fist. "I'm on my way."

When he went back to the bedroom, he walked with heavy steps, steadied himself on the side of the bed, and told Brooke. She put her hand on his hand and looked out at the darkness through the window. She didn't know what to say.

"I have to go," said Drew. "You can stay if you want."

"No. I better go, too, but thanks." She leaned over the side of the bed to grab her clothes from the floor. "I'll try to get more sleep at my place. Seems like today might be a long one."

"No kidding." Drew put on his shirt. "Do you want coffee?"

Brooke didn't answer. When Drew looked over at her, she was holding up a string bikini bottom.

"Whose is this?" asked Brooke with the bikini bottom hanging from where she pinched it between her thumb and index finger.

Drew hesitated when he saw the expression on Brooke's face—a conflicted mix of incredulous amusement and utter defeat—which made him fear they'd lose everything they started that night. "Oh, um, that must be Bella's—you know—that local TV news reporter. She stayed with me a couple of weekends ago. It was nothing. A two-night stand. Really *not* my type."

"You mean, that reporter woman I always see on breaking news?"

Drew nodded sheepishly.

"*She* stayed with you for the *weekend*? I guess she must've been staying with you to not notice she was *missing* her *bikini bottom*. Ugh! I feel like such an idiot!" Brooke tossed the bikini bottom at the trash can in the corner and climbed out of bed, her long shirt covering her bare body below the waist. She looked at the floor for her clothes, didn't look at Drew. "Haven't I had enough already? This is exactly what I was saying last night." She found and shimmied into her underwear and stepped into her jeans. "There's always some other woman. I mean, it's like a different woman every week. Here I am thinking we're in love when I might just be the woman of this week."

"That's not fair, Brooke. You know that's not true because it isn't the same with you. None of those other women mean anything compared to you. I'm in love with you and only want to be with you."

She zipped up her jeans. "How am I supposed to believe that when another woman's bikini bottom is still in your bedroom?"

"Because I'm finally saying it. Do you want to know why I act differently with you? It's because I've never loved any other woman in my life the way I love *you*. You just have to take a risk and believe I'm telling you the truth."

"But your words—I can't believe just your words. I'm a scientist. I need proof. Evidence. That's what I believe in. You know what that is, *Detective*. So, if you're really in love with me like you say you are . . . then *act* like it. Show me with your actions." She released a tired sigh. "I need to go."

When she turned to leave the room, Drew reached for her hand. Their fingertips clasped. She looked at their hands and then at his face before she let go. Grabbing her bag from the chair, she walked out.

Drew watched her but didn't follow. He couldn't think of anything else to say—or *do*—that would change her mind. Standing still in the middle of his bedroom, he remembered Brooke's soft skin on his, her hair woven between his fingers while they kissed. But just now her eyes were dark with doubt and pain, anguished by the realization he could hurt her, and disappointed he already did.

CHAPTER

49

Tethered to the Dylan Creek Marina dock, *Bonnie* glowed like a ghost ship in the spotlights of news crews and emergency responders. Drew hurried into the fray, where Sampson attached himself like a barnacle to Drew's side, notebook out, and said, "It could be suicide."

Drew scowled at him; of course, Sampson would hope it was suicide, so he wouldn't be held responsible for losing track of their key witness long enough for him to be killed. Drew conveyed with his silence that he doubted the suicide theory, although part of him also wished for it to be true. Selfishly, suicide would be much easier to explain to the chief. On the other hand, suicide would be much more difficult to explain to Joe's family. Joe seemed too brash and confident to be suicidal. But Drew wasn't very good at reading people.

Paul met them on board *Bonnie*, where he ushered Drew to the gruesome catch of the day: Joe Willis drowned in his own shrimp net. His body, sprawled flat on the deck under a web of lines, had been hoisted from the sea and lowered to rest, dead on arrival.

"By the time he was discovered, he was long gone," said Paul. "There wasn't anything anyone could do."

"Who found him?" asked Drew.

"Riley did, about an hour ago." Paul pointed to where Riley sat on a dock bench, his head buried in his hands. "When he got to the boat, the nets were in the water, which he said isn't normal when the boat's docked, so he pulled them in and found Joe. He was probably already dead, but Riley was attempting CPR when paramedics arrived and took over. I'm pretty sure we were all too late, but we'll see what the autopsy shows."

Drew nodded while he listened. He noticed Sampson, quiet and uncomfortable, standing still and waiting. "How did this happen?" Drew asked Sampson. "Where was his security?"

Shifting his weight, Sampson flipped his notebook pages, then adjusted his glasses. "The officers escorted Joe to the boat. He said he was going to help Riley prepare for a shrimping trip but wouldn't be going on the trip because of, well, his situation and being out on bail. They were waiting in their patrol car just up in the parking lot and didn't see anyone come or go except Riley, who was supposed to be here to meet Joe."

"Riley won't do us any good at this point." Drew shook his head. "This is just carelessness. Joe was the only witness I had, and we couldn't protect him. Just one person, and we couldn't do it."

Sampson frowned and looked down at his feet. He had been in charge of security for Joe, but he knew this failure would ultimately fall on Drew.

Paul said, "I hear you, Young, but you did everything you could. The guy decided to come out here to the docks. He knew the risk."

"Or he came out here on purpose to kill himself," added Sampson.

"It ain't suicide," the coroner piped in from behind them.

"Jesus, Terry!" said Drew. "You keep sneaking up on me."

She chuckled, smirked, then got back to business. "I looked at him already. There's blunt force trauma to the head. No way he could do that to himself and still manage to climb in the nets and lower himself overboard. This is homicide. Probably someone professional—you know—a hit."

"Why do you say that?" asked Drew, alarmed.

"Well, boys, I've seen a lot of dead bodies, and I just know how to read 'em. An unplanned, amateur murder done in haste is usually messy, lots of evidence to give away the killer—blood, defense wounds, that sort of thing. But this one, I can't find anything other than the head wound. The water washed away a lot of other stuff, and there isn't a murder weapon or any blood on deck. Someone planned this and made sure to clean up and dispose of the body so it would be found . . . as a warning. Hit men usually have a message to send."

"A message to whom?" asked Sampson, his eyes wide behind his glasses.

"To anyone else they see as a threat or a snitch. Anyone who might get in the way of what they're trying to do."

"How do you even know that?" asked Drew.

"I was a medical examiner in Jersey before I moved down here." Terry pursed her lips and made bug eyes. "Saw some brutal stuff up there, the mob and all that, makes this one look merciful. Guys killed up there, they knew it was coming. And sometimes we only found parts. You get me?"

"Shit." Paul looked at Terry with new respect.

Drew's mind was blown by the idea that there'd been a professional hit at Dylan Creek Marina, of all places. Somehow it was linked to his investigation. This was much bigger than he originally thought. Drew looked at Paul with a plea in his eyes, hoping his firefighting friend would understand. "This is like wildfire. We don't know where it's headed next, and it's far from contained."

A few hours later, Drew parked in the driveway of the Willis residence. Woods surrounded the modest one-story brick house. A shutter leaned against the wall below the window it once framed, where a clean rectangular patch remained in sharp contrast to the rest of the dirt-stained brick. The harsh sun showed the worst in the house and yard—chipped shingles, rotted trim, and patches of grass amid rampant weeds.

He rang the doorbell and heard immediate commotion inside. Low voices argued. A door shut hard. Then Nadine Willis appeared and pushed the screen door on its whining hinges to let Drew in.

She didn't say a word, just closed the door behind Drew and stood there in the dim hallway, her eyes downcast to the floor.

Drew spoke first. "I want to offer my deepest—"

"Don't. I don't want to hear it." Nadine, frozen in place, looked to the ceiling then the walls, searching for anything to see other than Drew's face. She tried to will away all the kind words and well-meaning gestures and pity. Hearing a rush of sound from down the hall, she saw the watchful eyes of Mac and Cecilia peeking through the cracked-open bedroom door. The knit between her eyes softened at the sight of them.

Drew followed her gaze to the kids. He was suddenly thirteen again, hearing the serious voices of Mullinax and his mom rumble up through his bedroom floor, the whine of each step interrupted by his mom's mournful sniffle when she came upstairs to tell him that his dad was dead. Looking at the small faces of Mac and Cecilia, he wondered what they would remember most from this terrible, life-altering day.

He tried again. "I'm so sorry—"

"Don't!" She slammed her palm against the wall. The kids shut the door fast. "Some other officers already told me what happened. Nothing you say will make it any better."

Drew bowed his head and stood statue-still, waiting to see what Nadine would do next.

When she realized he wasn't spewing platitudes or making a hasty departure, she said, "Do you know they already asked me about life insurance? Some nerve, those people, telling me it was in place for something like this, that I should be grateful. But they don't get it, what that life insurance means to me." She clamped her lips on her last words to hold back tears.

Drew tried to offer some comfort. "It means you can provide for your children, and you won't have to worry about money."

"No." She shook her head. "It means my husband is *dead*." She clenched her fists and did not cry.

Drew put his hand on her arm, but she shrugged it away.

Lifting her chin, she shook off sorrow. "Anyway, I asked you to come over because I found something in our closet with the life insurance policy." She reached into the pocket of her worn cardigan sweater. "This."

She handed Drew a slightly concave hard object in a plastic bag, rough-textured and angular, about the size of a salad plate, with a handwritten note that read:

Dear Nadine,

If you have this note, I'm already gone or dead. Give this shell to Detective Young at Anders Isle PD and tell him it has Oliver's fingerprints on it. Tell him I reckon there's more to the story than I know, but I already messed things up enough for our family. That's why I have to go now, or I'll put you and the kids in more danger. I'm so sorry. Give my love to Mac and CeeCee and tell them I'm so proud of them. I did all this because I love you.

Joe

Drew looked up and met Nadine's sad eyes. They both knew this was a major clue as to why Joe would risk a trip to the marina in the middle of the night. He wasn't there to help Riley prepare for a trip. He didn't intend to go home afterward. He went there to board his boat and escape.

Joe's note confirmed the uneasy feeling Drew had been fighting from the start about Oliver being a killer. Something was off. Why would Oliver, a seasoned pro who kept to himself, resort to murder to protect *this* poaching scheme? Diane interrupted what seemed to be just another routine night of poaching for Oliver. He could have simply scared her, knocked her out, taken the turtle, and left her without any proof of a crime. But this loggerhead poaching was clearly more valuable—valuable enough for Oliver to kill to keep it quiet. Unless—Drew thought of the shelter and beer cans he found in the forest—Oliver had been watching Diane, stalking her. Maybe his attack was personal, a crime of opportunity based on obsession?

Drew thanked Nadine and walked briskly to his car, convinced that Oliver—whether blinded by money or mania—had gone too far, triggering the retaliation of a busted poaching ring that successfully silenced Joe and would probably stop at nothing to do the same to Oliver.

One thought kept pounding through Drew's head with each step: *What the hell am I missing?*

CHAPTER

50

Now that billable hours seemed irrelevant to his job security, Caldwell made it his singular mission to find some concrete information about Project Hurricane. He had called Ben Feldman again yesterday afternoon, but Ben wouldn't take his call, which made Caldwell even more suspicious.

Staying up most of the night, he carefully searched the firm's document database from home on his work laptop. At dawn, he went to his office to use his desktop computer to access the firm's case management system available only to associates and partners *inside* the firm's walls. After hours and hours of sifting through electronic documents and files, he only found the same password-protected Project Hurricane link in the database. He wouldn't try to guess the password. For all he knew, the system might warn Percival when an incorrect password was entered. Caldwell wouldn't take that chance. He wanted to keep Percival blissfully unaware of his search to preserve any evidence that might be out there about the mysterious project. Documents had a way of disappearing to prevent them from being discovered.

By lunchtime, he had nothing new on Project Hurricane—not a memo, not a contract, not even an email. Based on its name, it must involve property in the Carolinas. But, as lead associate for Art's deals in the Carolinas, why was he shut out of this one?

His office door remained closed all morning, much like the day before. In fact, he hadn't spoken to anyone on his floor other than his legal assistant since Tuesday. He stood up and stretched, took a step toward the floor-to-ceiling window forming one wall of his office, and gazed out at an eerie view of the tops of neighboring skyscrapers poking through an expansive layer of low-lying clouds. From his window, the world looked surreal, silent, and foggy, like a fantasy land or a movie depiction of heaven.

Pressing his forehead to the cold window glass, he flattened his palms against it, closing his eyes.

When his desk phone rang, he ignored it, just like the other calls that morning. He didn't even open his eyes.

For a few minutes, he leaned into the window, his caffeine-fueled energy squashed by the weight of exhaustion. He imagined himself free, floating over clouds and building tops, breathing fresh air, out there. What else was out there for him? For such a long time, for as long as he could remember, he dreamed of being exactly where he stood right now, in his own office on top of the world, with high-powered lawyers—his colleagues, his mentors, the best of the best—in offices lining the hall of his floor. He had everything he'd ever wanted. But did *he* want it? Or was he groomed, raised, to believe he *should* want it? Did he ever consider another option, another career, another final destination? He couldn't remember a time when he'd searched his own soul. And that, he realized, was his greatest failure. He failed to know himself. He made the ultimate philosophical mistake: he didn't examine his own life. And now, encircled by clouds of doubt about his ability, his needs, and his purpose, he felt as lost—as absent, though existing—as the cloud hidden bottom halves of the surrounding buildings.

He exhaled slowly.

A timid knock on his office door startled him, even with its softness. He opened his eyes, thinking he might've drifted to sleep for a few seconds while propped against the window.

Usually, his closed door meant no interruptions, but for every rule there was an exception. His legal assistant knew to knock if something needed urgent attention.

Settling into his desk chair, he cleared his throat. "Come in."

His assistant cracked the door open just enough for her face. "I have mail for you. It looks important." When she saw him seated expectantly at his desk and not on the phone, she slipped into his office and handed him a slick courier package marked *Confidential. Eyes Only.*

"Thank you," he said.

She nodded and left quickly, closing the door behind her.

Caldwell was aware of secret document classification. He didn't know a lot about it, but he knew *Eyes Only* meant the document was only to be seen by a specific reader. The package didn't have a return address.

Opening it, he found a business envelope addressed to him and again marked *Eyes Only* with a tamper-evident flap. The intact flap proved it hadn't been opened before arriving in his hands.

He tore the flap and pulled out four sheets of paper. Taped to the front page, a small note read: *I don't know what this project is about, but if it puts Art in jail, better late than never. The woman in the enclosed article is my former co-worker and a dear friend. Please burn this note and don't contact me again. —Ben*

The first paper showed confirmation of a wire transfer of funds from one numbered bank account to another, neither of which Caldwell recognized. The transfer took place nearly two years earlier for the hefty sum of fifty million dollars. Caldwell felt unsettled by this obscure secret financial transaction. But aside from his sense of invading someone's privacy, he didn't learn anything new from the series of numbers on the page.

He flipped to the second paper, which was a plat, a map of real estate, drawn to scale, showing the divisions, dimensions, and location of a large piece of land. Sometimes a plat depicted a proposed site for construction. Caldwell knew exactly how to read it, how to extract a whole picture of the land's purpose from the numbers and annotations. This plat showed clusters of dozens of lots divided and subdivided around oblong golf course fairways. The massive piece of property, bound along its east and north sides by the Atlantic Ocean, appeared to be the rough draft for a resort. Although the notes were sparse, the location was clear to Caldwell from the brief legal description beneath the title: Project Hurricane.

The final two pages—a printed copy of a newspaper article from two years earlier in the *Boston Globe*—began with the headline: "Charges Dropped Against Real Estate Tycoon Accused of Sexual Assault." The article explained how a former employee of Ogletree Acquisitions recanted her accusation that Art Ogletree forced himself on her after none of the DNA evidence matched Ogletree's voluntary DNA sample obtained by police. Although the woman also claimed Ogletree exposed himself to her in her office one night, she declined to pursue further action. Ogletree denied the allegations, insisting the woman fabricated the claims to retaliate for being fired based on poor work performance and win a large monetary settlement. Ogletree was cleared of all charges.

Shaking his head in disbelief, Caldwell slid the papers into the envelope, tucked it under his arm, grabbed his personal items, and made a swift exit from his office with only a cursory wave at his legal assistant. When he reached the relative privacy of his car, he called Bud Gibson, his college fraternity brother, and the only real estate broker he trusted in Anders Isle.

Bud answered, "Howdy, Mad Dog. I tell you what, that golf cart tour of Taylor Island is still the highlight of my week." He spoke as though they were just in mid-conversation.

"Glad to hear it, Gibb." The nickname Gibb evolved in college from Bud's last name and his resemblance at that time to Barry Gibb of the Bee Gees.

"So, how's it going?" asked Bud.

"I need a big favor."

"I'm your man. What can I do?"

"A title search for a piece of property in your county. I have a plat and legal description, but I can't send them by email or text. Highly confidential. Nobody can know about it. Meet me at your office," said Caldwell, wary of sharing too much over the phone.

"Are you in town?"

"Not yet," said Caldwell. "I'm on my way. I have to grab some clothes before I hit the road. Should get there around six."

"No problem. I'll be here."

"Thanks. I owe you one," said Caldwell.

"Bullshit. You put me on a boat with Linwood Kingston. This just makes us even."

After Caldwell hung up, he felt an instant pang of nervous regret. Should he show this to anyone else? Did he really want to know more about Project Hurricane?

Next, he called Brooke. She didn't respond to his message about dinner that night. The call went to voice mail this time too. He invited her again to meet him for dinner at eight o'clock at School and asked her to call or text to let him know if she'd be there.

There was something he needed to tell her—in person.

CHAPTER

51

At four o'clock Thursday afternoon on Front Beach, the staff from Anders Aquarium prepared for a scheduled sea turtle release. Two lucky rehabilitated female loggerheads were ready to return to the ocean. A mass of onlookers four layers deep lined ropes forming a V-shaped runway to the water. The event attracted sea turtle lovers from the greater Anders area, many of whom gathered on Front Beach an hour in advance to claim the best viewing spots. Kids wobbled on parents' shoulders and people readied phone cameras. It was a sight to behold. Anticipation thickened the crowd, all of whom were there to witness the beauty of loggerheads in good health, to experience the exhilaration of their recognition of home, to see their flippers paddle and bellies slide into foaming waves.

Brooke drove the aquarium's truck along a tire-flattened beach access path, then backed it up until the tailgate reached the entrance to the sandy runway. Three staff members rode in the flatbed beside two sea turtles in giant plastic tubs. Volunteers in bright-yellow turtle hospital T-shirts managed the watching crowd. It took four staff members to lift and carry the two huge adult loggerheads to the runway between the ropes, where they gently placed the turtles on the sand amid gasps of awe and squeals of delight. Those farther back in the crowd rose on tiptoes to catch a glimpse or held cameras high overhead to snap blind photos. Inside the ropes, a photographer from the local paper tracked the turtles' movements with shutter clicks.

And what a moment it was when the loggerheads lifted their scaled faces and breathed in familiar salt-laced ocean air. One of them opened and shut her beaked mouth, pushed up on her front flippers, and posed. The other dug her flippers into the sand and began a hasty, cartoonish belly-crawl, making people laugh. Brooke and the volunteers nudged the turtles, redirected them as needed, and cheered with the crowd when each swam into the waves. Agile in the water, flippers propelling them with ease, the loggerheads popped their heads above the surface beyond the breakers as if to bid farewell to their caregivers on land. A final look back or, perhaps, forward. Brooke loved that part the most, the bittersweet glimpse of each turtle once again free in the wild wonderland of ocean, once again home.

When the turtles were out of sight, Brooke turned to leave and saw Drew walking toward her from the boardwalk. He smiled the instant their eyes met. *Damn, he's so good-looking. Those blue eyes know me too well.* With his collared shirt tucked into long pants and his shoes on, he wasn't dressed for the beach. A backpack hung from one shoulder. While he strolled across the sand, Brooke's mind flashed to his strong hands gripping her hips, his mouth on her skin. Her quickening heartbeat was either excitement or dread. Trying to relax, she took a deep breath and smiled at him.

They hadn't spoken since their awkward parting in the early morning hours. Not a call or text or email or anything. This was their first face-to-face after having sex. It was all new territory for them as friends or lovers or whatever they were now. Brooke struggled all day with the unknown impact of crossing that line. It was a delicate dance—one she never did before—and one she couldn't do alone. She was unsure after the bikini bottom incident, and after all she'd learned about him and Diane, but she was happy to see him now.

When he reached her, he hugged her like usual. But this time he held on a little longer. She was the first to let go.

"Hi," he said, a bit flirtatious. "Gorgeous day you have here for a turtle release. I thought it was supposed to rain."

"I know, it seemed like it would, but the clouds burned off around noon and the sun's been out since then." Brooke couldn't stand talking about the weather, especially with friends.

"I heard it's supposed to be sunny all weekend."

"That'll be nice." Brooke crossed her arms, cocked her head at him, and squinted in the sun. "Are we really just going to talk about the weather like strangers in an elevator?"

"No, I don't want to talk about the weather." Drew hesitated and raked his hair off his face. "Listen, I didn't call or write today because I wanted to see you in person. You said words aren't enough, you need action, so here I am."

"Here you are."

"I meant everything I said last night."

Brooke could see he was serious. "Thanks," she said softly, "Me, too." Sighing, she looked down at a sun-bleached oyster shell, wedged it into the sand with her toe. "I think I overreacted about the bikini bottom. I'm sorry."

Drew chuckled. "Hey, I'm sorry, too. I was so embarrassed about that. I don't even know what to say."

"Let's just not say anything else about it, okay?"

"Okay." Drew reached for her hand, and they walked with interlaced fingers toward the parking lot. "You know, I thought the world might've ended because we finally slept together. I started looking for zombies in the fog this morning."

Brooke laughed, relieved to be talking like friends again. "Zombies are *so* overrated." She teased, purposely avoiding the rest of his comment. Their night together seemed like a dream that might disappear from memory if she tried to put it into words. She wanted to remember every single second of it.

"I bet that's what people said about vampires, too, but look what happened. Zombies are in, I'm telling you."

"Yeah, but zombies will never have the same appeal as vampires because zombies aren't sexy," said Brooke. "Who wants to make out with a decomposing dude whose arm is falling off? That's just gross. And if his arm falls off, then another *part* could fall off, too. Right?" Brooke wrinkled her nose and shook her head. "Not sexy."

Drew laughed and squeezed her hand. "Good point." He smiled.

They stepped onto the boardwalk, where he slipped his backpack off his shoulder and unzipped it. "Well, all zombies aside, I have this for you." He reached into his backpack. "Close your eyes."

When she did, he put something smooth and light in her hands. She opened her eyes to see a sparkling silver sea turtle on a thin necklace chain. It was the first gift Drew ever gave her. "Oh, I love it!" Turning the tiny turtle in her fingers, she studied its details. "Thank you so much." She hugged Drew and kissed him lightly on the cheek.

"You're welcome. I thought of you when I saw it." He helped her put it on, then reached into the backpack again. "I'm sorry to have to ask you this, especially now, but I need you to look at something else, for the investigation. Maybe you can help."

"Of course. Happy to help."

From his pack Drew pulled the oddly shaped shell—the one Joe left for him—now in a clear plastic bag marked *Evidence*. "I'm hoping you know what this is."

She took the bagged shell from Drew. "It's a scute," she said without a doubt, but his expression made it clear she needed to translate her science language. "A scute is an external plate, like a scale, made of keratin. This is a piece of a loggerhead sea turtle carapace, its top shell, a *lateral* scute to be precise. Where did it come from?"

"It was with Joe Willis's life insurance policy at his house. His wife gave it to me this morning. Joe left a note saying Oliver's prints are on it, and our crime lab already confirmed it. I guess Joe thought he might not live to tell a jury himself."

Stunned, Brooke looked at the scute in her hands. If this was related to the investigation, it must be part of a carapace from one of the loggerheads taken from the island. "Why would he still have this—a piece of a poached loggerhead's shell? Wouldn't they sell the *whole* turtle on the black market?" Brooke shook her head. "Nothing about this poaching scheme makes sense to me based on what I know about the value of different sea turtle species."

"Oh, wait 'til you hear *this*: Joe told me he was getting paid forty thousand dollars for each loggerhead."

"For each one?" She asked with astonished eyes.

"I thought that sounded high."

"High? That's insane!" Her voice rose, tightened. "How much was Oliver making?"

"Joe didn't say, but it had to be more."

"So, you mean to tell me that Joe and Oliver together were paid—let's just round up—one hundred thousand dollars *per loggerhead*?"

"Probably about that much. Yes." Drew answered.

"And thirteen turtles—that we know of—were taken in the past three years, which adds up to more than one million dollars in total poaching fees."

Drew nodded. "When you put it that way, I see a definite motive for murder. I just didn't realize that amount of money was so unusual for poached animals."

"It sure is, especially for loggerheads." Brooke handed the shell back to Drew. "But I still wonder why they kept the shell. I don't understand where the money's coming from if the whole turtle isn't being sold on the market. Loggerhead meat isn't valuable enough to earn anywhere near that kind of money. Maybe this piece of shell came from the unlucky thirteenth turtle I found, and some of the turtles are still alive, shipped off to *very* wealthy collectors willing to pay a fortune for loggerheads. Marine turtle tourism brings in about three times more annual income than turtle products. Sea turtles are worth more alive than dead."

"Sorry, but Joe made it clear the turtles they poached are all dead. Obviously, something about loggerheads appeals to these buyers. We need to figure out what that is."

"Do you think Joe found out too much about the buyers, so Oliver killed him?"

"Maybe. Joe's note said he suspected there was more to the story, but he didn't know. I think he underestimated the danger of his situation, probably feared for his life. And for good reason. The coroner seemed convinced it was a hit. I looked at the body and crime scene and would have to agree. The boat deck was bleached clean, not a spot of blood, not a single fingerprint or footprint anywhere. Definitely a professional job. But it happened in Anders City, not my jurisdiction, so not mine to solve. We'll share what we can with the city police, because Joe was our witness, but I doubt they'll ever find his killer."

Brooke's mouth dropped open. She wondered if they should be worried for their own safety.

Drew continued, "And my guess is the people who killed Joe are after Oliver too. He's on the run for his life. Oliver brought Joe into the loop, and Joe busted up the whole poaching ring by turning himself in. But Oliver started this whole mess by killing Diane, making some serious enemies with some serious resources. We need to find Oliver before they do."

Brooke nodded, dumbfounded by all she heard.

Tucking the shell into his backpack, Drew said, "Thanks for your help."

"You're welcome." She swallowed, distracted by the aquarium staff pulling stakes out of the sand and loading them into the truck. "I really need to get back to the beach to help pack."

"Wait, what're you doing tonight? Let me take you to dinner." Drew's eyes shone expectantly, fixed on her, reassuring her. She felt like she was the only person in the world with him.

"I can't tonight. I already have plans . . . with Caldwell."

Drew's entire demeanor changed from laid back and friendly to tense and defensive. "Really? After everything you told me last night, you're going out with *him*?"

"It's not like that," Brooke shifted her weight and frowned. "He called a couple times and insisted we go to dinner. I ignored his calls and just texted him back that I'd meet him for drinks at School. I'm only doing it because I want to ask him in person about Diane. I need to hear it from him." She saw Drew roll his eyes. "What's that for?"

"Well, you know what I think of that son of a bitch. No way he's telling you the truth even if you ask him to his face. But . . ." Drew's expression brightened. Pepping up, he put his arm around her shoulder and lowered his voice. "I have an idea. Since you're meeting him anyway, if you want to know for sure about him and Diane—and frankly, help me tie up a loose end in the investigation—get a DNA sample from him. We'll find out if he's the father of Diane's baby. If so, then I'd just *love* to bring him in for questioning since he was in the area last weekend and might've seen Diane."

"Are you serious? I don't know how to do that sort of thing."

"You won't have to do it. I'll set it up with the bartender at School. He'll swipe one of Caldwell's drink glasses."

"Isn't that a little crazy? I'm already nervous just thinking about it."

"Do you want to know for sure or not?"

Brooke remembered the brooch and her devastation from the night before. "I want to know," she said, determined.

"Then all you have to do is meet Caldwell at School and make sure he has a drink."

Nodding, Brooke pushed a strand of loose hair behind her ear. "Okay, let's do it."

CHAPTER

52

Just past six o'clock, Caldwell parked in the lot next to Bud's office building and climbed out of the low-slung seat of his BMW. He stretched his legs, tight and stiff after three hours of nonstop driving.

"Nice ride!" Bud waved to him from the front entrance, propping the door open with his foot.

"Hey, Gibb," said Caldwell.

They shook hands and shoulder-hugged the way men do when they're happy to see each other, but too uncomfortable for a full body hug. Caldwell followed Bud through a sterile front lobby to an office at the end of a long fluorescent-lit hallway.

"They lock the front door after five thirty, so I've been watching for you. How was the drive?"

"Easy, and probably too fast." Caldwell grinned. He liked to speed without getting caught.

"Lead foot."

Caldwell snorted. "I'm blaming the car." He dropped into one of the chairs in front of Bud's desk.

"Ha! No kidding." Bud swiveled his desk chair to face his computer, clicked a window on the screen. "So, what's up? You need a title search?"

"Well, I hope that's all it'll take. I don't care much about the history of ownership or whether it's good title. I just need to know who owns it now."

Caldwell wanted to reveal as few details as possible. The less Bud knew the better. "Here's the plat."

Bud took the sheet of paper and studied the shape and annotations, the location and description. Caldwell was sure Bud immediately recognized the property as the unruly swath of maritime forest at the north end of Anders Isle, divided into rows of rectangular lots and tongues of golf course fairways.

Noticing Bud's changed expression, Caldwell reminded him, "This is highly confidential, Gibb. I mean it. I don't even know for sure what we're looking at here."

Bud nodded with his eyes still on the plat. "I hear ya. My lips are sealed." He appeared to be both intrigued by the development project's potential for his own real estate gain and unnerved by the secrecy of it.

The property was a coveted target for development. Vicious resistance from locals bent on protecting the last remaining maritime forest on the island and its heavily used loggerhead nesting beach forced developers to scrap their plans. The protests and lawsuits, followed by the housing market crash, had a chilling effect on resort development along the Carolinas' coast for years. The main developer in that earlier fiasco was none other than the local real estate kingpin Linwood Kingston.

Bud asked, "Doesn't Linwood still own this property?"

"I thought he did," said Caldwell. "But he didn't mention it when I specifically asked him for a tour of his best local properties. That's partly why I'm here. A client is involved with this project. I want to know more about any other players." He wrung his hands, felt his lack of sleep giving way to nervous energy. "I'd do the search myself, but I know the Anders County title information isn't online. Plus, here's the thing: I shouldn't have a copy of this plat. That's all you need to know. The search must be done in person, and I can't be seen doing it, so you'll have to go to the county's Recorder of Deeds Office when it opens tomorrow and search through the records. Will you do that for me?"

"Glad to do it, Mad Dog. I'll make a copy of this." Bud slid the plat page onto his copy machine.

"Wait!" Caldwell leaped up, arm outstretched, coming off as not only stressed but also a little paranoid.

"Are you okay?"

Feeling his own forehead, Caldwell sat down again. "Sorry. Yeah, I'm okay. I just didn't get much sleep last night." He wiped his hand down his face, blew out a long breath, and pulled himself together. "It's fine. Make a copy, but shred it when you're finished, all right?"

"I'll shred it." Bud seemed worried about his friend. "So, what's going on? You said you're only partly down here for this, so what else?"

Caldwell shrugged. "It's been a long week. Work is . . . well, there's a lot going on. My dad's campaign events are tomorrow. I'll have to be there for all of it, the rally and fundraising dinner. Oh, and I'm meeting Brooke tonight for drinks."

Bud raised his eyebrows. "Really? Drinks with the ex-fiancée? Your idea or hers?"

"Mine. Well, dinner was my idea. She agreed to drinks."

"Ouch. No wonder you're on edge."

"I don't know what I was thinking. I ran into her last weekend at the marina, and we talked, and I thought we had more to talk about. Now, I'm not so sure."

"Well, maybe it's a good time to smooth things over and get used to being in the friend zone." Bud chuckled. "I'm messing with you. I liked her." Bud powered down his computer and started to pack his things. "Besides, weren't you seeing someone else down here?"

A loud ring tone erupted from Caldwell's phone. It was Percival, and to make matters worse, he was calling from his mobile phone, not the office. Fear jolted Caldwell to his feet. He looked around as though Percival might be watching. Maybe he knew Caldwell had a copy of the Project Hurricane plat or that he'd searched the database and talked to Ben Feldman. Maybe Art Ogletree found out Ben sent something to Caldwell and told Percival to get to the bottom of it.

"Excuse me, I have to take this," said Caldwell, a sheen of sweat on his brow. He hastily shook Bud's hand and opened the office door to leave. "Let me know about the title search tomorrow. And thanks for doing that." With a quick wave, he walked out while answering the phone.

"Well, well, the man of the hour," said Percival with sarcastic gusto.

Caldwell swallowed hard. "What do you mean?"

"Happy hour with the summers—aren't you coming?" Percival burped purposefully into the phone. "I've been here since four o'clock. Get your ass over here for your hour of happy, Duck. The summers were just talking about you, especially Vanessa."

Caldwell's head swam with relief that this call was just Percival's typical rallying cry for a drinking buddy and nothing more. In the background he heard the hum of music and a full bar crowd punctuated by loud talkers. He had no idea which summer Vanessa was—and he didn't know how he felt about being nicknamed Duck—but he knew how to play along. "You'll have to tell Vanessa I'll see her next time around. I'm at the coast for dad's campaign stuff. You know—business development central." Caldwell reached his car, slid in, and revved the engine.

"Oh no, this place full of drinking female summers is *business* development central. Make no mistake about it, Duck. You follow me?" Percival laughed at his own joke.

Caldwell heard ice clink on glass when Percival took another sip of whatever cocktail was the flavor of the day. "You're right. Y'all have fun for me. Don't do anything *you would* do."

"Aw, you got me. Be a good duck. Get some new clients," Percival said.

"You know it, boss."

Caldwell's Beemer purred like a mellow cat as he pulled out of the lot and drove toward town.

CHAPTER

53

People spilled onto the sidewalk in front of School Bar and Grill—some waiting for tables, others leaving after an early evening of food and drinks. Brooke slipped past the loitering crowd and pulled open the heavy front door. The chatter and music enveloped her while she craned her neck to find Caldwell's familiar face. She didn't see him yet, but caught a glimpse of Jack, the bartender. He was hard to miss with his sleeve tattoo and funky black Mohawk.

Pushing her way through throngs of standing drinkers and talkers, she reached the far end of the bar, closest to the windows, where two bar stools wore small signs marked *Reserved*. Before she sat down, Jack spotted her and walked over while shaking a drink. She smiled at him.

"You're Brooke, right?" he asked.

Brooke nodded. "I am."

"I was told to look for the supermodel tall girl with beautiful big brown eyes and a killer smile."

"That's a good line. Sounds like Drew." Brooke shrugged bashfully, all at once flattered by Drew's description and apprehensive about the whole purpose for Jack's involvement.

"I'm Jack. I'll be taking care of you tonight. Those are your seats. Take your pick."

"Thanks." She chose the stool at the very end of the bar, leaving the other for Caldwell.

"Can I get you something to drink?"

"Not yet, thanks, I'll wait." Then she remembered by waiting she'd end up with Caldwell paying for the drinks, which made it feel more like a date. "On second thought," she said before Jack moved too far away, "I'll have a Heineken. And open a tab for me please." She handed her credit card to him.

"You got it." Yanking a cold green bottle from the bar cooler, he popped the top and poured it expertly into a chilled pint glass. He set the glass on a coaster in front of Brooke while she thanked him again.

Behind the bar, from the back counter to the ceiling, liquor bottles lined mirrored wall-mounted shelves and glowed in LED lighting that subtly alternated intensity and color. A wordless zen-techno mix created an atmosphere of upbeat relaxation.

Brooke sipped her beer. The prickle of carbonation moved from her tongue to her throat while she swallowed her feelings: searing hurt and bitter betrayal from thoughts of Diane with Caldwell, anxiety about the plan to get a secret DNA sample, and a nagging sense of guilt—or perhaps hope—that there was some other logical explanation as to why Diane had the brooch. Nervous to see Caldwell, she had to act as if everything was normal. It had been years since they were out together.

Although Brooke didn't spend a lot of time on her choice of dress or hair and makeup, she wanted to look pretty. She certainly wasn't trying to rekindle any romance, but she needed confidence to balance her growing anticipation of how it would go. Light-headed already, she scanned the crowd again, then looked in her purse to find her phone. That's when she felt him approach. She felt his hand on her shoulder, heard him say her name, and before she could respond, she stood to hug Caldwell as the crowd pressed in around them. It was a quick hug, awkward, without pretense or planning. And a jolt of dread made her breath catch. When they stood face-to-face, she touched his arm out of habit, and they smiled at each other like long lost friends with a shared secret. He was exactly how she remembered him—clean cut, shining eyes, deep dimples, and a Southern swagger. His cologne stirred memories of long-ago parties and nights out on the town. Then reality flooded in—the brooch and Diane flashed to mind like a brain freeze—and she cleared her throat, sat down, and pointed to his stool.

"I saved you a seat," she said, "and opened a tab. First round is on me."

"Oh, there'll be rounds?" He nudged her. "You look great."

"Thank you." She glanced at him and smiled, then made eye contact with Jack down the bar before finishing the last of her beer.

Jack arrived and wiped the bar top in front of Caldwell but looked at Brooke. "Another Heineken?" He pointed to her empty glass.

"Yes, please." She reached for her glass too fast and knocked it over. Jack caught it. "Whoops! Sorry." She laughed at her own clumsiness.

Caldwell looked surprised. Brooke wondered if he was as nervous as she was.

Jack asked Caldwell, "What can I get for you?"

"Gin and tonic."

"And a menu please," said Brooke. "I'm starving."

Jack handed menus to them and moved down the bar to get their drinks.

Propping one elbow on the bar, Caldwell angled himself toward Brooke. "So, thanks for coming to meet me. It's been a while."

"It has been a while," said Brooke, not sure where to go with the conversation. She turned her attention to the menu, trying hard to keep herself from blurting out her pressing questions, tamping down her inner scientist.

Jack returned and placed their drinks on the bar. "Decide on any food yet?"

"Undecided," said Brooke. "It all looks delicious. What do you recommend?"

"The white bean hummus roll is awesome. Our small plates are crafted to look like sushi even if there isn't any fish involved. The hummus roll is flattened wheat bread with cucumber spears and white bean hummus, sliced like a sushi roll, so you get about eight individual pieces. Bacon wrapped scallops are also amazing."

Brooke looked at Caldwell, who gestured to the menu and said, "I'll eat whatever you get. It all sounds good to me."

"Let's get one of each." Brooke handed the menus to Jack.

"You got it," said Jack, turning to leave them.

Caldwell lifted his drink when Brooke reached for hers.

"Cheers."

"To . . ." Brooke hesitated.

"Don't know yet. We'll have to wait and see."

"Well, okay then, cheers to the unknown." She tapped her glass to his and took a sip, noticing he was unusually attentive compared to the Caldwell she remembered from past dates. He tried to hold her eye contact, but she dropped her gaze to the bar or feigned interest in the décor. Nothing about his demeanor indicated a woman he possibly slept with and impregnated, someone he cared about enough to gift his family's brooch, was murdered less than a week before. But he was a master of compartmentalizing and hiding his emotions, self-controlled sometimes to a fault, which made him a good lawyer.

Caldwell took a long slow sip of his drink and turned toward Brooke. She was guarded, which made him unsure about where to start. He no longer knew enough about her life to ask about anything specific, and neither of them were good at small talk. Still, he couldn't accept that they didn't have anything to say. This wasn't at all how he imagined the evening. He thought she was happy to see him at the marina, and that she'd open up to him the way she used to. But she *did* agree to meet for drinks. That meant something.

"I'm at a loss for words," he said, stating the obvious. "You seem different—in a good way. How are things going?" He took another sip of his drink.

Brooke softened visibly. "Things *are* different now. I'm different, more myself than I used to be. I'm in a good place—for me. It's home here, you know."

He nodded, listened.

"I mostly spend my time helping sea turtles, working at the aquarium, and researching when I can. This week has been . . ." She trailed off, gulped her beer. "Tough." Keeping her eyes on her glass, she bit back tears.

"What's wrong?" He placed his hand on her arm.

"Oh, I'm okay, it's just, there's a lot going on that's out of the ordinary." Brooke straightened on her stool and moved her arm away from Caldwell's hand. "I don't know if you heard, but we lost thirteen turtles to poaching and"—she looked at Caldwell, then at her glass again— "worst of all, a friend of mine was killed—Diane, the Turtle Lady. She was . . . we were really close."

Caldwell leaned back and crossed his arms. "Oh, God. I'm sorry, Brooke. I didn't know you knew her."

When she composed herself enough to look at him, she couldn't read anything in his eyes or posture to suggest he was grieving Diane's death. But, then again, she remembered when his Gam died. He simply clammed up. Caldwell had the uncanny ability to turn off his feelings, especially when it concerned the death of someone he cared about.

A brief silence stretched between them, leading them both to doubt and drink. When Caldwell ordered another, Jack strategically swiped Caldwell's empty glass and replaced it with a fresh one. Brooke breathed a quiet sigh of relief. At least the hard part was over.

The food appeared and provided a welcome chance for Caldwell and Brooke to keep their mouths occupied. Caldwell claimed to like the bacon-wrapped scallops best, but ate the hummus roll first. Brooke thought one could tell a lot about people from the way they eat. Does someone eat what he likes the most first, or does he save his favorite part for last? Drew always ate his favorite things first. He was spontaneous, did what he wanted, and lived in the moment. Caldwell saved his favorite part for last. He delayed gratification, denied himself pleasure, and was more cautious and calculated. He lived for the future. The contrast was so obvious to Brooke, especially now that she sat here with Caldwell after spending the past two years around Drew. She liked the way Drew ate.

When the rolls were gone, Brooke was halfway through her beer. Caldwell tapped his finger on the bar, then tossed back his second drink and said, "I should've come after you."

"Excuse me?" Turning to look at him, Brooke noticed he was preoccupied by something, perhaps even nervous.

"When you broke our engagement, when you moved away, I'm sorry I didn't come after you. I'm sorry I just let you leave. I was an idiot. My ego was bruised. I was too proud. I got angry instead of trying to make it work and said some mean things. I didn't listen to you when you were telling me what you needed all along." His eyes watched hers. "I know this is coming out of nowhere after two years, but if I don't tell you, it'll haunt me forever. It was all my fault. I realize now just how much we loved each other and how much I miss you. And . . . I *still* love you."

Stunned by Caldwell's confession, Brooke put her hand on his arm and took a deep breath. She didn't expect his regret or a relapse of love. Shaking her head casually, she smiled at him. "Thank you for saying that. All of it. Leaving you was the hardest thing I've done. For a long time afterward, I wondered if I'd made a huge mistake." She squeezed his arm. "I think we'll always feel some kind of love for each other. And it wasn't all your fault. We both let it go. I wasn't the one for you. We wanted completely different things."

"Did we?"

Brooke nodded. "Remember when you proposed to me? You said we'd make a perfect pair, but then we fought more and more as the wedding approached because you couldn't understand why I wasn't interested in every single planning detail offered up by your mother—the appropriate shade of tablecloth for the reception, the proper place settings to use, which brand of votive candle would burn brightest and longest."

"Oh yeah, my mom still talks about sitting in our dining room, judging candles with a stopwatch. Nuts."

They laughed.

"See, I couldn't care less about all that," said Brooke. "But you wanted me to care. And I felt your disappointment, the weight of your expectations—your family's expectations—for me as a wife and someday as a mother, and I knew I wouldn't meet them. You didn't need *me*. You needed a homemaker. You needed someone who likes to bake casseroles, keeps whites looking white, and cares about things like valances. I'm an outdoor girl. I love spending hours on the beach, sandy and sunburned in search of sea creatures. I'm messy. My work is important to me. You knew those things about me, but you still wanted me to fit into your version of what a wife should be. I couldn't make a home with you there, in that way, never living up to duties set by your family and losing myself in the process. My home is here, on this island."

"Well, shit." Caldwell shook his head. "I didn't even see that. I shouldn't have made you feel that way. I should've done better."

"No, it's not like that. You just are how you are, and I am how I am—neither one is good or bad, better or worse—just different in a way that wasn't going to change and didn't make us the perfect pair."

"I guess so." Caldwell picked at the edge of his coaster, then shrugged. "But I'm still glad I asked you to marry me."

"Thanks." Brooke patted his arm. "Me too."

They split the tab and walked out of School into a wall of warm air alive with the whirring trill of cicada songs. On the sidewalk, Caldwell reached for Brooke and hugged her goodbye.

Wrapping her arms around his wide, solid chest, she held tight for a few seconds, then let go first.

CHAPTER

54

Drew opened his eyes. It took a few seconds to remember where he was. A pewter sea turtle paperweight sat on the nightstand. The full-length mirror on the bedroom door reflected stripes of morning light through the blinds. He rolled over to face Brooke, asleep on her side, next to him. Her dark hair fanned across the pillow as if blown by wind. Listening to her slow even breaths, watching the slight shiver of her closed eyelids fringed with long lashes, he had to calm his urge to touch her face, to press his lips to hers, to wake her from the midst of a dream. Lying beside her, still, Drew realized he rarely saw Brooke this way: eyes shut, mouth parted but unsmiling, sun-bronzed skin. Expressionless. He could look at her for as long as he wanted, but he wasn't staring; he was seeing, admiring, memorizing.

Last night, after delivering Caldwell's DNA evidence from School to the crime lab, Drew came to Brooke's apartment. Both exhausted from the day's events, they just planned to sleep. She greeted him in pajamas, with a book in one hand. But the thrill of being together again sparked a tight hug and immediate kisses, stirring enough energy for Brooke to drop her book and lead him to bed. His fingertips remembered how her bare shoulder and the mound of her cheek were as soft as lamb's-ear. The pad of his thumb fit perfectly in the hollow of her throat, traced the dip in the center of her collarbone before he reached for a plump handful of her breast. Kissing with tenderness, they paused to capture each inch of pleasure while pushing and rubbing their bodies together in slow motion, trying to press and lengthen tingling sensations between them, then shifting. Sliding. Making love with need and comfort and deep inhaled gasps. In the afterglow, they fell fast asleep, curved toward each other in the middle of Brooke's bed, holding hands and touching knees, close enough to share a breath, or a dream.

From somewhere on the floor, Drew's phone rang, cutting through the peaceful hum of air conditioning and yanking him from quiet adoration into flustered action. He found it in the pocket of his pants by the second ring and recognized the coroner's number.

Brooke squinted at him with half-open eyes and a sleepy grin but didn't get up.

"Terry?" Drew answered, sitting on the edge of the bed.

"Good morning, Detective!" She sounded triple-espresso excited about something. Much too jovial for the early hour. "Thought I'd be the first to inform you—you hit the jackpot!"

"What does that mean?" Coming from Terry, it could be actual good news or sarcastic bad news.

"The evidence jackpot—bingo—whatever you wanna call it."

"Are you talking about the DNA I brought over last night?"

"Oh, hell no, the crime lab just got that, so it'll take a few hours for analysis. I'm talking about forensic evidence from the deceased."

"From *my* homicide victim?"

"Yes, dummy."

He imagined her rolling her eyes. "Well, there's a dead witness, too, so I'm just catching up."

"Okay then, stick with me, this is right in my wheelhouse. The other day, you asked me about the fingernail clippings I sent to the lab from your dead girl."

"Yes," Drew said. "I've been researching cases about homicide victims submerged in water and came across a study published in New Zealand where DNA evidence was found under the fingernails of female victims in two separate cases after the bodies were submerged in water for hours. I'm hoping Diane fought back, and I'm desperate for forensic evidence."

"Well, get ready for greatness because DNA was recovered from the cellular material under a fingernail from her right hand."

"You're telling me we have DNA evidence from Diane's fingernail that might belong to her killer?" Drew sat up straighter, fully awake now.

"Yup. There's a mixture of DNA from two individuals in unequal proportions. A rapid DNA test already matched the minor DNA contributor to Diane's blood sample, but the major DNA contributor is an unknown male. She scratched the bastard!" Terry's voice was practically giddy.

"I knew it! Of course, she did. That's—holy shit—that's unbelievable. It was a longshot, but this is like a miracle, this is like . . ."

"Science." Terry finished for him. "The beauty of science. I've seen my share of stellar detectives in this business, and I can tell you, you're one of them. You have a knack for this and a perseverance that's lacking in so many others. See, most people—even detectives—underestimate the value and persistence of evidence from underneath a deceased's fingernails. I learned a long time ago—up in Jersey—to routinely collect and analyze fingernail debris no matter what the scene. Lots of bodies were dumped in the river up there, you know. The sensitivity of current DNA technology led to successful DNA extraction from material under nails in all sorts of unlikely situations: after a body spent a month in wet conditions, was exhumed, or—in cases like the ones you mentioned—had been submerged for hours in fresh or salt water. And in many of those cases, DNA from under victims' fingernails 'hit to' or matched suspected individuals and solved the case."

"Well, thank you, Terry. This is amazing! Exactly what I need to corroborate Joe's witness statement, especially since he can't testify. I want to run Oliver's DNA against the unknown male sample to make the final forensic link to Oliver, which could help me force a confession out of him. I'll notify the crime lab to use something in Oliver's house for a DNA sample, or his saliva on the beer cans I found in the forest. Obviously, we can't get a buccal sample from his cheek until we arrest him."

"A personal item of his should be enough."

"This news could not have come at a better time. Thanks again."

"That's how jackpots work, right? They happen when you least expect them." She cackled and hung up.

Brooke placed her hand on Drew's back, kissing the space between his shoulder blades, the spot almost out of his own reach when scratching or applying sunscreen. "I only heard your side of the conversation, but it sounds promising."

"Way more than promising. This could be all I need. If a good sample of Oliver's DNA matches the DNA under Diane's nail—I'm done. Once we find Oliver, I'll have Joe's witness statement and solid forensic evidence to push for a confession. But even without one, he's as good as convicted. Case closed. My first homicide, solved within a week! The chief will be satisfied. Bad guy will get what's coming to him. Win-win." Looking at Brooke, he raised his eyebrows suggestively and added, "Not that I haven't already won."

She laughed. "Who? Me? Am I your prize?"

"Well, you're certainly proof I'm winning at life." He flashed a wide smile, loving her with his eyes.

"Aw, that's just . . . the sweetest. Get over here and claim your prize." Brooke pulled him back into bed, feeling him harden while they kissed.

Ducking under the covers, Drew found her warm, naked body, moved on top of her, and pinned her down with his hands, his mouth, and his hips until she squealed with delight.

CHAPTER

55

The stage was set for the Get Mad rally in front of Sand Dollar Grocery and Sundries. American flags flew from banners strewn around the rectangular parking lot and billowed from a row of posts behind the podium. The crowd had been growing slowly for two hours.

Sanny and Marla Otis beamed with pride from where they stood holding hands on the curb in front of their store, admiring the scene. An event like this attracted the most important people in town with its magnetic force. Media outlets claimed territory for the best vantage points. Campaign staff dressed in office attire walked stiffly in the heat, wearing headsets, and checking details on tablets. The sun bore down—hot and bright—on the busy patch of parking lot.

Walt, on security duty, ogled Bella across the lot where her camera crew set up to broadcast. Glancing at him with a seductive side-eye and smiling without showing her teeth, she smoothed her hair, then her skirt. Their exchange made it clear they'd been repaying each other's favors *all* week.

The crowd filled the space between the storefront and street. When Bud arrived just before noon, he angled through the pressing throng of people and shook hands with acquaintances while he made his way to where Caldwell stood in the shade of a tent near the stage. "Hey, Mad Dog!" He motioned to a clearing just outside the tent. Caldwell met him there. "I brought this to you in person, in case you need the hard copy."

Caldwell unfolded the sheet of paper from Bud. "Okay, so the property's owned by Project Hurricane LLC. Ugh. Figures." He looked expectantly at Bud. "Please tell me you know who the members are."

Bud shook his head. "Nope. Couldn't find a damn thing. I searched the title records, the deed records, even the LLC formation documents. But, you know, in South Carolina an LLC doesn't have to list any of its members' names on any formal public document."

"I know. Shit."

"That's all I've got." Bud shrugged.

"Well, thanks, man. I really appreciate your time and discretion on this. I guess my client could be the sole member of the LLC, but he already has an LLC for his South Carolina developments—I helped him form it—so why would he create a separate LLC for this project? And who sold the property to my client or deeded it over to the LLC as a member? Since Linwood's the last owner in the chain of title, I guess I'll have to ask him."

"Be careful. Don't burn that bridge."

"Oh, I won't. I'll talk it up as a potential deal. That should pique his interest." Caldwell clapped Bud on the shoulder. "Stick around. Dad's speaking soon. I'll make my way back over here after I find Linwood."

The heat of the day rose along with the excitement of the growing crowd. Some waved small flags while others hoisted children onto their shoulders for a better view. After an opening prayer, Mayor Patterson McPhee stepped up to the podium for introductory remarks.

Caldwell listened to the mayor's address while he worked his way along the perimeter of the lot, focused on Linwood—tall and cross-armed—in conversation with another middle-aged man under the awning of the Sundries storefront. Within earshot of Linwood, Caldwell heard the end of a crass comment about the heat. The other man walked off laughing with a thumbs-up.

Linwood turned abruptly and nearly bumped into Caldwell. "Well, look who it is!" Linwood gave him a firm handshake. "The best tour guide I've had in these parts."

"Thanks, Linwood, you're too kind. It was my pleasure—even though we were supposed to catch some damn fish. I'm sure I bored you silly with a drive around your own properties."

"I don't get out there to see my developments all that much. Heck, I hadn't been to Taylor Island in, oh, I can't even remember how long." He pointed to the stage. "Aren't you supposed to be over there with your daddy?"

"Not really. This is all about him. Nobody knows who I am."

"Just you wait until this election really gets going. I imagine you'll wish you could've stayed unknown. Your dad has a clear shot at the White House, you know. He's the party favorite." Linwood rocked back on his heels.

"That's what I hear." Caldwell felt the title search and plat papers crinkle in his pocket.

They listened to the mayor spew his gratitude for Senator Madden's visit.

"So, how's business?" Caldwell tried his best to sound casual.

"Busy, which is good, because there ain't much business going on without the busy, right?" Linwood smirked.

"That's the truth. In fact, funny you should put it that way. There's been a lot of busy for me, too, some of which might interest you. This one high-roller client of mine is looking for new prospects right here on Anders. He told me the other day he has his eye on the north end, the maritime forest property. He's looking to build a mega resort, but I told him you own it, and if anyone's developing it, you are." Then Caldwell lowered his voice. "That is, unless you're in the market for a buyer or a partner. I'm happy to make introductions."

"Oh, Lord," Linwood said, eyes to the sky. "That property's worthless. I tried every angle to develop it—wasted almost a decade trying—but it was just a giant pain in the ass. You probably don't know about all the problems I had over on Taylor Island. That was back when I was younger with more energy for the fight, and before there were actual records of turtle nests. But, let me tell you, that north end property was another Taylor waiting to happen. It's covered with maritime forest and sea turtle nests—a double whammy to those anti-developer tree-huggers. Hell, you'd think I was plotting to steal their children when I suggested building a golf course. I couldn't get a single permit approved without protests, pushback, and lawsuits." Linwood pursed his lips in disgust. "That property nearly bankrupted me—it would've when the market collapsed, if it wasn't for your dad."

"Really?" Caldwell looked at Linwood with a blank expression, then from Linwood to his dad—Senator Madden—just visible behind the stage where he waited for his big entrance.

"He bought it from me."

Caldwell tried not to show his shock but knew he had failed.

"Don't worry. There wasn't any reason you would know about it. The bank threatened to foreclose, so I asked Mad to keep it quiet. I told him it was a rotten egg, but he said he wasn't interested in building on it—just wanted to help an old friend." Linwood followed Caldwell's gaze to the senator, then softened his tone. "You know, that was the nicest thing a friend ever did for me."

Just then, Mayor McPhee announced, "It's my pleasure to introduce the future president of the United States, Senator Madden!" The mayor clapped and stepped aside.

Taking the stage amid uproarious whoops and hollers, Senator Madden waved both hands in the air and gave thumbs-up to climactic cheering from the crowd. As hot as it was and with their bodies packed together in a dusty lot, everyone seemed re-energized and invigorated by the senator's appearance.

He shook the mayor's hand before turning to the podium. "Mayor McPhee, my family, and friends, and all you great men and women out there, good afternoon. It's my honor to be here with you today. Sanford and Marla Otis, thank you for sharing your storefront and parking lot for this special occasion. Actually," he paused and shaded his eyes with his hand to search the crowd, "I'd love for my family to come up to join me onstage, to see this view and be part of this moment. Come on up!" He pointed to his wife. "Lydia, bring the girls. Where's Junior?"

"That's my cue," Caldwell said to Linwood.

"Uh-oh, looks like people are going to know who you are now." Linwood chuckled.

Caldwell gave a reluctant wave.

"There you are, Junior, come up!" The crowd parted as much as it could to let him squeeze through to the stage steps. "All of you come up and let me introduce you." Senator Madden took his wife's hand. "Here they are, folks: my wife, Lydia, our twin daughters, Elizabeth and Annabelle, and our son, Caldwell. They're a tremendous support system."

The senator clapped for his family along with the crowd. The Maddens stood together, waving and smiling, until the senator gestured for them to exit.

He returned to the podium. "From my family to yours, thank you for being here. I'm holding this rally in memory of Diane Raydeen, your local Turtle Lady, to honor her love for sea turtles, something I hope to keep in mind while I champion the effort to protect threatened and endangered species and their essential habitats." The crowd cheered in response. "If you're here today, it means you're ready to get mad. Or maybe you're already mad. And it may not be an angry mad, it may be a mad care or a mad need—there's something you feel must be done. You want answers, but—even more than that—you want action." Louder cheers erupted. "You care about your island, your town, your state, your country. You care about the environment, taxes, education, and gun laws. These are big topics, but something big can be done if we each take one small step, together, and then another and another. Pretty soon, all our small steps will add up to big change."

Caldwell scanned the faces of enthralled onlookers from his vantage point in the shadow of a tent beside the stage. It never ceased to amaze him how intently they listened. He had heard it all before. His dad's campaign speeches were basically a remix of the same sentences adjusted for location and demographics. They'd added a few new concepts since the senatorial campaign as well as the catchy Get Mad slogan, but his dad delivered the message with predictable language and gusto. Caldwell had been to at least fifteen rallies and could almost repeat the speeches word for word. If he was ever called upon to speak for his dad, he was confident he could do so on short notice.

Still, the people watched Senator Madden with such intensity and singular focus, none of them—not even the media—noticed when Detective Drew Young tapped Caldwell on the shoulder, flashed his badge, and asked Caldwell to come in for questioning.

CHAPTER

56

"Did you make it clear to Mr. Madden that he isn't being charged?" asked Chief Mullinax, presiding in his office before Drew and Sampson while Caldwell waited in the interview room. "He isn't under arrest, isn't in our custody, but is only here for investigatory questioning, correct?"

"Yes, sir," said Drew. "I told him he might have information we need since he happened to be at School last Friday night about the same time Diane was there." What Drew didn't say was that he used a little personal clout to convince Caldwell to cooperate by telling him Brooke wanted his help with this, too, since Diane was her good friend. "Caldwell agreed to a voluntary interview. As an attorney, he knows the drill. He's free to leave anytime."

"Good. Don't push too hard. We already know Oliver is the killer."

"And we have forensic evidence that should prove it," said Drew, thinking of the fingernail DNA. "Sampson, will you follow up with the crime lab about that?"

"Sure, Detective." Sampson made a note.

Drew continued, "As for Joe, we don't know who killed him or why. There still seems to be a missing piece to that whole story."

"I heard your angle about big money in the poaching ring," said Mullinax. "That certainly creates enough motive to go around and could be related to Joe's death. I'm not saying Oliver killed Joe, but Oliver is the only suspect for the Turtle Lady murder. So, let's stay focused." Leaning forward, Mullinax folded his forearms on the edge of his desk. "Listen, you two, just because Mr. Madden might've been involved with the victim doesn't mean he's guilty of anything more than knocking up his girlfriend. We're just trying to find out if he knows where she was between leaving School that night and going to North End Beach, or why she went out there alone in the dark. Last thing I need is the senator's son being falsely accused of a crime. Got it?"

"Yes sir," said Drew and Sampson in unison.

"So, which one of you will be going in there to talk to him?"

"I'm sending Sampson in," said Drew. "He's humble and precise, which should put Caldwell at ease. Plus, my personal relationship with Caldwell's ex-fiancée could cloud my judgment or make him hold back. I'll get more out of observing him during the interview."

"I see. Good decision," said Mullinax, eyeing Drew with a sense of fatherly pride. "Well, Mark, you have your marching orders. Go in there and find out what he knows."

"On my way," said Sampson. He knocked a chair over when he stood to leave, muttered something, then fumbled his notebook when he bent to pick up the chair.

Drew and Mullinax exchanged a look, then moved to watch through the one-way glass as Sampson entered the interview room. Caldwell stood to shake Sampson's hand, but was met with an awkward, limp handshake in return. Sampson barely made eye contact and hastily introduced himself. They sat across from each other at the square table.

"Mr. Madden," began Sampson, flattening his hands on his notebook.

"Please, call me Caldwell."

Drew could tell from Caldwell's casual demeanor he already sized up Sampson and wasn't feeling threatened. Sampson was having the intended effect. Caldwell, like any good lawyer, appeared composed and ready to take control of the interview.

"All right." Sampson pushed up his glasses and cleared his throat. "Caldwell. Where were you last Friday night between the hours of eight and midnight?"

"At a business dinner at School Bar and Grill in Anders City."

"Great, great, that's what I thought." Flipping open his notebook, he pulled out a photo. He slid it across the table to Caldwell. It was a head shot of Diane. "Have you seen this woman before?"

"Yes, on the news."

"Her name is Diane. Did you know her?"

"No."

"Did you see Diane at School last Friday night?"

"No."

"Did you speak to her that night?"

Caldwell sat up straighter. "Not that I recall."

"What do you mean?" Sampson wrote something in his notebook.

"Well, I was told I'm being questioned because we were both at the restaurant that night. I can't be sure she didn't talk to our group at some point, but I don't remember seeing her there. I don't remember speaking to her."

Drew listened intently to Caldwell's carefully chosen words and wondered why he seemed to be covering himself in case there was evidence of him speaking to Diane that night. Caldwell still appeared comfortable, but he was alert, cautious.

Sampson flipped a few pages in his notebook until he reached a stapled set of papers. "Had you ever spoken or corresponded with Diane before that night?"

Caldwell eyed the papers in Sampson's hand. "No?" He said it with such little conviction that Sampson's brow furrowed.

Sampson peered at Caldwell through glasses that slightly magnified his eyes. "Are you sure? You don't sound sure."

"I told you already, I didn't know her."

"But that can mean a lot of things. You could chat with someone or even just text and email someone, perhaps even a client, and still claim to not really know that person. People have all sorts of funny notions about what it means to know someone." Sampson scratched his temple. "For instance, you and I have been talking for five minutes or so, but six months from now, if asked, you wouldn't say you know me, right?"

"Okay." Caldwell put his hands up in a gesture of half surrender and adjusted his posture to speak directly to the one-way glass, knowing Drew—and whomever else—must be on the other side. "I don't know what this is, but I'm not playing a game of semantics here."

"Oh no, I'm not playing games. I'm very serious. And we need your help," said Sampson. Drew saw the flustered and perhaps even scared part of Caldwell flash in his eyes. This was the reaction Drew hoped to see. Sampson made Caldwell doubt himself, made him defensive, and by doing so unleashed his own inner interrogator. "Maybe this will jog your memory." Sampson placed the stapled papers on the table in front of Caldwell. "These are Diane's phone records. The highlighted lines are calls from an outside number to Diane. You'll see the same number pop up at least five times in the past month. There were at least twenty times as many texts from that number, but I thought it would be overkill to print that list. Anyway, this was the last outside number to call Diane's phone before her death and, here's the thing: it's registered in your name."

Drew admired Sampson's delivery.

Caldwell, wide-eyed, snapped his head up from the paper to look at Sampson and then at the one-way glass. "That's crazy." He read the number again. "That's not my number. Someone stole my identity or used my name for a false account. Here's my phone." He reached in his pocket for his phone and held it up for Sampson to see. "Call that number and you'll see it isn't my phone."

"You're right," agreed Sampson. "This doesn't prove anything. We can't rely on a phone number because—like you said—there's a reasonable explanation of stolen identity. You're saying that's what this is?"

"That's absolutely what this is," said Caldwell.

"Okay, okay, it wasn't your number. What about this?" Fumbling in his bag under the table, Sampson retrieved a glistening mahogany box. "Someone ransacked Diane's apartment looking for something. I think we found what they wanted. Is this yours?" Sampson opened the box to reveal the shining butterfly brooch.

Panic registered in Caldwell's face. "That's my family's—my grandmother's—brooch. Where did you get that?"

"You should know. You gave it to Diane. When she lent it to her closest friend, she claimed it was her own family heirloom. Why would she do that?"

"I don't know," said Caldwell. "I'm not sure what you're getting at. There's been a horrible mistake. I didn't do anything wrong."

"Perhaps you didn't. I'd imagine you were in a tight spot. Secretly dating the best friend of your ex-fiancée can be complicated. It's not necessarily wrong, but not right either. Let's just say I understand why you would keep your distance after your girlfriend's sudden and mysterious death, given you could be implicated. But we aren't accusing you of that. We just want to know where she went after School and why she was out there in the dark at the end of the island all alone, and it appears you know a lot more about her than you're telling us."

"She wasn't my girlfriend." Caldwell crossed his arms and shook his head at the one-way glass, as if suggesting he knew Drew was trying to set him up. "Like I said, I didn't know her or anything about her."

"That's what you say, and, you know what? I'd accept your word for it: you didn't know Diane, you didn't call her, you didn't give her the brooch," said Sampson, setting the box aside and flipping to another set of stapled papers, "but this last little bit of evidence . . . well, I have to tell you, it makes me doubt what you say. I'm not a scientist, but I'm confused by how this could happen." He tossed the papers across the table to land on top of the phone records. "DNA paternity test results indicate you're the father of Diane's unborn child."

Alarmed, Caldwell stood up to leave.

"Should we stop him?" Drew asked Mullinax.

"No. Let him go. We don't have enough to charge him with anything yet." Mullinax pinched his chin in his hand and exhaled through his nose.

Drew wondered: what was the truth from Caldwell and what was the standard deny-deny-deny, even in the face of hard evidence, deny? He knew Caldwell was trained to think like a lawyer, and to react like one, too.

At the door, Caldwell paused, indignant and self-righteous. "I don't know what y'all were trying to pull here today, but I won't be coming back without a lawyer, without a whole team of lawyers."

And with that said, he stormed out.

CHAPTER

57

At the aquarium, Brooke was distracted most of the day by her mind's replay of the previous night. She never expected Caldwell to tell her openly how he felt, to come right out and say he still loved her. Did she dismiss him too quickly? Did she say the right things? But her answer was the same no matter how many times she thought it all through: she didn't want to be married to Caldwell. They had their time, and it passed. Not to mention, he might've been sleeping with Diane.

Brooke's heart was set on Drew, especially after last night, and this morning.

In her distraction, Brooke almost overdosed one of the turtles, went up to the main floor twice only to forget why, and called an intern Drew by mistake. She was so obviously preoccupied that one of the staff members asked if she was feeling okay. Nobody was surprised when she decided to leave a few hours earlier than usual.

On her way home, her thoughts turned back to the missing turtles and the investigation. The same question continued to plague her: why were the loggerheads of Anders Isle at the center of a million-dollar poaching ring? Out of the seven species of sea turtles, the *hawksbill* had been hunted almost to extinction for its shell, known as tortoiseshell—a glossy patterned spray of mocha brown and straw yellow—coveted and carved into jewelry, combs, furniture inlays, and sunglasses until the species was finally protected as critically endangered. Poachers also stole unhatched sea turtle eggs by the hundreds, selling them as a delicacy for purported aphrodisiac effects. But none of the loggerhead nests were disturbed and—after seeing the scute yesterday—it was possible none of the shells were sold. It appeared these poachers were being paid obscene amounts of money to simply kill logger-heads—to get rid of them.

Maybe the purpose of the poaching wasn't to sell, but to exterminate.

Gripping the wheel tighter, Brooke crossed the connector bridge, certain she was onto something. Extermination. Yes. It seemed as obvious to her now as the long, stark white neck of a single snowy egret in the expanse of tall, lime green marsh grass.

Just as she reached the island, Drew called. When she answered, she could tell he was in detective mode by his clipped, no-nonsense words.

"Are you someplace private?" He asked, a vacuum of wind in the background.

"Yes, in my car on my way home."

"Good. I'm coming over to your place as soon as I can. Linwood Kingston's secretary, Marion, just called to let me know who owns the maritime forest property. Well, it's owned by an LLC, so there isn't a specific person yet, but the registered agent is Percival Jones, who, as I found out after a little digging, is Caldwell's boss. Marion said they heard rumors of development, a resort. This whole thing might be much bigger than we think and could include some dangerous players with a lot to lose. One of them might even be Caldwell."

"You're scaring me."

"Just sit tight. I'll be there soon. Oh, and I'm so sorry to tell you this, but you should know Caldwell's DNA matched to Diane's baby."

Parking askew at her apartment and hurrying out of her car, Brooke's hands shook as she tried to unlock her front door. When the key finally caught and turned, she rushed inside, locked the door again, and closed all the blinds. Sitting carefully on the couch in the dim room, she caught her breath. Her mind raced, heartbeat thumping in her ears. She shuddered to think what more might be revealed when Drew arrived, when they could put their theories together.

CHAPTER

58

After driving around for almost an hour, thinking about what to tell his dad, Caldwell parked at Anders Isle Marina and took the water taxi to Taylor Island. He stepped off the boat just past two o'clock in the afternoon. Calm inlet waves lapped gently at the dock pilings. A pelican perched on the tallest telephone pole across the way. Caldwell breathed in the familiar odor of low-tide mud.

Like the sights and smells of Taylor Island, the water taxi dock had been the same for as long as Caldwell could remember. Although hurricanes and erosion forced renovations and rebuilding from time to time, the sunbaked docking area kept its simplistic charm. A single dock as wide as a king-size bed stretched out from a grove of trees with a welcome hut at its base for residents and their guests. He checked in with the security guard and climbed onto the golf cart brought around for his arrival.

Caldwell bumped along the graveled dirt road to his family's beach house, sensing the sameness of the place in sharp contrast to the difference in him. Head swimming, he felt dizzy and pulled over. With a deep breath, he wiped his brow. He'd skipped lunch, but it was more than hunger that gnawed at his insides. It was emptiness—deep down, hollow emptiness—and a bite of fear.

When he entered the house, nobody was home from the rally. He ate a sandwich, drank a glass of water, and made a phone call. Wandering from the kitchen to his dad's office to the master bedroom, he smelled a faint trace of his mother's perfume and followed it back to the main living room. Banks of windows flooded the house with light, framing a picture-perfect scene from dunes to beach to ocean and beyond.

The first time Brooke walked into this house, she'd gasped at the view, then stood at the windows and watched the waves while Caldwell watched her. He imagined her standing there now, her shape outlined by beach and sunlight. That was only a few months into their relationship when he could still surprise her. On most of their dates, they learned something new from each other, not just about each other, but new stories and facts about the world. He told her his favorite bits of history. She lit up when she talked about the latest scientific discovery. But one thing he didn't talk about was how he really felt about her. Sure, he eventually said he loved her, but not often or how much. And he didn't tell her when she needed to hear it most, when she was leaving him. He thought it would be enough to tell her last night, hoped to hear her say she felt the same way, but it turned out he'd waited too long.

Caldwell hid his feelings well, though inside he held regret and a desperate need to let go of his constant re-examination of his mistakes. It was an exhausting internal battle, one he thought he had finally won when he concluded that losing Brooke was one of his biggest mistakes. Now, with Brooke lost for good and—on top of that—the police evidence pounding in his head, he was near a breaking point. His hands shook while he poured himself a drink and sat on the couch.

A few minutes later, the familiar creak of the front door echoed through the foyer. Adjusting his phone on the coffee table, Caldwell focused on what to say to his dad.

Senator Madden sauntered in, dropped his keys on a side table, and exhaled hard. He saw Caldwell on the couch. "Hey, Junior! There you are. I didn't see you after the rally. Where'd you go?"

Caldwell didn't look at his dad. "Are you alone?" he asked, then took a sip of his drink.

Bitter. Chilled.

"Yes, your mother took the girls shopping. Why?"

"I was just at the police station. I need your help."

"What happened? Are you okay?"

His dad's concern made it all feel worse. He tossed back the rest of his drink. "I need your help to understand why the police have evidence linking me to the woman killed last weekend and why they're telling me that I got her pregnant."

Senator Madden walked to the window, jaw clenched, arms crossed. He stared out at a container ship on the horizon—as big as an office building floating on its side, off to sea, headed somewhere far away—a lonely, giant ship.

"Did you hear me?" Caldwell stood up, but kept a distance, reined himself in. He never spoke to his dad this way. "They think I was involved with that woman, Diane, and with her murder. I don't know anything about her, but based on the evidence I saw, you do. Phone records, DNA, even Gam's brooch. You need to tell me what's going on."

"I didn't want to hurt your mother," Senator Madden said in monotone.

Caldwell scoffed at his dad's response. "I think it's too late for that." He'd memorized the phone number on the records in evidence and, before his dad arrived at the house, Caldwell called it. The ringing led him to a phone buried deep in his dad's desk drawer. He pulled that phone out of his pocket now and held it up. "And what about me? Did you think about me when you used my name to set up this phone to call your lover? Did you care about hurting *me*?"

His dad turned to face him, saw the phone. "I don't know what to say, Junior. Of course I didn't want to hurt you." He swallowed his last words through strained lips, shifting his eyes from Caldwell to the floor. "I had an affair with her. I got her pregnant. I made a mistake, a huge mistake."

Caldwell tried to make sense of the relief he felt in hearing his dad admit to the affair. Time slowed. Planting his feet, he kept pressing. "Why did you call her the night before she was killed? The police said the last call she answered was from this phone number." He set the phone down on the table.

"It was a goddamned mess," Senator Madden said while he sat down across from Caldwell, hunched over with his elbows propped on his knees. "I made special arrangements for Diane to get an abortion that day, but she canceled the appointment. She wanted to keep the baby. I had a lot to drink that night. I thought I could change her mind. So, I called her to ask her to meet me at 5:00 a.m. at our usual spot—North End Beach—where we could talk. Normally, I picked her up there in the boat and brought her back here to the house, but you were staying here. That's why she went to North End by herself in the dark."

Caldwell heard the words, but he couldn't believe them. "You were here last weekend?"

"Yes, briefly. I sobered up enough to drive up and meet her."

"From Charlotte?"

"No, from Savannah. I was there for my coastal Georgia campaign event, so only about two hours away."

"In the middle of the night?"

"We had to be discreet."

Caldwell felt disoriented by the many secrets his dad was keeping, the double life he'd been leading. And he was drinking heavily again, which always impaired his usually astute judgment. Caldwell didn't know what might come out of his dad's mouth next.

"The thing is," Senator Madden leaned back in his chair and stared up at the ceiling, shaking his head while he thought out loud, "I was going to end the affair, convince Diane to go through with an abortion, go our separate ways. I did so much for her. She loved her turtles, so I pulled strings to push through the federal grant for her turtle group. I gave her gifts and loans and time." Looking at his son with wild and pleading eyes, he gestured with his hands like he was giving a speech. "I did all that for her, and she wanted *more!*" His eyes widened. "Diane wanted love, wanted me to leave your mother, in the middle of this campaign. I never intended to be with her. I mean, it started with a lot of passion, but then she became moody and unpredictable, especially after she got pregnant. Diane knew she could ruin me if she went public. She even knew about my drinking problem. She threatened everything I worked so hard for. She put my family, my reputation, in jeopardy."

"So, did you talk to her that morning?"

"She wasn't there." Senator Madden shook his head and crossed his arms.

"I assumed she decided not to come, just to spite me. And when it turned out she was dead, well, I knew I'd be a suspect if I came forward." He clamped his hand to his chest. "My campaign, my marriage, my entire political career would be *over*!"

Caldwell was shocked to see his dad come unglued, to hear him use politics as an excuse for shirking personal responsibility. He didn't know how to react. Every time he heard his dad speak the name Diane, he felt like he'd been punched. "What about the phone, Dad? I don't understand. You could've used any name, or a burner phone. Why involve me?"

Senator Madden looked squarely at Caldwell with a void of conscience in his eyes that made the room feel colder. "I needed a red herring," he said flatly.

"What?" Caldwell's throat tightened. Suddenly, his anger gave way to a palpable fear.

"When I found out Diane was pregnant, I put the phone in your name. I knew if her pregnancy ever became news, I'd need to take the focus off me. I panicked. I found out that since fifty percent of your DNA comes from me, there's a high possibility for a false positive on a paternity test if the lab only has *your* DNA. The phone would lead to a DNA sample from you and, without one from me, there'd appear to be a good match. It would all stop with you. I mean, it wasn't full proof, but the odds were in my favor it would work. And it did." He saw Caldwell's stunned expression, softened his tone. "But, Junior, it was just a precaution until the abortion. I never thought it would come to this."

"Well, that's just great, Dad. Nice planning." Caldwell rubbed his palms on his legs. "So, what the fuck do we do now?"

"Let them believe what they want to believe. It's all circumstantial." His dad tried to sound convincing. "Besides, if they try to charge you with something, we'll have the best lawyers money can buy."

"No way! No fucking way! This is crazy!" Caldwell began to sweat. His dad's callous and unapologetic response, his flippant protection of himself at his own son's expense, left Caldwell reeling. "I didn't know that woman! You have to tell them everything. I want out of it. You leave me out!"

"Junior, look at me. I need you to do this for me." He steadied his eyes on

Caldwell's. "Think of our family, your sisters, your mother. You can keep us all together and keep this from getting worse. Just claim that the baby was yours."

"How can you ask me to do that?" Caldwell shot to his feet, indignant.

"I'm not really asking you." The senator stood up, kept his gaze fixed on Caldwell. "I'm telling you, Junior, it's done. Just go along with it and everything will be fine. Trust me."

But Caldwell didn't. Not anymore. He'd tried his whole life to be the son he thought his dad wanted him to be, but it would never be enough. Now, he was being told not only to conform to the family way but also to take the burden of and blame for his self-serving dad's egregious mistakes. The alternative was to torpedo his family's life as they knew it and his dad's bid for the White House. It was too much to bear.

"Junior?"

Caldwell stared blankly at the windows, the rolling ocean view. He grabbed his phone and the red herring phone from the coffee table, stuffed them in his pockets, and left the house without another look at his dad.

"Junior!"

It was the last thing Caldwell heard before the door creaked on its hinges and slammed behind him.

CHAPTER

59

When Brooke heard a knock at her door, relief streamed through her.

Drew, at last.

Crossing the room, she pulled the door open. "I'm so glad you're . . ."

Caldwell.

She froze. Fear paralyzed her for an instant in a primal moment of fight or flight. She didn't expect to see him again, certainly not in person—alone—at her apartment. Did he find out about the DNA sample and come to confront her? Was he angry? She thought about Drew's warning. Could she be in danger?

"Caldwell?" She swallowed, attempting to act nonchalant, and used her best pleasant-surprise grin. "What are you doing here?" She leaned on the door, hesitant to let him in.

"I'm sorry to show up like this." He fidgeted, glanced at her, visibly upset. "May I come in?"

"Um, I don't know if that's such a good idea. Drew will be here any minute."

"Oh, well, that might be okay." He scratched his neck. "I mean, I might need to talk to him, too, so . . ."

Brooke sensed he was anxious, not angry. "Are you okay?"

He dropped his head, sighed. "No, Brooke, I'm not." When he looked up again, his eyes were on hers, pleading for her to see him, the Caldwell she once loved. "I need to talk to you. You're the only one I trust."

"All right." Brooke stepped aside and let him in.

"Thanks." He stuffed his hands in his back pockets, pulled out two phones and set them on Brooke's coffee table. "This is going to be difficult for you to hear—and to believe."

Brooke braced herself for his confession, prepared to hear him say he was the one who got Diane pregnant. "Go on." Sitting on the nearest chair, she shut her eyes for a few seconds, then opened them to see Caldwell watching her.

He sat on the couch across from her. Tapping his phone to access a voice recording, he kept his finger hovering over the screen while he said, "Your friend, Diane . . ."

Here it comes, thought Brooke. She couldn't believe he was saying it. Holding her breath, she focused on Caldwell's mouth as it formed each word.

"She was on the beach alone when she was murdered because my dad told her to meet him there. He was having an affair with her. She was pregnant with his child. And now he wants me to take the blame for it all to shield him from political ruin."

Eyes wide, Brooke exhaled in disbelief and shock. "What?" She inched to the edge of the chair with breath bated.

"I just came from our beach house. He told me everything, but he didn't know I was recording it. Listen." Caldwell tapped his phone again and his dad's voice rose into the room. The whole conversation was there—from the moment Senator Madden walked into the house until the moment Caldwell walked out.

Leaning toward the phone, listening to the truth, Brooke's emotions clashed as a thrill of relief was quickly replaced by disgust. Senator Madden had an affair with Diane and was planning to let his own son take the fall for it. She took a deep breath to ease the knot in her stomach.

Caldwell held up the other phone. "This is the phone Dad put in my name to connect me to Diane." Then he reached into his front pocket and removed something sealed in a plastic bag for her to see. "And before he even admitted to the affair, I took his hairbrush from the master bathroom for a sample of his DNA to prove the baby was his and not mine."

Overwhelmed by the moment, Brooke crossed the room to sit beside Caldwell. She put her arms around him, hugged him close, felt his arms encircle her, and his chin rest on her shoulder.

She let go and looked at him, placing a hand on his knee. "What can I do to help?"

Before Caldwell could answer, there was an urgent knock at the door.

"Brooke, it's me!"

At the sound of Drew's voice, Caldwell stiffened, then fiddled with his phone to prepare the recording for Drew.

"Coming," said Brooke.

She let Drew in.

Clearing the doorway, Drew saw Caldwell on the couch and shot a skeptical look at Brooke. "What's *he* doing here? Don't let him manipulate you." Drew pointed an angry finger at Caldwell. "You have a hell of a lot of nerve showing up here after all you've done!" Drew started toward Caldwell, looking ready to kick his teeth in.

"Wait! Hold on." Brooke placed her palms flat on Drew's chest and followed his eyes to get his attention. "Caldwell didn't do anything."

"Bullshit!" said Drew. "Don't believe him for a second. We have the evidence."

"Not all of it," she said. "You need to hear the conversation he just had with his dad. Senator Madden is the baby's father. *He* was having an affair with Diane. Caldwell brought his dad's hairbrush for DNA to prove it." She gestured to the bagged brush and felt Drew's tense muscles slacken under her palms. "Caldwell, play the recording," said Brooke, not taking her eyes off Drew.

The voices of Senator Madden and Caldwell filled the room again until the sound of the slamming door.

"Damn." Shaking his head, Drew looked at Caldwell with pity in place of his original contempt. "I'm sorry." But something Drew heard in the recording felt like a house of cards collapsing in his chest. "Let me see that phone." He pointed to the red herring phone, then slipped his hands into a pair of latex gloves.

Caldwell handed it to him.

Drew scrolled recent calls, stopping at a number he recognized that was called late Friday night before the murder and again, hours later, early Saturday morning. "Brooke, what's Diane's number?"

She told him, and he saw Diane's number on the list of calls, but it wasn't the one he was recognizing, which made Drew wonder who else the Senator had been secretly calling or dating. Where did Drew see this vaguely familiar number? He asked Brooke and Caldwell, but neither of them recognized it. Wary of calling the mystery number and possibly alerting someone to his pursuit, he decided to wait and check phone records in his case file for a match.

Enclosing the phone in an evidence bag, Drew looked at Caldwell. "Now," he said, ruffling his hair and blowing out an exhale, preparing for what felt like a suspect interview, "tell me about Project Hurricane LLC."

Caldwell held Drew's stare, but a slight wince in Caldwell's expression belied his surprise to hear those words come from Drew's mouth. Reluctantly, likely unsure of the legal ramifications of showing a client's confidential documents to a detective, but seeming to already be on shaky ethical ground, Caldwell reached into his pocket again.

He flattened a stack of four papers on the coffee table with the plat on top. "What's that?" asked Drew.

"This is Project Hurricane, the plans for a luxury golf resort community on property that covers the entire north end of Anders Isle. It's owned by Project Hurricane LLC. All I know so far is that one member of the LLC is an influential Boston-based real estate magnate named Art Ogletree, an important client to my firm whose cases I usually oversee, but I'm locked out of this one. I've been trying to figure out why." Caldwell pointed to the project name and the long edge of property rimmed by coastline. "Linwood Kingston was the previous owner. At the rally today, he told me the beach along this property is prime sea turtle nesting ground, and the property itself is one of the last maritime forests on the east coast. He dreaded the environmental red tape to develop it—said it was nearly impossible to get through—which is why he let my dad take the whole thing off his hands when the real estate market crashed."

"Wait, let me get this straight," Drew said, "Linwood sold the property to Senator Madden? Then how did it end up in the LLC?"

"Art is one of dad's *it's-who-you-know* friends, influential and wealthy. So, yes, Linwood sold it to dad, but I don't know whether dad sold it to Art and Art moved forward with development through an LLC, or if dad is a member of the LLC and working with Art to build this resort. I don't understand why it matters to *you* who owns this property and what they're doing with it. I was looking into it because of my job issues, my dad issues, but what's the connection to your investigation?"

Drew and Brooke exchanged a look of mutual trepidation and curiosity.

Brooke's eyes shifted from Caldwell to the Project Hurricane plat to Drew, where she saw in Drew's face that he had also put together the property and poaching connection. She said, "Loggerheads were being poached *because* of this property deal. They weren't being sold on the black market. They were being *exterminated.*"

"Exactly," Drew kept putting the pieces together for Caldwell. "It looks like the developer, the LLC—Art and any other members—*hired* poachers to target sea turtles because no turtle nests would mean less red tape and a faster path to development. They made big plans to clear the maritime forest and develop a resort community—like you said—that would probably make them hundreds of millions."

Brooke added, "In the past, I remember similar plans by developers were met with powerful protests and lawsuits to protect the maritime forest and especially the turtles' nesting beach. The public backlash delayed and prevented development to the point where investors lost millions of dollars. That's why the poachers were being paid exorbitant fees for each sea turtle. See, loggerheads nest one summer season out of every two to three years, so, by killing off thirteen mature female loggerheads over the past four years they tried to create the illusion that Anders Isle, and specifically North End Beach, is no longer being used by loggerheads as a key nesting habitat. The poachers were being paid to wipe out the island's current nesting population, and they almost did."

"Fuck." Caldwell cupped his face in his hands, no doubt absorbing the reality of what they were telling him. It seemed Art and possibly his dad were involved in a scheme that resulted in murder. "This is all starting to make sense now." Sitting up again, he spread the other pages on the table. "I'm not supposed to have any of these. Ben, one of Art's associates, sent them to me, mostly to get even with Art. One page is the plat of the property, one is a bank transaction for fifty million dollars, and the last two are copies of an article about charges that were dropped against Art Ogletree for his alleged sexual misconduct with a former employee, Ben's close friend."

"Interesting." Drew crossed his arms. "I bet once we follow the money, trace the accounts, we'll find payments being made from Project Hurricane LLC to the poachers, probably all offshore banking."

Caldwell nodded. "And I'm pretty sure Art was also contributing his own large chunk of change to my dad's presidential campaign, either in exchange for ownership of the property or, if my dad is an LLC member, in exchange for all the local *help* with the turtles. This would be one of the crown jewels in Art's real estate portfolio. My dad wouldn't have wasted his time with any of this if there wasn't something huge in it for him. Art knows where lots of the bodies are buried when it comes to convincing people to make crucial endorsements for a presidential candidate. His kind of clout can make or break an election. Dad always says it's not *what* you know that matters, but *who* you know. At this point, nothing surprises me about what he's done—or might do—to win the White House."

Leaning back in her chair, Brooke shook her head in dreadful comprehension of the big picture. Then, most unexpectedly, she let out a single laugh. "Those arrogant developers actually thought they could get rid of enough sea turtles to make it easier to build their resort. They must feel like idiots since the turtles keep outsmarting them and coming back to nest each summer. Never underestimate the resilience of nature." She smiled back tears for her triumphant turtles.

Caldwell shrugged. "I don't know what they were thinking. I'm supposed to handle all of Art's business in the Carolinas, but I knew *nothing* about this property. In fact, I was intentionally kept in the dark about it by my firm, maybe because Art didn't want my dad involved, or maybe at my dad's request. But I can't honestly say I would've done the right thing if I'd known, with millions in potential profit at stake." He bent forward, resting his elbows on his knees, looking down. "Money and power." He shook his head. "I've been on that path—to be just like my dad—but I want out. I want something else, something for myself, something good to come from all this mess."

"Money and power," Brooke repeated. In the wrong hands, they ruin lives, manipulate societies, and rarely deliver the happiness they seem to promise. Why hadn't people figured that out yet? She leaned over and touched Caldwell's arm. "You aren't like your dad."

"Thanks." Caldwell's gaze met hers for a few seconds before drifting across the room.

Drew put his hand on Brooke's shoulder. "I know you aren't going to like this, but we need more proof to link the poaching to the property deal."

"We should follow the turtles," Brooke suggested. "Figure out where the poachers would take them after capturing them on the beach. If we can find dead turtles, or even pieces of them, left behind, we'll have some evidence the turtles weren't being sold or traded, which will support our theory."

"Good thinking. The poachers must've kept some physical piece of each turtle, some souvenir, to verify each kill and get paid for it."

Brooke nodded. "Well, if I were a poacher planning to trade animals on the black market or hide carcasses from the authorities, I'd want to be prepared to get them out of the country as soon as possible. The fastest way to do that here is by water. So . . ."

"The port!" Drew's face brightened. "Oliver works at the port."

"That's right! I just saw him there Sunday during one of my turtle rescues. He was pushing crates into a warehouse—number eight. I remember because I named the rescued turtle Eight."

"I sure do love your turtle names." Drew pulled his phone out of his pocket. "The port is massive, no way to know where to look first, and a great place to hide something you don't want anyone to find. Might as well start at warehouse eight and go from there. I'll text Paul to let him know we're coming to look around for some turtles."

"What else do you need from me?" Caldwell stood up, eager and ready to help.

Drew finished his text and pointed to the coffee table. "That brush, those papers"—he spoke to Caldwell in a terse voice, all business, still harboring suspicion and hesitant to trust him—"and a complete copy of your recorded conversation with Senator Madden. I could take your phone, but I might need to reach you later, so stay available in case I want more information."

"All yours." Caldwell handed over the papers and brush, which Drew tucked safely into evidence bags.

Brooke looked from Drew to Caldwell, marveling at how these two men, both of whom she cared about and admired, were standing there in her apartment, trying to work together.

An awkward moment of silence hung between them until Drew opened the door and ushered them out. "After you, Brooke." He winked at her.

In the parking lot, Brooke reached for Caldwell on his way to his car. "Thank you for trusting me . . . for everything." Squeezing his arm, she leaned closer and kissed him lightly on the cheek before climbing into Drew's passenger seat.

CHAPTER

60

Riding in Drew's truck, listening to radio songs mixed with the engine's low rumble, Brooke closed her eyes, not from fatigue, but for focus. The day was building to a crescendo, a crest, a precipice at which she teetered on the cusp of some full understanding, some final discovery of the truth of what had been happening to the turtles, and of what had happened to Diane. Vibrations from the truck's speed matched the trembling in her body. Alertness like a sixth sense kept her racing for answers, searching for the finish line.

Drew's hand dropped onto her thigh. His thumb brushed across her bare skin between her knee and shorts. Opening her eyes, she covered his hand with hers, turned her head toward him, catching his glance, his smile. She surveyed his profile, let her gaze drift along the outline of a face she knew so well she could draw it blindfolded.

He squeezed her leg, made her flinch and giggle, knowing her most ticklish spot. Then he bunched up his face, puckered his lips, and said in a deep voice, "Now, be *serious*, Dr. Edens. This is no laughing matter."

"Oh, stop, you big flirt." Brooke tossed his hand off her leg. "This *is* serious!" But trying to still her face straight, she immediately cracked up, unable to contain her giddiness being with Drew on their way to find justice for thirteen unlucky loggerheads and for Diane.

The Port of Anders City rose from the river's edge as a multicolored cityscape. Shipping containers were stacked in a grid like giant Lego creations, forming blocky hotels made of solid colors flanked by rows of gray warehouses. Since Drew had to stop at his office and get a search warrant, it was half past five o'clock when they arrived at the port's south entrance, where Paul took the lead in his jeep, escorting Drew's truck to warehouse eight.

After handshakes and hellos beside the warehouse, Paul said to Brooke, "Wasn't our next meet up supposed to be for something fun? That usually doesn't start with a search warrant." He chuckled.

Shrugging, Brooke smiled and suggested, "Maybe next time? But you'll have to convince your buddy here," she nudged Drew, "not to bring a search warrant to the party."

"I'll do my best," Paul said while unlocking the side door of the warehouse. "This is a pre-inspection storage space so most of the items are in labelled crates or boxes but aren't scheduled yet for packing and delivery. Think of it like a giant storage unit for companies who need a place to keep inventory or overstock." He opened the door to a dark space with a polished concrete floor. "The lights work on a timer, so you turn it like this," Paul twisted a dial on the wall to illuminate a cavernous industrial interior with exposed steel beams across the ceiling, "and they should be on for an hour, but seem to have a mind of their own, so if you need more time there's a light dial at each door."

"Thanks, Asher." Drew stepped inside with Brooke close behind him.

"Glad to help. Take a look around and just call or text if you need me. I'll be at the guard house 'til six." He left with a quick nod and let the door click shut.

The temperature-controlled air smelled of fresh cut wood and foam packing peanuts. Chills sprouted across Brooke's skin in the cool stillness. Their footsteps echoed, amplified by bare walls and ceiling, until a fan rattled on from somewhere above them and drowned smaller sounds in its blowing white noise.

Touching her arm, Drew said, "Let's start this way." He pointed straight ahead to signs labeled with letters of the alphabet attached to metal shelving that ran the length of the warehouse.

Moving toward the section labeled P–T, they hoped to find a crate stored under the name: Project Hurricane LLC.

Brooke saw the first aisle—almost as long as a football field—between two shelving sections and realized this search might take a while. Only a few steps behind Drew, she turned right at the shelves marked P-T, not rushing, but sensing a shared anticipation about what they might find.

Pausing next to the first large crate, Drew read the label. "This company name starts with T, so we need to go to the opposite end of this row."

Brooke nodded, following his lead.

Halfway down the aisle, he paused again. "In the range of letter R."

Although they didn't need to be quiet, their task and surroundings subdued their moods, evoking the heady silence of a library.

Drew stopped abruptly. Fifty feet in front of them, almost at the end of the storage section for letter P, a crate was pried open on one side, revealing something periwinkle blue. Sticking his arm out to his side to shield Brooke and keep her back at a safe distance, Drew felt for his pistol grip with the other hand while they approached the open crate.

"Someone beat us to it," said Drew, walking faster as if the crate's contents might vanish.

The open crate, as tall as Drew, was filled with oddly shaped blue objects interlaced in two piles to maximize space and stuffed with packing peanuts, some of which spilled out and swirled around their feet like grotesque snowflakes. He quickly inspected the crate's label while putting on latex gloves, also handing a pair to Brooke.

"What does it say?" asked Brooke, stretching her hands into the gloves.

"Company name is Project Hurricane LLC." Drew shot her a victory look. "And listen to this, the customs form describes the contents as: *plastic recycle.*"

"I seriously doubt *that*," said Brooke, scowling. "Let me see one."

Reaching inside the crate, Drew carefully pulled out one of the objects the same way he would slide a Jenga block from its stack, as though the whole tower might fall with one false move. A spray of packing peanuts showered to the floor. Using his phone to photograph everything, he gave the object to Brooke.

As soon as her hands felt its solid weight, its gentle curve, she knew what it was. Even disguised with a chalky blue coating of paint, the distinctive brownish-orange hue of a loggerhead shell was visible underneath. "These are scutes from our missing turtles."

"We were right," Drew said, looking at the blue shell in Brooke's hand and then at her. "Project Hurricane is behind this whole poaching scheme." Pivoting back to the crate, he started to count the individual shell pieces. "How many turtles do you think this is? It looks like they broke each whole shell into smaller pieces."

Brooke didn't answer.

Drew heard the sickening slap of a hard shell on concrete and turned to see Brooke's wide terrified eyes above a giant hand clamped over her mouth. With a stomach-dropping lurch of dread, he saw Oliver standing behind her, gripping her face in one hand, and holding a knife to her neck with the other.

Time slowed and warped.

Brooke's eyes darted, her breath heavy inhales and exhales through her nose. Arms stiff at her sides. Hands tightly fisted.

Oliver towered over her, taller and wider than her in every way, more than twice her size. The knife resembled a toy in his sausage-like fingers, one simple slice away from severing Brooke's artery and killing her in an instant.

Drew did not move. Horrified by the sight of Brooke's slender body dwarfed in the shadow of mammoth Oliver, he steadied himself and looked above Brooke's head into eyes dark as coal. Deadly, uncaring eyes. "Oliver," he said, controlling his tone, aware any sudden misstep, any harsh word, could be fatal. Fear screamed through him like a braking train. "What can I do to make you let her go?"

"You listen to me." Oliver's snarled lips barely moved over his clenched teeth.

"I'm listening." Drew said evenly, keeping his eyes on Brooke, who closed hers.

"That crate, that's my ticket out of here. I'll get millions in exchange for delivering those shells. Then I can disappear. No way I'm giving that up."

"I hear you. I understand. But you'll be on the run. What if I can offer you something better? You know everything I need to know. With your help, we can catch the people behind all this, get you a deal. I know you didn't act alone."

"Nobody's gonna believe me!" Oliver's head shook furiously, his fingers tightening over Brooke's mouth.

A whimper caught in her throat.

Gasping at the sound of Brooke's pain, Drew softened his voice. "*I* believe you. But if you do this, if you hurt Brooke, if you kill her, I won't be able to help you."

"Because I'm a murderer. Right?" Oliver spit the words at Drew.

"I don't think you're a murderer." Taking a deep breath, Drew tried to calm Oliver. "You were caught in a situation where Diane saw what you were doing on the beach, and you knew she would tell. The money at stake, the danger to you if the poaching was discovered, made you act out of haste and desperation. You never meant for anyone to get hurt. She surprised you, and you reacted in the heat of the moment."

"I wasn't surprised by her." Oliver sneered, squinting his hollow eyes. "I *knew* she was coming."

Drew's airway constricted. His voice came out like a croak. "How did you know?"

"I was supposed to *scare* her, that's all. Scare her into the forest before she ruined everything. And then . . ."

"And then, what, Oliver?" His mind reeling, Drew needed to keep Oliver talking.

"I had to do it, get rid of her body, or else I'd be dead. I'd be killed next." Slack-jawed now, Oliver seemed to be replaying the scene in his head, mumbling, shifting his feet. "I had to do exactly what I was told."

"Who told you?" Drew gently pressed. "I need to know who." Even though Drew had a hunch, he wanted to hear it from Oliver.

Stiff-lipped, Oliver shook his head. "Like I said, nobody's gonna believe me. I *only* did what I was supposed to do. I was set up!" Pleading now with Drew, Oliver's eyes looked through him, anguish flared with each word. "Those shells, the money, it's my only way out!"

Oliver jolted Brooke, making her wince. Her eyes flew open.

"Okay, okay, Oliver, watch me. *Please.*" Drew slowly raised his palms. Heart thumping. Breath shallow. "You want this crate? You can have it. If you let go of Brooke, you can have it. I'm backing up . . . please just let her—"

Suddenly, the lights clicked off and everything went black.

Brooke screamed.

Drew heard her body slump to the floor followed by a loud drum beat of footsteps running away. "Brooke!" He shouted, frantic, groping for his flashlight on his belt, shining it in her direction.

A door opened nearby with a yawn of daylight, then slammed shut.

"Brooke!" Leaping to her, kneeling beside her, he lifted her up just as she grabbed for him. "Oh, my God! Are you okay?"

At first, she could only nod, shaking in his arms while he clung to her in the dark. Then her voice returned, hoarse and panic-stricken, "I think so." She sighed.

"Let me see." Drew flashed the light on her neck and face, making her squint and block her eyes with her hand. "What's this blood on your shirt? Did he cut you?"

"No. I grabbed the knife." She took a deep breath. "I think I got his arm. Serves him right."

Letting out a relieved chuckle, Drew kept searching carefully under her chin and along her neck, didn't see any marks. "Not a scratch on you, thank goodness." He squeezed her shoulders. "Just a minute. I'll find the lights."

He hurried with his flashlight to where he'd seen the door open in the wall behind them and turned the dial. Pushing the door open, he saw Oliver loping away in the distance, already fifty yards down the thoroughfare and headed toward the far edge of the port.

Dashing back into the warehouse, he met Brooke jogging toward him. "Here, bag up the knife and take my keys." He tossed an evidence bag and his keys to her. "Go lock yourself in my pickup. I'm going after Oliver."

"Okay," she nodded. "Be careful!"

He waved and raced through the door.

While he ran, he called Paul, talking fast and loud as soon as Paul answered.

"Secure the port, Asher! Oliver's here!"

"What?" Paul asked.

"He just held Brooke at knifepoint."

"Oh, shit! Is she okay?"

"Yes, but he's getting away! I'm in pursuit on foot near the westernmost container crane. I have him in my sights, but I'm not close enough yet. Call for back-up and meet me over here."

"Done."

Alarms blared from every corner of the port.

Pounding across the pavement with ease, Drew sped up to a full sprint, his surfer-fit body propelled by fierce determination and adrenaline. He closed in on Oliver, who only looked back at Drew once and couldn't run any faster, couldn't hide.

Within twenty feet of Oliver, Drew squared his stance and aimed his gun at Oliver's back, yelling, "Freeze! Put your hands up! Now!"

Oliver staggered to a stop, his chest and shoulders visibly heaving with each breath while he lifted his arms, one bloodied, and hung his head. He didn't say a word or make eye contact while Drew handcuffed him just as Paul's jeep screeched to a halt beside them. Patting Oliver down, Drew found Oliver's phone and put it into an evidence bag, then stuffed him into the back seat of the jeep.

CHAPTER

61

By the time Paul's jeep pulled up to warehouse eight, blue and red flashing lights and sirens from police cruisers and emergency vehicles exploded around them like fireworks. Yanking Oliver out of the jeep, Drew handed him over to a couple of patrol officers with instructions for transport to the county jail, receiving pats on the back and even some applause.

But Drew waved them all off, knowing he wasn't finished yet.

After arranging for Project Hurricane's crate and shell evidence to be collected and taken to the crime lab, Drew thanked Paul for his help and started toward his truck when he heard, "Detective, wait!" He turned to see eager Sampson emerge from the sea of uniforms, waving at Drew with his notebook.

Watching Sampson shuffle toward him, Drew was reminded of the first day on the dock almost a week ago when Sampson had flagged him down the same way.

Adjusting his glasses, Sampson cleared his throat while jostling his notebook open. "Okay, Detective, since you stopped by the office a few hours ago, I did everything you asked. So, first, as you suspected, the phone number you recognized on that red herring phone matched to a number on Joe Willis's phone record, but it seems to be a burner phone, good for thirty days at most."

"Do you have the number there in your notebook?" asked Drew. "I think I know whose it is, but I need to *know* I know." He smiled, thinking of the chief's constant badgering about think versus know.

Sampson flipped a page. "It's right here."

"Call it."

"Sure, Detective. Hang on." Sampson pulled out his own phone and called the mystery number.

A muffled ring tone emanated from Drew's pocket. He fished out the evidence bag containing Oliver's phone, which was buzzing and ringing with Sampson's phone number bright on the screen. "Gotcha!" Drew pressed his lips together with a single nod.

Sampson's eyes rounded behind his glasses while he ended the call. "Good thinking, Detective."

"What about Diane's phone record?" asked Drew.

"Well, like you asked, I went back to look for any calls made to her phone the day of her murder after 5:00 a.m., the approximate time of her death. The only numbers that came up belonged to your friend, Brooke, and to Diane's mom."

"I'm not surprised," said Drew, fitting that piece perfectly into the puzzle. "And the DNA results?"

"Yes, Detective, right here." He handed a few papers to Drew. "As you requested, the lab used the rapid DNA machine and rushed the analysis report."

Drew read: "The male component of the DNA profile from the deceased's fingernail matched to the DNA profile of one male individual obtained from a sample in police evidence." Drew saw the name of the identified male individual in bold font. In his hands, Drew held irrefutable DNA evidence proving Diane had scratched this man while he strangled her to death. "I knew it!" Looking down again at the report, he could hardly believe the gravity of this result.

"Does that mean . . ." Sampson saw Drew nod slowly. "Wow."

"Oliver asked for a lawyer already, so I won't be able to question him until he has one, but, before that, I got enough out of him in Paul's jeep. I have everything I need." Drew held up the DNA report. "Please keep this between us until I have a chance to brief the chief."

"You can count on me, Detective," Sampson said, closing his notebook.

"I know I can. Thank you." Drew shook Sampson's hand, then walked to his truck and climbed into the driver's seat, clutching the DNA report like a faulty grenade that, if mishandled, could blow up at the wrong time.

Sitting in the passenger seat, Brooke stared through the windshield at the thinning scene. "He wouldn't have done it, you know. Oliver wouldn't have killed me." She looked at Drew.

"Why do you say that?" Drew searched her eyes.

"I think, no, I know," she rubbed her neck as if remembering, "he put his thumb between the knife blade and my skin the whole time."

Drew furrowed his brow, then relief surged through him in the ebb of adrenaline. Reaching for her, hugging her harder than he ever had and rocking her in his arms, he said against her ear, his voice cracking, "I've never been so scared in my life. If anything had happened to you, Brooke, I don't know how I'd ever make it." He nuzzled his face in her hair, kissed her cheek and lips, holding back tears.

She pulled away enough to look him in the eyes, those sea glass blue eyes she loved, and saw them welling for the first time. Cupping his jaw in her palm, she smiled. "I'm right here. I'm fine, and I'm not going anywhere."

He sighed and smiled back at her, turning his mouth into her hand to kiss her soft palm. Then he straightened in his seat, shifted into drive, and made a wide turn to leave the port.

Drew's hunch that began at Brooke's apartment when he heard the recording of Senator Madden's conversation with Caldwell, became a certainty with the exclamation point of the DNA report. After linking the poaching to the property deal, deciphering phone records, and re-examining evidence, Drew finally fit all the pieces into place. It was a different and much bigger picture than he'd expected.

Oliver's voice repeated in Drew's head: *I only did what I was supposed to do . . . Scare her into the forest . . . Get rid of her body . . . I was set up.*

While Drew drove, he and Brooke discussed everything they'd figured out, walking through a timeline of events leading up to Diane's death, and reviewing the evidence they had to prove it. Brooke watched the salt marsh from the side window as they crossed the connector bridge to Anders Isle.

Tidal creeks held the fading light of day in their curves of water, sipping sun from the horizon. A strip of dark blue ocean rose like wainscoting on a wall of pale blue sky.

Drew finished, "So that's why this isn't over until we know the members of Project Hurricane LLC. Art Ogletree is one of them, and Senator Madden, who made calls to Oliver with the red herring phone, is another. But, while we have the murderer pinned down, we still don't know all the players involved. Did Art know about the poaching scheme, or was he just the money guy funding the LLC and Madden's campaign? Are there any *other* LLC members?"

Absorbing the magnitude of what had happened, and what still lay ahead, Brooke steeled her nerves. "What's our next move?"

"Well, while Oliver was handcuffed in Paul's jeep, I *strongly suggested* he tell me the details of his planned delivery of the turtle shell pieces."

"And?" Brooke studied his eyes with riveted curiosity.

"He was instructed to pack the shells in two golf club travel bags and hide them near the service dock behind Taylor Island Golf Resort clubhouse where, at ten o'clock *tonight*, someone is supposed to meet him to exchange the shells for an envelope containing a new bank account number, access codes, and proof of a balance of five million dollars." Drew raised his brows for emphasis.

"Who's meeting him?"

"He wasn't given a name, but we're going to find out because, here's the thing, I happen to know there's a private fundraising event tonight at the Tiger clubhouse. A roast for Senator Madden with an exclusive, high profile guest list. All the local police departments were notified about it. I'm sure Art will be there along with Caldwell, Kingston, and anyone who's anyone already in town or within private jet distance. So, I'm thinking—" Drew smiled.

"No," said Brooke, reading his mind and shaking her head. "We aren't crashing the party."

"We are. Put on your ball gown. I'll bring the *party favors*. I have at least one arrest to make, and we've got to see who comes for the shells. I know you don't want to miss this grand finale." Drew loved to tease her, especially when she secretly wanted to do exactly the thing she so protested.

Brooke rolled her eyes, but she knew this would be unforgettable. "Okay then. I'll be your undercover date."

"Good." He glanced at her warmly. "We have them right where we want them. Everyone will be drunk as skunks with their guards down by the time we get there. And I'm ready to wrap up the loose ends of this whole investigation." Drew pulled into the parking lot of Brooke's apartment complex. "Meet me at Anders Isle Marina at nine o'clock. That should give me enough time to secure the warrants and arrange for back-up. Paul can probably take us over to Taylor Island on his boat."

"I'll be there." Looking at Drew with a soft smile, she felt a rush of apprehensive excitement and burning-bright love.

For the night ahead, they would need each other. They were two local kids in love, the same Brooke and Drew from decades ago on imaginary missions to defeat bad guys in a schoolyard game. But this time, they were about to change the world.

CHAPTER

62

Cicada songs buzzed through the dusk surrounding Taylor Island Golf Resort, rivaled by the buzz of chatter spilling out from the Greek Revival-style clubhouse. The white-columned clubhouse entrance overflowed with the din of donors drawn to roast Senator Madden before a well-heeled, dolled-up audience of moneyed elite. An elegant Swarovski crystal chandelier cast its soft light over the foyer where Caldwell worked his charm bestowing handshakes and shoulder squeezes on each couple he greeted as they made their way inside.

A river of people flowed into the grand ballroom to find their seats strategically arranged around tables crowned with stalks of calla lilies in fluted vases. The scene was reminiscent of a wedding reception.

Caldwell introduced himself as the senator's son, making small talk and forcing laughter as appropriate. But he kept a cool distance from his dad, who stood with Art Ogletree in a circle of fawning guests.

Someone across the room tapped a spoon to wineglass to ring in the roast.

First to the mic was Mayor McPhee, who set the bar high with his funny insults about the senator's preference of Taylor Island over Anders Isle, complete with a slide show beamed onto the screen behind him. After the mayor, the lineup included congressmen, businessmen, and family friends, like Linwood Kingston, who poked fun at the senator's claim to be a capitalist protecting the environment.

Linwood raised his glass and proposed a toast. "To the fox guarding the hen house!"

The crowd snorted and laughed and drank.

Senator Madden watched with delight from the front center table, basking in the attention and glory of his blossoming political ambitions.

A fingernail moon hung in the dark sky above Taylor Island while Brooke and Drew rode in Paul's boat along the Intracoastal Waterway behind the clubhouse. The No Wake Zone forced a slow approach. Conversation was subdued by the mission ahead and by wondrous pinpricks of starlight scattered throughout the umbrella of night.

As they motored quietly into the private dockage area, Drew tapped Brooke's arm. "See that?" He pointed to a large sport fishing boat securely moored in a nearby slip. "A Boston Whaler 420 Outrage with features, accents, and a name like that *must* belong to Art Ogletree." Above a row of four outboard engines, the name *ART of the Reel* stood out in bold, black lettering across the sleek ice blue stern.

"Of course," Brooke nodded, smoothing the wind-blown frizz from her hair, wishing she could smooth the knots in her stomach.

Paul tied off to cleats while Brooke and Drew stepped onto the dock. "Are you sure you don't want me to wait?" asked Paul.

"Positive," said Drew. "A couple of my officers are already in position as security, ready for my signal if we need them. Plus, I don't want to spook the suspect. But thanks for offering and for the ride."

"Anytime, bro. Good luck with it." He untied his boat, climbed on board, and gave them a single wave while slowly backing into the waterway.

Thinking of loyal lady luck, Drew smiled, then turned to Brooke. "Fifteen minutes 'til the exchange." He linked his arm with hers.

Navigating her way along the wood dock in heels, Brooke tried not to trip on plank seams while adjusting the bodice of her strapless dress to make sure her bra wasn't showing. She'd only worn this gown once before at an aquarium gala and forgot how many times that night she'd gently tucked and pulled at it.

Pinned to the left breast of her dress was the twinkling butterfly brooch. Every so often, she touched it lightly to be sure it was still there.

It all came down to this. After a long week full of doubt, upset, and questions, the answers weren't at all what she expected. But she learned to adapt to the unexpected.

Holding hands, Brooke and Drew followed a stone-paved path lined with festive torch lights from the private dockage up to the majestic back patio of the clubhouse. From inside, smatterings of laughter rose and fell between bouts of applause.

Leaning in, Drew gently touched the small of Brooke's back and whispered, "Have I told you how beautiful you look in that dress?"

"Thank you." Chuckling a little, she tugged at the bodice again. "I'm mostly uncomfortable."

"Well, you look like you belong here."

"That's the idea. And what about you, handsome?" She nudged him gently with her hip. "I like you in a tux."

"Definitely not my style," he said. "But I did add my own accessories." Winking at her, he patted his side, where Brooke knew he stashed his badge, handcuffs, and gun.

"I'm nervous," she said.

"Don't worry, we'll blend right in." Drew shifted his eyes to the back entrance. "Look over there." Brooke was surprised by the relief she felt to see Walt standing guard with another officer. "Just past Walt is the path to the service dock. If we take a stroll to the far end of the patio, we'll have a clear view of anyone who goes that way. And after we make this bust, we'll go inside to deliver the punch line for the biggest roast of all."

Brooke exhaled slowly. "Okay. I'm ready."

With the speeches in full swing, most guests were seated inside feasting and drinking and laughing. Only a few couples dotted the patio area. Grabbing a half-finished glass of wine from an abandoned tall table and handing it to Brooke as a prop, Drew led her to the far corner overlooking the lawn and waterway. "Now, we wait." He gave her a reassuring smile.

Facing Brooke and the clubhouse, Drew acknowledged Walt with a slight nod, then watched the back entrance over Brooke's shoulder. Banks of windows framed the inside hallway, beaming golden-lit activity into the darkness like a movie screen. A jazz quartet clattered out of the French doors, lugging instrument cases and music stands. Following close behind them, a silver-haired man in a double-breasted tuxedo checked his Rolex and hurried toward the path to private dockage.

"That might be our shell guy," Drew whispered, keeping a careful eye on the man until he was halfway to the dock. Brooke caught sight of the man, then looked down. "When he gets too far behind me, you take over and tell me where he goes."

Brooke nodded, letting out a fake giggle to maintain their image as a couple in easy conversation while her eyes tracked the man's movements to one of the moored boats. "It's Mr. *ART of the Reel*." Widening her eyes at Drew, she pretended to sip her secondhand wine.

"Is he *leaving*?" Drew's voice tightened.

Searching the space where she'd seen the man climb aboard, Brooke spotted him emerge again from the boat. "No, there he is. Now, he's on the boardwalk along the water's edge toward, it looks like, the service dock."

"Well, well," said Drew, wrapping one arm around Brooke's waist. "Let's go."

Walking casually from the patio to the path, they watched the man disappear into a fringe of trees and shadows around the service dock entrance almost fifty yards away. A dimly lit manicured lawn stretched across the space between the clubhouse and the waterway, leaving very few places to take cover. They needed to sneak closer to the location of the exchange without drawing anyone's attention. Best to hide in plain sight by meandering their way along the path, as any couple might do.

Reaching the shadows near the dock's entrance, Drew paused to check the time. Five minutes past ten o'clock. Through a cluster of sawgrass and sabal palms, he could see the long black rectangle of a dock surrounded by the still mirror of water. And, at the end of the dock, there stood a dark male shape with his back to them.

Then the man turned to peer in their direction. Blinded by light pouring from the clubhouse behind them, he said, "Oliver?"

That single word cut through the quiet of the night.

It was not only a name and a question but also an answer.

It was all Drew needed to hear.

And the man seemed to realize his mistake almost immediately when he saw Drew step onto the dock followed by Brooke. "Oh," he said, "Excuse me. I thought you were someone else."

"I am." Drew lifted his badge. "I'm detective Drew Young, Anders Isle PD. Are you Art Ogletree?"

Rubbing his abnormally large ear lobe, the man cleared his throat. "Yes."

"Then you are *exactly* who I thought you were. Please keep your hands where I can see them." He radioed for Walt.

"What's this about?" Art tried to sound calm, but Brooke heard a scrape of alarm in his voice.

"Project Hurricane," said Drew.

Art didn't say another word. He clamped his lips and dropped his head, allowing Drew to place him under arrest without any resistance. When Drew patted Art down, he found Art's phone and the envelope meant for Oliver with bank details and a balance of five million dollars.

Just as Walt arrived and hauled Art off the dock, Art's phone vibrated in the evidence bag. Drew saw a text banner on the locked screen from Mayor Pat McPhee with the message: "Meeting finished? Madden's up next. Where are you?"

"Hold on, Walt," Drew caught up with them. "One question for Mr. Ogletree." Art gazed across the lawn, not engaging. "Is Mayor McPhee in on this too? The LLC? The poaching?" Drew showed Art the text.

Art looked from his phone to Drew without a reaction, his shrewd business acumen rendered useless. Any flash of temper would only make things worse.

Returning Art's stare, Drew added, "We'll find out one way or another, but it would serve you well to tell us."

Art looked at the ground, then nodded.

"Take him away," said Drew.

Brooke thought she heard Art whimper while Walt marched him discreetly up the side lawn to a patrol car waiting in the front driveway.

The roast festivities were winding down and the guests were reasonably sloshed from the ceaseless flow of alcohol when Brooke and Drew arrived at the ballroom. Choosing a vantage point in an archway by the foyer, they had a view of the whole party of wealthy insiders.

Caldwell—already center stage—proceeded to announce Senator Madden as the final speech of the night. "I wasn't sure my dad would make it through all your jabs," he finished, hearing a few chuckles at the lead-up to the senator's appearance on stage. "But I'm sure y'all will be riveted, as always, by what he has to say."

The jovial audience clapped a warm welcome for Senator Madden, who took over the mic from Caldwell with a knowing smile and a pat on the back. Caldwell returned to his seat and tossed back the last swallow of his Old Fashioned.

Facing his sea of patrons, Senator Madden quieted their applause, a glaze of mild intoxication in his dull eyes. "Good evening, all you good people—family and friends. Thank you for being here. And thanks for what you had to say. You can make fun of me all you want as long as it comes with a generous campaign contribution." Some laughter trickled through the room. "But seriously, I have a few words and slides to share. Many of you traveled from far and wide just to attend this event. So please, indulge me and allow me to express my gratitude while I have you here."

The screen lit up behind the senator with the red, white, and blue slogan: "Get Mad for President!"

Brooke bit her lip and fumed. "I don't think I can listen to this."

Drew turned to her, "Remember." He placed his hand over his heart like he might pledge allegiance, both to convey his love for her and to remind her of the butterfly brooch pinned over her own heart. "It won't be much longer."

She nodded and took a slow deep breath. Brushing her fingers across the brooch, she narrowed her eyes, anxious to expose the hypocrisy and deception that led to Diane's murder and the killing of so many loggerheads.

Senator Madden stoked the crowd. "Let me start by saying I've accomplished a lot so far during my term as senator, thanks to your continued support." Speaking with confidence, he didn't slur, but the pace and manner of his speech—his tendency to hold his grin a beat too long—gave the impression he was using more effort than usual to form sentences and remain coherent. "I'd especially like to thank the sponsors on this list," he gestured to the next slide on the screen behind him, "for this extravagant event tonight. Let's give them a round of applause." The senator clapped along with the audience, then continued, "We're at a crucial point of momentum on the campaign trail and this dinner helped us meet *and exceed* our fundraising goals. We still have a long road ahead, but it's worth it for a better America."

A slide blinked onto the screen with a series of stock photos of quintessential American city skylines, wildlife, and landscapes superimposed on an American flag.

"To those of you from South Carolina, this neighboring sister state to my home state of North Carolina, I've enjoyed having a small foothold here on Taylor Island for the past decade or so. Thank you for always making me feel welcome with your famous hospitality." He pointed to a slide of a pineapple—symbolic of hospitality—surrounded by photos of sunlit beaches, bright green salt marshes, gulls, dolphins, and even the state reptile of South Carolina: the loggerhead sea turtle. "The natural beauty of this state is one of our country's greatest treasures and inspires me to stay the course to preserve the environment and to champion a reverence for wildlife."

Brooke's chest tightened into a fist of anger radiating to her extremities. The senator's duplicity made heat rise in her cheeks. Brooke wasn't a hateful person, but she'd never hated anyone as much as the senator. It took every ounce of her self-control to restrain her furious screams.

Just then, from behind her, Walt said to Drew in a loud whisper, "Showtime. A couple officers are standing by to grab Mayor McPhee." He winked at Brooke, but she didn't smile.

Neither did Drew. "Good work, Walt," he said in a serious, all-business tone, remaining focused on the task at hand.

A final slide filled the screen with the phrase "Thank You!" in huge starspangled letters while Senator Madden concluded with his usual rallying cry. "We're all mad for something. You're here tonight because you believe in this campaign, and you believe in me. I'm humbled by your devotion. My family thanks you. I thank you. America will thank you!" Everyone raised their glasses and drank. "Get Mad for a better America!" He smiled wide, waved both hands, and gave a thumbs-up.

The audience hooted and hollered, clapping their wild approval as he made his way off stage.

Drew intercepted the senator along the perimeter of the ballroom with Walt and Brooke in his wake. "Senator Madden, I'm Detective Young." Pulling his badge from his jacket, Drew motioned to the foyer. "Will you come with us please?"

Through a nearby doorway, Brooke caught a glimpse of two uniformed officers leaving the clubhouse with Mayor McPhee, whose reddened face and pinched expression made it clear he knew they knew he was complicit in the poaching scheme.

Amid the end-of-party commotion, everyone was too preoccupied and drunk to notice the confrontation between the senator and detective. Everyone except Caldwell, who weaved awkwardly across the room between tables and guests, keeping his surprised eyes on Brooke and Drew.

The senator also seemed surprised. "May I ask why?"

Drew answered, "The party's over, Senator."

"That's right. It is." But the senator didn't move. "Wait a minute," pointing at Brooke, he let out a messy laugh, somewhat drunk with confusion. "You're Brooke. The one that got away. Where's Junior? Is this some kind of joke? Oh, he got me *good*."

Brooke had heard enough. "This isn't a joke. I'm not Caldwell's one-that-got-away." She fumed. "I'm Dr. Edens, a sea turtle biologist and Diane Raydeen's friend. And you won't be getting away with anything, asshole." She glared at Senator Madden, who dropped his cold eyes to her dress.

The butterfly brooch turned his bewilderment to stone.

Drew admired Brooke's delivery, then commanded the senator's attention. "Senator," he said impatiently. "You're coming with us."

Walt gripped the senator by his upper arm and guided him forcefully toward the hall.

"The hell I am." Senator Madden jerked his arm away.

Drew boxed him in and lowered his voice. "I really don't want to make a scene. Do you?"

Caldwell reached them just in time, nodding nervously at Brooke and Drew, knowing what was about to happen. "Dad," he said, urging his words to get through, "they know about Project Hurricane and the loggerhead poaching."

"It's even worse than that," said Drew.

Brooke saw a mask of shock cover Caldwell's face.

Stepping closer to the senator, Drew tilted his head to look at the skin around the senator's shirt collar, then smirked. "Let's just say, we know who made that scratch on your neck. And why."

The senator's hand shot up reflexively to cover his neck. Startled, he pivoted, but Walt blocked the way. Like a caged animal, he glowered at his captors, the finality sinking in.

Drew continued, "We have Art. We have the mayor. And we have Oliver." He watched the senator wince. "We know all about your affair with Diane—the gifts, the pregnancy, and her refusal to abort your baby. We know you convinced her to meet you at North End Beach and told Oliver to scare her into the forest. You were counting on Joe as a witness to assume Oliver chased her down and killed her. Because *you* were nowhere to be seen. Even Oliver didn't know you were going to be there. You set it all up to frame Oliver for Diane's murder. He knew how it would look, that everyone, including Joe, would assume he killed her, and nobody would believe him—an outsider, a known poacher—over a U.S. senator, a presidential candidate. Plus, Oliver was being paid to keep quiet about the poaching scheme and to disappear. So you hid in the forest and waited. You had appearances on your side, like your mask, your shield. A perfect murder relies on appearances. We only see what the killer wants us to see. But appearances are often at loggerheads with the truth. The truth is: Oliver chased Diane toward the forest as he was told to do, but you were there when they made it just past the first head-high dune. *You* knocked her down, *you* strangled her to death, and *you* ordered Oliver to get rid of her body. But you didn't call Diane's number at all after that morning because you knew she was dead. And you certainly didn't count on her fighting back."

Senator Madden's vacant stare moved from Drew to Caldwell, whose mouth gaped in complete and utter disbelief. Then Caldwell inhaled sharply like a wave pulling back from the sand, steadying himself on a nearby chair. Brooke patted his shoulder.

Resentful and grasping at some semblance of control, Senator Madden straightened his tuxedo jacket and said in a curt voice, "Junior, call my lawyer."

But Caldwell didn't answer, couldn't even look at his dad again. He turned his back and walked away into the muttering swirl of a lingering, oblivious crowd.

Drew shook his head, fed up with the senator's audacity. Signaling to Walt to make the arrest, Drew simply said with deliberate sarcastic bite, "Get Mad."

Brooke couldn't suppress her satisfied smile.

Walt handcuffed the stiff and defiant Senator Madden, escorting him through a side door. "You're under arrest for the murder of Diane Raydeen. You have the right to remain silent. Anything you say can and will be used against you . . ."

It's been said that when a group of people laughs together, each person looks at the person in the group to whom they feel closest. That night, as the party ended and the ballroom cleared after the pun that was Senator Madden, Brooke stood looking at Drew. And he was looking back at her.

He always had been.

Immersed in mixed emotions about all that had happened, Brooke unpinned the butterfly brooch from her dress. Squeezing it in her palm, she felt its faceted gems indent her soft flesh and set her free.

EPILOGUE

TWO MONTHS LATER

At first light, the glassy inlet reflected stacks of lavender clouds against a pastel pink horizon. Brooke sat near the dunes and pushed her feet into dry sand, looking out across the wide ethereal expanse of North End Beach to the water where the dark oblong shape of Taylor Island met the ocean. Two dolphins arced in unison through low tide, surfacing with blowhole puffs, their sleek bodies silhouetted against the silver-topped sea.

Beside Brooke, a lone turtle nest was overdue for hatchlings to erupt in their mad dash to the ocean. For the past week, she'd been checking the nest at dawn each day after her morning run, waiting for a spot of sunken sand or the scribbled paths of hatchling tracks—any sign the nest was ready to boil.

This would be her first hatching nest without Diane.

Brooke was sick of the endless news cycles about Senator Madden's indictment, the Turtle Lady Murder, the poaching ring's prominent members, and the collateral death of Joe Willis. Every time she came across a report by Bella Michaels, she cringed and changed the channel, fighting the urge to throw a shoe at the television.

Of course, the senator blanketed himself with attorneys and continued to contest his long list of felony criminal charges including conspiracy to kill a federally protected species, violation of federal campaign financing laws, and—most damning—first degree murder. His trial would start next month. His political reputation had been destroyed, and he withdrew from the presidential race.

Through it all, Caldwell had been nothing short of brave. He took the heat from his family, and from many of their high-society friends, for agreeing to testify against his father and hold him accountable for his actions. His humiliated mother eventually came around to Caldwell's side and retained a divorce attorney. The Monday after the infamous roast, Caldwell gave his two weeks' notice at the big firm and joined his friend Bud Gibson in the real estate game. His first order of business was to untangle the property deal that formed the heart of Project Hurricane, the motivation for so much murder. Art Ogletree, who evidently cut all ties with the senator, and Mayor Pat McPhee, who resigned in disgrace, claimed to know about the poaching scheme but not about the related murders. They were deposed and, in exchange for complete immunity, agreed to grant access to all of the LLC's financial transactions and accounts. According to a recent newspaper article, Caldwell struck a deal with Art and Pat to buy them out of Project Hurricane LLC at a bargain price, and—with majority ownership of the company—he donated the maritime forest property to a land conservation trust. The whole north end of Anders Isle would be permanently retained by the land trust as: Diane Raydeen Nature Reserve.

Brooke smiled with pride. Diane's name would be forever linked with protecting forest wildlife and the beach habitat of nesting and newborn loggerheads. Her legacy as the Turtle Lady would live on well beyond anything she could've imagined.

From the direction of the beach access path behind her, Brooke heard the jingle of keys. She turned to see Drew—barefoot in board shorts and a T-shirt—walking toward her from the dunes.

"I thought I might find you here," he said, grinning.

"Hey." Brooke stood up to brush sand off her legs. "Weren't you sleeping in today after our late night out with Paul and his new girlfriend?"

Drew grabbed her and pulled her close. They kissed gently.

"I was, but when I woke up and you weren't there, I wanted to be here with you." Keeping his arm hooked around her, he pressed his nose against her hair.

"I'm glad you're here."

The glowing August sun began to rise from the ocean like a smear of orange fire, burning through clouds and growing brighter. The day broke open. Then the turtle nest broke open.

"Look!" Brooke pointed to the nest, where a pile of palm-sized, sand-caked hatchlings paddled their flippers in the air, slapping each other on the head. About a hundred baby turtles climbed out on top of the heap, until they boiled over and tumbled down onto the sand, making swift belly crawls in all directions.

"Wow," said Drew softly.

Without the moonlight to guide them to the water, some of the hatchlings became disoriented on the beach and were heading inland.

"Help me steer them toward the ocean, like this . . ." Using her feet as bumpers in front of hatchlings that had gone astray, Brooke herded them back toward the ocean.

Drew joined in.

When the hatchlings reached the final stretch, they sped up to the lapping waves, pulled by instinct like a leash, then ducked under and glided with ease until they were out of sight.

Exhilarated, Brooke and Drew stood ankle-deep in the water, watching the last baby turtle as it swam hastily away.

Drew stripped off his shirt and tossed it on the beach. He took Brooke by the hand, coaxing her. "Come here." They waded in up to their thighs. The waves soaked her running shorts while Drew led her deeper, until the water was waist high.

She couldn't resist.

Brooke's shirt clung to her stomach, the wetness spreading up to her chest. It was restrictive, saturated. Crossing her arms in front, she grabbed the hem, peeling off her shirt, then sports bra, and throwing them toward shore. Half-naked in only her shorts, she caught her breath when a passing swell moved across her bare breasts. In the shallow edge of the vast ocean, Brooke felt small and insignificant, but free.

Drew couldn't take his eyes off her. He splashed her playfully, spraying her face and hair with delicious saltwater. She splashed back and squealed when he reached for her. They wrapped their arms around each other while he kissed her neck and caressed her back. Chills covered her skin. Their bodies pressed together from head to toe.

Drew whispered in her ear, "Will you move in with me, Brooke? Let's live together."

She squeezed him tighter, feeling his warm chest against hers, sealed to her with slick bits of sea. It was exactly what she wanted. "Yes," she said with joyful eyes.

"Yes!" He threw his arms up in victory, then cupped her face in his wet hands and kissed her tenderly.

They hugged, touched, and loved each other, in the ocean beside their island while the sun came up and the tide began to turn.

For Brooke, home had always been a feeling of deep connection to a sacred place. She returned to Anders Isle as a homecoming, but she found home to be so much more than just a place. She found home in the people she loved, especially Drew. She found home to be something worth fighting for, worth protecting. She found home to be not only changed by time but also more exposed by it. Time revealed the resilience of sea turtles, restored her sense of self, and laid bare the lengths to which people will go for money, for power, and for love. But, while time had been the true test of what endured, death lent a stark urgency and importance to the meanings of home and of love.

While she held Drew in her arms, the moon-pulled tide rising around them, she gazed out across the waves at the distant horizon.

She felt loved. Wanted. She was where she belonged.

And she couldn't taste the difference between the saltwater and her tears. She was home.

Home.

THE END

ACKNOWLEDGMENTS

I don't remember the first time I saw the ocean. When I was born, my parents lived in a condo at a place called Lands End, aptly named since it sat on a point where a wide grass lawn gave way to a small sand beach edging a lake that must have looked as big as an ocean to me then. Water to the horizon. It was there I learned to swim and to read (well, memorize) my favorite book, *The Story of Ferdinand* by Munro Leaf. Dad was in law school, and mom had a master's degree she would later use as a middle school English teacher. From the beginning, I was born to love water and books.

A lake was my introduction to the ocean, which I saw by age six, much like a children's book was my introduction to storytelling. These introductions soon led to my fascination with ocean creatures and my need for writing, both of which have been constant personal pursuits of mine for as long as I can remember, even while working as a lawyer and raising a family. I guess it was as inevitable as the tides, as inevitable as my first glimpse of the ocean, that I would someday write a novel, but it wasn't until the idea for this novel hatched from the sands of my imagination that I truly believed I could call myself a writer. I have so many people to thank for helping me along the way.

Holding my published book in my hands is one of my wildest dreams come true! But, as all writers know, making it to publication is not something we do alone or in a vacuum. After years of writing and editing (and editing and editing), my dream has come to fruition with some luck and endless support from those listed here and from everyone who has influenced and inspired me. I am so thankful.

To my agent, Russell Galen, who changed my life with his email and these five words: "You had me at turtles." Thank you, Russ, for your insightful feedback after reading each draft, for answering my questions and providing expert guidance, for seeing potential in my writing, and for loving sea turtles, nature, and science as much as my characters and I do. I am forever grateful that I had you at turtles!

To my editor, Elizabeth Hollerith, thank you for your excitement about my book and its characters, for your patience with my questions, and for your thoughtful revisions to each draft. It was meant to be that my book would end up in the hands of an editor with experience as a former turtle team volunteer. My gratitude extends to Michael Nolan and to the publishing team at Evening Post Books, including Alex Lanning and Gill Guerry, for your support in marketing and design.

To the team at Ebook Launch, thank you for creating a hauntingly beautiful cover design that makes me hope people will judge this book by its cover. You took my vague ideas and formed the picture I didn't even know I had in my head until I saw it.

To Diana Deaver, thank you for sharing your talent as a photographer, capturing in my author photos all the drama and beauty of the golden hour on a windy beach. My gratitude extends to Pamela Lesch for the perfect makeup.

Thank you to the team at Buzzworthy Studio for an enticing website design and for your innovative and customized approach to marketing.

A heartfelt thanks to Heather MacQueen Jones, an artist who transformed my basic photos of turtle tracks on a sunrise beachscape into gorgeous paintings. Thank you, Heather, for sharing your talent in search of my cover design and for your encouragement and marketing ideas.

Big thanks to my readers. If you're holding this book (whether hard copy or electronic), or listening to an audio version, I appreciate your time and hope you enjoy the story. While I write, I keep you in mind, trying to entertain you, to move you, to keep you guessing—and turning pages—to the end.

Thank you to my teachers and professors who encouraged me to write and taught me the beauty of language, especially James Gasque. I'm grateful to those professors in college and law school who allowed me to write creative versions of final papers for their courses, and to my Duke drama professor, Jeffery West, who scribbled in the margin of my class journal: "P.S. I think you're a born writer."

A special thanks to my friend and published author, Maya Myers, whose precise edits to early drafts of this book helped me sculpt a tighter narrative and whose questions led to a deeper understanding of my characters.

Thank you to our former neighbor, Craig Mielcarek with the City of Charleston Police Department, for reading sections of my book and providing helpful edits and information.

Thank you to Joan Mebane for welcoming me into your home and taking me with you to a nest-sitting as your guest, where you not only introduced me to the world of local turtle teams but also gave me the thrill of seeing my first nest "boil" with baby turtle hatchlings. To Nancy Hutchison Fahey, the Turtle Lady of Wrightsville Beach, NC, who was also there that night, thank you for inviting me to join in, for answering my many plot-related sea turtle questions, and for your heart and time dedicated to protecting sea turtles.

An ocean of thanks to the turtle ladies of the Island Turtle Team on Isle of Palms and Sullivan's Island for all that they do to protect sea turtles and for welcoming me as a volunteer for the past decade: Mary Pringle, Barbara Bergwerf, Barbara Gobien, Beverly Ballow, Linda Rumph, Jo Durham, Tee Johannes, Cindy Moore. My gratitude extends to my turtle team walking partners, Carolyn Eshelman and Cathy Harris, who make the morning hours fly by in conversation, and to all of the turtle teams and volunteers striving to protect sea turtles everywhere. Thank you to Kelly Thorvalson for her dedication to sea turtle conservation at the South Carolina Aquarium. To Sally Murphy, who pioneered South Carolina's sea turtle programs and battled for the turtle excluder device law, thank you for your memoir *Turning The Tide*, which served as a valuable reference during my research.

A special thanks to Christel Cothran, also a turtle lady with the Island Turtle Team and a writer, who was my first walking partner during nesting season. Thank you, Christel, for your friendship and support, for sharing this writing journey with me, for hours of great conversation while looking for turtle tracks, and for getting to that dinner table in Amelia Island to let David Baldacci know why I was running late.

My deepest gratitude to Mary Alice Monroe, who is a champion of the environment, a prolific *New York Times* bestselling author, a turtle lady with the Island Turtle Team, and my mentor and friend. Thank you, Mary Alice, for offering your generous support and enthusiasm for my writing, for providing my very first blurb, and for your warmth and experienced advice. You prove that one person can make a big difference.

Thank you to Shelby Van Pelt, whose magnificent debut novel *Remarkably Bright Creatures* draws readers into the beauty and mystery of the ocean through the eyes of an octopus and the human he befriends. I'm forever grateful for your generosity, your excitement about my book, and your incredible blurb.

To John Hart, who is an author of six *New York Times* bestsellers, thank you for your encouragement and for always offering to help, including the very first time you drove through a giant rainstorm to speak to our group of lawyer-writers in Charlotte.

To Zibby Owens, who is a powerhouse podcaster, author, publisher, bookstore owner, and basically just does it all, thank you for being a champion of books and authors, for your kindness, for inviting me to your podcast, and for somehow feeling like a longtime friend after only a quick first meeting. When I listen to your podcast, I think of you as the woman with a smile in her voice.

Thank you to Patti Callahan Henry for your support of my writing and for answering my questions from the first time I reached out to you. My gratitude extends to Ron Block and the entire team at Friends & Fiction for inviting me to a podcast episode and for creating an incredible outlet for readers and authors.

A special thank you to the following authors who inspire me with their stories and have been generous with their time and friendship: Judy Goldman, Angela May, Stephanie Alexander, Stacy Willingham, Josephine Humphreys, Chic Cariaga, Gervais Hagerty, Wendy Nilsen Pollitzer, Kris Manning, and

Pino Ragona (who always makes me feel like a celebrity at his restaurant, Giovanni's of Covent Garden).

To Dr. Kathryn Moore and Dr. Jeannine Monnier, thank you for your guidance and expertise.

Many waves of appreciation for the Navarro family—especially Ben, Kelly, Emma, and Meggie. Thank you for embracing our family like your own, for your generosity, friendship, and support in every way, and for the many experiences and adventures that have influenced and enriched not only my writing but our lives.

For Kevin Mooney, Jessica Klein, and Nathaniel Mooney—your luminous Kayleigh stayed in mind while I wrote this book. Thank you for keeping her light and love alive in this world. I think of her when I see the moon, guiding sea turtles home. As you told me, she wrote: "Look to the moon if you are lost. She holds all power."

Thank you to my amazing friends throughout my life for your love and support. I cherish each friendship and wish I could list every one of you by name. The friends listed here influenced this book in both direct and indirect ways. Some were early readers of various drafts while others simply listened and offered encouragement or advice. I'm grateful to these friends for spending time with me, for big laughter, for entertaining stories, for reading all or part of my book, and for giving me so much inspiration and love along the way. I hope you each know how much you mean to me. Thank you: My TGs—Nellie Lanier Harasimowicz and Gretchen Watters; My "Book Club"—Heather Atchison, Heather Burchfield, Kim Burchfield, Jeni Cutting, Marci Easterling, Tabitha Ehman, Kennedy Reynolds, and Ashley Shults; Will McKibbon - always; My Wemoon sea sisters—Jenny Brown, Becky Baird, Susan Haidary, Tara "T1" Miller, Tara Miller "T2" Thomas, and Ann DuPre Rogers; Braeden Brice Kershner for music and motivation; Our best babysitters ever—Chloe Tribolet, Brittany Smith, Deidra Stillwagoner, and Erica Whiteside; My dear friends—Jenn Russ, Elizabeth Vinson Lonsdorf, Jason Lynn, Emily Fletcher, Kevin Mooney, Jen McCartha-Pearce, James Johnson, Eliza Edgar, Josie Owens, Kim Smith Vroon, Paige Emerson, Brittany Gooding, Alexis Berman, Beth Kesser, Julia Donley, Aimee

Phelan-Deconinck, Dave Sieling, Steve Dollar, Heidi Baer, Yani Dilling, Mike Champion, Glenn Raus, Jeddie Suddeth, David and Esther Zimmer.

Most of all, thank you to my family.

To my mom, Jane Ness, who taught me how to write and who showed me how to be strong and kind. I owe my love of books and writing to you. Thank you for always being there for me as a mother, as a confidante, and as a constant source of wisdom, enthusiasm, and humor. Thank you for your unconditional love and friendship. You are my greatest inspiration. As you know, I love you to the moon and back.

Thank you to my dad, Dale Ness, who passed away before I finished the first draft of this book. As my biggest champion, full of unconditional love, he supported me in every way, wanting most of all for me to be happy. He taught me optimism, self-reliance, and, ultimately, that life is short. I miss him every day. More than a decade ago, when he read the first one hundred pages of this book, which was all I'd written at the time, I knew he liked it when he simply said: "Finish your book." So, I did. I'm always looking for owls.

To my sister and brother, Sarah Ness Luke and Dale Ness Jr., thank you for being my first best friends and for endless laughs and so many memories made together. We always have a good time. I love you so much.

To my extended family, I'm forever grateful for your love and support. Thank you to Pete and Nancy Ayers; Kerri, Dale III, and Ford Ness; Kevin, Kellen, and Brady Luke; Andrew Ayers; Ashley, Hank, Jackson, Wyatt, and Kylie Hodges; Kathryn, Chris, Cole, Hayley, and Eleanor Hamrick; Monica McCarthy; Sarah Hoover; Peter Ness; Teal Ness; Charlotte Ness; and Ieko Shields; Wayne and Linda Ayers; and Kenny Lineberger.

To my wonderful children, Taylor and Dylan, you are my heart. Better than any characters I could imagine. It is the joy of my life to watch you grow into your own people full of personality and possibility. You are my favorite daughter and favorite son. Thank you for being funny and patient, for doing your best, and for giving me so much love. You make me very happy. I'm the luckiest mom. I will always be proud of you for being just who you are. I love you always and forever no matter what.

Thank you to my husband, my love, Peter Ayers, for always supporting my dreams, for taking over the daily routines of family life each time I unexpectedly go down a writing rabbit hole, and for being a trusted reader and sounding board for possible twists and revisions. I'm so happy to be on this life adventure with you, Sweet Pete. I love you, I love you, I love you. Keep tappin'.

A Note to Readers

If you would like to learn more about how to conserve and protect sea turtles and the ocean, please consider these organizations, volunteer your time with a local turtle team, or donate your resources:

- Island Turtle Team - Isle of Palms and Sullivan's Island: islandturtleteam.org
- South Carolina Aquarium: scaquarium.org
- DNR SC Marine Turtle Conservation Program: dnr.sc.gov
- 4Ocean: 4ocean.com
- The Ocean Agency: theoceanagency.org
- The Karen Beasley Sea Turtle Rescue & Rehabilitation Center: seaturtlehospital.org
- Nicholas School of the Environment, Duke University Marine Lab: nicholas.duke.edu
- Mission Blue: missionblue.org
- Sea Turtle Conservancy: conserveturtles.org
- Ocean Conservancy: oceanconservancy.org
- A New Earth Project: anewearthproject.com
- The Nature Conservancy: nature.org
- National Oceanic and Atmospheric Administration (NOAA): noaa.gov
- Oceanic Society: oceanicsociety.org

When you visit a beach, please remember to keep the beach CLEAN, DARK, and FLAT for sea turtles coming ashore to nest.

- CLEAN: Take trash and other items with you when you leave the beach for the day.
- DARK: Keep lights out for turtles at night.
- FLAT: Fill in your large holes and knock down your sand creations.